# Regency Reputations

# Regency Reputations:

# Secrets and Scandal

LOUISE ALLEN

MILLS & BOON

First Published in Great Britain 2021
By Mills & Boon, an imprint of HarperCollins*Publishers*
1 London Bridge Street, London, SE1 9GF

www.harpercollins.co.uk

HarperCollins*Publishers*
1st Floor, Watermarque Building,
Ringsend Road, Dublin 4, Ireland

REGENCY REPUTATIONS: SECRETS AND SCANDAL
© 2021 Harlequin Books S.A.

*Regency Rumours* © 2013 Melanie Hilton
*Tarnished Amongst the Ton* © 2013 Melanie Hilton

ISBN: 978-0-263-30303-2

**MIX**
Paper from
responsible sources
FSC® C007454

# REGENCY RUMOURS

For the staff at Wimpole who were a mine of information and who were so patient with my endless questions

# CHAPTER ONE

*February 2nd, 1801—the Old North Road,*
*Cambridgeshire*

THE CHAISE RATTLED and lurched. It was an almost welcome distraction from the stream of bright and cheerful chatter Isobel's maid had kept up ever since they left London. 'It isn't *exile* really, now is it, my lady? Your mama said you were going to rusticate in the country for your health.'

'Dorothy, I know you mean to raise my spirits, but *exile* is precisely the word for it.' Lady Isobel Jervis regarded the plump young woman with scarce-concealed exasperation. 'To call it *rustication* is to draw a polite veil over the truth. Gentlemen rusticate when they have to escape from London to avoid their creditors.

'I have been banished, in disgrace, and that is exile. If this was a sensation novel the fact that it is completely undeserved and unjust would cast a romantic glow over the situation. But this is not a novel.' She stared out through the drizzle at the gently undulating farmland rolling past the post-chaise window. In reality the injustice only increased her anger and misery.

She had taken refuge in the country once before, but that had been justified, essential and entirely her own doing. This, on the other hand, was none of those things.

'That was the sign to Cambridge we've just passed,' Dorothy observed brightly. She had been this infuriatingly jolly ever since the scandal broke. Isobel was convinced that she had not listened to a word she had said to her.

'In that case we cannot be far from Wimpole Hall.' Isobel removed her hands from under the fur-lined rug and took the carriage clock from its travelling case on the hook. 'It is almost two o'clock. We left Berkeley Street at just before eight, spent an hour over luncheon and changing horses, so we have made good time.'

'And the rain has eased,' Dorothy said, bent on finding yet another reason for joy.

'Indeed. We will arrive in daylight and in the dry.' The chaise slowed, then swung in through imposing gateposts. From her seat on the left-hand side Isobel glimpsed the bulk of a large brick inn and a swinging sign. 'The Hardwicke Arms—we are in the right place, at least.'

As they passed between the gateposts Isobel began to take more interest in the prospect from the window: it would be her home for the next two months.

The tree-dotted parkland rose gently on the left-hand side. She glimpsed a small stone building on the top of one low knoll, then, as the carriage swung round, the house came into view.

'Lawks,' Dorothy observed inelegantly.

'It *is* the largest house in the shire,' Isobel pointed out. 'I thought it might be a small palace from what Mama said, but it looks curiously welcoming, don't you think? Quite like home at Bythorn Hall.' It was no simple mansion, to be sure, but the red brick looked warm, despite the chill of the sodden February air.

The chaise drew up close to the double sweep of steps that led to the front door. *Too soon.* Isobel fought the sudden wave of panic. The Earl and Countess of Hardwicke had offered her shelter for the sake of their old friendship with her parents—Philip Yorke, the third earl, had met her father, the Earl of Bythorn, at Oxford—so they were hardly strangers, she told herself, even if she had not met them for several years.

'Be on your best behaviour, Dorothy,' she warned. 'The earl has been appointed the first Lord Lieutenant of Ireland, so he will soon be the king's representative.'

'Foreign, that's what Ireland is,' the maid said with a sniff. 'Don't hold with it.'

'It is part of the new United Kingdom,' Isobel said repressively. 'You enjoyed the celebrations at the beginning of the year, do not pretend that you did not! I must say I would like to see Dublin when the earl and countess move there in April, but they will have far more important things to worry about then than a house guest.'

In fact it was very kind of Lord Hardwicke and Elizabeth, his witty blue-stocking countess, to give sanctuary to their old friend's disgraced daughter at such a critical juncture in their lives. It might suit the Jervises to put it about that Isobel was helping the countess with her preparations, but she was sure she would be more of a distraction than a help.

She had wanted to flee to her friend Jane Needham's cheerful country manor in the depths of the Herefordshire countryside. It was remote, it was safe and it held warmth and love. But Mama had been adamant: if scandal forced her daughter to retreat from London, then she would do so, very ostentatiously, under the wing of a leading aristocratic family.

The doors opened, footmen came down the steps, and Dorothy began to gather up their scattered shawls and reticules as Isobel tied her bonnet ribbons and strove for poise.

It was too late to back away now: the carriage door was opened, a footman offered his arm. Isobel put back her shoulders, told herself that the shivers running down her spine were due entirely to the February chill and walked up the steps with a smile on her lips.

'My dear Isobel! The cold has put roses in your cheeks—let me kiss you.' The entrance hall seemed full of people, but Lady Hardwicke's warm voice was an instant tonic, lifting spirits and nerve. 'What a perfectly ghastly day, yet you have made such good time!'

Caught before she could curtsy, Isobel returned the embrace wholeheartedly. 'Thank you, ma'am. It was an uneventful journey, but it is a great relief to be here, I must confess.'

'Now please do not *ma'am* me. Call me Cousin Elizabeth, for we are related, you know, although rather vaguely on your mother's side, it is true. Come and greet my lord. You are old friends, I think.'

'My lord.' This time she did manage her curtsy to the slender man with the big dark eyes and earnest, intelligent face. Philip Yorke was in his mid-forties, she recalled, but his eager expression made him look younger.

'Welcome to Wimpole, my dear Isobel.' He caught her hands and smiled at her. 'What a charming young woman you have grown into, to be sure. Is it really four years since I last saw you?'

'Yes, sir. After Lucas…after Lord Needham's funeral.' As soon as she said it Isobel could have bitten her tongue. Her host's face clouded with embarrassment at having reminded her of the death of her fiancé and she hurried into speech. 'It is delightful to meet you again in happy circumstances—may I congratulate you upon your appointment to the lieutenancy?'

He smiled in acknowledgement of her tact. 'Thank you, my dear. A great honour that I can only hope to be worthy of.' Behind him one of the two men standing beside the butler shifted slightly. 'You must allow me to introduce our other guests.' The earl turned to motion them forwards. 'Mr Soane, who is doing such fine work on the house for us, and Mr Harker, who is also an architect and who is assisting in some of Mr Soane's schemes for improvements in the grounds. Gentlemen, Lady Isobel Jervis, the daughter of my old friend the Earl of Bythorn.'

'My lady.' They bowed as one. Isobel was fairly certain that she had shut her mouth again by the time they had straightened up. Mr Soane was in his late forties, dark, long-faced and long-chinned, his looks distinctive rather than handsome. But Mr Harker was, without doubt, the most beautiful man she had ever set eyes upon.

Not that she had any time for handsome bucks these days, but even a woman who had vowed to spurn the male sex for ever would have had her resolution shaken by the appearance of this man. He was, quite simply, perfection, unless one would accept only blond hair as signifying true male beauty. His frame was tall, muscular and elegantly proportioned. His rich golden-brown hair was thick with a slight wave, a trifle overlong. His features were chiselled and classical and his eyes were green— somewhere, Isobel thought with a wild plunge into the poetic, between shadowed sea and a forest glade.

It was preposterous for any man to look like that, she decided while the three of them exchanged murmured greetings. It was superfluous to be quite so handsome in every feature. There must be *something* wrong with him. Perhaps he was unintelligent—but then, the earl would not employ him and Mr Soane, who had a considerable reputation to maintain and who had worked for the earl at Hammels Park before he succeeded to the title, would not associate with him. Perhaps he was socially inept, or effeminate or had a high squeaky voice or bad teeth or a wet handshake…

'Lady Isobel,' he said, in a voice that made her think of honey and with a smile that revealed perfect teeth. He took her hand in a brief, firm handshake.

Perfection there as well. Isobel swallowed hard, shocked by the sudden pulse of attraction she felt when she looked at him. A purely physical reflex, of course—she was a woman and not made of stone. He would be a bore, that was it. He would talk for hours at meals about breeding spaniels or the importance of drainage or the lesser-known features of the night sky or toadstools.

But the perfect smile had not reached his eyes and the flexible, deep voice had held no warmth. Was he shy, perhaps?

The two architects drew back as the countess gave instructions to the butler and the earl asked for details of her journey. Isobel realised she could study Mr Harker's profile in a long mirror hanging on the wall as they chatted. What on earth must it be like to be so good looking? It was not a problem that she had, for while she knew herself to be tolerably attractive— *elegant* and *charming* were the usual words employed to describe her—she was no great beauty. She studied him critically, wondering where his faults and weaknesses were hidden.

Then she saw that the remarkable green eyes were fixed and followed the direction of his gaze, straight to her own reflection in the glazing of a picture. She had been staring at Mr Harker in the most forward manner and he had been observing her do it.

Slowly she made the slight turn that allowed her to face him. Their gazes locked again as she felt a wave of complex emotion sweep through her. Physical attraction, certainly, but curiosity and a strange sense of recognition also. His eyes, so hypnotically deep and green, held an awareness, a question and, mysteriously, a darkness that tugged at her heart. Loneliness? Sadness? The thought flickered through her mind in a fraction of a second before they both blinked and she dismissed the fancy and was back with the social faux pas of having been caught blatantly staring at a man. A man who had been staring at her.

The polished boards did not, of course, open up and swallow her. Isobel fought the blush that was rising to her cheeks with every ounce of willpower at her disposal and attempted a faint smile. They were both adult enough to pass this off with tolerable composure. She expected to see in return either masculine smugness coupled with flirtation or a rueful acknowledgement that they had both been caught out staring. What she did *not* expect was to see those complex and haunting emotions she had observed a moment earlier turn to unmistakable froideur.

The expression on Mr Harker's face was not simply haughty, it was cold and dismissive. There was the faintest trace of a sneer about that well-shaped mouth. She was no doubt intended to feel like a silly little chit making cow's eyes at a handsome man.

Well, she was no such thing. Isobel lifted her chin and returned his look with one of frigid disdain. *Insufferable arrogance!* She had hardly been in the house five minutes, they had exchanged a handful of words and already he had taken a dislike to her. She did not know him from Adam—who was he to look at her in that way? Did he think that good looks gave him godlike superiority and that she was beneath him? He no doubt produced an eyeglass and studied women who interested him without the slightest hesitation.

'Shall we go up?'

'Of course, ma'am…Cousin Elizabeth,' Isobel said with the warmest smile she could conjure up. 'Gentlemen.' She nodded to the earl and Mr Soane who were in conversation, ignored Mr Harker, and followed her hostess through into the inner hall and up the wide staircase.

That snub on top of everything else felt painfully unjust. What was wrong with her that men should treat her so? Isobel stumbled on the first step and took herself to task. *She* had done nothing to deserve it—

they were simply unable to accept that a lady might not consider them utterly perfect in every way.

There was a faint odour of paint and fresh plaster in the air and she glanced around her as they climbed. 'Mr Soane has done a great deal of work for us, including changes to this staircase,' the countess remarked as they reached the first-floor landing. She did not appear to notice that her guest was distracted, or perhaps she thought her merely tired from the journey. 'There was a window on the half landing on to an inner court and that is now filled in and occupied with my husband's plunge bath, so Mr Soane created that wonderful skylight.' She gestured upwards past pillared balconies to a view of grey scudding clouds. They passed through double doors into a lobby and left again into a room with a handsome Venetian window giving a panoramic view across the park.

'This is your sitting room. The view is very fine when the sun shines—right down the great southern avenue.' Lady Hardwicke turned, regarding the room with a smile that was almost rueful. 'This was one end of a long gallery running from back to front until Mr Soane put the Yellow Drawing Room into what was a courtyard and then, of course, the upstairs had to be remodelled. We seem to have lived with the builders for years.'

She sighed and looked around her. 'We had just

got Hammels Park as we wanted it and then Philly's uncle died and he inherited the title and we had to start all over again here ten years ago.'

'But it is delightful.' Lured by sounds from next door, Isobel looked in and found that her pretty bed-chamber had an identical prospect southwards.

Dorothy bobbed a curtsy as they entered and scurried through a door on the far side to carry on unpacking. Isobel saw her evening slippers already set by the fire to warm and her nightgown laid out at the foot of the bed.

'Catherine, Anne and Philip will have been sorry not to be here to greet you.' The countess moved about the room, shifting the little vase of evergreens on the mantelpiece so it reflected better in the overmantel mirror and checking the titles of the books laid out beside the bed. 'We did not expect you to make such good time in this weather so they went out after luncheon to call on their old governess in Royston.'

'Cousin Elizabeth.' On an impulse Isobel shut the connecting door to the dressing room and went to catch the older woman's hand so she could look into her face. 'I know you wrote that you believed my account of the affair—but was that simply out of your friendship for Mama? You must tell me honestly and not try to be kind. Mama insisted that you would never expose your daughters to a young woman who had participated in a veritable orgy, but I cannot help but wonder if you perhaps think that there was no smoke without some flicker of fire?

'Do you believe that I am completely innocent of this scandal? I feel so awkward, thinking you might have reservations about my contact with the girls.' She faltered to a halt, fearful that she had been gabbling. Guilt for sins past and hidden, no doubt. But this scandal was here and now and the countess, however kind, had a reputation for strict moral principles. It was said she did not even allow a beer house in the estate village.

'Of course I believe you would never do anything immoral, Isobel.' Her conscience gave an inward wince as the countess drew her to the chairs set either side of the fire. 'But your mother was so discreet I have no idea exactly what transpired. Perhaps it is as well if I know the details, the better to be prepared for any gossip.'

Isobel stared into the fire. 'When Lucas died I was twenty. I stayed in the country for almost a year with my old school friend Jane, who married Lucas's half-brother. You will recall that he drowned in the same accident. Jane was pregnant, and their home was so remote: it helped both of us to be together.

'I wanted to remain there, but Mama felt strongly that I should rejoin society last year because I had missed two Seasons. I hated it—I was older than the other girls, none of the men interested me in the slightest and I suppose I allowed it to show. I got a reputation for being cold and aloof and for snubbing gentlemen, but frankly, I did not care. I did not want to marry any of them, you see.

'Mama thought I should try again this year and, to ease me in, as she put it, I went to the Harringtons' house party at Long Ditton in January. I knew I was not popular. What I did not realise was that what might have been acceptable in a beauty with a vast fortune was merely regarded as insulting and irritating in a tolerable-looking, adequately dowered, second daughter of an earl.'

'Oh, dear,' Lady Hardwicke murmured.

'Quite,' Isobel said bitterly. 'It seems that instead of being discouraged by my snubs and lack of interest, some of the gentlemen took them as an insult and a challenge and resolved to teach me a lesson. I was sitting up reading in my nightgown late one night when the door opened and three of them pushed in. They had all been drinking, they had brought wine with them and they were bent, so they said, on "warming me up" and showing me what I had been missing.'

A log collapsed in a shower of sparks, just as one had in the moment before the door had burst open that night. 'I should have screamed, of course. Afterwards the fact that I did not seemed to convince everyone that I had invited the men there. Foolishly I tried to reason with them, send them away quietly before anyone discovered them. They all demanded a kiss, but I could see it might go further.

'I pushed Lord Halton and he collapsed backwards into a screen which smashed with the most terrific noise. When half-a-dozen people erupted into my room Halton was swigging wine from the bottle where he had fallen, Mr Wrenne was sprawled in my chair egging on Lord Andrew White—and he had me against the bedpost and was kissing me, despite my struggles.

'One of the first through the door was Lady Penelope Albright, White's fiancée. No one believed me when I said I had done nothing to encourage the gentlemen, let alone invite them to my room. Lady Penelope had hysterics, broke off the engagement on the spot and has gone into such a decline that her parents say she will miss the entire Season. Lady Harrington packed me off home at dawn the next day.'

'Oh, my dear! I could box Maria Harrington's ears, the silly peahen. Had she no idea what the mood of the party was? I suppose not, she always had more hair than wit.' Lady Hardwicke got to her feet and paced angrily to the window. 'And what now? Do your parents think this will have died down by mid-April when we go to Ireland and you return home?'

'They hope so. And I cannot run away for ever. I suppose I must face them all some day.' Isobel put a bright, determined smile on her face. The thought of going into society again was daunting. But she could not live as a recluse in Herefordshire, she had come to accept that. She had parents and a brother and sister who loved her and who had been patient with her seemingly inexplicable desire to stay away for far too long.

She might wish to be removed from the Marriage Mart, but not under these humiliating circumstances. And London, which she enjoyed for the theatres and galleries, the libraries, the shops, would become a social minefield of embarrassment and rejections.

'That is very brave,' the countess said. 'I could call out all those wretched young bucks myself—such a pity your brother is too young to knock their heads together.'

'I would certainly not want Frederick duelling at sixteen! It is not as though I feel any pressing desire to wed. If I had found a man who was the equal of Lucas and this had caused a rift with him, then I would have something to grieve over, but as it is...'

*As it is I am not faced with the awful dilemma of how much of my past life to reveal to a potential husband.*

# CHAPTER TWO

ISOBEL STARED INTO the fire and finally said the things she had been bottling up inside. She had tried to explain at home, but it seemed her mother would never understand how she felt. 'I suppose I should be fired up with righteous indignation over the injustice of it all. I was so hurt and angry, but now I feel no spirit for the fight any more. What does it matter if society spurns me? I have not felt any burning desire to be part of it for four years.'

She bit her lip. 'The men believe I am putting on airs and think myself above them, or some such foolishness. But the truth is, even if I did wish to marry, they all fail to match up to my memories of Lucas. I still remember his kindness and his intelligence and his laugh. People say that memory fades, but I can see his face and hear his voice.'

'But you are no longer mourning him, only regretting,' the countess suggested. 'You have accepted he is gone.'

'Oh, yes. I know it, and I have accepted it. There

was this great hole full of loss and pain and now it is simply an empty ache.' And the constant nagging doubt—had she done the right thing in those months after Lucas's death? The decisions had seemed so simple and yet so very, very hard.

'I do not want to go through that again. Or to settle for something less than I felt for him.' Isobel turned, reached out to the older woman. 'Do you understand? Mama does not, she says I am fanciful and not facing up to reality. She says it is my duty to marry.'

'Yes, I understand.' Lady Hardwicke gave her hand a squeeze. 'But I should not give up on men *quite* yet,' she added with a shake of her head. 'Do you mind if I tell Anne in confidence what happened at the house party? She is almost eighteen now and will be making her come-out in Dublin. She might pick up something from gossip in friends' letters and I would have her know the truth of matters. It will serve as a warning to her.'

'To fawn on young gentlemen in case they turn on her?' Isobel enquired.

'To lock her bedroom door at night and to scream the moment she feels any alarm,' the countess said with a smile.

'No, I do not mind.' Isobel returned the smile. The older woman was right to reprove her for that note of bitterness. If she became a sour old maid as a result of this, then those rakes would have made her exactly what they jeered at her for being.

'I will have tea sent up and hot water. Relax and rest until dinner time, then you will feel strong enough to face at least some of my brood. Charles and Caroline must have nursery tea and wait until the morning to meet you, but I will allow Lizzie and Catherine to have dinner with us, and Anne and Philip will be there, of course.'

'And the architects?' Isobel asked with studied non-chalance.

'Yes, they will join us. Mr Soane will travel back to London tomorrow. It is never easy to persuade him to stay away from his wife and his precious collection of art and antiquities in Lincoln's Inn Fields, but Mr Harker is staying. I confess, I wish he were not *quite* so good looking, for the girls are all eyes and attitudes whenever they see him, but to do him credit, he gives them not the slightest encouragement, which is just as well, considering who he is.'

She swept out, adding, 'Do not hesitate to ring if you need anything, my dear, I am so pleased to have you here.'

Isobel sank back into the chair, puzzled. *Who Mr Harker is? He* was an architect, but so was Mr Soane. Architects of good breeding—or even the sons of bricklayers like Mr Soane, if they were cultivated and successful—were perfectly acceptable socially, even at the dining table of an earl. Mr Harker's accent had been impeccable, his manners—if one left aside his hostile gaze—without reproach, his dress immaculate. He was a gentleman, obviously, and as eligible as a houseguest as Mr Soane. But who *was* he? Isobel shrugged. 'Why should I care?' she asked the crackling fire. 'He is insufferable whoever he is.'

The clock in the inner hall struck seven as Isobel reached the foot of the stairs. Where was everyone? There were no footmen to be seen and the doors ahead and to the right were closed, giving her no clues.

'If you say so...' A low masculine rumble. At least two of the party were down already, she realised with relief. It was always so awkward, standing around in a house one did not know.

Isobel followed the voices into the front hall and realised they came from the rooms to the left of the entrance. The cues lying on the billiard table in the first hinted that perhaps some of the gentlemen had only recently left. The conversation was clearer now, coming from the room beyond. The door stood ajar.

'...pleasant young lady, she will be companionship for Lady Anne, no doubt.' That was Mr Soane. Isobel stopped in her tracks. Was he talking about her?

'She is a good six years older than Lady Anne,' Mr Harker replied with disastrous clarity. 'One wonders what she is doing unwed, although I imagine I can hazard a guess. She has too bold an eye—no doubt it attracts the wrong sort of attention, not honourable proposals.'

*'You...'* Isobel bit back the words and applied her eye to the crack between door and hinges.

'You think she might prove to be an embarrassment?' the older man asked. He sounded concerned. 'I have seen the lengths you have to go to to prevent young ladies from becoming...um, attached.'

'I have no intention of allowing her to so much as flirt with me. She was staring in the most brazen manner in the hall—presumably she thinks it sophisticated. That, or she is on the shelf and signalling that she is open to advances.'

Harker was strolling around the room, looking at the pictures that hung on the panelling. For a moment the exquisite profile came into view, then he vanished with a flick of dark blue coat tails.

*You arrogant, vain swine!* Isobel's fingers uncurled, itching to slap that beautiful face.

'I do hope not.' A slice of Soane's long, dark countenance appeared in the slit, furrowed by a frown. 'Lady Hardwicke would be most upset if there was any untoward flirtation. You know her reputation for high standards.'

'And it would rebound on you by association, Soane, as I am your protégé. I have no intention of risking it, have no fear. It is hardly as if she offers irresistible temptation in any case.' Both men laughed, covering Isobel's gasp of outrage.

'A pity gentlemen cannot have chaperons in the same way as the ladies,' Soane remarked. 'Being a plain man myself, I never had any trouble of that kind. Find yourself a wife, preferably a rich one, and settle down as I have, that is my advice, but I have no doubt you enjoy your freedom and your dashing widows too much, eh, Harker?'

'Far too much, sir. Besides, finding the right wife, in my circumstances, will take more application than I am prepared to expend upon it just now.'

*As if anyone would have you!* The words almost left Isobel's mouth as the sound of their voices faded away. Her vision was strangely blurred and it took a moment to realise it was because her eyes had filled with tears of anger and hurt. It was so unjust to be stigmatised as a flirt, or worse, simply for staring at a man. And then to be labelled as *on the shelf* and too ordinary to offer any temptation to a connoisseur, such as Mr Harker obviously considered himself to be, was the crowning insult.

It took a few moments to compose herself. Isobel turned back the way she had come, unwilling to risk walking into them again. Was that cowardice or simply the wisdom to keep well away from Mr Harker while her palm still itched to slap him?

There was a footman in the hall when she emerged. 'May I help you, my lady? The family is in the saloon, just through here, ma'am.'

Ushered back through the inner hall, Isobel found herself in a pleasant room with a large bay window. It was curtained now against the February darkness, but she assumed it would look out onto the gardens and park stretching off to the north.

The earl was poring over what looked like architectural drawings with Mr Soane and a fresh-faced youth was teasing a giggling girl of perhaps twelve years—Lord Royston and Lady Lizzie, she guessed.

The countess sat on a wide sofa with Lady Anne and her fifteen-year-old sister, Catherine, who were making a show of working on their embroidery.

Mr Soane must have come through a connecting door, but there was no sign of the viper-tongued Mr Harker. Where was he? Isobel scanned the room, conscious of butterflies in her stomach. The evidence of nerves gave her another grudge against Mr Perfection.

The children saw her first. 'Ma'am.' Philip bowed. 'Welcome to Wimpole Hall.'

'Are you our Cousin Isobel?' Lizzie was wide-eyed with excitement at being allowed to a grown-up party. Isobel felt her stiff shoulders relax. *He* was not here and the children were charming.

Giles Harker straightened up from his contemplation of the collection of Roman *intaglio* seals in a small display table set against the wall. Lady Isobel had entered without seeing him and he frowned at her straight back and intricate pleats of brown hair as she spoke to Philip and Lizzie. She was a confounded nuisance, especially in a household presided over by a lady of known high standards. Lady Hardwicke's disapproval would blight his chances of commissions from any of her wide social circle. She might be a blue-stocking and a playwright, but she was the daughter of the Earl of Balcarres and a lady of principle.

The Yorke daughters were charming, modest and well behaved, if inclined to giggle if spoken to. But this distant cousin was another matter altogether. At his first sight of her a tingle of recognition had gone down his spine. She was dangerous, although quite why, Giles would have been hard pressed to define. There was something in those wide grey eyes, her best feature. Some mystery that drew his unwilling interest.

Her frank and unabashed scrutiny had been an unwelcome surprise in an unmarried lady. He was used to the giggles and batted eyelashes of the young women making their come-outs and made a point of avoiding them. His birth was impossibly ineligible, of course, even if his education, style and income gave him the entrée to most of society. But he was unmarriageable and dangerous and that, he was well aware, was dinned into the young ladies he came into contact with.

Yet those very warnings were enough to make some of them think it irresistibly romantic that the illegitimate son of the Scarlet Widow was so handsome and so unobtainable.

For certain married ladies Giles Harker was not at all unobtainable—provided his notoriously capricious choice fell on them. Something the son of the most scandalous woman in society learned early on was that one's value increased with one's exclusivity and he was as coolly discriminating in his sins as his mother was warmly generous in hers. Even in her fifties—not that she would ever admit to such an age despite the incontrovertible evidence of an adult son—her heart was broken with delicious drama at least twice a year. His remained quite intact. Love, he knew from observation, was at best a fallacy, at worst, a danger.

Lord Hardwicke and Soane straightened up from their litter of plans, young Lord Royston blushed and the countess smiled. 'Come in, my dear. Philip, bring that chair over to the sofa for Cousin Isobel.'

Giles watched as she walked farther into the room with an assurance that confirmed him in his estimate of her age. 'Thank you, Lord Royston,' she said as he brought her chair. 'And you are Lady Lizzie?'

'Yes, ma'am.'

'I think I must be Cousin Isobel to you and Philip, for your mama assures me we are all related. Will you take me and introduce me to your sisters?'

Giles let the lid of the display table drop for the last fraction of an inch. Lady Isobel turned at the small, sharp sound. There was a friendly smile on her lips and it stayed, congealed into ice, as her gaze passed over him without the slightest sign of recognition.

A most-accomplished cut direct. It seemed an extreme reaction. He had sent her that chilling look in the hall out of sheer self-defence, as he did with any over-bold young woman who seemed interested. Mostly they took the hint and retreated blushing. This one seemed to have taken deep offence instead. She turned back and went to take her seat, sinking on to it with trained elegance.

For the first time in a long time Giles felt a stirring of interest in an utterly ineligible woman and it made him uneasy. That meeting of eyes in the hallway had been astonishing. He had intended to warn off yet another wide-eyed virgin and instead had found his snub returned with interest and hostility. Why she was so forward, and why he was so intrigued, was a mystery.

The earl began to pour drinks for the ladies without troubling to ring for a footman. Giles strolled over. 'Allow me to assist, sir.' He took the two glasses of lemonade for the youngest girls, noting how tactfully their father had used wine glasses to make them feel grown up. He came back and fetched the ratafia for Lady Anne and Lady Isobel, leaving the earl to serve his wife.

'Lady Isobel.' He proffered the glass, keeping hold of it so that she had to respond to him.

'Thank you.' She glanced up fleetingly, but did not turn her body towards him. 'Would you be so good as to put it on that side table, Mr Harker?' He might, from her tone, have been a clumsy footman.

Giles put the glass down, then spun a chair round and sat by her side, quite deliberately rather too close, to see if he could provoke her into some reaction. He was going to get to the bottom of this curiosity about her, then he could safely ignore her. As good breeding demanded, Lady Isobel shifted slightly on the tightly stuffed blue satin until he was presented with her profile.

Now she was rested from her journey she was much improved, he thought, hiding a connoisseur's assessment behind a bland social smile. Her straight nose was no longer pink at the tip from cold; her hair, freed from its bonnet, proved to be a glossy brown with a rebellious wave that was already threatening her hairpins, and her figure in the fashionable gown was well proportioned, if somewhat on the slender side for his taste.

On the other hand her chin was decided, her dark brows strongly marked and there was a tension about her face that suggested that she was braced for something unpleasant. Her mouth looked as though it could set into a firm line of disapproval; it was full and pink, but by no stretch of the imagination did the words *rosebud* or *bow* come to mind. And she was quite definitely in at least her fifth Season.

Lady Isobel took up the glass, sipped and finally turned to him with a lift of her lashes to reveal her intelligent dark grey eyes. 'Well?' she murmured with a sweetness that did not deceive him for a second. 'Have you studied me sufficiently to place me in your catalogue of females, Mr Harker? One well-bred spinster with brunette plumage, perhaps? Or do I not quite fit into a category, so you must bring yourself to converse with me while you decide?'

'What makes you think I have such a catalogue, Lady Isobel?' Giles accepted a glass of claret from the earl with a word of thanks and turned back to her. Interesting that she described herself as a spinster. She was perhaps twenty-four, he guessed, five years younger than he was. The shelf might be in sight, but she was not at her last prayers yet and it was an unusual young woman who would admit any danger that she might be.

'You are studying me with scientific thoroughness, sir. I half expect you to produce a net and a pin to affix me amongst your moth collection.'

*Moth*, he noted. *Not butterfly. Modesty? Or is she seeing if I can be provoked into meaningless compliments?*

'You have a forensic stare yourself, ma'am.'

Her lips firmed, just as he suspected they might. *Schoolmarm disapproval*, he thought. Or embarrassment, although he was beginning to doubt she could be embarrassed. Lady Isobel seemed more like a young matron than an unmarried girl. She showed no other sign of emotion and yet he could feel the tension radiating from her. It was strangely unsettling, although he should be grateful that his unwise curiosity had not led her to relax in his company.

'You refer to our meeting of eyes in the hall? You must be tolerant of my interest, sir—one rarely sees Greek statuary walking about. I note that you do not relish being assessed in the same way as you study others, although you must be used to it by now. I am certain that you do not harbour false modesty amongst your faults.'

The composure with which she attacked began to nettle him. After that exchange she should be blushing, fiddling with her fan perhaps, retreating from their conversation to sip her drink, but she seemed quite calm and prepared to continue the duel. It confirmed his belief that she had been sounding him out with an intention to flirt—or more.

'I have a mirror and I would be a fool to become swollen-headed over something that is due to no effort or merit of my own. Certainly I am used to stares,' he replied. 'And do not welcome them.'

'So modest and so persecuted. My heart bleeds for you, Mr Harker,' Lady Isobel said with a sweet smile and every appearance of sympathy. Her eyes were chill with dislike. 'And no doubt you find it necessary to lock your bedchamber door at night with tiresome regularity.'

'That, too,' he replied between gritted teeth, then caught himself. Somehow he had been lured into an utterly shocking exchange. A well-bred unmarried lady should have fainted dead away before making such an observation. And he should have bitten his tongue before responding to it, whatever the provocation. Certainly in public.

'How trying it must be, Mr Harker, to be so troubled by importunate members of my sex. We should wait meekly to be noticed, should we not? And be grateful for any attention we receive. We must not inconvenience, or ignore, the lords of creation who, in their turn, may ogle as much as they please while they make their lordly choices.'

Lady Isobel's voice was low and pleasant—no one else in the room would have noticed anything amiss in their conversation. But Giles realised what the emotion was that had puzzled him: she was furiously angry. With him. Simply because he had reacted coldly to her unladylike stare? Damn it, she had been assessing him like a housewife looking at a side of beef in the butchers. Or did she know who he was and think him presumptuous to even address her?

'That is certainly what is expected of ladies, yes,' he said, his own temper rising. He'd be damned if he was going to flirt and cajole her into a sweet mood, even if Lady Hardwicke noticed their spat. 'Certainly unmarried ones—whatever their age.'

Her chin came up at that. 'A hit, sir. Congratulations. But then a connoisseur such as yourself would notice only ladies who offer *irresistible temptation*. Not those who are *on the shelf and open to advances*.'

She turned her shoulder on him and immediately joined in the laughter over some jest of Philip's before he had time to react to the emphasis she had put on some of her phrases. It took a second, then he realised that she was quoting him and his conversation with Soane a few minutes earlier.

*Hell and damnation.* Lady Isobel must have been outside the door. Now he felt a veritable coxcomb. He could have sworn he had seen the glitter of unshed tears in her eyes. Now what did he do? His conscience stirred uneasily. Giles trampled on the impulse to apologise. It could only make things worse by acknowledging the offending words and explaining them would simply mire him further and hurt her more. Best to say nothing. Lady Isobel would avoid him now and that was better for both of them.

# CHAPTER THREE

'DINNER IS SERVED, my lady.' There was a general stir as the butler made his announcement from the doorway and the party rose. Giles made a hasty calculation about seating plans and realised that ignoring Lady Isobel might be harder than he had thought.

'We are a most unbalanced table, I am afraid,' the countess observed. 'Mr Soane—shall we?' He went to take her arm and the earl offered his to Lady Isobel. Giles partnered Lady Anne, Philip, grinning, offered his arm to fifteen-year-old Catherine and Lizzie was left to bring up the rear. When they were all seated Giles found himself between Lady Isobel and Lizzie, facing the remaining Yorke siblings and Mr Soane. Conversation was inevitable if they were not to draw attention to themselves.

Lizzie, under her mother's eagle eye, was on her best behaviour all through the first remove, almost unable to speak to him with the effort of remembering all the things that she must and must not do. Giles concluded it would be kinder not to confuse her with conversation, which left him with no choice but to turn and proffer a ragout to Lady Isobel.

'Thank you.' After a moment she said, 'Do you work with Mr Soane often?' Her tone suggested an utter lack of interest. The question, it was obvious, was the merest dinner-table conversation that good breeding required her to make. After his disastrous overheard comments she would like to tip the dish over his head, that was quite clear, but she was going to go through the motions of civility if it killed her.

'Yes.' Damn it, now he was sounding sulky. Or guilty. Giles pulled himself together. 'I worked in his drawing office when I first began to study architecture after leaving university. It was a quite incredible experience—the office is in his house, you may know—like finding oneself in the midst of Aladdin's cave and never knowing whether one is going to bump into an Old Master painting, trip over an Egyptian sarcophagus or wander into a Gothic monk's parlour!

'I am now building my own practice, but I collaborate with Soane if I can be of assistance. He is a busy man and I owe him a great deal.'

Lady Isobel made a sound that might be interpreted, by the wildly optimistic, as encouragement to expand on that statement.

'He employed me when I had no experience and, for all he knew, might prove to be useless.'

'And you are not useless?' She sounded sceptical.

'No.' *Hell, sulky again.* 'I am not.' Deciding what to do with his future during that last year at Oxford had not been easy. It would have been very simple to hang on his mother's purse strings—even her notorious extravagances had not compromised the wealth she had inherited from her father, nor her widow's portion.

Somehow the Dowager Marchioness of Faversham kept the *bon ton*'s acceptance despite breaking every rule in the book, including producing an illegitimate child by her head gardener's irresistibly handsome soldier son, ten months after the death of her indulgent and elderly husband. She was so scandalous, so charming, that Giles believed she was regarded almost as an exotic, not quite human creature, one that could be indulged and permitted its antics.

'I work for my living, Lady Isobel, and do it well. And I do not relish indolence,' he added to his curt rejoinder. He would have little trouble maintaining a very full, and equally scandalous, social life at the Widow's side, but he was not prepared to follow in her footsteps as a social butterfly. Society would have to accept him as himself, and on his own terms, or go hang if they found him too confusing to pigeonhole.

'You had an education that fitted you for this work, then?' Lady Isobel asked, her tone still inquisitorial, as though she was interviewing him for a post as a secretary. Her hands were white, her fingers long and slender. She ran one fingertip along the back of the knife lying by her plate and Giles felt a jolt of heat cut through his rising annoyance with her, and with himself for allowing her to bait him.

*Stop it, there is nothing special about her. Just far more sensuality than any respectable virgin ought to exude.* 'Yes. Harrow. Oxford. And a good drawing master.'

Lady Isobel sent him a flickering look that encompassed, and was probably valuing, his evening attire—from his coat, to his linen, to the stick-pin in his cravat and the antique ruby cabochon ring on his finger. Her own gown and jewellery spoke of good taste and the resources to buy the best.

'What decided you on architecture?' she asked. 'Is it a family tradition?'

No, she quite certainly did not know who he was or she would never have asked that. 'Not so far as I am aware. My father was a soldier,' Giles explained. 'I did not realise at first where my talents, if I had any, might lie. Then it occurred to me that many of the drawings in my sketchbooks were buildings, interiors or landscapes. I found I was interested in design, in how spaces are used.' His enthusiasm was showing, he realised and concluded, before he could betray anything more of his inner self, 'I wrote to Mr Soane and he took me on as an assistant.' He lowered his voice with a glance down the table. 'He is generous to young men in the profession—I think his own sons disappoint him with their lack of interest.'

And now, of course, many of his commissions came from men he met socially, who appreciated his work, liked the fact that he was 'one of them' and yet was sufficiently different for it not to be an embarrassment to pay his account. Giles was very well aware that his bills were met with considerably more speed than if he had been, in their eyes, a mere tradesman. And in return, he stayed well clear of their wives and daughters, whatever the provocation.

'So, have you built your own house, Mr Harker?'

'I have. Were you thinking of viewing it, Lady Isobel?'

'Now you are being deliberately provocative, Mr Harker.' Her dark brows drew together and the tight social smile vanished. 'I am thinking no such thing, as you know perfectly well. This is called *making polite conversation*, in case you are unfamiliar with the activity. You are supposed to inform me where your house is and tell me of some interesting or amusing feature, not make suggestive remarks.'

'Are you always this outspoken, Lady Isobel?' He found, unexpectedly, that his ill temper had vanished, although not all his guilt. He was enjoying her prickles—it was a novelty to be fenced with over dinner.

'I am practising,' she said as she sat back to allow the servants to clear for the second remove. 'My rather belated New Year resolution is to say what I mean. Scream it, if necessary,' she added in a murmur. 'I believe I should say what I think to people to their faces, not behind their backs.'

*Ouch.* There was nothing for it. 'I am sorry that you may have overheard some ill-judged remarks I made to Mr Soane earlier, Lady Isobel. That is a matter for regret.'

'I am sure it is,' she said with a smile that banished any trace of ease that he was beginning to feel in her presence. If she could cut with a smile, he hated to think what she might do with a frown.

'However, I do not feel that any good will be served by rehearsing the reason you hold such...*ill-judged* opinions.' Giles took a firm grip on his knife and resisted the urge to retaliate. He had been in the wrong—not to feel what he did, but to risk saying it where he might be overheard. Now he must give his head for a washing. He braced himself for her next barb. 'You were telling me about your house.'

*Excellent tactics*, he thought grimly. *Get me off balance while you work out how to knife me again.* 'My house is situated on a small estate in Norfolk. My paternal grandfather lives there and manages it for me in my absence.' It was also close enough for him to keep an eye on his mother on those occasions she descended on the Dower House of Westley Hall for one of her outrageous parties, causing acute annoyance and embarrassment to the current marquess and his wife and scandalised interest in the village. When she was in one of her wild moods he was the only person who could manage her.

'Your father—'

'He died before I was born.' It had taken some persuasion to extract his grandfather from the head gardener's cottage at Westley and persuade him that he would not be a laughing stock if he took up residence in his grandson's new country house. 'My grandfather lives with me. His health is not as robust as it once was.' Stubborn old Joe had resisted every inch of the way, despite being racked with rheumatism and pains in his back from years of manual labour. But now he had turned himself into a country squire of the old-fashioned kind, despite grumbling about rattling around in a house with ten bedchambers. Thinking about the old man relaxed him a little.

'How pleasant for you,' Lady Isobel said, accepting a slice of salmon tart. 'I wish I had known my grandfathers. And does your mama reside with you?'

'She lives independently. Very independently.' Things were relatively stable at the moment: his mother had a lover who was a year older than Giles. Friends thought he should be embarrassed by this liaison, but Giles was merely grateful that Jack had the knack of keeping her happy even if he had not a hope of restraining her wilder starts. To give the man his due, he did try.

'She is a trifle eccentric, perhaps?'

'Yes, I think you could say that,' Giles agreed. How quickly Lady Isobel picked up the undertones in what he said— No wonder she was able to slip under his guard with such ease when she chose.

'My goodness, you look almost human when you grin, Mr Harker.' She produced a sweet smile and turned to join in the discussion about the Irish language the earl was having with his eldest daughter.

*You little cat!* Giles almost said it out loud.

He had succeeded—far more brutally than he had intended—in ensuring he was not going to be fending off a hand on his thigh under the dinner table, or finding an unwelcome guest in his bedchamber, but at the expense of making an enemy of a close friend of the family. Now he had to maintain an appearance of civility so the Yorkes did not notice anything amiss. He could do without this—the tasks he had accepted to help Soane were going to be as nothing compared with the challenge of keeping his hands from Lady Isobel's slender throat if she continued to be quite so provocative.

She was idly sliding her fingers up and down the stem of her wine glass as she talked. The provocation was not simply to his temper, he feared.

Giles took a reviving sip of wine and listened to young Lizzie lecturing John Soane on the embellishments she considered would make the castle folly on the distant hill even more romantic than it already was.

That was one possibility, of course: wall up Lady Isobel in the tower and leave her for some knight in shining armour to rescue. Which was a very amusing thought, if it were not for the fact that he had a sneaking suspicion that through sheer perversity she would never wait around for some man to come to her aid. She would fashion the furniture into a ladder, climb out of the window and then come after him with a battleaxe.

She laughed and he turned to look at her, the wine glass halfway to his lips. That laugh seemed to belong to another woman altogether: a carefree, charming, innocent creature. As if feeling his regard, she turned and caught his eye and for a long moment their glances interlocked. Giles saw her lips part, her eyes darken as though something of significance had been exchanged.

A stab of arousal made him shift in his chair and the moment was lost. Lady Isobel turned away, her expression more puzzled than annoyed, as though she did not understand what had just happened.

Giles drank his wine. He knew exactly what had occurred; two virtual strangers had discovered that they were physically attracted to each other, even if one of them might not realise it and both of them would go to any lengths to deny it.

There were people in her bedroom. Voices, too low to make out, a tug on the covers as someone bumped into the foot of the bed. Isobel opened her eyes to dim daylight and a view of lace-trimmed pillow. With every muscle tensed, she rolled over and sat up, ready to scream, her heart contracting with alarm.

There was no sign of the party of rowdy bucks who had haunted her dreams. Instead, three pairs of wide eyes observed her from the foot of the bed, one pair so low that they seemed on a level with the covers. *Children*. Isobel let out a long breath and found a smile, restraining the impulse to scoot down the bed and gather up the barely visible smallest child and inhale the warm powdered scent of sleepy infant.

'Good morning. Would one of you be kind enough to draw the curtains?'

'Good morning, Cousin Isobel,' Lizzie said. 'I knew it would be all right to wake you up. Mama said you should sleep in and eat your breakfast in your room, but I thought you would like to have it with us in the nursery.'

The contrast between her own dreams of drunken, frightening bucks invading her bedroom, of the presence of Giles Harker somewhere in the mists of the nightmare, and the wide, innocent gaze of the children made her feel as though she was still not properly awake.

'That would be delightful. Thank you for the invitation.' Isobel rubbed the sleep out of her eyes and regarded the other two children as they came round the side of the bed. 'You must be Caroline and Charles. I am very pleased to meet you.'

Charles, who was four, if she remembered correctly, regarded her solemnly over the top of his fist. His thumb was firmly in his mouth. He shuffled shyly round the bed to observe her more closely. Isobel put out one hand and touched the rosy cheek and he chuckled. She fisted her hands in the bed sheets. He was so sweet and she wanted...

Caroline beamed and dragged the wrapper off the end of the bed. 'You'll need to put this on because the passageways are draughty. But there is a fire in the nursery.'

The children waited while she slid out of bed, put on the robe, ran a brush through her hair and retied it into a tail with the ribbon before donning her slippers. 'I'm ready now.'

'We can go this way, then we will not disturb Mama.' Lady Caroline led her out of the door on the far side of the bedchamber, through the small dressing room and out of another door on to what seemed to be the back stairs. 'We just go through there and up the stairs to the attic—'

There was the sound of whistling and the soft slap of backless leather slippers on carpet. Across the landing a shadow slid over the head of the short flight of stairs that must lead to the suites at the back of the house. Someone was coming. A male someone. Trapped in the doorway, with a chattering seven-year-old in front of her, a small boy hanging on to her skirts and Lizzie bringing up the rear, Isobel just had time to clutch the neck of her wrapper together as Mr Harker appeared.

He stopped dead at the sight of them, his long brocade robe swinging around his bare ankles. His face was shadowed with his unshaven morning beard, his hair was tousled and an indecent amount of chest was showing in the vee of the loosely tied garment.

He must be naked beneath it. 'Good morning, Lady Isobel, Lady Lizzie, Lady Caroline, Master Charles. I hope you do not represent a bathing party.'

Cousin Elizabeth had said something about a plunge bath in this area, so that was presumably where he was going. He might have had the decency to have turned on his heel the moment he saw them, Isobel thought, resentment mingling with sensations she tried hard not to acknowledge. Now she was in the position of having to exchange words with a scarcely clad man while she was in her nightwear. The fact that her wrapper was both practical and all-enveloping was neither here nor there.

'We are going to the nursery for breakfast,' she said, her gaze, after one glimpse of hair-roughened chest, fixed a foot over his head. 'Lead the way, please, Caroline.'

'Good morning, Mr Harker,' the children chorused. Isobel scooped up little Charles as a shield and they trooped across the landing, past the architect and through into the sanctuary of the door to the attic stairs. She was furiously aware that she was peony-pink and acting like a flustered governess. All her anger-fuelled defiance of him over dinner was lost in embarrassment.

They climbed the stairs and Caroline took them around the corner and on to a landing with a skylight overhead and a void, edged with rails and panelled boards, in the centre. As she tried to orientate herself Isobel realised it must be above the inner hallway her room opened on to, with the snob-boards to prevent the servants looking down on their employers.

'Papa had Mr Soane make him a plunge bath in the old courtyard that used to be behind the main stairs.' Lizzie waved a hand in the general direction. 'I think it would be great fun to learn to swim in it, but Mama says it is for Papa to relax in, not for us to splash about.'

*Now I have the mental picture of Mr Harker floating naked in the warm water... Thank you so much, Lizzie.*

'Here we are. This is where Caroline and I sleep, and here is Charles's room and here is the nursery. Nora, we have brought Lady Isobel, I told you she would like to have breakfast with us.'

A skinny maid bobbed a curtsy. 'Oh, Lady Lizzie! I do hope it is all right, my lady, I said you'd be wanting to rest, but off they went...'

'That is quite all right. I would love to have breakfast here.' The children and their staff appeared to occupy this entire range of south-facing rooms with wonderful views over the long avenue and the park towards Royston. A pair of footmen carried in trays.

Charles twisted in her arms and she made herself put him down.

'I told them to bring lots of food because we had a special guest. Those are my designs for the tower—Mr Soane says I show a flair for the dramatic,' Lizzie pronounced, pointing at a series of paintings pinned on the wall. 'I expect I get that from Mama. She writes plays, you know and sometimes when we have a house party they are acted in the Gallery. Papa says she is a veritable blue-stocking. We will go for a walk this morning and I will show you the tower.' Lizzie finally ran out of breath, or perhaps it was the smell of bacon that distracted her.

'That would be very pleasant, provided your mama does not need me.' Isobel sat down at the table. 'It would be wonderful to get out in the fresh air and it looks as though the morning will be sunny, which is such a relief after yesterday's drizzle.' And there was the added advantage that if she was out of the house she would be at a safe distance from Mr Harker's disturbing presence.

While she ate she contemplated just how maddening he was. He was arrogant, self-opinionated, far too aware of his own good looks, shockingly outspoken and did not do his robe up properly. He was, in fact, just like the drunken bucks at the house party, only sober, which was no excuse, for that meant he should know better. He also made her feel strangely unsettled in a way she had almost forgotten she could feel. There was no doubting that his relaxed, elegant body would strip to perfection, that his skin would feel—

Isobel bit savagely into a slice of toast and blackcurrant conserve. What was the use of men except to make women's lives miserable? She contemplated Master Charles, chubby-cheeked, slightly sticky already, full of blue-eyed innocence. Little boys were lovely. She felt a pang at the thought of what she was missing.

Kind fathers and husbands like her own papa, or Lord Hardwicke, were obviously good men. Lucas had been almost perfect. But how on earth was one to tell what a candidate for one's hand would turn out to be like? Most males, by the time they turned eighteen, appeared to be rakehells, seducers, drinkers, gamblers...

Perhaps she could become an Anglican nun. They did have them, she was sure, and it sounded safe and peaceful. A mental image of Mr Harker, laughing himself sick at the sight of her in a wimple, intruded. She would look ridiculous and she would be quite unsuited to the life. Besides, she would not be free to travel, to visit Jane and the children. An eccentric spinster then. She had enough money.

Only she did not *want* to be a spinster. She would

rather like to fall in love again with a good man and marry. Her daydream stuttered to a halt: he would doubtless want children. But where did she find one she could trust with her heart and all that was most precious to her? And even if she did find this paragon, was he going to want her when he knew the truth about her?

# CHAPTER FOUR

'MORE COFFEE, COUSIN ISOBEL?'

'Thank you, Lizzie.' Her mind was going round in circles. Isobel forced herself into the present. 'At what time shall we go for our walk?'

'Shall I meet you in the garden at ten o'clock?' the girl suggested. 'I must explain to Miss Henderson, my governess, that I am going on an educational nature expedition with you.'

'You are?'

'There are the lakes—we will see all kinds of wild birds,' Lizzie said with irrefutable logic. Isobel found herself experiencing a pang of sympathy for the unfortunate Miss Henderson.

A visit to Lady Hardwicke's unusual semi-circular sitting room, almost next to her own, reassured Isobel that her hostess did not require her assistance, and that Lizzie was permitted to escape from French conversation for one morning.

Isobel snuggled her pelisse warmly around herself as she stepped out into the garden that lay between the north front and the parkland. It wanted at least fifteen minutes until ten o'clock and there was no sign of Lizzie yet. The bleak, wintry formal beds held little attraction, but the shrubbery that lay to one side behind the service wing looked mysterious and worthy of exploration.

A glimpse of a small domed roof intrigued her enough to brave the dense foliage, still dripping on to the narrow paths after yesterday's drizzle. The building, when she reached it down the twisting paths, was small, low and angular with an odd dome and no windows that she could see. It looked vaguely classical, but what its function might be, she had no idea. The gloomy shrubbery seemed an odd place for a summer house. Perhaps it was an ice house.

Isobel circled the building. Under her boots the leaf mould yielded damply, muffling her footsteps as she picked her way with caution, wary of slipping.

The sight of a pair of long legs protruding from the thick clump of laurel bush that masked the base of the structure brought her up short. The legs were visible from midthigh, clad in brown buckskin breeches. The polished boots, smeared with mud, were toes down—their owner must be lying on his stomach. As she stared there was a grunt from the depths of the bush—someone was in pain.

A keeper attacked by poachers? A gardener who had fainted? Isobel bent and pushed aside the branches with her hands. Even as she crouched down she realised that gamekeepers and gardeners did not wear boots of such quality. She slipped, landed with an ungainly thump, threw out a hand and found she was gripping one hard-muscled, leather-clad thigh.

'Oh! Are you all right?' The man was warm at least—perhaps he had not lain there very long. There did not seem to be any room to move away now she was crouched under the thick evergreen foliage.

The prone figure rolled over and she went with him in a tangle of thin branches to find herself flat on her back, her body pinned under the solid length of a man who was quite obviously neither fainting nor wounded, but very much in possession of his senses. All of them.

'My dear Lady Isobel, have you come to assist me with the plumbing?' Harker drawled as he looked down at her through the green-shadowed gloom. After a fraught moment he raised his weight off her and on to his elbows.

'Plumbing?' Isobel stared at him. 'What on earth are you talking about? Let me go this—ouch!'

'You are lying on a hammer,' he explained. 'If you will just move your shoulder a trifle... There. Is that more comfortable?'

'No, it is not. Will you let me up this instant, Mr Harker!'

'The ground is quite dry under these evergreens and you are lying on sacking.' There was the hint of a smile tugging at one corner of those sculpted lips. 'You are being very demanding—I really do not feel you can expect anything better if you will insist on an alfresco rendezvous with me in early February.'

Isobel tried to sit up and succeeded merely in pressing her bosom against his chest. Harker's eyes darkened and the twitch of his lips became an appreciative smile. She fell back, opened her mouth to scream and then remembered Lizzie—the last thing she wanted was to frighten the child by bringing her to this scene.

Furious at her own powerlessness, she put up her hands and pushed against his shoulders. He did not shift. Isobel felt her breath become shorter. *Oh, the humiliation*—she was positively panting now and he doubtless thought it was with excitement. Even more mortifying was the realisation that he would be right—her instincts were responding and she *was* finding this exciting. This was her punishment for daydreaming about his body. The reality was just as deliciously hard and lean and—

'Get off!' She felt aroused, flustered and indignant, but she did not feel afraid, she realised as the green eyes studied her. 'I have not the slightest intention nor desire of making a rendezvous with you, Mr Harker, inside or outside.'

'Then whose thigh did you think you were fondling?' he asked with every appearance of interest.

'*Fondling?* How dare you! I lost my balance.' The feel of those taut muscles under the leather was imprinted on her memory. 'I thought a gardener had fainted, or hit his head, or a gamekeeper had been attacked by poachers or something.' His body was warm and hard and seriously disturbing to a lady's equilibrium, pressed against her just there…and the wretch knew it. He shifted slightly and smiled as she swallowed. Oh, yes, he was finding this *very* interesting. No doubt she should be flattered.

'And there I was, thinking that the sight of me in my dressing gown was enough to lure young ladies into a damp shrubbery,' Harker said. 'I was, of course, about to decline what I assumed was your most flattering offer.'

'Decline?' She stared at him. That he could imagine for one moment that she had actually followed him there in order to…to…canoodle… Indignation became fury. 'Why—?'

'Why? Because well-bred virgins are far more trouble than they are worth.'

'Oh!' The insufferable arrogance of the man!

'This is probably madness, but as we are here, it

seems a pity to waste the moment.' She realised too late that her hands were still on his shoulders and tried to pull herself away, but there was nowhere to go. He bent his head and took her mouth, all with one smooth, well-practised movement.

The last man to kiss her had been both drunk and clumsy. Harker was neither. His mouth was hot and demanding and sent messages straight to her belly, straight to her breasts, as though wires connected every nerve and he was playing with them. Panic at her own response threatened for a fleeting moment and then she got one hand free, twisting as she did so. The smack of her palm against the side of his face was intensely satisfying.

'You...you *bastard*,' she spat, the moment he lifted his head. The word seemed to rock him off balance. The green eyes darkened, widened and he pushed himself up and away from her. The wave of anger brought her to her feet, shoving against him for balance as she crashed out of the shrubs onto the path. 'Is this revenge because I took you to task for your insulting words to Mr Soane last night? You arrogant, lustful, smug *bastard*!' It was a word she never used, a word she loathed, but now she threw it at him like a weapon.

'Cousin Isobel? Are you in the shrubbery?' Lizzie's voice sounded as though she was coming towards them.

'Stay there,' Isobel said fiercely, jabbing a finger at him. 'Just you stay there.' Harker straightened up, one hand rubbing his reddening cheek, his mouth twisted into a rueful smile. The mouth whose heat still seemed to burn her own.

Isobel turned on her heel and almost ran along the twisting path to meet the child. The tug of the ribbons at her throat stopped her in time to rescue her bonnet. She brushed leaf mould from her skirts, took a deep breath and stepped out onto the lawn.

'Here I am. I went exploring.' Somehow her voice sounded normal, if a little over-bright.

'Oh, I expect you found the Water Castle. *Castello d'Aqua*, Mr Soane calls it. He had it built to supply the boiler when the plunge bath was put in, but it hasn't been working very well.' Lizzie chattered on as she led the way across the garden and out of the gate into the park. 'Papa said the pressure was too low and the steward should call a plumber, but Mr Harker said he'd see if he could free up the valve, or something. I expect having a bath this morning reminded him.'

That must have been what he was doing in the bushes, not lying in wait for passing females to insult. Apparently he could manage to do that with no prior warning whatsoever.

They let themselves out of the iron garden gates and Lizzie led the way across the park that lay between the house and the hill surmounted by the folly tower. A small group of deer lifted their heads and watched them warily.

'What a delightful park.' Isobel kept her side of the conversation going while she forced her somewhat-shaky legs to keep up with Lizzie's exuberant pace.

Harker had leapt to the most indecent conclusion about her motives—her desires, even. He had not let her get more than a word out, he had taken advantage of her in the most appalling way.

She had stood up to him last night—was this then to be her punishment? To be taken for a lightskirt? Or was this insult simply retaliation for her refusal to meekly treat him as wonderful? That made him no better than those wretched bucks who had invaded her bedroom and she realised that that was disappointing. Somehow, infuriating though he was, she had expected more of him.

She had responded to him, she thought, incurably honest, as she trudged in Lizzie's exuberant wake through a gate and across a narrow brick bridge crossing a deep stock ditch. Had he realised? Of course he had—he was experienced, skilful and had slept with more women than she had owned pairs of silk stockings. So now she could add humiliation to the sensations that would course through her when she next saw Mr Harker and he, no doubt, would use it to torment her mercilessly for as long as the game amused him.

She toyed with the idea of telling Cousin Elizabeth, then realised that she did not come out of the incident well herself, not unless she was prepared to colour the encounter so she appeared a shrinking violet and he a ravisher.

'See—is it not splendid?' Lizzie gestured to the tower and ragged length of curtain wall that crowned the far hill. 'But I think Papa should have Mr Soane build an entire castle. Or Mr Harker could do it. He is younger so perhaps he is more romantic. It would not be an extravagance, for all the gamekeepers and under-keepers could live in it, which would be a saving in cottages.'

'Do you not think the keepers might find it uncomfortable?' Isobel enquired as they took the winding sheep path down towards the sheet of water. She resisted the temptation to remark that, in her opinion, Mr Harker was as romantic as a ravaging Viking horde.

'That had not occurred to me. You are very practical, Cousin Isobel.' Practicality did not seem to appeal much to Lizzie. She frowned, but her brow cleared as the lake opened out in a shallow valley before them. A long narrow ribbon of water ran away to their right. Ahead and to the left was a smaller, wider lake.

'When Mr Repton was here to do the landscaping he said we should have a ship's mast on the bank of the lower lake.'

'A rowing boat or a skiff, you mean?'

'No, a proper big ship's mast so the tops of the sails would be seen from the house and it would look as though there was an ocean here.' Lizzie skipped down the somewhat muddy path. 'Papa said it was an extravagant folly. But I think it would be magnificent! I liked Mr Repton, but Papa says he has expensive ideas, so Mr Sloan and Mr Harker have come instead. You see, there is a bridge here.'

As they got closer Isobel could see that the valley had been dammed and that the smaller lake was perhaps fifteen feet above the lower one, with a bridge spanning the point where the overflow ran from one to the other.

Lizzie gestured expansively. 'Mr Repton said we need a new bridge in the Chinese style.' She ran ahead and leaned over the rail to look into the depths below.

Isobel dragged her mind away from trying to decide whether she ought to tell Cousin Elizabeth about Mr Harker's kiss, however badly it made her appear. 'That does look a trifle rickety. Do be careful. Lizzie!'

As she spoke the rail gave a crack, splintered and

gave way. Lizzie clung for a moment, then, with a piercing shriek, tumbled into the water and vanished under the surface.

'Lizzie!' Isobel cast off her bonnet and pelisse as she ran. 'Help! Help!' But even as she shouted she knew they had seen no one at all in the broad sweep of park, let alone anyone close enough to help.

Could the child swim? But even if she could, the water was cold and muddy and goodness knew how deep. There were bubbles rising, but no sign of Lizzie. Isobel ran to the edge, waded in and forced her legs, hampered by her sodden skirts, through the icy water. She couldn't swim, but perhaps if she held on to the bridge supports she could reach out a hand to Lizzie and pull her up.

Without warning the bottom vanished beneath her feet. Isobel plunged down, opened her mouth to shriek and swallowed water. Splinters pierced her palm and she lost her hold on the wooden supports. The light was blotted out as the lake closed over her head.

Giles cursed under his breath and held the grey gelding to an easy canter up the sweeping slope. Had he completely misread her? Had Lady Isobel simply chanced to come upon him in the shrubbery and lost her balance as she maintained? He had thought it a trick to provoke him into kissing her and that her protests had been merely a matter of form. But now his smarting cheek told him her protests had been real enough. So had her anger last night. He had let his desires override his instincts and he had completely mishandled the situation.

*Bastard*. He had learned to accept and ignore that word, to treat it with amusement. But for some reason it had stung more from her lips than the flat of her hand on his cheek had done

He should seek her out and apologise. *Hell*. If he did, then she would either slap his face again or she would be all too forgiving and…and might kiss him again with that delicious mixture of innocent sensuality and fire.

No. Too dangerous. Concentrate on work and forget one provoking and unaccountably intriguing woman who, it was becoming painfully clear, he did not understand. She was no schoolroom miss—she would soon forget it, or at least pretend to.

He reined in as the grey reached the earthworks that marked the base of the old windmill. From here there was a fine view north over the lakes to the Gothic folly and, stretching south along the edge of the woodland, an avenue of trees leading to his destination, the Hill House.

The avenue stretched wide and smooth, perfect for

a gallop. Giles gathered up the reins, then stopped at the sound of a faint shriek. A bird of prey? A vixen? He stood in his stirrups and scanned the parkland. There was nothing to be seen.

'Help!' It was faint, but it was clear and repeated, coming from the direction of the lakes. A woman's voice. Giles dragged the gelding's head round and spurred down the slope, heedless of wet grass, mud and thorn bushes. The deep stock ditch opened up before them and the grey gathered his hocks under him and leapt, then they were thundering down towards the lake.

As Giles reined in on the flat before the dam he could see no signs of life—only a bonnet and pelisse lying discarded at the water's edge.

There were footprints in the mud, small woman's prints, and a disturbance, bubbles, below the centre of the bridge where the rail was broken. Giles flung himself out of the saddle, wrenched off his coat and boots and strode into the lake. The muddy water churned and two figures broke the surface for a few moments, the larger flailing desperately towards the bridge supports, the smaller limp in her grasp before they sank again. Lady Isobel and Lizzie.

It took a dozen strokes to reach them. Giles put his head down and dived under, groped through the muddy water and touched a hand, so cold that for a

moment he thought it was a fish. He kicked and broke
the surface hauling the dead weight of both woman
and child after him.

'Take her,' Isobel gasped as they broke the surface
and she thrust the child's body into his reaching arms.
When he tried to take hold of her too, she resisted.
'No, there's weed tangled round her. I couldn't…
You'll need both hands to pull her free.'

Treading water, Giles wrenched and tugged and the
slight body was suddenly floating in his arms. 'Hang
on!' he ordered Isobel as though he could keep her
afloat by sheer force of will. He towed Lizzie back to
the shore, dumped her without ceremony and turned
back to Isobel. She had vanished.

# CHAPTER FIVE

NUMB, SHAKING WITH cold and fear for Isobel, Giles launched himself back into the water in a shallow dive. She was beyond struggling now as he caught one slender wrist and pulled her, gasping and choking, back to the surface again.

As soon as they reached the shallows she managed to raise herself on hands and knees and shake off his hold. 'Go and see if she's breathing. Help her—I can manage.'

Giles stumbled to the shore and dragged Lizzie farther up onto the grass, turned her over his knee and slapped her hard between the shoulder blades. 'Come on, breathe!' She coughed, retched up quantities of muddy water, then began to cry.

'Lizzie, it is all right, Mr Harker rescued us,' a hoarse voice croaked beside him. 'Come here now, don't cry.' Somehow Isobel had crawled up the bank to gather the child in her arms, petting and soothing. 'There, there. We'll get you home safe to your mama, don't worry.'

Giles found his coat and wrapped it round them. Lady Isobel's hair hung in filthy sodden curtains around her face, her walking dress clung like a wet blanket to her limbs and she was shuddering with cold, but her voice was steady as she looked up at him. 'Please, go for help, Mr Harker.' She dragged the coat off her own shoulders and around the child.

He stared at her for a moment, a bedraggled, exhausted Madonna, somehow the image of desperate motherhood and feminine courage. 'Felix will take all of us at a walk, it will be faster.' He dragged on his boots and unsaddled the gelding to make room for the three of them. 'Let me get you up first, then I'll hand Lizzie to you. Can you manage?'

Lady Isobel let him drag her to her feet, then boost her onto the horse. She ignored the display of bare flesh as her skirts rode up her legs and held out her hands to steady Lizzie as the child was put in front of her. Giles vaulted up behind.

Felix, well trained and willing, plodded up the slope with his burden while Giles tried to hold Isobel and Lizzie steady as their shivering increased. Through his own wet shirt he could feel how cold Lady Isobel was growing, but she did not complain. He could hear her murmuring reassurance to Lizzie, the words blurred as she tried to control her chattering teeth.

'Thank God you can swim,' he said as the house

came in sight. He steered Felix towards the service wing where there would be plenty of strong hands to help.

'I c-can't.'

'Then why the hell did you go in?' Giles demanded, his voice roughened with shock.

'I th-thought I might be able to reach her if I held on to the bridge supports. She did not c-come up, you see. By the time I had got to the house and brought help she would have drowned. But the bottom shelved and I was out of my depth—as I went down I found her.' She broke off, coughed, and he did his best to support her until the racking spasms ceased. 'I untangled enough of the weed to push us up to the surface, but then I could not keep us there.'

Every other female of his acquaintance would have stood on the lakeside and screamed helplessly while the child drowned. 'Isobel, that was very brave.'

She did not react to the way he addressed her—she was probably beyond noticing such things. 'There didn't seem to be any other option—she was my responsibility.' The retort held a ghost of her tart rejoinders of the night before and Giles smiled with numb lips even as a pang of shame reminded him how easily he had judged this woman.

She seemed to slump and Giles tightened his arms around them. 'Steady now.' Isobel let her head fall back on his shoulder and she leaned against him as though seeking for the slight heat he could give her. He wanted to rip off their clothes, hold her against his bare flesh to force his remaining warmth into her. 'Almost there now, my brave girl.'

As they rode into the yard the boot boy gawped, a scullery maid dropped an armload of kindling, but one of the footmen ran forwards shouting, 'Here! Everyone—quick—and bring blankets! Hurry!'

Hands reached for Lizzie and Isobel and he let them be taken before he threw a leg over Felix's withers, dropped to the ground and ran to find the countess.

Isobel rather thought she had fainted. One minute she was held against Mr Harker's comfortingly broad chest, and he was calling her his brave girl, the next hands were lifting her down and then she found herself in the countess's sitting room with Cousin Elizabeth ordering hot baths and towels and more coals for the fire and no recollection of how she had got there.

'I'm sorry,' she managed to say when the hubbub subsided enough to make herself heard. Her voice sounded raspy and her throat was sore. 'The rail on the bridge broke and Lizzie tumbled in. Mr Harker...'

Mr Harker had saved her and the child. She looked

at Lizzie, white-faced, her vulnerable, naked body and thin little arms making her look much younger than her years. She wanted to hold her, convince herself the child was safe, but that was not her right. Lizzie had her mother to hold and comfort her. Her mother was with her, every day, saw every change in her growing child, felt every emotion…

'Mr Harker said you went in after Lizzie even though you cannot swim,' Cousin Elizabeth said. She looked up from the tub where she was on her knees helping the nursery nurse rub her daughter's pale limbs amidst clouds of steam. Isobel blinked back the tears that had blurred her vision and with them the pang of jealousy towards the older woman with her happy brood of children all around her. 'She owes her life to you both.' The shock was evident on the countess's strained face, even though she managed to keep her voice steady.

'Let me help you into the bath.' Lady Anne, who had been peeling off Isobel's sodden, disgusting clothes, pulled her to her feet and urged her towards the other tub set before the fire. 'Papa insisted on sending his valet to look after Mr Harker. Tompkins went past just now muttering about the "State of Sir's Breeches" in capital letters. One gathers that Mr Harker's unmentionables may never be the same again.'

As Anne must have intended, the women all laughed and Isobel felt herself relax a little as she slid into the hot water. To her relief Lizzie began to talk, her terrifying brush with death already turning into an exciting adventure. 'And Mr Harker galloped up like a knight in shining armour and dived into the lake…'

He must have done—and acted without hesitation or neither of them would be here now. He might be a rake, and an arrogant one at that, but he had been brave and effective. And kind in just the right way: brisk and bracing enough to keep them both focused.

Isobel bit her lip as Anne helped her out of the tub and into the embrace of a vast warm towel. She was going to have to thank Mr Harker, however hard that would be. 'Sit by the fire and let me rub your hair dry,' Anne said as she and the maid enveloped Isobel in a thick robe.

Finally Lizzie was bundled off to bed. Her mother stopped by Isobel's chair and stooped to kiss her cheek. 'Thank you, my dear, from the bottom of my heart. Will you go to bed now?'

'No. No, I want to move around, I think.' She was filled with panic at the thought of falling asleep and dreaming of that black, choking water, the weed like the tentacles of a sea monster, her fear for the child. As Lizzie had slid through her hands she had thought she had lost her. She shuddered. To lose a child was too cruel and yet they were so vulnerable. *No, stop thinking like that.*

'If you are sure.' The countess regarded her with concern. 'You are so pale, Isobel. But very well, if you insist. Perhaps you could do something for me—I know my husband will have said all that is proper, but will you ask Tompkins to tell Mr Harker that I will thank him myself tomorrow? For now I must stay with Lizzie.'

'Yes, of course. As soon as I am dressed,' Isobel promised. Anne pressed a cup of tea into her hands and stood behind her to comb out her hair.

'Mr Harker is very handsome, don't you think?' the younger girl remarked as soon as they were alone.

'Oh, extraordinarily so,' Isobel agreed. To deny it would be positively suspicious. 'Although I find such perfection not particularly attractive—quite the opposite, in fact. Do you not find his appearance almost chilly? I cannot help but wonder what lies behind the mask.' What was he hiding behind that handsome face? Puzzling over his motives kept drawing her eyes, her thoughts, to him. He had courage and decision, he was beautiful, like a predatory animal, but he was also rude, immoral...

'How exciting to have your come-out in Dublin,' she said, veering off the dangerous subject of rakish architects. 'And with your papa representing his Majesty, you will be invited to all the very best functions.'

The diversion worked. Anne chatted happily about her plans and hopes while Isobel let the strength and courage seep slowly back into her as the warmth gradually banished the shivers.

Mr Harker's rooms would be on the north side of the house, judging by his appearance en route to the plunge bath. There were three suites on the northern side and the westernmost one of those belonged to the earl. So by deduction Harker must be in either the centre or the eastern one. Isobel hesitated at her sitting-room door and was caught by Dorothy as her maid bustled past with an armful of dry towels.

'Lady Isobel! How did you get yourself dressed again? You should be in your own bed and wrapped up warm. Come along, now, I'll tuck you up and fetch some nice hot milk.'

'I would prefer to warm myself by exploring the house a little and for you to see what can be done with my walking dress. I fear it must be ruined, but I suppose it might be salvageable.'

There was a moment when Isobel thought Dorothy was going to argue, then she bobbed a curtsy and retreated to the dressing room with pursed lips, emanating disapproval.

Isobel's footsteps were muffled as she crossed the landing. Somehow that made the nerves knotting her stomach worse, as though she was creeping about on some clandestine mission. But she had to thank Mr Harker for saving her life and she had to do that face-to-face or she would be uncomfortable around him for her entire stay at Wimpole. It did not mean that she forgave him for that kiss, or for his assumptions about her.

It occurred to Isobel as she lifted her hand to knock on the door of the central suite that this visit might reinforce those assumptions, but she was not turning back now.

She rapped briskly. A voice within, somewhat smothered, called 'Come!' Isobel rapped again. The door opened with a impatient jerk and Mr Harker stood on the threshold, a towel in his hand, his damp-darkened hair standing on end. He was in his shirt sleeves, without his neckcloth. Like this he seemed inches bigger in both height and breadth.

'Isobel?'

'Do not call me—' She took a breath, inhaled the scent of sandalwood and soap and moderated her tone. She was here to make peace, she reminded herself, not to lash out to prove to herself just how indifferent she was to him. 'I have a message from the countess and something I wish to say on my own account. Lady Hardwicke wants very much to thank you herself, but she feels she must be with Lizzie today and she hopes you will understand if she does not speak with you until tomorrow. I think you may imagine her emotions and will therefore forgive her sending a message.'

He tossed the towel away towards the corner of the room without taking his eyes from her face. 'I do not need thanking and certainly do not expect her to leave the child in order to do so. How is Lady Lizzie?'

'Much better than one might expect, after that experience. She will be perfectly all right, I believe.' She could turn tail and go now. Isobel took a deep breath instead. 'And I, too, must thank you, Mr Harker, on my own account. I owe you my life.'

'I was in the right place to hear you, that is all. Anyone would have done the same.' He frowned at her. 'You should not be here.'

For him to be preaching the proprieties was intolerable! 'Please, do not be afraid I have come with any improper purpose, Mr Harker. Surely even your elevated sense of self-esteem would not delude you into thinking that after this morning's experiences I have either the desire or the energy to attempt to seduce you.'

The acid in her tone made him blink and the sweep of those thick dark lashes did nothing to moderate her irritation with him. 'Rest assured,' she added rather desperately, 'I have no intention of crossing the threshold. Your...virtue is perfectly safe.'

He studied her in silence for a moment. Isobel pressed her lips together to control the other things she would very much like to say on the subject of men who made assumptions about ladies with no evidence and then discussed them with their friends and then ravished them in wet shrubberies and made them feel...made them...

'What a relief,' he said finally. 'I was about to scream for help.' She glared at him. 'However, I believe I have an apology to make.'

'Oh? So you are sorry for that outrage in the shrubbery, are you?' It was very hard to hang on to a sense of gratitude when the wretch stood there, the gleam in his eyes giving the lie to any hint of penitence in his voice.

'I am sorry for coming to an incorrect conclusion about your intentions. I cannot be sorry for the kiss, for I enjoyed it too much.'

'If that is intended to flatter, Mr Harker, it failed. I imagine you enjoy virtually any kisses you can snatch.' She should turn on her heel and walk away, but it was impossible to leave him before she had made her indifference to him clear beyond any possible doubt. It was very strange—the last time she had felt this stubborn and light-headed had been after an incautious second glass of champagne on an empty stomach.

'I do not find you in the slightest bit attractive and, even if I did, my upbringing and my personal standards would prevent me acting in any way that might hint at such foolishness,' she stated, crossing her fingers tightly in the folds of her skirt. 'If your delusions about your personal charms have suffered a correction, I can only be glad of it for the sake of other females you may encounter.' It must be the effect of expressing her irritation so freely, but she was feeling positively feverish. Isobel shivered.

Instead of taking offence at her lecture, or even laughing at her, Harker took a step closer, his face serious. 'Why are you not in your bed, Isobel?'

'Because I do not need to mollycoddle myself. And grateful as I am to you for rescuing me, I did not give you the use of my name.'

'If you desire to thank me for getting wet on your behalf, I wish you will let me use it. My name is Giles and I make you free of that,' he said as he lifted one hand and laid the back of it against her cheek. 'You are barely warm enough, Isobel. I am sorry for this morning, and last night. I have become...defensive about single ladies. I was wrong to include you with the flirts and, worse, upon no more evidence than a very frank stare and a willingness to stand up to me.'

Somehow his hand was still against her cheek, warm and strangely comforting, for all the quiver of awareness it sent through her. If her limbs felt so leaden that she could not move, or brush away his hand, then at least she could speak up for herself. 'Surely you are not so vain as to believe that good looks make you somehow superior and irresistible to women? That every lady who studies your profile or the width of your shoulders desires you?' Oh, why had she mentioned his shoulders? Now he knew she had been looking.

He did not take her up on that revealing slip. 'Unfortunately there are many who confuse the outer form, over which I have no control, and for which I can claim no credit, for the inner character. And, it seems, there are many ladies who would welcome a certain amount of…adventure in their lives.' He shrugged. 'Men are just as foolish over a pretty face, uncaring whether it hides a vacuous mind or fine intelligence. You must have observed it. But the pretty young ladies are chaperoned,' he added with a rueful smile.

'And no one protects the handsome men?' Isobel enquired. She had managed to lift her hand to his, but it stayed there instead of obeying her and pushing his fingers away. She felt very strange now, not quite in her own body. There was a singing in her ears. She forced herself to focus. 'You are telling me that you are the victim here?'

'We men have to look after ourselves. I am vulnerable, certainly. If I acquire a reputation for flirting, or worse, with the unmarried daughters of the houses where I work, I will not secure good commissions at profitable country estates.' His mouth twisted wryly. 'Repelling single young ladies has become second nature and a certain cynicism about the motives of those who show an interest is, under the circumstances, inevitable.'

'What circumstances?'

Giles had caught her left hand in his, his fingers long and strong as they enveloped it. 'You do not know? Never mind.' Isobel thought about persisting, then restrained herself—probably this was something that would reveal her as painfully naive. Giles drew her closer and slid his hand round to tip up her chin. 'You are exhausted and probably in a state of shock. Why will you not rest?'

'I do not want to dream,' Isobel confessed. 'I have night…' The man must be a mesmerist, drawing confessions out of her as she stood there, handfast with him. She should go at once, stop talking to him about such personal matters. If only her body would obey her, because she wanted to go. She really wanted...

'You suffer from nightmares?'

'When I have a lot on my mind.' Her voice sounded as though it was coming from a long way away. She stared at Giles Harker, who was moving. Or perhaps the room behind him was. It began to dawn on her that she was going to faint.

'You are in no fit state—' Harker caught her as her knees gave way and gathered her against his chest. He ought to put her down because this was improper. She should tell him... But he was warm and strong and felt safe. Her muddled brain questioned that— Giles Harker was not safe, was he?

There was the sound of footsteps on the great staircase below them, muted voices carrying upwards. Giles stepped back into his room, pulling her with him, and closed the door. 'Damn it, I do not want us found by a brace of footmen with you draped around my neck and me half dressed.' His voice was very distant now.

'Put me down, then,' Isobel managed as she was lifted and carried into another room, deposited on something. A bed?

'Stay there.'

'I do not think I could do anything else...' It was

an effort to speak, so she lay still until he came back and spread something warm and soft over her.

'Go to sleep, Isobel. If any nightmares come, I will chase them away.'

*He will*, promised the voice in her head. It was telling her to just let go, so she did, and slid into a darkness as profound as the blackness of the lake water.

# CHAPTER SIX

GILES LOCKED THE door from his dressing room on to the landing and studied the sleeping woman stretched out on the chaise. Isobel must be utterly drained to have fainted like that. He supposed he should have done something, anything, rather than carry her into his room, but it was a trifle late to worry about that now and they were probably safe enough. The family would be too concerned about Lizzie to wonder where their guest had got to and his borrowed valet believed him to be resting and would not disturb him.

He sat down in a chair, put his elbows on his knees and raked his fingers through his damp hair. Nothing had changed, so why the devil was he ignoring the self-imposed rules that had served him so well all his adult life? Isobel was a single young lady of good family and one, it would appear, that he had misjudged. The wild sensuality he had sensed in her must have either been his own imagination or she was unaware of it in her innocence.

He shot a glance through the door into the dressing room, but she seemed deeply asleep. He was discovering that he liked her, despite her sharp tongue and unflattering view of him. He admired her courage and her spirit, enjoyed the sensation of her in his arms. But all of that meant nothing. She should be, literally, untouchable and they both knew it.

Why, then, did she make him feel so restless? He wanted something, something more than the physical release that his body was nagging about. There was a quality, a mood, about Isobel that he simply could not put his finger on. Giles closed his eyes, sat back, while he chased the elusive emotions.

'Mr Harker. Giles! Wake up, you are having a nightmare.'

Giles clawed his way up out of a welter of naked limbs, buttocks, breasts, reaching hands and avid mouths. 'Where the hell am I?'

'In your bedchamber at Wimpole Hall.' He blinked his eyes into focus and found Isobel Jervis kneeling in front of him, her hands on the arms of the chair. His body reacted with a wave of desire that had him dropping his hands down to shield the evidence of it from her as she asked, 'What on earth were you dreaming about? It sounded very...strange.'

'I have no idea,' he lied. 'How long have we been asleep?' Long enough for her to have lost the pallor of shock and chill. Her body, bracketed by his thighs, was warm. *Hell*. 'You should not be here.' And certainly not kneeling between his legs, as though in wanton invitation to him to pull her forwards and do the outrageous things his imagination was conjuring up.

'I am well aware of that, Mr Harker! It is four o'clock. I heard the clocks strike about five minutes ago when I woke. Are you all right? You were arguing about something in your sleep.'

'I am fine,' Giles assured her. Already his head was clearing. It was the familiar frustrating dream about trying to break up a party at the Dower House, the one that had got completely out of hand. It was after that fiasco that he began to lay down the law to his mother—and to his surprise, she had listened and wept and things had become marginally better. But that night, when he had to cope with a fire in the library, a goat in the salon—part of a drunken attempt at a satanic mass—and the resignation of every one of his mother's long-suffering staff, had burned itself into his memory.

'I was supposed to be making sure you did not dream,' he apologised. 'And you had to rescue me instead.'

'I had no nightmares,' she assured him. 'But it was a good thing that your voice woke me.' Her hair had dried completely and the loose arrangement was beginning to come down in natural waves that made him want to stroke it as he might a cat's soft coat. Isobel shook it back from her shoulders and a faint scent of rosemary touched his nostrils, sweet and astringent at one and the same time, like the woman before him.

'You must go before anyone starts looking for you.' He kept his hands lightly clasped, away from temptation.

Isobel nodded and sat back on her heels and the simple gown shifted and flowed over breast and thighs. Giles closed his eyes for a moment and bit back a groan.

'I will go out of your dressing room and across the inner landing to my sitting room. Provided no one sees me leaving your chamber, there are any number of ways I could have reached my own door.'

'You have an aptitude for this kind of intrigue,' Giles said in jest. Isobel got to her feet in one jerky movement and turned towards the door in a swirl of skirts. He saw the blush on her cheek and sprang up to catch her arm. 'I am sorry, I did not mean that as it sounded. You think clearly through a problem, that is all.'

'Yes, of course.' She kept her head averted, but the tension in her body, the colour in her cheek, betrayed acute mortification. 'I have a very clear head for problems.' The unconcern with which she had knelt before him had gone—now she was uncomfortably aware of him as a man.

'Isobel.'

She turned, her eyes dark and her mouth tight. He no longer thought it made her look like a disapproving governess. This close, he could read shame behind the censorious expression.

'I am sorry.' How she came to be in his arms, he was not certain. Had she moved? Had he drawn her close—or was it both? But with her there, warm and slender, those wide, hurt grey eyes fixed questioningly on his face, it seemed the most natural thing in the world to kiss her.

Isobel must have sensed his intent, although once his arms had encircled her she did not move for a long moment. Then, 'No!' She jerked back against his hold, as fiercely as if he had been manhandling her with brutal intent. 'Let me *go*.'

Giles opened his hands, stepped back. 'Of course.' There had been real fear in her eyes, just for a moment. Surely she did not think he would try to force her? Perhaps she had recovered enough to realise just how compromising it was to be in a man's bedchamber.

Or was this all a tease, a way of punishing him for

his kiss that morning? But then she would have to be a consummate actress. Puzzled, uneasy, he knew this was not the time to explore the mystery that was Isobel Jervis. In fact, now was the time to stop this completely before his curiosity about her got the better of him.

He opened the door and looked out. 'It is safe to leave.'

'Thank you,' Isobel murmured and brushed past him without meeting his eyes.

That was, of course, the best possible outcome. All he had to do now was to maintain a civil distance. He could only hope he was imagining the expression in her eyes and that he could ignore the nagging instinct that he should be protecting her from whatever it was that caused it.

'You're not having anything to do with that man, are you, my lady?' Dorothy set the breakfast tray across Isobel's lap with unnecessary firmness. 'You go vanishing goodness knows where yesterday when you should have been resting and I worry you were with him. He's too good looking for any woman to be around—it shouldn't be allowed. You can't trust any of them—men—he knows you're grateful for him saving you and the next thing you know he'll be—'

'I told you, I had a nap in one of the other rooms,

Dorothy.' Isobel made rather a business of wriggling up against the pillows and setting the tray straight on her knees. 'Will you please stop nagging about it?'

'What your sainted mama would say if she knew, I do not know.'

'And how could you?' Isobel said between gritted teeth. 'There is nothing to know.'

'He's no good, that one. He's not a gentleman, despite all those fine clothes and that voice,' Dorothy pronounced as she bustled about, tidying the dressing table. 'They don't say much in front of me in the servants' hall, me being from outside, but I can tell that there's something fishy about him.'

'Dorothy, if Lady Hardwicke trusts Mr Harker sufficiently to entertain him in her own home, with her daughters here, I really do not feel it is your place to question her judgement.'

'No, my lady.'

'And one more sniff of disapproval out of you and you can go straight back to London.'

Silenced, the maid flounced out, then stopped to bob a curtsy in the doorway.

'May I come in?' Cousin Elizabeth looked round the door and smiled when she saw Isobel was eating. 'It seems everyone is much recovered this morning, although I have forbidden Lizzie to leave her room today.'

'How is she?' Isobel's sleep had been disturbed by vivid dreams of loss, of empty arms and empty heart. She felt her arms move instinctively as though to cradle a child and fussed with the covers instead.

'She is fine, although a trifle overexcited. What would you like to do, my dear? Stay in bed? I can bring you some books and journals.'

The sun was pouring through the window with a clarity that promised little warmth, but exhilarating views. 'I thought I might take another walk, Cousin Elizabeth. If you do not require me to assist you with anything, that is. Perhaps Anne or Philip might join me?'

'Of course, you may go and enjoy this lovely weather, just as long as you do not overtire yourself.' She looked out of the window and nodded, as though she could understand Isobel's desire to be outside. 'Philip would join you, but his father has sent him to his studies—his tutor's report on his Latin was very unsatisfactory, poor boy. And Anne has fittings with the dressmaker all morning—I declare she has not a single thing fit to wear for her come-out.'

'Never mind. I do not mind exploring by myself,' Isobel said. 'It is such a sunny day and who knows how long the weather will hold at this time of year.'

'Do you want me to send one of the footmen to go with you?'

'Goodness, no, thank you. I will probably dawdle about looking at the view and drive the poor man to distraction.'

The countess smiled. 'As you wish. The park is quite safe—other than the lake! Mr Harker and my husband will be in a meeting this morning.' She delivered this apparent non sequitur with a vague smile. 'And now I fear I must go and have a long interview with the housekeeper about the state of the servants' bed linen. Do not tire yourself, Isobel.'

Isobel came down the front steps an hour later, then stopped to pull on her gloves and decide which way to go.

Over to her left she could glimpse the church with the stables in front of it. Time enough for viewing the family monuments on Sunday. A middle-aged groom with a face like well-tanned leather came out from the yard and touched his finger to his hat brim.

'Roberts, my lady,' he introduced himself. 'May I be of any assistance?'

'I was trying to decide which way to walk, Roberts.' Isobel surveyed the long avenue stretching south. It would make a marvellous gallop, but would not be very scenic for a walk. The park to the north, towards the lake, she did not feel she could face, not quite yet. To the east the ground was relatively flat and wooded, but to the west of the house it rose in a promising manner. 'That way, I think. Is there a good view from up there?'

'Excellent, my lady. There's very fine prospects indeed. I'd go round the house that way if I was you.' He pointed. 'Don't be afeared of the cattle, they're shy beasts.'

Isobel nodded her thanks and made for the avenue of trees that ran uphill due west from the house. At the first rise she paused and looked back over the house and the formal gardens.

Why, she wondered, had Cousin Elizabeth made a point of mentioning where Giles Harker would be that morning? Surely she did not suspect that anything had transpired between them beyond his gallant rescue?

And what *had* happened? Gi…Mr Harker seemed to accept that she was not some airheaded flirt. She was, she supposed, prepared to believe that he suffered from an irritating persecution by women intent on some sort of relationship with a man of uncannily good looks. But that kiss in the shrubbery, the look in his eyes as they stood at the door of his room, those moments made her uneasily aware that she could not trust him and nor could she trust herself. He was a virile, attractive male and her body seemed to want to pay no attention whatsoever to her common sense.

There was something else, too, she pondered as she turned and strode on up the hill, her sturdy boots giving her confidence over the tussocky grass. There was another man behind both the social facade and the mocking rake, she was sure. He had a secret perhaps, a source of discomfort, if not pain.

Isobel shook her head and looked around as she reached the top of the avenue and the fringe of woodland. The less she thought about Giles Harker the better and she had no right to probe another's privacy. She knew what it was to hold a secret tight and to fear its discovery.

To her right was an avenue along the crest, leading to the lake and, beyond it, she could see the tower of the folly. To her left the view opened out beyond the park, south into Hertfordshire across the Cambridge road. A stone wall showed through a small copse. She began to walk towards it, then saw that it was the building she had noticed from the chaise when she had first arrived. As she came closer to the grove of trees it revealed itself as a miniature house with a projecting central section and a window on either side.

It was set perfectly to command the view, she realised, but as she got closer she saw it was crumbling into decay, although not quite into ruin. Slates had slipped, windows were broken, nettles and brambles threatened the small service buildings tucked in beside it.

Isobel walked round to the front and studied the structure. There was a pillared portico held up by wooden props, a broken-down fence and sagging shutters at the windows. The ground around it was trampled and muddy and mired with droppings and the prints of cloven hooves.

And through the mud there were the clear prints of a horse's hooves leading to where a rope dangled from a shutter hinge: a makeshift hitching post.

Giles Harker's horse? Why would he come to such a sad little building? Perhaps he was as intrigued by it as she was, for it had a lingering romance about it, a glamour, as though it was a beautiful, elegant woman fallen on hard times, perhaps because of age and indiscretion, but still retaining glimpses of the charms of her youth.

But he was not here now, so it was quite safe to explore. Isobel lifted her skirts and found her way from tussock to tussock through the mud until she reached the steps. Perhaps it was locked. But, no, the door creaked open on to a lobby. The marks of booted feet showed in the dust on the floor. Large masculine footprints. Giles.

With the delicious sensation of illicit exploration and a frisson of apprehension that she was about to

discover Bluebeard's chamber, Isobel opened the door
to her right and found the somewhat sordid wreck-
age of a small kitchen. The middle door opened on
to a loggia with a view of the wood behind the building and the door to the left revealed a staircase. The
footprints led upwards and she followed, her steps
echoing on the stone treads. The door at the top was
closed, but when she turned the handle it opened with
a creak eerie enough to satisfy the most romantic of
imaginings.

Half amused at her own fears, Isobel peeped round
the door to find a large chamber lit patchily by whatever sunshine found its way through the cracked and
half-open shutters.

It was empty except for a wooden chair and a table
with a pile of papers and an ink stand. No mysterious
chests, no murdered brides. Really, from the point of
view of Gothic horrors it was a sad disappointment.
Isobel cast the papers a curious glance, told herself
off for wanting to pry and opened the door on the
far wall.

'Oh!' The room was tiny and painted with frescoes
that still adhered to the cobwebbed walls. A daybed, its silken draperies in tatters, stood against the
wall. 'A love nest.' She had never seen such a thing,
but this intimate little chamber must surely be one.
Isobel went in, let the door close behind her with a

click and began to investigate the frescoes. 'Oh, my goodness.' Yes, the purpose of this room was most certainly clear from these faded images. She should leave at once, they were making her feel positively warm and flustered, but they were so pretty, so intriguing despite their indecent subject matter...

The unmistakable creak of the door in the next room jerked Isobel out of a bemused contemplation of two satyrs and a nymph engaged in quite outrageous behaviour in a woodland glade. She had heard nothing—no sound of hooves approaching the building, no footsteps on the stairs. The wind perhaps... but there had been no wind as she walked up hill. The consciousness that she was not alone lifted the hairs on the nape of her neck.

# CHAPTER SEVEN

'I KNOW YOU are in there, Isobel.' Giles Harker's sardonically amused voice made her gasp with relief, even as she despised herself for her nerves and him for his impudence.

'How did you know?' she demanded as she flung the door wide.

He was standing hatless in the middle of the room in buckskins and breeches, his whip and gloves in one hand, looking for all the world like an artist's model for the picture of the perfect English country gentleman. He extended one hand and pointed at the trail of small footprints that led across the room to the doorway where she stood.

Isobel experienced a momentary flicker of relief that she had resisted the temptation to investigate what was on the table. 'Good morning, Mr Harker. I came up here for the view, but I will not disturb you.'

'I thought we were on first-name terms, Isobel. And I am happy to be disturbed.' Was there the slightest emphasis on *disturbed*? She eyed him warily. 'It is an interesting building, even in this sorry state. Whether I can save it, or even if I should, I do not yet know.'

So this was what he was about, the rescue of this poor wreck. 'It is charming. It is sad to see it like this.'

'It was built as a prospect house and somehow was never used very much for forty years. Soane had suggestions for it some time ago, Humphrey Repton countered with even more ambitious ones. His lordship points out that it cost fifteen-hundred pounds to build, so hopes that I, with no previous experience of the place, will tell him what can be done that will not cost a further fifteen-hundred pounds.' He smiled suddenly and she caught her breath. 'Now what is it that puts that quizzical expression on your face?'

'It is the first time I have heard you sound like an architect.'

'You thought me a mere dilettante?' The handsome face froze into pretended offence and Isobel felt the wariness that held her poised for flight ebb away as she laughed at his play-acting. Surely he was safe to be with? After all, he had let her sleep untouched when she was at her most vulnerable yesterday and the moment when they had stood so close and she had thought he was about to kiss her had been as much her own fault as his. But it had troubled her sleep more than a little, that moment of intimacy, the sensual expertise she knew lay behind the facade of control.

'I knew Mr Soane would not associate with you, nor the earl employ you, if that was so. But you are the perfect pattern of the society gentleman for all that. You should not object if that is all you are taken for.'

'Appearances are deceptive indeed. You should look out for the glint of copper beneath the plating when you think you are buying solid silver,' he said with an edge to his voice that belied the curve of his lips. He turned to the table before she could think of what to reply. 'You are that impossibility, it seems—a woman without curiosity.'

'Your papers? Of course I was curious, but curiosity does not have to be gratified if it would be wrong to do so.'

'Even if these are simply sketches and elevations?'

'For all I knew they might be the outpouring of your feelings in verse or love letters from your betrothed or even your personal accounts.'

'I fear I am no poet and there is no letter from a patient betrothed, nor even—do not think I cannot read that wicked twinkle in your eyes, Isobel—billets-doux from females of quite another kind.'

'I have no idea what you are talking about,' she

said repressively. 'Tell me about this house. Or is it not a house?'

'A prospect house is a decoration for a view point, not for living in. As was fashionable when it was built, this room was designed as a banqueting chamber. It *is* rather splendid.' He swept a hand around the space which was perhaps twenty feet square. 'Repton's plans would make this open for picnics. He proposed moving the pillars up from the front portico to frame the opening and turning the ground floor into an estate worker's cottage.'

'Oh, no.' Isobel looked around her at the wide fireplace and the walls that had once been painted to resemble green marble. 'I love this as it is. Could it not be repaired?'

'I share your liking. But I fear the initial building was so poorly done that repair or alteration may be a positive money pit for the earl.'

'And there I was imagining it renovated and turned into a little house. I love looking at houses,' she confessed. 'I think I must be a natural nest-builder.' She could imagine herself, an almost-contented spinster, in a little house like this. But she would be alone with a cat, not with the sound of a child's feet running towards her—

'You found the painted room.' He strolled past her and into the little chamber she had been examining.

Isobel shook off the momentary stab of sadness and followed. She would not be a prude, she would simply ignore the subject matter of the tiny, intricate scenes that covered the mildewed walls. 'The frescos are in the Etruscan style,' he explained. 'I think this room was intended for trysts, don't you?'

'Or as the ladies' retiring room,' Isobel suggested.

'So prosaic! I hoped you would share my vision. Or perhaps you have examined the designs and are shocked.'

It rankled that he should think her unsophisticated enough to be shocked. 'Your vision is of a history of illicit liaisons taking place here?' Isobel queried, avoiding answering his question.

'Do you not think it romantic?' Giles leaned his shoulder against the mantel shelf and regarded her with one perfect eyebrow lifted.

'Thwarted young lovers might be romantic, possibly, but I imagine you are suggesting adulterous affairs.' She could easily imagine Giles Harker indulging in such a liaison. She could not believe that he was celibate, nor that he repulsed advances from fast widows or wives with complacent husbands, however much he might protest the need to keep young ladies at a safe distance.

'Not necessarily. How about happily married couples coming here to be alone, away from the servants

and the children, to eat a candlelit supper and redis-
cover the flirtations of their courtship?'

'That is a charming thought indeed. You are a romantic after all, Mr Harker. Or a believer in marital bliss, perhaps.' She kept her distance, over by the
window where the February air crept through the
cracks to cool her cheeks.

'Giles. And why *after all*? An architect needs some
romance in his soul, surely?'

'Yesterday your views on the relationships between
men and women seemed more practical than romantic.' Isobel picked at a tendril of ivy that had insinu-
ated itself between the window frame and the wall.

'Merely self-preservation.' Giles came to look out
of the window beside her, pushing the shutter back
on its one remaining hinge. 'How is it that you have
avoided the snare of matrimony, Isobel?'

Surprised and wary, she turned to look at him.
'You regard matrimony as a snare for women as well
as for men? The general view is that it must be our
sole aim and ambition.'

'If it is duty and not, at the very least, affection that
motivates the match, then I imagine it is a snare. Or
a kindly prison, perhaps.'

*A kindly prison.* He understood, or could imagine, what it might mean for a woman. The surprise

loosened her tongue. 'I was betrothed, for love, four years ago. He died.'

'And now you wear the willow for him?' There was no sympathy in the deep voice and his attention seemed to be fixed on a zigzagging crack in the wall. Oddly, that made it easier to confide.

'I mourned Lucas for two years. I find it is possible to keep the memory of love, but I cannot stay in love with someone who is no longer there.'

'So you would wed?' He reached out and prodded at the crack. A lump of plaster fell out, exposing rough stone beneath.

'If I found someone who could live up to Lucas, and he loved me, then yes, perhaps.' *He would have to love me very much indeed.* 'But I do not expect to be that fortunate twice in my life.'

'I imagine that all your relatives say bracingly that of course you will find someone else if only you apply yourself.'

'Exactly. You are beset with relatives also, by the sound of it.'

'Just my mother and my grandfather.'

Which of those produced the rueful expression? she wondered. His mother, probably. He had described her as eccentric.

'If this paragon does not materialise, what will you do then?' Giles asked.

'He does not have to be a paragon. I am not such a ninny as to expect to find one of those. They do not exist. I simply insist that I like him and he is neither a rakehell nor a prig and he does not mind that I have…a past.'

'Paragons of manhood being fantastic beasts like wyverns and unicorns?' That careless reference to her past seemed to have slipped his notice.

Isobel chuckled. 'Exactly. I have decided that if no eligible gentleman makes me an offer I shall be an eccentric spinster or an Anglican nun. I incline towards the former option, for I enjoy my little luxuries.'

Giles laughed, a crow of laughter. 'I should think so! You? A nun?'

'I was speaking in jest.' How attractive he was when he laughed, his handsome head thrown back, emphasising the strong line of his throat, the way his eyes crinkled in amusement. Isobel found herself smiling. Slowly she was beginning to see beyond the perfect looks and the outrageous tongue and catch glimpses of what might be the real man hiding behind them.

There was that suspicion about secrets again. What would he be hiding? Or was it simply that his faultless face made him more difficult to read than a plainer man might be? 'I thought about a convent the other day when I was reflecting on just how unsatisfactory the male sex can be.'

'We are?' He was still amused, but, somehow he was not laughing at her, but sharing her whimsy.

'You must know perfectly well how infuriating men are from a female point of view,' Isobel said with severity, picking up the trailing skirts of her riding habit to keep them out of the thick dust as she went to examine one of the better-preserved panels more closely. Surely they could not all be so suggestive? It seemed they could. Was it possible that one could do that in a bath without drowning?

'You have all the power and most of the fun in life,' she said, dragging her attention back from the erotic scene. After a moment, when he did not deny it, she added, 'Why is the thought of my being a nun so amusing?'

Giles's mouth twitched, but he did not answer her, so she said the first thing that came into her head, flustered a little by the glint in his eyes. 'I am amazed that the countess allows this room to be unlocked. What if the girls came in here?'

'The whole building has been locked up for years. Lady Hardwicke told the children that they were not to disturb me here and I have no doubt that her word is law.'

'I think it must be, although she is a very gentle

dictator. So—will you recommend that the place is restored?'

'I do not think so.' Giles shook his head. 'It was badly built in the first place and then neglected for too long. But I am working up the costing for the earl so he has a fair comparison to set against Repton's ambitious schemes.'

'But that would be such a pity—and you like the place, do you not?'

'It is not my money. My job is to give the earl a professional opinion. I am not an amateur, Isobel. I am a professional, called in like the doctor or the lawyer to deliver the hard truths.'

'But surely you are different? You are, after all, a gentleman—'

Giles turned on his heel and faced her, his expression mocking. 'Do you recall what you called me when I kissed you?'

'A…*bastard*,' she faltered, ashamed. She should never had said it. It was a word she had never used in cold blood. A word she loathed.

'And that is exactly, and precisely, what I am. Not a gentleman at all.'

'But you are,' Isobel protested. He was born out of wedlock? 'You speak like a gentleman, you dress like one, your manner in society, your education—'

'I was brought up as one, certainly,' Giles agreed.

He did not appear at all embarrassed about discussing his parentage. Isobel had never heard illegitimacy mentioned in anything but hushed whispers as a deep shame. How could he be so open about it? 'But my father was a common soldier, my grandfather a head gardener.'

'Then how on earth…? Oh.' Light dawned. His *eccentric* mother. 'Your mother?' His mother had kept him. What courage that must have taken. What love. Isobel bit her lip.

'My mother is the Dowager Marchioness of Faversham.' Isobel felt her jaw drop and closed her mouth. An aristocratic lady openly keeping a love child? It was unheard of. 'She scorns convention and gossip and the opinion of the world. She has gone her own way and she took her son with her.' He strolled back into the large chamber and began to gather up the papers on the table.

'Until you left university,' Isobel stated, suddenly sure. A wealthy dowager would have the money and the power, perhaps, to insist on keeping her baby. Not everyone had that choice, she told herself. Sometimes there was none. 'She did not want you to study a profession, did she?' She made herself focus on the man in front of her and his situation. 'That was when you went your own way.'

'Perceptive of you. She expected me to enliven society, just as she does.' He shrugged. 'I am accepted widely—I know most of the men of my age from school and university, after all. I am not received at Court, of course, and not in the homes of the starchier matrons with marriageable girls on their hands.'

Isobel felt the colour mount in her cheeks. No wonder he was wary of female attention. If his mother was notorious, then he, with his looks, would be irresistible to the foolish girls who wanted adventure or a dangerous flirtation. Giles Harker was the most tempting kind of forbidden fruit.

'Of course,' she said steadily, determined not to be missish. 'You are not at all eligible. I can quite see that might make for some…awkwardness at times. It will be difficult for you to find a suitable bride, I imagine.'

'Again, you see very clearly. I cannot marry within society. If I wed the daughter of a Cit or some country squire, then she will not be accepted in the circles in which I am tolerated now. There is a careful balance to be struck in homes such as this—and I spend a lot of my time in aristocratic households. We all pretend I am a gentleman. A wife who is not from the same world will not fit in, will spoil the illusion.'

'It will be easier as your practice grows and your wealth with it.' Isobel bit her lip as she pondered the problem. 'You could wed the daughter of another successful professional man, one who has the education and upbringing to fit in as you do.'

Giles stopped in the act of rapping a handful of papers on the desk to align them. Isobel's reaction to his parentage was undeniably startling—it was almost as though she understood and sympathised. 'Do you plot all your friends' lives so carefully for them? Set them all to partners?'

'Of course not. It is just that you are a rather different case. Unusual.' She put her head on one side and contemplated him as though trying to decide where to place an exotic plant in a flower border or a new ornament on a shelf. 'I would never dream of actually matchmaking.'

'Why not? It seems to be a popular female preoccupation.'

Now, why that tight-lipped look again, this time accompanied by colour on her cheekbones? 'Marriage is enough of a lottery as it is, without one's acquaintances interfering in it for amusement or mischief,' she said with a tartness that seemed entirely genuine.

'You are the victim of that?' Giles stuffed his papers into the saddlebag he had brought up with him.

'Oh, yes, of course. I am single and dangerously close to dwindling into a spinster. It is the duty of every right-thinking lady of my acquaintance to find me a husband.'

There was something more than irritation over being the target of well-meaning matchmaking, although he could not put his finger on what it was. Anger, certainly, but beneath that he sensed a deep unhappiness that Isobel was too proud to show.

'Ah, well,' Giles said peaceably, 'we are both safe here, it seems. The Yorke girls are well behaved and well chaperoned and there are no eligible gentlemen for the countess to foist upon you.'

'Thank goodness,' Isobel said with real feeling. 'But I am disturbing you when you have work to do. I will go on with my walk now I have admired the view from up here.'

'I do not mind being disturbed.' He thought he had kept the double meaning out of his voice—he was finding her unaccountably disturbing on a number of levels—but she bit her lower lip as though she was controlling a sharp retort. Or just possibly a smile, although she turned abruptly before he could be quite certain. 'Where are you going to go now?'

'I do not know.' Isobel stood looking out of the window.

'The avenue running north from here is pleasant. It skirts the wood.'

'And leads to the lake.'

'That frightens you?'

'No. No, of course not.' The denial was a little too emphatic.

'Then you did not dream?' Giles buckled the saddlebag, threw it over his shoulder, picked up his hat and gloves and watched her.

'No…yes. Possibly. I do not recall.'

'I will come with you,' he said. 'I have been sitting too long.'

'But your horse—'

'I will lead him. Come and see the best view of the Gothic folly.'

Isobel followed him down the stairs and out into the sunshine, allowed him to take her hand as they negotiated the mud and then retrieved it as she fell in beside him. They walked beneath the bare branches of the avenue, Felix plodding along behind them, the reins knotted on his neck, the thin February sunlight filtering through the twigs.

# CHAPTER EIGHT

AFTERWARDS GILES FOUND it difficult to recall just
what they talked about on that walk. His memories
seemed to consist only of the woman he was with.
Isobel seemed to be interested in everything: the deer
grazing in the park, the lichen on the tree trunks, the
view of the roofs of the Hall, complex and interlock-
ing, the reason why he had named his horse as he
had and what an architect must learn. He made her
laugh, he could recall that. She stretched his knowledge of botany with her questions and completed
his verse when he quoted Shakespeare. But under it
all there was still a distance, a wariness. She was no
fool, she knew she was playing with fire being with
him, but it seemed, just now, as if she was suspend-
ing judgement.

She held her bonnet against the breeze. 'A lazy
wind—it does not trouble itself to go around,' she
said. 'Oh.' The lakes spread out below them in the
valley, chill and grey.

'And there is the folly.' Giles pointed to the tower

on the opposite hill to bring her eyes up and away from the source of her apprehension. 'Shall we go and look at it?'

If you fell off a horse, then the best thing was to get right back on, and the narrow bridge where the broken timbers showed pale, even at this distance, was her fall. 'Of course, if you are too tired...'

Isobel's chin went up. 'Why not?'

They followed the path down into the stock ditch and through the gate in the fence at the bottom. Felix's hoofprints from the previous day were clear in the turf. It had been a good jump, Giles thought as they climbed out at the other side.

Isobel was silent as they walked down the hillside towards the lake. Then, as the muddy patch where they had clawed their way out came in sight, she said, 'I thought she had drowned. I thought I was not going to be able to save her. What if you had not heard us?' The words tumbled out as though she could not control them and he saw her bite her lip to stem them. Her remembered fear seemed all for Lizzie, not for herself, and he recalled how she had cradled the child on the bank. For the first time it occurred to him that a single woman might mourn her lack of children as well as the absence of a husband.

'Don't,' Giles said. 'What-ifs are pointless. You

did save her, you found her and hung on until I got there. Now run.'

She gasped as he caught her hand and sprinted down the last few yards of the slope, along the dam, on to the wooden bridge, its planks banging with the impact of their feet. Moorhens scattered, piping in alarm. A pair of ducks flew up and pigeons erupted from the trees above their heads in a flapping panic. Giles kept going, past the break in the rail and on to the grass on the other side.

He caught Isobel and steadied her as she stopped, gasping for breath. 'You see? It is quite safe.' Felix ambled in their wake.

'You—you—' Her bonnet was hanging down her back and she tugged at the strings and pulled it off. She was panting, torn between exasperation and laughter. 'You idiot. Look at my hair!'

'I am.' The shining curls had slipped from their pins and tumbled down her back, glossy brown and glorious. Her greatest beauty, or perhaps as equally lovely as her eyes. Isobel stood there in the pale February sunlight, her face flushed with exertion and indignation, her hair dishevelled as though she had just risen from her bed, her breasts rising and falling with her heaving breath.

*Kiss her*, his body urged. *Throw her over the saddle and gallop back to the Hill House and make love to her in the room made for passion.* 'You are un-used to country walks, I can tell,' he teased instead, snatching at safety, decency, some sort of control. 'I will race you to the folly.' And he took to his heels, going just fast enough, he calculated, for her to think she might catch him, despite the slope.

There was no sound of running feet behind him. So much the better—he could gain the summit and give himself time to subdue the surge of lust that had swept through him. Just because Isobel was intelli-gent and poised and stood up to him he could not, *must not*, lose sight of the fact that she was a virgin and not the young matron she often seemed to be.

The thud of hooves behind him made him turn so abruptly that his heel caught in a tussock and he twisted off balance and fell flat on his back. Isobel, perched side-saddle on Felix's back, laughed down at him for a second as the gelding cantered past, taking the slope easily with the lighter weight in the saddle.

*God, but she can ride*, Giles thought, admiring the sight as she reached the top of the hill and reined in.

'Are you hurt?' Her look of triumph turned to con-cern when he stayed where he was, sprawled on the damp grass.

'No, simply stunned by the sight of an Amazon at full gallop.' He got to his feet and walked up to join her. 'How did you get up there?' She had her left foot in the stirrup and her right leg hooked over the pommel. Her hands were light on the reins and she showed no fear of the big horse. Her walking dress revealed a few inches of stockinged leg above the sturdy little boot and he kept his gaze firmly fixed on her face framed by the loose hair.

'There's a tree stump down by the fence. Felix obviously thought someone should be riding him, even if his master was capering about like a mad March hare.'

'Traitor,' Giles said to his horse, who butted him affectionately in the stomach. 'Would you care to explore the folly, Isobel?'

She sent an interested, curious glance at the building, then shook her head. 'We had better go back or we will be late for luncheon, will we not? Perhaps I can look at it tomorrow.'

Pleasure warred with temptation. They could be together safely, surely? He had self-control and familiarity would soon enough quench the stabs of desire that kept assailing him. It was too long since he had parted with his last mistress, that was all that ailed him. The challenge to make Isobel smile, make her trust him, was too great.

'I am not too busy to walk with you. Or we could ride if you prefer?'

'Oh, yes. If only it does not rain. I had better get

down.' She lifted her leg from the pommel and simply slid, trusting him to catch her. Obviously his dangerous thoughts were not visible on his face. Her waist was slender between his hands. He felt the slide of woollen cloth over silk and cotton, the light boning of her stays, and set her down with care.

It took him a minute to find his voice again, or even think of something to say. 'What have you done with your bonnet, you hoyden?' Giles asked halfway down the hill as they walked back towards the lake. Isobel pointed to where the sensible brown-velvet hat hung on a branch beside the path. 'And what are you going to say to Lady Hardwicke about your hair if she sees you?'

'Why, the truth, of course.' Isobel sent him a frowning look. 'Why should I not? Nothing happened. We ran, my bonnet blew off, my hair came down. It is not as though we are in Hyde Park. Or do you think she will blame you in some way?'

'No, of course not. She trusts you, of course—she would suspect no impropriety.' Now why did that make her prim up her lips and blush?

'Exactly,' Isobel said, her voice flat. But when they reached the garden gate and Giles turned to walk Felix back to the stables, she caught his sleeve. 'Thank you for chasing my nerves away at the bridge.'

'That is what friends do,' he said. That was it, of

course: friendship. It was novel to be friends with an unmarried woman but that was surely what this ease he felt with Isobel meant.

She smiled at him, a little uncertain. He thought he glimpsed those shadows and ghosts in her eyes still, then she opened the garden gate and walked away between the low box hedges.

*A friend*. Isobel was warmed by the thought as she walked downstairs for breakfast the next morning. It had never occurred to her that she might be friends with a man, and certainly Mama would have the vapours if she realised that her daughter was thinking of an architect born on the wrong side of the blanket in those terms.

But it was good to see behind the supercilious mask Giles Harker wore to guard himself. After a few minutes as they walked and talked she had quite forgotten how handsome he was and saw only an intelligent man who was kind enough to sense her fears and help her overcome them. A man who could laugh at himself and trust a stranger with his secrets. She wished she could share hers—he of all men would understand, surely.

He was dangerous, of course, and infuriating and she was not certain she could trust him. Or perhaps it was herself she could not trust.

Giles was at the table when she came in, sitting with the earl and countess, Anne and Philip. The men stood as she entered and she wished everyone a good morning as the footman held her chair for her.

'Good morning.' Giles's long look had a smile lurking in it that said, far more clearly than his conventional greeting, that he was happy to see her.

The morning was fine, although without yesterday's sunshine. They could ride. Isobel did not pretend to herself that she did not understand why the prospect of something she did almost every day at home should give her such keen pleasure. Perhaps she felt drawn to him because Giles was of her world but not quite in it, someone set a little apart, just as she was by her disgrace. She wanted to like him and to trust him. Could she trust her own judgement?

'Might I ride today, Cousin Elizabeth?'

'This morning? Of course. You may take my mare, she will be glad of the exercise. I have been so involved with the endless correspondence that this change in our life seems to be producing that I have sadly neglected her. And it is not as though my daughters enjoy riding, is it, my loves?'

A heartfelt chorus of 'No, Mama!' made the countess laugh. 'One of the grooms will accompany you, Isobel.'

Isobel caught Giles's eye. 'I...that is, Mr Harker is

riding out this morning, ma'am, I believe. I thought perhaps...'

She feared the countess would still require a groom as escort, but she nodded approval. 'I will have Firefly brought round at ten, if that suits Mr Harker?'

'Thank you, ma'am, it suits me very well. Shall I meet you on the steps at that hour, Lady Isobel?'

'Thank you,' she said demurely and was rewarded by a flickering glance of amusement. Was she usually so astringent that this meekness seemed unnatural? She must take care not to think of this as an assignation, for it was nothing of the kind. *Friendship*, she reminded herself. That was what was safe and that, she had to believe, was what Giles appeared to be offering her.

'Mama, I have been thinking,' Lady Anne said. 'With Cousin Isobel and Mr Harker here we might have enough actors to put on a play. We could ask the vicar's nephews to help if we are short of men. Do say *yes*, it is so long since we did one.'

'My dear, it is not fair to expect poor Mr Harker to add to his work by learning a part. He and Papa are quite busy enough.'

'You have a theatre here, Cousin Elizabeth?' Isobel asked, intrigued.

'No, but we have improvised by hanging curtains between the pillars in the Gallery.'

'That was where we had the premiere performance of Mama's play *The Court of Oberon*,' Lizzie interrupted eagerly. 'And then it was printed and has been acted upon the London stage! Is that not grand?'

'It is wonderful,' Isobel agreed. Many families indulged in amateur dramatic performances, especially during house parties. She caught Giles's eye and smiled: he looked appalled at the possibility of treading the boards.

'Perhaps on another visit, Lizzie,' the countess said. 'I am writing another play, so perhaps we can act that one when it is finished.'

'The post, my lord.'

'And what a stack of it!' The earl broke off a discussion with his son to view the laden salver his butler was proffering. 'And I suppose you will say that all the business matters have already been dispatched to my office? Ah well, distribute it, if you please, Benson, and perhaps my pile will appear less forbidding.'

'Feel free to read your correspondence,' Lady Hardwicke said to her guests as her own and her daughters' letters were laid by her plate.

After a few minutes Isobel glanced up from her mother's recital of a very dull reception she had attended to see Giles working his way through half-a-dozen letters. He slit the seal on the last one and it seemed to her, as she watched him read, that his entire body tensed. But his face and voice were quite expressionless when he said, 'Will you excuse me, Lady Hardwicke, ladies? There is something that requires my attention.'

Isobel returned to her own correspondence as he left the room. It was to be hoped that whatever it was did not mean he would have to miss their ride. She told herself it was not that important, that she could take a groom with her, that it was ridiculous to feel so concerned about it, but she found she could not deceive herself: she wanted to be alone with Giles again.

The earl departed to the steward's office, Philip to his tutor and Cousin Elizabeth and Anne for a consultation with the dressmaker. Isobel followed behind them a little dreamily. Where would they ride this morning? Up to the folly and beyond, perhaps. Or—

'Lady Isobel.' Giles stepped out from the Yellow Drawing Room. 'Will you come to the library?'

It was not a request; more, from his tone and his unsmiling face, an order. 'I—' A footman walked across the hallway and Isobel closed her lips on a sharp retort. Whatever the matter was, privacy was desirable. 'Very well,' she said coolly and followed him through the intervening chambers into the room that was one of the wonders of Wimpole Hall.

But the towering bookcases built decades ago to

house Lord Harley's fabled collection were no distraction from the sick feeling in the pit of her stomach. Isobel could not imagine what had so affected Giles, but the anger was radiating from him like heat from smouldering coals.

'What is this autocratic summons for?' she demanded, attacking first as he turned to face her.

'I should have trusted my first impressions,' Giles said. He propped one shoulder against the high library ladder and studied her with the same expression in his eyes as they had held when he had caught her staring at him in the hall. 'But you really are a very good little actress, are you not? Perhaps you should take part in one of her ladyship's dramas after all.'

'No. I am not a good actress,' Isobel snapped.

'But you are the slut who broke up Lady Penelope Albright's betrothal. You do not deny that?' he asked with dangerous calm.

When she did not answer Giles glanced down at the letter he held in his right hand. 'Penelope is in a complete nervous collapse because you were found rutting with Andrew White. But I assume you do not care about her feelings?'

Isobel felt the blood ebbing from her cheeks. That foul slander…and Giles believed it. 'Yes, I care for her distress,' she said, holding her voice steady with an effort that hurt her throat. 'And I am very sorry that she chose such a man to ally herself with. But you must forgive me if I care even more that Lord Andrew mauled and assaulted me, ruined my reputation and that very few people, even those who I thought were my friends, believe me.'

'Oh, very nicely done! But you see, I have this from my very good friend James Albright, Penelope's brother—and he does not lie.'

'But he was not there, was he? He knows only what Penelope saw when she came into my room that night: four people engaged in a drunken romp. Only one of them, myself, was not willing and the other three—the men—were set on giving a stuck-up spinster a good lesson, a retaliation for snubbing their patronising flirtation.

'That is the truth and if you have not the perception to know it when you hear it, then I am sorry, but there is nothing I can do.' Isobel turned on her heel. One more minute and she was going to cry and she was *damned* if she would give Giles Harker the satisfaction of knowing he had reduced her to that. A fine friend he had turned out to be!

'Who would believe such a tale?' he scoffed as he caught her by the arm and spun her back to face him. 'No one there did and they were on the spot.'

'You think it improbable they would be deceived?'

Yes, after all there *was* something she could do, something to shake that smug male complacency.

'Of course,' Giles began as Isobel threw herself on his chest, the suddenness of it knocking him off balance back against a bookcase full of leather-bound volumes. 'What the devil—'

As he tried to push her away she used the momentum of his own movement to swing around in his grip until she was pressed by his weight against the books, then she threw her arms around his neck, pulled his head down and kissed him hard, full on the mouth.

For a moment Giles resisted, then he opened his lips over hers and returned the kiss with a ruthless expertise that was shocking and, despite—or perhaps because of—her anger, deeply arousing. Isobel had been kissed passionately by her betrothed, but that was four years ago and she had loved him. The assault of Giles's tongue, his teeth, the fierce plundering exploration, fuelled both anger and the long-buried desire that had been stirring with every encounter they had shared. When he lifted his head—more, she thought dizzily, to breathe than for any other reason—Isobel slapped him hard across the cheek.

'Now, if someone comes in and I scream, what will they think?' she panted. His face was so close to hers that she could feel his breath, hot on her mouth. 'What will they have seen? Giles Harker, a rake on the edge of society, assaulting an innocent young lady who is struggling in his arms. Who will they believe? What if I tear my bodice and run out, calling for help? You would be damned, just as I was.

'I do not have to justify myself to you. But I was sitting in my room, reading by the fireside in my nightgown, and three men burst in. I thought I could reason with them. I did not want a scandal, so I did not scream—and that was my mistake. And for that I am condemned by self-righteous hypocrites like you, Giles Harker. So now will you please let me go?'

For a long moment he stared down at her, then those gorgeous, sinful lips twisted. 'Yes, I believe you, Isobel. I should never have doubted you.'

*Kiss me again*, a treacherous inner voice said. *Listen to your body. You want him.* 'You called me a slut. You just kissed me as though I was one.' She did not dare let go of her bitterness.

'I believe you now.' He looked at her, all the anger and heat gone from his face. 'I am sorry I doubted you. Sorry I called you... No, we won't repeat that word. But I am not certain I can be sorry for that kiss.'

'Unfortunately, neither can I,' Isobel admitted and felt the blood rise in her cheeks. 'You kiss very... nicely.' And as a result her body had sung into life in a way it had not done for a long time. 'No doubt you have had a great deal of practice. But kindly do not think that is why I...why I did what I did just now. I could think of no other way to prove my point.'

'Nicely?' Giles seemed a trifle put out by the description. 'We will not pursue that, I think. I should not make light of what has happened to you. I was wrong and you have been grievously slandered. What is your family doing about it?'

Isobel shrugged and moved away from him to spin one of the great globes that stood either side of the desk. It was easier to think away from all that intense masculinity. The man addled her brain. She had let herself be almost seduced into friendship and then he believed the worst of her on hearsay evidence. And instead of recoiling from her angry kiss he had returned it. He was not to be trusted. Not one inch.

'They denied it everywhere they could, of course. But my brother is a schoolboy, my father a martyr to gout. Neither of them is going to be taking up a rapier in my defence! Besides, my hostess threw me out the next morning, so the lie is widely believed. There is nothing to be done except take refuge where I am trusted—here with old friends of my parents.'

# CHAPTER NINE

GILES PACED DOWN the length of the library to the other globe, the celestial one showing the heavens, and spun it viciously. 'Something should be done.' Hell's teeth, he had called an innocent woman a foul name, he had accused her on hearsay evidence. He was having trouble getting past his own self-loathing for that, and for wanting to kiss her again. Kiss her... and more. That made him a rutting beast like Andrew White and he was not. Please God, he was not that.

'Why is your old friend not calling out the man who betrayed his sister? Andrew White seems to be getting away scot-free,' Isobel demanded. It was a reasonable question.

'James is almost blind. He can see well enough to get around, but that is all. His sight was failing when we were at Harrow and it has deteriorated since.'

'Poor man. I had no idea. I was aware that he did not come into society, of course,' Isobel said, instantly compassionate. She was sweet when she was soft—

pitying for James, tender with the child. He wanted that softness, but all she would give him was the fire.

'He is a scholar, a great mind. When we were children at school he held the bullies at bay because they were frightened of his rapier intelligence and his sharp tongue. He protected me with his wits when I was new, terrified and a victim because of my parentage. As I grew in size and confidence I defended him with my fists. Fortunately he can afford to keep secretaries and assistants so his studies are not affected by his sight. He is working on a new translation of the Greek myths.'

'A true friendship,' Isobel murmured, her head bent over the spinning globe, her long index finger tracing a route across continents. Was she imagining an escape from all this? 'Will you help me? Tell Lord James you believe me? If he can convince his parents and Penelope, then it might do some good.' She sounded doubtful that he would support her, even now.

'Of course.' *Of course. But that is not enough. You are mine. I saved your life so you are mine.* The anger boiling inside him became focused. He would tell James, of course, and Penelope, whom he had known since she was six, but there must be justice for Isobel. White and the other two had got off from this almost unscathed.

Out of the corner of his eye he saw Isobel put back her shoulders and straighten her back as if bracing herself to carry this burden of disgrace. Alone, she believed. But she was not alone any more. The fierce sense of possessiveness was unsettling, but he had never saved someone's life before—perhaps that accounted for the way he felt about Isobel now.

'You are very brave,' he said and her chin came up with a defiance that tugged at his heart.

'I refuse to go into hiding because I am the victim of an injustice, so what else can I do but carry on? Besides, if I was truly courageous I would be in London now, brazening it out, would I not?' Isobel threw at him.

'I think you are too much of a lady to be brazen about anything. And what well-bred virgin would not shy away from such behaviour?' Now, what had he said to make her blush so? 'It takes a wicked widow like my mother to carry off that kind of thing.'

She gave herself a little shake. 'There is nothing to be done about the situation beyond you telling your friend the truth. Look, the sun is shining—I think I will ride after all.'

'Then I hope the weather holds for you. I find I must go to London this morning.' There *was* more he could do and it seemed that Isobel had no one else to do it for her. Besides, Giles thought, the fierce posses-

siveness burning hot inside him, this would be both
his right and a pleasure. The experience of defending
a lady was not new, but it was an ironic twist that this
time he would be on the side of innocence instead of
mitigating his mother's latest outrages.

'It is not a problem with your business that takes
you there, I see,' she said, watching him with narrowed eyes. 'That was the smile of a man who positively relishes what is in front of him.'

'Oh, yes,' Giles agreed. 'I am looking forward to
it, although it is an unexpected development.' It was
easy to resist the temptation to tell her what he was
intending to do. This could all be covered by his
willingness to stand up for his friends the Albrights.
Isobel's name need not come into it.

'How mysterious! Or perhaps you are simply missing your mistress.'

'No.' He made himself smile at the jibe. 'It is a secret, but I will tell you when I get back.' He would
have to do that, for she needed to know that the insult and the calumny had been answered. Giles lifted
a hand to touch her cheek, pale and sweetly curved,
but she flinched away as though she feared even that
caress.

He wanted to protect her, needed to possess her.
It seemed his wants might be satisfied, but never his

needs. Nor should they be, of course, he thought with a stab of regret.

Behind them the library doors opened and he let his hand fall away as Isobel pretended a renewed interest in the globe.

'Ah! There you are, Harker.'

'My lord?'

'Excuse me, Isobel my dear—a matter of urgent business.'

'But of course. I hope your journey to London is uneventful, Mr Harker.' Isobel smiled politely and turned from him. 'I will see if they can spare me a groom—the morning is too fine to waste the opportunity of a ride.'

In the silence that followed the swish of her skirts through the door the earl strode across the room and half sat on the edge of the big desk.

'London? I need you here, Harker. My steward tells me that my banker is due the day after tomorrow to discuss how the financial affairs of the estate will be handled in my absence in Ireland. I need to confirm the figures Soane left with me for the further building work and to make a final decision on the Hill House and the other matters you were looking into for me. I must have the funds and authorities in place to allow matters to proceed without my agents having to endlessly send to Dublin for my agreement on every detail.'

'I will be back by then, my lord.' He could be in London by that night, have a day to do what he had to do and a day at most to travel back. 'I assure you of it.'

'You are certain? You will forgive me if I press you, but it would be extremely inconvenient if this were delayed and Delapoole had to return to town.'

'My word upon it, my lord.'

'Excellent. I will let you get on then. Safe journey, Harker.'

Giles walked up the steps into Brookes's, one hand unobtrusively under Lord James Albright's elbow. It was all the guidance his friend needed, other than a murmured word now and again to help him orientate himself in the blurred world he refused to allow to defeat him.

'Good evening, my lord, Mr Harker.' The porter came forwards for their hats and canes.

'Evening, Hitchin. Lord Andrew White in?'

'Yes, my lord. He is in the library with Mr Wrenne and Lord Halton, I believe.'

'Excellent,' James remarked as they made their way down the corridor. 'Three birds with one stone.

I've never felt so helpless before—I wish I could get my hands on that swine White myself.'

'I'll hold him for you,' Giles offered with a grin as he opened the library door. The room was empty except for the three men lounging in deep leather armchairs by the fireside. They looked round as the friends entered and Giles saw the mixture of wariness and defiance on White's face when he realised who his companion was.

He guided James's hand to rest on the back of a chair, then walked across. The three got to their feet to face him. 'Harker. Do they let you in here? I thought this was a club for gentlemen.'

'Quite patently it is not,' Giles countered. 'They appear to have admitted the three of you and you are lying scum who think nothing of assaulting a lady and blackening her reputation. Or perhaps you crawled in here through the sewers like rats?'

'Wrenne, be so kind as to pull the bell, will you?' White drawled, but Giles could see the wariness in his eyes. The beginning of fear. 'Get a porter to throw out this bastard.'

'And what about me?' James asked. 'Do you expect the porters to expel two club members on no grounds whatsoever?'

'This is damned awkward, Albright.' White's bluff tone was at odds with the look of dislike he shot at James. 'Your sister took exception to a situation that was completely misinterpreted, made a scene, accused me of lord knows what, broke off the engagement— If I had been permitted to come and explain at the time, this could all have been put behind us.'

'You could hardly blame Penelope for her reaction,' Albright said with dangerous calm. 'You were found in another woman's bedchamber.'

'All a bit of fun that got out of hand. If Penelope had been a bit more sophisticated about it, we would still be betrothed.'

'And what a pity that would be,' James remarked. 'This is bad enough, but at least she discovered that you were a philandering cheat before she was irretrievably tied to you.'

'The devil!' White strode across the room until he stood immediately in front of James. Giles shifted his position so he could watch the other two—he did not want a brawl in the club, but if James lost hold of the threads of his temper, that is what they might well have. 'No one calls me a cheat! If you weren't as blind as a bat I would call you out for that, Albright.'

'And I would refuse your challenge, White. My grievance predates yours. You will apologise both to my sister and to the lady who you so grievously offended that night, or give me satisfaction.'

'I will do no such thing,' White blustered. 'And meet *you*? You couldn't hit a barn door with a blunderbuss.'

'I fear you are correct,' James said with such politeness that Giles felt his mouth twitch in amusement. 'However, as in all cases where a duellist cannot fight because of infirmity, my second will take my place.'

'And who is that?' White swung round as Giles cleared his throat. 'You? I'll not meet a bastard on the field of honour.'

'No?' Giles drawled. 'Then it will be all around town within the day that you and your friends are cowards who will not fight, even when the odds are three to one. My friend did not make it clear, perhaps, that the challenge includes all of you. The choice of weapons is, of course, yours, as is the order in which you meet me. We stay at Grillon's tonight and I expect word from you as to place, time and weapons by nine tomorrow morning. I have no time to waste on you—the matter will be concluded by dawn the day after tomorrow.'

He took James's arm and guided him out of the door, closing it on an explosion of wrath. 'That went well, I think.' The picture of Isobel struggling in that lout's grip while he pawed at her was still painfully vivid in his imagination, but at least the gut-clenching anger had been replaced with the satisfying anticipation of revenge for her. He hoped they would choose rapiers; he would enjoy playing with them, making it last.

'Exceedingly well. I might not be able to see much, but I could tell that rat's face changed colour. Where shall we dine tonight?'

'We are being followed.' Giles took a firmer grip on James's arm. In the darkness with only occasional pools of light, or the wind-tossed flames of the torches carried by passing link-boys, his friend was completely blind.

'Who? How many?'

'Five, I think.' Giles turned a corner, aiming for King Street and the bright lights around the entrance to Almack's. They had been eating in a steak house in one of the back streets that criss-crossed the St James's area. Now they were only yards from some of the most exclusive clubs, gracious houses and the royal palace, but surrounded by brothels, drinking dens and gambling hells. It was not an area to fight in—not with a blind man at his side.

'As to who it is, I suspect our three friends and a pair of bully boys they've picked up.' He lengthened his stride. 'We rattled them, it seems. We're almost to King Street, James. If anything happens you'll be able to make out the lights if you just keep going down the slope and you'll be on the doorstep of Almack's.'

'And leave you? Be damned to that,' James said hotly.

'Go for help—hell, too late, here they come.'

There was a rush of feet behind them. Giles swung round, pulled the slim blade from the cane he carried and pushed James behind him as he let his sword arm fall to his side. The two big men, porters by the look of them, skidded to a halt on the cobbles, their shadowed faces blank and brutal.

Beyond three figures lurked, too wary to approach. Giles stepped back as though in alarm, flailed wildly with the cane and the big men laughed and rushed him. The rapier took the nearest through the shoulder, then was wrenched from Giles's hand as the man fell against his companion. As the second man fended off the slumped body Giles jabbed him in the solar plexus with the cane, kneed him in the groin as he folded up, then fetched him a sharp blow behind the ear as he went down.

'Stay behind,' he said sharply to James as his friend moved up to his side. The three men who had held back rushed them, so fast that he was only just aware as they reached him that they were masked. His fist hit cloth, but there was a satisfying crunch and a screech of pain as the man—White, he suspected—

fell back. Then one of the others had him in a bear hug from behind and the other began to hit him.

Through the blows and the anger he kept control, somehow, and began to fend off the man in front of him with lashing feet and head butts when he got close enough. Dimly he was aware of the sound of breaking glass and James's voice, then he wrenched free and could use his fists.

James shouted again, there was a thud and swearing, a fast-moving shadow and pain in his face, sharp and overwhelming. Giles's fist connected with the chin of the man in front of him and he saw him fall. As he went down the alleyway was suddenly full of figures and the flare of light.

James was there at his side, gripping his arm, and a stranger who seemed strangely blurred, stood close, a torch in his hand. 'Gawd! They've made a right bloody mess of you, guv'nor.'

'Made more of a mess of them,' Giles said, his voice coming from a long way away. Then there was silence.

Giles had believed her. Isobel hugged that to herself through the rest of the day and into the next, allowing his faith to warm her like a mouthful of brandy. He believed her and he would convince Penelope's family of her innocence. Somehow that was less important than Giles's acceptance, although it should not have been.

She could not deceive herself: Giles Harker aroused feelings in her that no unmarried lady should be feeling—anger and exasperation amongst them. But there was more, something between friendship and desire that every instinct of self-preservation told her was dangerous.

Perhaps it *was* simply desire. Isobel sat and sorted tangled embroidery silks for the countess without taking conscious note of the vivid colours sifting between her fingers. He aroused physical feelings in her and that, of course, was wrong and sinful.

If she was the unawakened innocent that he believed her, then perhaps she would not have recognised this ache, this unsettled feeling, for what it was. Or she would have been shocked at herself and put it out of her mind, convinced that she was simply attracted by a handsome face and fine figure.

But she was not innocent and not a virgin. She had made love with her betrothed twice and, although Lucas had been almost as shy and inexperienced as she, it had been intense and pleasurable and had left her body wanting more. In her grief, and through the heartrending decisions to be made after his death, those feelings had vanished. Unaroused and unimpressed by the men she met when she returned to society, Isobel had assumed that passion had died for her.

But it seemed that desire had only been sleeping and all it had taken was a kiss from the right man to awaken it. Giles Harker had not been the first man to kiss her since Lucas Needham's death, but he was the only man who made her feel like this.

What did that mean? Isobel held up two hanks of orange silk and tried to focus on whether they were exactly the same shade. She knew how she felt: happy and apprehensive, warm and slightly shaky. Very restless. Her lips retained the feel of his, her tongue the taste of him.

Isobel shifted uncomfortably in the deep arm-chair. He was a rake, he had behaved disgracefully as well as heroically, and he made her want to cross verbal swords with him at every opportunity. She knew, none better, the dangers of giving in to physical passion—she should find an excuse and leave Wimpole before she was tempted any further.

*Coward*, an insidious little voice murmured in her head. *Why not enjoy being with him, even snatch a few kisses? You are far too sensible to—*

'Cousin Isobel, you are wool-gathering!' It was Anne, laughing at her. Isobel looked down at her lap and found greens carefully paired with blues, the orange arguing with a rich purple and pinks looped up with grass-green.

'So I am! Listen—is that a carriage arriving?' They were in the South Drawing Room and the sound of wheels and of the front doors opening came clear in the still of the house.

'Who on earth can that be?' Anne glanced at the clock. 'Past three. Too late for a call and we are expecting no one for dinner.'

'And Mr Harker is not due back until tomorrow.' Isobel dumped the silks unceremoniously into their basket and went to peep out of the window. 'Very unladylike of me, I know! Now who is that? I do not recognise him.'

'Neither do I.' Anne came to look over her shoulder. 'The groom is helping him down, even though he is quite a young man. I do believe he is blind—see his stick? But we do not know anyone who is blind, I am sure.'

'It must be Lord James Albright. Mr Harker mentioned that he had a blind friend of that name. But...' Her voice trailed off. If James Albright had heard from Giles of her innocence and had called to tell her so, surely he could not have arrived so speedily and uninvited by the Yorkes? Unless he had met Giles in town and had set out that morning without pausing to write.

'What on earth is going on?' Anne tugged her hand. 'Come on, we will find out better from the hallway—see, four footmen have gone out *and* Mama!'

'They are helping someone who is sick or injured,' Isobel said. Her feet did not want to move. Her stomach was possessed by a lump of ice. It was Giles, she was certain, and something was horribly wrong.

# CHAPTER TEN

ISOBEL CLUTCHED THE draped brocade at the window while Peter, the brawniest of the footmen, backed out of the carriage, supporting a tall figure. *At least he is alive.* Only then could she admit to herself the depth of her sudden irrational fear. With the thought her paralysis ended. It was Giles and he was injured. His head was swathed in bandages, his legs dragged as the men held him. *'Giles.'* She brushed past Anne, uncaring about the other girl's startled expression, and ran through the anteroom into the hall.

'Giles!'

'I can walk upstairs perfectly well,' he was saying to the footmen on either side of him. 'I do not need carrying up in a chair, I assure you.' His voice was slurred. As she ran forwards she saw his face was bruised. He did not seem to hear her, or see her.

*'Giles.'*

'Leave him.' Cousin Elizabeth caught her arm while she was still yards away. 'He is hurt, but the last thing he needs is women fussing over him. Peter and Michael will get him upstairs. The doctor has been sent for. I will go and have Mrs Harrison gather up salves and bandages and plenty of hot water.'

'But—'

'It is nothing mortal, I assure you, ma'am,' an unfamiliar voice said behind her. 'He is in a great deal of discomfort, but there are no deep wounds. Sore ribs, broken nose, bruising, cuts—so my doctor tells me. He should not have travelled today, but he said he had given the earl his word he would be here tomorrow and he's a stubborn devil.'

'You are Lord James Albright?' Giles had vanished unsteadily around the turn of the stair. The man who stood to one side, leaning on a light cane, wore thick spectacles on a pleasant face that showed both bruises and a graze along the jaw. When he held out his hand to her she saw his knuckles were raw. 'You have been in a fight? Is that what happened to Giles…Mr Harker?'

'The same fight,' he said with a grin. 'I might be nearly as blind as a bat, but when you put a big enough target in front of me, I can hit it.' As she took his hand he closed his fingers around hers, as if to detain her. 'I think you must be Lady Isobel?'

'Yes.'

'Then I have an apology to make to you on behalf of my sister.'

'There is no need. I understand why she thought as she did. But why have you and Giles been fighting?'

'Is there somewhere we can sit and talk?'

'Of course, forgive me. Lady Anne, do you think a room could be prepared for Lord James, and some refreshments sent to the South Drawing Room?'

'Yes, of course. I'll arrange that and then go and help Mama.' Anne hurried away.

'Through here, Lord James.' Uncertain how much assistance he would need, Isobel laid her hand on his arm and guided him to where she and Anne had been sitting. 'Are you in need of any medical attention yourself?' The bruises seemed alarming as he settled into the armchair with the last of the fading light on his face.

'It is nothing some arnica will not help,' he said with a smile, then fell silent as the tea tray was brought in, candles lit and the fire made up.

Isobel served him tea, then forced herself to wait patiently while he drank.

'You are wondering why I am here and what Harker and I have been doing,' James Albright said after a minute. 'He came to London yesterday to tell me the truth of what occurred when my sister's engagement was broken. At the time Penelope was adamant that she did not want any action taken against White, that in drink and high spirits he must have been entrapped by—forgive me—a designing female. She just wanted to put it all behind her.

'But once I heard the truth, that he had not only been unfaithful to my sister but had plotted to assault another woman in the process, then I knew I must challenge the three men involved. My family honour was involved twice over—once in the insult to Penelope and secondly in the role we unwittingly played in your disgrace.'

'But, forgive me, you are—'

'Almost blind. Quite. But, as my second, Harker could legitimately take up the challenge on my behalf. He would have called them out in any case, but that would raise questions about his, er…relationship with you. This way we both achieved satisfaction and the matter appeared to be entirely related to the insult to my sister.'

'His relationship with me?' What had Giles said to this man? *What* relationship?

'You are friends, are you not?'

'Oh. Yes, of course.' Isobel's pulse settled back down again.

'We challenged them and they apparently decided it would be easier if we suffered an unpleasant accident and fell foul of some footpads. Foolish and dishonourable, and even more foolish in practice. They thought that two large bully boys would make mincemeat out of one blind man and an architect with a pretty face. Unfortunately for them they were not at school with us. I learned to defend myself in a number of thoroughly ungentlemanly ways and Giles, when he is angry, fights like a bruiser raised in Seven Dials.'

'And you beat them—five of them?'

'Almost. It turned nasty by the end, but then the noise brought out a crowd from the nearby ale houses and, er, another place of entertainment and they soon worked out who the aggressors were and the odds against us. White, Wrenne and Halton have been taken up by the watch for assault and affray and their two thugs proved to be wanted by the magistrates already.'

'But Giles—how badly is he hurt?'

'Sore ribs where he was kicked. He was kicked in the head, too, I suspect, so he is probably concussed. The broken nose. Bruises and grazes all over. But that will all heal.'

A chill ran down her spine. What was Albright not saying? 'And what will *not* heal?' Isobel demanded bluntly.

'Oh, it will all knit up again. It is just that his face…there was a broken bottle.'

It seemed it was possible to become colder, to feel

even more dread. 'His eyes?' she managed to artic-
ulate.

'His sight is all right, I promise. As to the rest—I
couldn't see well enough to judge.'

'No, of course not. Thank you for explaining it all
to me so clearly.'

'Harker said you were not a young lady to have the
vapours and that you would want the truth whole.'

'Indeed, yes. Please, allow me to pour you some
more tea. Or would you prefer to go to your room
now?' Giles expected her to be strong and sensible
and so, of course, she would be.

The evening seemed interminable. The doctor
came and went after speaking to the countess, the
earl and Lord James. Dinner was served and eaten
amidst conversation on general matters. The explanation that Mr Harker and Lord James had been set
upon by footpads was accepted by the younger members of the family and everyone, once concern for Mr
Harker's injuries had been expressed, seemed quite
at ease. The earl was delighted with his intellectual
guest and bore him off to the library after dinner to
discuss the rarer books.

Isobel thought she would scream if she had to sit
still any longer with a polite smile on her lips, attempting to pretend she had nothing more on her

mind than helping Lady Anne with her tangled tatting. She wanted to go to Giles so badly that she curled her fingers into the arm of the chair as though to anchor herself.

Finally Cousin Elizabeth rose and shooed her elder daughters off to their beds. 'And you too, Isobel, my dear. You look quite pale.'

'Cousin Elizabeth.' She caught the older woman's hand as the girls disappeared, still chattering, upstairs. 'How is he? Please, tell me the truth.'

'Resting. He is in some pain—the doctor had to spend considerable time on the very small stitches on his face, which was exhausting for Mr Harker of course. He will be able to get up in a day or so.'

'I must see him.'

'Oh, no!' Lady Hardwicke's reaction was so sharp that Isobel's worst fears flooded back. 'He needs to rest. And, in any case, it would be most improper.'

'And those are the only reasons?'

'Yes, of course.' But the countess's gaze wavered, shifted for a second. 'Off to bed with you now.' As they reached the landing she hesitated. 'Isobel… You have not become unwisely fond of Mr Harker, have you? He is not…that is…'

'I know about his parentage. I hope we are friends, ma'am,' Isobel said with dignity. 'And he helped Lord

James clear my name, so I am grateful and anxious about him.'

'Of course.' Reassured, Cousin Elizabeth patted her hand. 'I should have known you would be far too sensible to do anything foolish. Goodnight, my dear.'

*Anything foolish. She is worried that I have become attached to him in some way. And I have. I desire him, I worry about him. I want to be with him.*

At her back was the door to his room. In front, her own with Dorothy waiting to put her to bed. Isobel walked across the landing and laid her right palm against the door panels of Giles's room for a moment, then turned on her heel and walked back to her own chamber.

'What an evening of excitements, Dorothy,' she remarked as she entered, stifling a yawn. 'I declare I am quite worn out.'

Half an hour later Isobel crept out of her room, her feet bare, her warmest wrapper tight around her over her nightgown. At Giles's door she did not knock, but turned the handle and slipped into the room on chilly, silent feet.

There was a green-shaded reading lamp set by the bed, but otherwise the room was in darkness, save for the red glow of the banked fire that was enough to show the long line of Giles's body under the covers. His left arm lay outside, the hand lax, and the sight of the powerful fingers, open and still, brought a catch to her breathing. It was unexpectedly moving to see him like this, so vulnerable.

On the pillow his head was still, with a bandage around the forehead, down over one cheek and around his neck. It was lighter than the heavy turban he had been swathed in when he arrived—Isobel tried to take comfort from that as she crept closer. The doctor had paid no attention to anything but getting his dressings right, it seemed—Giles's normally immaculate golden-brown hair stuck out incongruously between the linen strips.

She felt the need to smooth it, touch it and feel the rough silk, convince herself that he was alive and would soon be well, although he lay so immobile. Even as she thought it Giles moved, caught himself with a sharp breath. His ribs, or perhaps it was just the accumulation of bruised muscles.

'Lie still,' Isobel murmured and took the last few steps to the bedside. His unbandaged cheek was rough with stubble and unhealthily hot when she laid her palm against it. They had placed him in the centre of the wide bed and she had to lean over to touch him.

'Isobel?' His eyes opened, dark and wide in the lamplight, the pupils huge. 'Go 'way.'

'Did the doctor drug you?' It would account for the wide pupils, the slur in his speech. 'Are you thirsty?'

'Stubborn woman,' he managed. 'Yes, drug. Tasted foul…thirsty.'

There was a jug on the nightstand. Isobel poured what seemed to be barley water and held it to Giles's bruised lips. He winced as it touched, but drank deeply.

'Better. Thank you. Now go 'way.' His eyelids drooped shut.

'Are you warm enough?' There was no answer. She should go now and let him sleep. There was nothing she could do and yet she could not leave him. He had fought for her honour and for his friend who could not demand satisfaction for his sister. If she had only screamed when those men broke into her room, then none of this would have happened.

'Idiot man,' she murmured. 'You try to convince me that you are a rake and then you almost get yourself killed for honour.'

Giles shifted restlessly. He should not be left like this. There was a chair by the fireside, she could sit there and watch him through the night; she owed him that.

She eyed the bed. It was wide enough for her to lie beside him without disturbing him. Isobel eased on to the mattress, pulled the edge of the coverlet up and over herself. When Giles did not stir she edged closer, turned on her side so she could watch his shadowed face and let herself savour the warmth of his body.

It was very wrong to feel like this when he was injured, she knew that. It was not only wanton, it was unbefitting of a gentlewoman. She should be concerned only with nursing a sick man, not with wanting to touch every inch of him, kiss away every bruise and graze, caress him until he forgot how much he hurt.

She must not do it. But she could lie there, so close that their breath mingled, and send him strength through her presence and her thoughts. Tomorrow she must face the consequences of his defence of her, of the debt she now owed him and her own jumbled emotions, but not tonight.

'Oh, my Gawd!'

Giles woke with a jerk from a muddled, exhausting dream into pain that caught the breath in his throat and the sound of the valet's agitated voice. He must look bad to shake that well-trained individual.

He kept his eyes closed while he took stock. Ribs, back, a twisted shoulder, aching jaw, white-hot needles down the side of his face and a foul headache. Nothing lethal, then, only bruises, cuts and the effects of the good doctor's enthusiastic stitchery and drugs on top of a thoroughly dirty fist fight. But he had little inclination to move, let alone open his eyes. All that would hurt even more and, damn it, he had earned the right to ignore the world for a few minutes longer.

'My lady!'

That brought him awake with a vengeance as the bedding next to him was agitated and a figure sat upright.

'Oh, hush, Tompkins! Do you want to rouse the entire household?'

'No, my lady. That's the last thing I'd be wanting,' Tompkins said with real feeling. 'But you can't be in here, Lady Isobel! What would her ladyship say?'

'I was watching over Mr Harker last night and I fell asleep,' Isobel said with composure, sitting in the midst of the rumpled bedding in her nightgown and robe. Giles closed his eyes again. This had to be a nightmare. 'She would say I was very remiss to lie down when I became sleepy and we don't want to upset her, do we?'

'No, my lady,' said the valet weakly.

'So you will not mention this, will you, Tompkins?'

'No, my lady.'

Neither the valet nor the woman in bed with him— *in his bed*—were paying him the slightest attention. Giles gritted his teeth and pushed himself up on his elbows as the valet went to draw back the curtains. 'What the devil are you doing here, Isobel?'

'I wanted to make sure you were all right.' Her voice trailed away as she stared at him in the morning light and the colour ebbed out of her cheeks, leaving her white. 'Of all the insane things to do, to tackle five men like that!' She sounded furious.

'Insane? I did not have a great deal of options. I could have run away and left James, I suppose.' Damn it, he had fought for her and she was calling him an idiot?

'That is not what I meant.' Isobel slid from the bed and he turned his head away and tried to push himself upright, humiliated to find himself too weak to sit up and argue with her.

'Sir, you shouldn't try to sit up,' Tompkins said. By the sound of it he was trying to envelop Isobel in Giles's robe.

'Pillows,' Giles snapped, mustering his strength and hauling himself up. 'And a mirror.'

'Now I don't think that would be wise, sir.'

'Your opinion is not relevant, Tompkins. A mirror. At once.'

'Sir.' The valet piled pillows behind him, handed him a mirror and hovered by the bedside, his face miserable.

'Unfasten this bandage.'

'Giles—'

'Sir—' Giles lifted his hand to try to find the fastening and the man shook his head and leaned over. 'The doctor will have my guts for garters, sir.'

The process was unpleasant enough to make him feel queasy. When the dressing was finally unwrapped Giles lifted the glass and stared at the result. His nose had been broken, his mouth was bruised, but down the right side of his face where he had expected to find a single cut on his cheek, perhaps reaching to his cheekbone, were two savage parallel slashes from just above his eyebrow, down his cheek to his jaw.

'The swelling and the stitches made it look worse than it is, sir, I'm sure.' Tompkins rushed into speech. 'The doctor's very good, sir, lots of tiny stitches he took. Lucky it missed your eye, sir. A miracle, the doctor said that was.'

A miracle. A miracle that had changed his face for ever in seconds. Giles stared back at familiar eyes, a familiar mouth, eyebrows that still slanted slightly upwards. As for the rest… He had always taken his looks for granted. His glass had told him he was handsome. Some women called him beautiful. It was nothing to be proud of: his looks came from his parents and good fortune and had proved enough of a nuisance in the past. He would get used to the changes.

He had forgotten Isobel until she stammered, 'No... Giles...' She fled for the door, wrenched it open and, with the barest glance around to check outside, ran from the room.

So this new face sent a courageous young woman fleeing from the room in revulsion, a young woman who was not a lover, but who had called him her friend. That hurt, he discovered, more than the injuries themselves. 'Put back the bandage, Tompkins,' he said harshly. 'Then bring me hot water, coffee, food.'

'But, sir, you should be resting. Her ladyship told Cook to prepare some gruel.'

'Tompkins, I have a job to do and I cannot do it on gruel. His lordship requires my attendance today. Either you bring me proper food or I will go down to the kitchen myself and speak to Cook. And send for the doctor. I cannot go about looking like an Egyptian mummy.'

The valet left, shaking his head. Giles lay back against the pillows and told himself that it did not matter. He would heal in time and scars and a crooked nose were not the end of the world. But he could not forget the look on Isobel's face when she had stared at him, appalled. That felt as though something had broken inside him.

# CHAPTER ELEVEN

By BREAKFAST ISOBEL was no nearer overcoming the guilt. Giles's beautiful face was scarred for life and it was her fault. He had done it for her. The shock of how injured he was, her own helplessness, had made her angry—with herself as well as, irrationally, with him.

She should not have shouted at him, she thought penitently as she looked across the table to where James Albright sat, coping efficiently with bacon and eggs after a few moments' discreet exploration of the table around him with his fingertips. Giles had fought for him, too.

Cousin Elizabeth pressed Lord James to stay on, but he shook his head. 'You are very kind, but I will leave after luncheon if that is convenient. I must go and tell my family the truth of this matter.' He smiled in Isobel's direction before turning back to his hostess. 'I am sorry to trouble you for so long, but my groom tells me that one of the horses has cast a shoe and they must send to the village blacksmith. I thank you for your hospitality under such trying circumstances,' he added.

'Helping an injured man, and one who is a friend of the family now, is no hardship, Lord James. And I know Mr Harker insisted that you bring him, although what on earth he was thinking about, I cannot imagine. Surely he did not think that he would be in any state to work with my husband and his advisers today—' She broke off and stared at the door. 'Mr Harker!'

'Good morning. I apologise for my appearance.' Giles walked into the room with a deliberation that Isobel realised must be the only alternative to limping. She found she was on her feet and sat down again. He did not spare her a glance.

Giles had discarded the swathes of bandage, although there was a professional-looking dressing across his injured cheek. The swelling around his nose was less, although the bruising was colourful. He sat down next to his friend and touched his hand briefly.

'Mr Harker, you should go back to bed immediately! What can you be thinking of?'

'Lady Hardwicke, I assure you I am quite capable of working with the earl and his advisers.' He accepted a cup of tea from Anne and reached for the cold meats.

The countess shook her head at him, but did not argue further, apparently recognising an impossible cause when she saw one. 'Benson, please tell his lordship that Mr Harker will be joining him and Mr Delapoole after breakfast.'

Isobel ate in silence, almost unaware of what food passed her lips. Giles not so much ignored her as managed to appear not to notice her presence. When he rose to leave she got to her feet with a murmured excuse to her hostess and followed him out, padding quietly behind him until he reached the Long Gallery.

'Giles! Please wait.'

He stopped and turned. 'Lady Isobel?' The beautiful voice was still slightly slurred.

'Don't. Don't be like that.' She caught up with him and laid her hand on his arm to detain him. 'Why are you angry with me? Because I have not thanked you for what you did for me? Or because I slept in your room? I am sorry if it was awkward with Tompkins. If you had to give him money, I will—'

'What were you doing in my room? In my bed?'

'I was not in it, I was on it.' She knew she was blushing and that her guilty conscience was the cause. She desired him. She had lusted after him. 'I was worried about you. I came to your room to make certain you were all right. You were thirsty so I gave you something to drink. You were drugged and I thought someone should watch over you. The bed was wide. I only expected to doze, not sleep so soundly that anyone would find me in the morning.'

'A pity you did not turn up the lamp and see at once just how repulsive I look now: then you could have fled there and then and not waited until Tompkins and daylight revealed the worst.' His bloodshot eyes fixed her with chilly disdain as she gaped at him. 'You have had time to pluck up the courage to look at me. Pretty, isn't it?'

'You thought I was repulsed? Giles, for goodness' sake! No, it isn't *pretty*, it is a mess. But it will get better when the bruises come out and the swelling subsides. Your nose will be crooked, but surely you are not so vain that will concern you?'

'And the scars?' he asked harshly.

'Will they be very bad? The stitches will make it look and feel worse at first. My brother had them in his arm last year and they looked frightful. But now all there is to show is a thin white line.'

'Isobel, I am not a sixteen-year-old boy needing reassurance.' Giles turned away, but she kept her grip on his sleeve.

'No, you are a—what?—twenty-nine-year-old man in need of just that! Physical imperfections are no great matter, especially not when they have been earned in such a way. You will look so much more dashing and rakish that your problems with amorous ladies will become even worse.'

'Then why did you look at me as you did this morning? Why did you flee from my room?' he demanded.

'Because it was my fault, of course! You had been hurt, you must have been in such pain, and it was all because of me. I know you felt you had to defend your friend's sister, but if I had not told you my story you would never have known. I was angry with myself, so I shouted at you.'

'Of all the idiotic—'

'I am not being idiotic,' she snapped, goaded. 'You could have been killed, or lost an eye.'

'Isobel, I could not let them do that to you and not try to defend you. How could I not fight?' Giles turned fully and caught her hands in his. The chill had gone from his expression, now there was heat and an intensity that made her forget her anger. But with it, her vehemence ebbed away.

'You hardly know me. We have been friends for such a short time,' Isobel stammered.

'Friends? Is that really what you think we are?' She

could see the pulse beat in his temple, hard, just as her heart was beating. 'I saved your life—that makes you mine. I want to be so much more than friends with you, Isobel, did you not realise?'

'You do? But—'

'But it is quite impossible, of course,' he said with a harsh edge beneath the reasonable tone. 'You might be mine, but I can never have you. You do not have to say it. I am who I am—you are what you are. You must forgive me for speaking at all,' he added with a smile that did not reach his eyes. 'I have embarrassed you now.'

'No. No, you have not.' What did he really mean? What did he want, feel? She did not know, dared not ask. This was not some smooth attempt at seduction, this was bitter and heartfelt—the words seemed dragged from him against his will.

'I want you as more than a friend. I had hoped that I had hidden it. I knew I should not feel it. But I cannot help it,' she added despairingly.

'I should never have kissed you.'

'Two kisses are not what makes me feel like this.' She put her hand to her breast, instinctively laying it across the heart that ached for him.

'You fought very hard against what you feel?' he asked. His hands had come up to her shoulders. He was holding her so close that her skirts brushed his boots and she had to tip her head back a little to look into his face. The taut lines had relaxed into a wary watchfulness.

'Not as hard as I should have,' Isobel admitted. 'But I was afraid you would think me like the women you have to avoid, the ones who pursue you.'

'I doubt any of them would stand here, this close, with me looking like this,' Giles said with a return to the bitterness.

'I have seen better shaves,' Isobel admitted, seeing what humour might do. No good was going to come of this, she knew that. How could it? He was, as he said, who he was. But that was for tomorrow. Today she knew only that she was desired by this man. 'And I could wish your mouth was not so bruised.'

'Just my mouth?' He raised an eyebrow and winced.

'I would like to kiss you,' Isobel admitted, beyond shame at saying it. 'But I do not want to hurt you.'

'Kiss it better,' he suggested, pulling her closer and bending his head so his words whispered against her lips.

She slid her hands up to the nape of his neck to steady herself and trembled at the unexpected, vulnerable softness of the skin beneath her fingertips. With infinite care she met his lips with her own: the

slightest pressure, the gentlest brush. He sighed and
she opened to him and let him control the kiss.

This was so much more than that passionate exchange in the library, that foolish tumble in the shrubbery. So much more intimate, so much more trusting.
Giles made a sound deep in his throat, a rumble of
masculine satisfaction, and she met the thrust of his
tongue with her own, learning the taste of him, the
scent of his skin, the rhythm of his pulse. Their lips
hardly moved as the silent mutual exploration went
on, but Giles's hands travelled down her back until
he held her by the waist, drew her tighter against his
body.

He was lean and long and fit and Isobel pressed
against him out of need and yearning and felt the
heat and the hardness of his need for her. She wanted
to get closer, to wrap herself around him, but she
stopped herself in time, recalling his ribs.

'What is it?' Giles lifted his head.

'Your ribs. Lord James said you had been kicked.'

'If you can be thinking about my ribs while I am
kissing you, it does not say much for my lovemaking.'
Giles bent and brushed his uninjured cheek against
hers, his mouth nuzzling at the warm angle of her
neck and shoulder.

'You want to make love to me?' How brazen she

was to ask such a thing. How wonderfully liberating it felt to do so.

'I would give a year of my life for one night in your arms.' His voice was muffled against her skin as she lifted her hand to touch his hair.

Isobel gasped. It was all her fantasies about Giles, all her wicked longings, offered to her to take. All she needed was the courage to reach out.

Almost as soon as he said it, she felt him hear his own words. The enchanted bubble that surrounded them shattered like thin glass. Giles's body tensed under her hands, then he released her and stepped back.

'I am sorry. I should never have spoken, never touched you.' His face was tight with a kind of pain that his physical injuries had not caused. 'I did not mean— Isobel, forgive me. I would not hurt you for the world.' He turned on his heel and walked away without looking back, up the gallery and into the book room that led to the library.

She stared after him, still shaking a little from the intensity of that kiss, unable to speak, unable to call him back.

He had only wanted a brief amorous encounter and his sense of honour had stopped him before they both were carried away. Isobel sank down on the nearest chair, stared unseeing at a landscape on the opposite wall and tried to tell herself she had just had a narrow escape.

The earl broke up the meeting shortly before noon. Giles suspected that such a short morning's work was on his behalf, but he could not feel sorry for it. Between the lingering effects of the doctor's potions, the pains in his body and his anger with himself over Isobel, it had been an effort to think straight at all, although the other men did not appear to notice anything amiss.

Of all the damnably stupid things to have done. But somehow he had not been able to forget that moment of waking to find her beside him in the big bed. All his good resolutions, all his self-deception that he could treat her as a friend, had fled to leave only a raw, aching need for her.

He could have controlled it, he told himself savagely, as he turned left out of the steward's room and, on impulse, took the steps up from the basement. He emerged into the grey light of a blustery, cold day that threatened rain before nightfall. Giles jammed his hands into his breeches' pockets. He *would* have controlled it if she had not chosen that moment to come to him, her face full of hurt at the way he had coolly ignored her.

That vulnerability, that honesty, the way she confronted him so directly had somehow wrenched equal frankness from him. And because she was older than most of the unmarried girls he encountered, because he had been so open with her, he had let himself believe that they could have an affaire.

And of course she was too innocent to understand where their kisses were leading—even if she was not, it would have been wrong. By his own action he had cleared her name of all disgrace—now she could go back into society, find a husband, marry.

She was a lady and that meant marriage—but not to him, he told himself savagely. Not to him and she knew it, had remembered it when he had blurted out his desire for her. He had thought he had come to terms with his birth and with the limits it placed upon him: it seemed he was wrong.

'Idiot,' he muttered, kicking gravel. Of course a woman like her would not offer herself to a man she did not love. She had thought him her friend, nothing more, and he had betrayed her trust. 'Damnation.' What had he done?

'Harker, I could follow you across Cambridgeshire just from the muttered oaths.' He looked up to find

James, his cane in his hand, standing in front of him. 'What is the matter? Are you in pain?'

'Not as much as I deserve to be. What are you doing out here?' Giles took in his friend's thick greatcoat and muffler. 'It is no weather for a walk.'

'I went over to the stables to see how they were progressing in the search for a blacksmith. What's the matter with you? If you want to talk about it, that is.'

He could trust James, more than he could trust his own sense, just at the moment. 'Strictly between ourselves I've made a mull of things with Lady Isobel. More than a mull. Are you warm enough to walk? I don't want to risk being overheard.'

'Of course.' James fell in beside him as he walked past the stables and the church down the drive to the east. 'Have you told her you love her?'

'*What?* Of course not! I'm not in love with her. I do not fall in love with well-bred virgins. In fact, I do not fall in love with anyone.' James snorted. 'I want her, that's the trouble, and she caught me with my guard down and I damn nearly propositioned her.'

'Clumsy,' James remarked. 'And unlike you. But of course she, being female and having more intuition than the average male, presumably took your intentions to be honourable.'

'I don't know what she took them to be,' Giles retorted, goaded. 'She knows who I am, so how could she believe them to be anything but dishonourable? And what makes you think she wants me? Your fine understanding of female sensibility?'

'Not being able to see means I use my ears, my dear Harker. And I listen to the silences between the words as well. You two are, as near as damn it, in love with each other. What are you going to do about it?'

'Nothing. Because you are wrong, and even if you were correct, even if I was fool enough to allow myself to fall in love, I would do nothing. I am not even going to apologise for what happened between us in the Long Gallery and perhaps that will bring her to her senses. And stop snorting, it is like having a conversation with a horse. I'll leave as soon as I can.'

'So you make love to her and then snub her. An excellent plan if you wish to break her heart, although I doubt Lady Isobel deserves that.'

'Then what do you suggest?' Giles demanded.

'Marry her.'

# CHAPTER TWELVE

'MARRY HER? ARE you insane?' Giles slammed to a halt. 'Isobel is the daughter of an earl.'

'And so? She's a second daughter, she's perilously close to being on the shelf and she's had a brush with scandal. From what my sister tells me she was only doing the Season reluctantly in any case. Perhaps her father would be delighted for her to marry an up-and-coming architect with society connections, a nice little estate and a healthy amount in the bank.'

'You *are* insane,' Giles said with conviction.

'All right.' Albright shrugged. 'Go right ahead and break her heart because you won't risk a snub from the Earl of Bythorn.'

'Snub? I'd be lucky if he didn't come after me with a brace of Mantons and a blunt carving knife. I would in his shoes.'

'Coward,' James said.

'I am trying to do the honourable thing,' Giles said between gritted teeth. 'And that includes not knocking your teeth down your throat. You're the only man who can get away with calling me a coward and you know it.'

'If you want to do the honourable thing, then you want to marry her,' Albright persisted. 'Let's go back inside, it is raw out here and it must almost be time for luncheon.'

'Of course I do not.' Giles took the other man's arm and steered him down a path towards the back of the house. 'I am not in love. I have never been in love, I do not intend on falling in love. I intend,' he continued with more force when that declaration received no response, 'to make a sensible marriage to a well-dowered young woman from a good merchant family. Eventually.'

'That's three of you who'll be unhappy then,' James retorted as they went in through the garden door. 'Give me your arm as far as my room, there's a good fellow.'

Lord James was particularly pleasant to her over luncheon, Isobel thought. Perhaps he was trying to make up for the misunderstanding over the house-party incident. Sheer stubborn pride made her smile and follow all his conversational leads. She wished she could confide in him, for he seemed both intelligent and empathetic and he knew Giles so well. That was impossible, of course—he would have no more time for her foolish emotions than Giles had and, besides, she could not discuss Giles with anyone.

She had bathed her red eyes and dusted her nose with a little discreet rice powder. Giles would never guess she had been weeping, she decided, studying her own reflection in the overmantel glass.

'You think this new census is a good idea?' he was saying now in response to Lord James's speculation on how accurate the results of the government's latest scheme might be. He sounded not one wit discomforted by what had occurred that morning. Isobel tried to be glad of it.

'What do you think, Mr Harker?' she challenged him, frustrated by his impenetrable expression. He was treating her as though she was unwell, fragile, which was humiliating. It seemed to her that when he spoke to her his voice was muted. His face, when their eyes met, was politely bland. But she knew him too well now to believe he was indifferent to what had passed between them that morning. There were strong emotions working behind the green, shuttered eyes.

'I think that it will all depend on the competence of the parish priest entrusted to fill in the return in each place,' he said now. 'Better if each person was questioned individually. Or every householder, at least.'

'You think that would expose more of the truth?'

Isobel asked. 'That people would reveal their circumstances honestly?'

'Perhaps not,' Giles said slowly. 'And perhaps it is a mistake ever to ask for too much honesty.' Isobel had no difficulty reading the meaning hidden in his words. He had been honest about his desires, had led her to the point of seduction and now he was regretting it.

'Sometimes people do not know the truth because they are too close to it,' Lord James observed, making her jump. She had forgotten that she and Giles were not alone. 'The observer often sees more of the picture, don't you think?'

'So gossips and old maids like to say in order to justify their meddling,' Giles said harshly.

Startled, Isobel glanced between the two men. Albright's mouth twisted into a wry smile, but he did not appear to feel snubbed by what had sounded like a very personal remark. Giles, on the other hand, looked furious with his friend. Something had passed between them that morning, it was obvious.

The earl looked up from his plate of cold beef, unconscious of the undercurrents flowing around his luncheon table. 'The census? Very good idea in my view. I'd be glad if they did it in Ireland, then I might have a better idea of what to expect of conditions and problems there. I may suggest it when we see how this works out.'

The talk veered off into discussion of Irish politics, social conditions and, inevitably, sporting possibilities. Isobel placed her knife and fork neatly on her plate, folded her hands on her lap and watched Giles.

He guarded his feelings well at the best of times, except for his betraying eyes. But now, with his face so damaged and his eyes bruised, she was not at all sure she could read him at all. Except to know he was unhappy. *Good*, she thought, and went back to chasing a corner of pickled plum tart around her plate with no appetite at all.

In the general stir at the end of the meal Isobel found herself beside James Albright. 'I hope you have a safe journey home, Lord James.'

'Rest assured I will make your innocence known to Penelope and all my family,' he said. 'And we will ensure the facts are spread far and wide. Unless, of course...' he lowered his voice '...you would prefer to stay ruined?'

'Whatever can you mean, sir?'

'It might widen your choice of marriage partner, perhaps,' he suggested with a slight smile.

'Are you suggesting what I think you are?' Isobel

demanded. *Marriage?* 'There is no question of a match between myself and…and anyone.'

'No? Of course *anyone* would say that, too, and, if…er, *anyone's* defences were not down, he would never have got himself into a position where he betrayed his feelings to me quite so blatantly, as I am sure you realise.'

'As we are speaking very frankly, Lord James,' Isobel hissed, furious, 'the feelings betrayed to me were not those which lead to a respectable marriage— quite the opposite, in fact!'

'Oh, dear. Hard to believe that anyone could make such a mull of it, let alone my friend. He is usually more adroit,' Lord James observed. Isobel glanced round and found they were alone in the room. His sharp hearing must have told him that also, for he raised his voice above the murmur he had been employing. 'If I am mistaken in your sentiments, Lady Isobel, then pray forgive me. But if I am not, then you are going to have to fight for what you want. Not only fight your parents and society, but fight Harker as well.'

'I have no intention of throwing myself at a man who only wants me for one thing,' she said. 'And I do not want him at all, so the situation does not arise.'

'You know him better than that. Try to forgive him

for his clumsiness this morning. If his feelings were
not engaged he would have been…smoother.'

'How did you—?' She took a deep breath. 'My
feelings are not engaged.'

'I found him in some agitation of mind. He told me
he had erred and distressed you—I could fill in the
rest. He let himself dream and hope and then woke
up to the problems which are all for you, not for him.
Giles Harker has a gallantry that will not allow him
to harm you, so, if you want him, then you must take
matters into your own hands.'

'Lord James—are you insinuating that I should
seduce him?' Isobel felt quite dizzy. She could not
be having this conversation with a man who was a
virtual stranger to her.

The unfocused eyes turned in her direction. 'Just
a suggestion, Lady Isobel. It all depends what you
want, of course. Forgive me for putting you to the
blush, but Giles Harker is an old and dear friend and
I will happily scandalise an earl's daughter or two if it
leads to his happiness. I wish you good day, ma'am.'

With Lord James's departure the men went back
to their meeting and Lady Hardwicke swept up
Catherine, Anne, Lizzie and Isobel, ordered them
into bonnets, muffs and warm pelisses and set out for
the vicarage to call on Mrs Bastable, the vicar's wife.

'I have sadly neglected my parish duties these past few days and it is Sunday tomorrow,' she remarked as she led her party down the steps. 'What with Lizzie's drama and all our preparations for the move and the pleasure of having Isobel with us and now Mr Harker's accident, the Clothing Fund has been sadly neglected.'

'Was it an accident, Mama?' Lizzie demanded. 'Mr Harker, I mean. You said it was footpads who broke his nose and cut his face like that.'

'It was accidental in that he fell amongst criminals who tried to hurt him,' her mother said repressively.

'And Lord James was the Good Samaritan who rescued him?'

'I rather think he was rescuing himself quite effectively,' Isobel said, then closed her lips tight when Anne shot her a quizzical glance.

'And the bad men?'

'Have been taken up and will stand their trial, as all such wicked persons should,' her mother pronounced.

'The wages of sin is death,' Caroline quoted with gruesome relish.

'Really, Caro!'

'It is from the Bible, it was mentioned in last Sunday's sermon,' Caroline protested. 'Mr Harker is very brave, isn't he, Cousin Isobel?'

'Very, I am certain.'

'And he was very handsome. Miss Henderson said he's as handsome as sin. But will he still be so handsome when they take the bandages off?'

Lady Hardwicke's expression did not bode well for the governess, but she answered in a matter-of-fact tone, 'He will have scars and his nose will not be straight. But those things do not make a man handsome: his morals and character and intelligence are what matter.'

She pursued the improving lecture as they made their way across the churchyard and through the wicket gate into the vicarage garden. Isobel brought up the rear, her mind still whirling from that extraordinary conversation with James Albright.

Had he really meant that Giles was in love with her? Worse, he seemed to believe she shared those emotions.

The vicar's wife was grateful for help with the results of a recent clothing collection and, after serving tea, set her visitors to work that was familiar to Isobel from her own mother's charitable endeavours.

Isobel helped sort clothing into a pile that would be reusable by the parish poor after mending and laundering. The remaining heaps would be organised by the type of fabric so that when they had been washed the parish sewing circle could make up patchwork covers, rag-rugs or even suits for small boys from a man's worn-out coat.

It was worthy work and the kind of thing that she would be organising if she married a wealthy land-owner, as she should. Lord James had spoken of marriage. An architect's wife would not have these responsibilities, although Giles had said he had a small country estate, so perhaps there were tenants. What would the duties of an architect's wife be? Not organising the parish charities, or giving great dinner parties or balls, that was certain. Nor the supervision of the staff of a house the size of Wimpole Hall, either. Not any of the things she had been raised to do, in fact.

This was madness. She would not marry save for love—on both sides—and Giles Harker wanted one thing, and one thing only.

'Cousin Isobel, you are daydreaming again,' Anne teased. Isobel saw she was waiting for her to take the corners of a sheet that needed folding. 'What on earth were you thinking of? It certainly made you smile.'

'Of freedom,' Isobel said and took the sheet. They tugged, snapping it taut between them, then came together to fold it, their movements as orderly as a formal minuet.

'Goodness, are you one of those blue-stockings?' Anne put the sheet in the basket and shook out a much-worn petticoat. 'I do not think this is any use for anything, except perhaps handkerchiefs.'

'Me, a blue-stocking? Oh, no. And I was not thinking of freedom from men so much as from expectations.' Anne looked blank. 'Oh, do not take any notice of me, I am wool-gathering.'

'I think everyone is behaving most strangely,' Anne said and tossed the petticoat onto the rag pile. 'There is the fight Mr Harker was involved in—and Lord James. I do not believe for a moment that it was simply bad luck with footpads, do you? Then you are daydreaming all the time and Mama is lecturing and there are peculiar conversations that seem to be about one thing, but I don't think are, not really. Like you and Mr Harker talking about the census and honesty.'

'Well, you know why I am here,' Isobel said. 'I have a lot on my mind, so I suppose that makes me seem absent-minded. And men are always getting into fights. It was probably over a game of cards or something. And I expect Cousin Elizabeth has a great deal to worry about with your father's new post, so that makes her a little short. And as for peculiar conversations, I cannot imagine what you mean.'

Anne looked unconvinced, but went back to sorting shirts while the countess tried to persuade the vicar's wife that she could take over judging the tenants' gardens for a prize, as Lady Hardwicke did every year.

Isobel picked up some scissors and began to unpick the seams of a bodice, letting Mrs Bastable's protestations that she knew nothing about vegetable marrows and even less about roses wash over her head.

Was she falling in love with Giles? Had Lord James, with whatever refined intuition his blindness had developed in him, sensed it when she could only deny it? Had Lord James really been serious when he had told her to take the initiative? Now Giles was no longer in shock, half-drugged and in so much pain, he would not take the first step—whatever his feelings, his defences were up.

*I don't want to fall in love with him! That* can't *be what I feel.* She had not felt like this over Lucas, so torn, so frightened and yet so excited. But then, Lucas had been completely eligible, there had been no obstacles, no secrets. No reasons to fight against it. Or was she simply in lust with the man and finding excuses for her desires?

'Cousin Elizabeth, I would like to speak to Mr Harker alone after dinner, if you will permit. He will not let me thank him properly for what he did— perhaps if I can corner him somewhere I can say what I need to.'

The countess put down her hairbrush and regarded Isobel with a frown. 'That will be all, Merrill.' Her dresser bobbed a curtsy and went out, leaving the two women alone in the countess's bedchamber.

'He has certainly put you in his debt and a lady should thank a gentleman for such an action, I agree,' Lady Hardwicke said, a crease between her brows. 'But a tête-à-tête is a trifle irregular.'

'I have been alone with him before,' Isobel pointed out.

But the countess was obviously uneasy. Perhaps she suspected, just as Lord James did, that there was something more between Isobel and Giles. 'A walk or a ride in the open are one thing, but in the house… Oh, dear. Perhaps one of the downstairs reception rooms would not be so bad—if you can persuade him to stand there long enough to be thanked! But for a man determined on escape there is a way out of all of them into another room. Unless you speak to him in the antechapel—there is no way out of that except into the gallery of the chapel and no one could object to a short conversation in such a setting.'

'Thank you, Cousin Elizabeth. Now all I have to do is lure him in there.'

Isobel left the countess shaking her head, but she did not forbid the meeting.

# CHAPTER THIRTEEN

GILES SCHOOLED HIS face into an expressionless mask when Isobel, assisting the countess at the after-dinner tea tray, brought him a cup. He wanted to look at her, simply luxuriate in watching her, not have to guard every word in case he made things even worse.

He braced himself for murmured reproaches, or even hostility. 'Have you formed an opinion on the crack in the antechapel wall?' she asked without preamble. 'It sounds quite worrying, but perhaps the earl is refining too much upon it.'

'What crack?' It was the last thing he expected to hear from her lips. Giles put the cup down on a side table and the tea slopped into the saucer.

'Oh, he was saying something about it before dinner. I understood that he had asked you to look at it.' Isobel sat down beside him in a distracting flurry of pale pink gauze and a waft of some delicate scent. Now he did not want to look at all: he wanted to hold her, touch her. Did she not realise what she was doing to him? Was she trying to pretend nothing had happened in the Long Gallery?

'I was not aware of it,' he said, forcing his brain to deal with structural problems.

'Perhaps he did mention it and the blow to your head has made you forget it,' she suggested.

That was a disturbing thought. His memory was excellent, but then, he had believed his self-control to be so also and that episode with Isobel had proved him very wrong on that score.

'Or perhaps he meant to ask you, then decided it was not right while you feel so unwell,' she said with an air of bright helpfulness that made him feel like an invalid being patronised.

'I will go and look at it now.' Giles got to his feet and went into the hall. He took a branch of candles from the side table and opened the door into the chamber that led to the family gallery overlooking the chapel.

Once the room had been the State Bedchamber, but the great bed had long been dismantled and was somewhere up in the attics. Giles touched flame to the candles in the room and began to prowl round, trying to find cracks in the plaster, not think about Isobel's soft mouth, which seemed to be all he could focus on.

There in the left-hand corner was, indeed, a jagged

crack. It would bear closer investigation in daylight, he decided, poking it with one finger and watching the plaster flake.

'Is it serious?'

'Isobel, you should not be in here.' In response she closed the door behind her, turned the key in the lock and slipped it into her bodice. 'What the devil are you doing?' Behind him was the double door into the gallery pew. Short of jumping fifteen feet to the chapel's marble floor, he was trapped, as she no doubt knew full well.

'I need to talk to you.' She was very pale in the candlelight and the composure she had shown over the tea cups had quite vanished. Giles saw with a pang that her hands were trembling a little. She followed his gaze and clasped them together tightly. 'About this morning.'

'I am sorry— I allowed my desires to run away with me. I had no right to kiss you, to hold you like that. It will not happen again.'

'That is a pity,' she said steadily. 'I would very much like you to do it again. I think I am in love with you, Giles. I am very sorry if it embarrasses you, but I cannot lie to you, I find. Not even to salve my pride.'

He stared at her, every bone in his body aching to go to her, to hold her, every instinct shouting at him to tell her… What? That he loved her? Damn James for even suggesting it. Of course he was not in love—he simply could not afford the luxury of hopeless emotion. But he did not want to hurt Isobel. 'I am very sorry, too,' he said, staying where he was. 'I never wanted to wound you.'

'I might be wrong, of course. I might not be. I thought perhaps…you…' Saying it brought the colour up under the delicate skin of her cheeks, soft pink to match her gown. He thought he had never seen her look lovelier or more courageous.

'No,' he said and kept his voice steady and regretful. He did not know what he felt, but surely it was only desire and friendship and liking. The emotion was stronger than any he had ever felt for a woman, but that was simply because he had never saved the life of one before, never fought for her honour, never met a woman like Isobel.

Isobel valued honesty above her own pride, but he could protect her from herself. 'No, I do not love you, Isobel. And that is a mercy, is it not? We could not possibly marry.'

'If you had not cleared my name and restored my reputation, and we did love each other, then perhaps we might have done.'

*Hell, she's been talking to James, the interfering romantic idiot that he is.*

'But not if I do not love you,' he pointed out. It felt

like turning a knife in his chest, the pain of denying her, the knowledge that he was hurting her. 'And I do not think you love me, either. You feel desire, as I do, and it is easier for a woman to accept if you dress it up as love.'

'Do not patronise me! If I desire you I am not such a hypocrite as to pretend it is something else,' she flashed back at him. Her eyes were very bright, although if it was because they were full of tears, she did not shed them and he dared go no closer to see, in case she should read in his face how much he cared and took that for love. 'But you want me.'

'Oh, yes, and you know that too well for me to attempt to deny it. I want you so much it keeps me awake at night. So much that I ache and I cannot concentrate. But, Isobel, I might be many things, but I do not seduce virgins.'

'No,' she said, and smiled wryly. 'I am sure that you do not.'

'You will forget me soon enough,' he offered, flinching inwardly at the banality of the words.

'You think so? I thought we could talk this through with honesty, but it seems I misjudged you. Goodnight, Giles.'

She removed the key from her bodice, unlocked the door and walked away, leaving him, for once in his life, unable to think of a word to say.

\* \* \*

Giles did not come back to the saloon afterwards. Isobel smiled and nodded to Cousin Elizabeth to reassure her that her mission to thank him had been successful, stayed to drink one cup of tea and then made her excuses and went up to bed.

He said he did not love her, but then he would say that whatever he felt, it was the honourable course of action in his position. And he said he wanted her— although he was quite correct and she hardly needed him to tell her that. If they made love, it would be hard for him to hide his true feelings, she was certain. She could try to seduce him, and if he made love to her then he would be trapped between a rock and a hard place—to marry her would be, in his eyes, dishonourable, but then not to marry her after sleeping with her would be equally bad.

And to put Giles in that position would be very wrong of her whether he loved her or not. Isobel wrestled with her conscience while Dorothy brushed out her hair and helped her into her nightgown. 'I cannot do it.'

'What, my lady?'

'Never mind. Something I had been wondering about.'

'You look sad, my lady. Aren't you pleased that Lord James knows the truth? It will be all over town in a twinkling, then you can go back and do the Season, just like all the other young ladies.'

'I do not want to, Dorothy.' It was the first time she had said it out loud, but it sounded so right. She had tried hard to please her parents, but the thought of entering the Marriage Mart again with this aching in her heart was agony. How could she even contemplate marriage to another man? She had thought she would never get over Lucas's death. Now that she had and had found Giles, it was impossible to believe she would recover from it. It must be love, she thought drearily. But love should make you happy, not confused and angry and scared.

'Now, my lady, that is foolishness indeed!' Dorothy bustled about tidying up until Isobel thought she would scream. 'All young ladies want to get married and have children.' An ivory hairpin snapped between Isobel's fingers. 'You had a nasty time at that horrid house party and then you almost drowned and then there's the shock of poor Mr Harker coming back with his face all ruined. No wonder you are feeling out of sorts, my lady. You'll find a nice titled gentleman with a big estate and live happily ever after with lots of babies.'

'I don't want lots of babies. I just want my—' Isobel caught herself in time. 'His face is not ruined,' she snapped. 'The bruises and swelling will go down, the scar will knit and fade in time.'

'Yes, but he was so handsome. Perfect, like a Greek god.' The maid sighed gustily. 'Terrible blow to his pride, that will be.'

'He has more sense than to let such a thing affect him,' Isobel said, hoping it was true. Then a thought struck her. Surely Giles did not think she was saying she thought she loved him because she felt guilty that he had been wounded defending her good name? No, that was clutching at straws and she would go mad if she kept trying to guess at his motives. All she had was the bone-deep conviction that he did care for her and no idea how she could ever get him to admit it.

'I will go to bed and read awhile. Thank you, Dorothy, I will not need you again tonight.'

The maid took herself off, still talking about the joys of the London Season. Isobel stuffed another pillow behind her back and tried to read. *It might as well be in Chinese for all the sense it is making*, she thought, staring at the page and wondering why she had selected such a very gloomy novel in the first place.

The sound woke her from a light sleep that could only have lasted an hour at the most, for the candles were still burning. What was it? A log collapsing into fragments in the fire? No, there it was again, a scratch at the door panels. Isobel scrambled out of bed and went to open the door, half expecting Lizzie, intent on a midnight feast.

Giles stood on the threshold in the brown-and-gold brocade robe open over pantaloons and shirt, his feet in leather slippers. In the dim light his eyes sparked green from the flame of the candle he held.

'What on earth is wrong? Does Lady Hardwicke need me?'

'No. May I come in?' The clock on the landing struck one.

'Quickly. Before someone sees you.' Isobel pulled him inside and closed the door before the thought struck her that he was even more compromising on this side of the threshold. 'Giles, you should not be here.' How could he be so reckless? He spoke about her reputation and then he came to her room in the small hours. Isobel let her temper rise: it was safer than any of the other emotions Giles's presence aroused.

'I am aware of that.' He put down the candle and went to stand in front of the fire. 'I could not sleep because of you.'

'A cold bath is the usual remedy for what ails you, is it not?' she demanded.

He gave a short, humourless bark of laughter. 'Guilt, I find, trumps lust for creating insomnia.'

'What are you feeling guilty about and why, if I may be frank, should I care?' Isobel pulled on a warm robe and curled up in the armchair, her chilly feet tucked under her. There stood Giles, close enough to touch, and there was her bed, rumpled and warm, and if that was not temptation, she had no idea what was.

He stooped to throw a log on the fire and stirred it into flame with the poker. The firelight flickered across his bruised, grim face and made him look like something from a medieval painting of hell, a tormented sinner. 'You might care. I lied to you. I care for you very much, Isobel.'

It seemed she had been waiting to hear those words from him for days, but now all that filled her was a blank, hurt misery. Isobel blinked back the welling tears. 'I had not thought you so cruel as to mock me.' The heavy silk of the chair wing was rough against her cheek as she turned her head away from him.

'Isobel—no! I am not mocking you.' The poker landed in the hearth with a clatter as Giles took one long stride across to the chair to kneel in front of her.

'Then you are cynically attempting to make love to me.' She still would not look at him. If he had come to her room with a heartfelt declaration of love then he would not have looked so grim.

'That would make me no better than those three, tricking my way into your room.' His hands, strong and cold, closed over hers and she shivered and looked down at the battered knuckles. 'Isobel, my Isobel, look at me.'

With a sigh she lifted her eyes to meet his. 'Whatever your feelings, Giles, they do not seem to make you very happy.'

'That is true,' he agreed. 'And it is true that I care for you, and like you and want you, all those things. And it shakes me to my core that you might love me.'

'Then why deny it? Why hurt me, play with my feelings like this?'

He released her hands, rocked back on his heels and stood up to pace back to the fire. 'Because what I feel for you is not love and I dare not let either of us believe that it is. Because even if it was, I can see no way to find any happiness in this, however we twist and turn. I do not want to play with your feelings, I would never hurt you if I could help it. But we can do nothing about it. I believed it for the best if you thought I did not care—you might forget about me. Then I realised how much that wounded you and I could not bear not to tell you that I do care, that I want you, that in some way I do not understand, you are mine.'

The hard knot of misery inside her was untwisting, painfully, as hope warred with apprehension. *I am his, he wants me, he likes me, but he does not believe he loves me?* 'And what you feel for me is not love?' she asked.

'I do not think I know how to fall in love,' Giles said flatly. 'I have been with more women than I care to admit to you, Isobel. And I have never felt more than desire and a passing concern for them, pleasure in their company.'

*How carefully he guards his heart*, she realised with a flash of insight. *He knows he is ineligible for any of the women he meets socially, so he does not allow himself the pain of dreaming.*

'You think it is hopeless, then? My love for you, your...feelings for me?' *Yes*, she thought as she said it. *Yes, I do love him.*

'Of course it is hopeless. Even if I was a perfectly respectable second son, say, earning my own living as an architect, your father would consider it a poor match. As it is, he would never permit you to ally yourself to me. And you deserve a man who loves you. We can be strong about this, Isobel. Avoid each other, learn to live our separate lives.'

'Will you not even *try* to find some way we can be together?' Isobel scrambled out of the chair and went to stand in front of him. The heat of the fire lapped at her legs, but every other part of her was cold and shivery. 'If we talk about it, perhaps we can see some way through.'

'No. It would be wrong to wed you.'

'I am of age, I can decide who to marry. Love grows. I would take a risk on yours.'

'Your father would cut you off,' Giles said. 'Disown you.'

'Do you want my money, then?' she jibed at him, wanting to hurt him as he was so unwillingly hurting her.

'No—but I do not want to deprive you of it.'

'As your wife I would hardly starve,' she pointed out. 'And I am not at all extravagant. We would not be invited to all the most exclusive events, so that would be a saving in clothes—'

'Do not jest,' Giles said, shaking his head at her. But she could see the reluctant curve of his mouth. Misery and pessimism did not come easily to him. 'A scandal would affect my business and then how could I support you?'

'You are imagining the worst.' Isobel shook his arm in exasperation. 'What if marriage to the daughter of an earl was good for your business? I would keep the other women at bay, I would entertain, I know all the people who might commission you. You say you do not think you will ever fall in love—well then, why not take the nearest thing to it?'

'Stop it, Isobel.' Giles put both hands on her shoulders and looked down into her face. 'You are talking yourself into an emotion you do not feel. I will go back to London. In a week or two you will go home and take part in the Season and you will find an eligible, titled husband and live the life you were born to live.'

'No. I will not,' she stated with conviction. 'I was waiting for a man to fall in love with. One who loved me. One I could confess my secret to and who might accept me despite it. I do love you, I know that now—this could not hurt so badly if it was simply desire. But I cannot believe that after Lucas, and now you, that I will find a third man to love, and one who feels the same. So I am resolved to give up on the Season. I will become a spinster, a country mouse who will dwindle quietly away as a good daughter and sister. One day, no doubt I will be an aunt and much in demand.'

'You are talking rubbish.' Giles's voice was rough. 'What secret?'

'That I am not a virgin.' There was the other thing as well, the thing that tore at her heart, but she could not tell him that, however much she loved and trusted him. 'Lucas and I were lovers in the weeks before he died, you see. Men seem to place such importance on that, in a bride. I could hope that someone who loved me would understand, but not a man who was making a marriage for other reasons. I could lie, I suppose, and hope he would not notice. I could pretend to be ignorant and innocent—but that is hardly the way to begin a marriage, by deceiving one's husband.'

She shrugged, his hands still heavy on her shoulders. The truth, but not the whole truth. But Giles, of all men, would not understand why she had done what she had done, why she had made the dangerous, desperate choice that she had.

He stood there silent and she wondered if she had shocked him. Was he like all the rest, the respectable ones who would condemn her for the sin of loving? 'I have disappointed you,' she stated, unable to wait for the condemnation on his tongue, the rejection on his face.

'Then you misjudge me,' Giles said. 'You were in love with him. He was a fortunate man. I can feel jealousy, I will admit that. But how can I condemn you? But you are right about one thing—it would have to be a deliberate act of deception to pretend to your husband that you are completely unawakened. Even holding you in my arms, kissing you, I felt the sensuality, the awareness of your own body's needs and of mine.'

'Giles?'

'Mmm?' He drew her in close and held her warm

and safe against his bruised body and she felt his
breathing as she slid her arms under his robe and
around his waist. Suddenly it was all very simple.

'Make love to me.'

# CHAPTER FOURTEEN

GILES'S HEARTBEAT KICKED and his hands tightened. 'Isobel, think of the risk. You making love with the man you were going to marry is one thing. But I'll not chance getting you with child.'

'There are ways of making love that hold no risk,' she said. It was easier to be bold with her burning face hidden against his shirt front. 'We...Lucas and I, made love like that the first time.'

'You trust my self-control?' His voice rumbled in his chest against her ear and she felt the pressure as he rested his uninjured cheek against her hair. He had not rejected her out of hand. Her pulse quickened, the heaviness of desire settled low inside her. If he touched her intimately he would feel the evidence of her desire for him. And she wanted him to touch her, shamelessly.

'Yes.' The second time with Lucas, neither of them had had any self-control. But it had not mattered, they told themselves, lying tangled in a happy daze afterwards. They would be married within weeks. 'Am I asking too much of you?'

'There is nothing you could ask me that is too much, except to forget you. This is only going to make things worse for us, you know that?'

'I know. But it will not be worse until tomorrow.'

Giles gave a muffled snort of laughter. 'Feminine logic,' then gasped as she pulled a handful of shirt from his breeches and put her hands on his bare skin. 'Isobel, if we are found out—'

'Lock the door. Lock the door and make love to me, Giles.' Isobel stepped back out of his arms. 'Please. Make me yours, as much as we can.'

As he went to the door she blew out all but two of the candles.

'Isobel?' Giles turned back, the key in his hand.

'I am shy—a little,' she confessed and knew her blush added veracity to the half-truth. She did not want to risk what he might read from her body.

'There is no need,' he said, smiling at her as he let his robe drop then pulled his shirt over his head. 'It is all right,' he added as she ran forwards with a cry of distress at the sight of his ribs, marked black and blue with bruises. 'Bruised, not broken. Let me see you, Isobel.'

Her robe slithered to the floor. Under it all she wore was her nightgown, warm and sensible flannel for February. 'Ah. My little nun,' Giles teased and pulled it over her head before she could protest. 'Oh, no, not a nun. My Venus.'

'I am not that,' Isobel protested, her hands instinctively shielding her body, even as she warmed with shocked pleasure at Giles's expression as he looked at her in the shifting shadowlight.

'Slim and rounded and pale.' His hands traced down over her shoulders, down her arms, over her hips. His touch was warm now. 'When I first saw you I thought you were too thin and your nose was red from the cold. You seemed quite plain to me. I must have been blind.'

'And I thought you were a cold statue, too perfect to be real.' She let her hands stray to his chest and played with the dusting of dark hair. 'So cold.' His breath hitched as her fingernail scratched lightly at one nipple.

'No. Not cold,' Giles said thickly. 'Hot for you.' He kissed her, held her tight against him so her breasts were crushed against the flat planes of his chest and her thighs felt the heat of his through the black silk of his evening breeches. The thin fabric did nothing to disguise the hard thrust of his erection against her belly. This was no shy and tentative young lover, this was a mature, experienced man. Isobel moaned into his mouth, pressed herself against him.

She wanted him, needed him inside her so she could possess and be possessed, know that she was his. But they must not, she knew it. Whatever she did, she must not put Giles into a position where he felt honour-bound to marry her, come what may. Somehow—if only he would come to realise that he loved her—they would find a way, but not like that.

Giles slowed the kiss, gaining control after the first shock of their lips meeting. He edged her against the bed until she tumbled backwards and he followed her, rolling her into the centre of the mattress and coming to lie beside her.

'Your breeches.' Isobel felt for the fastenings, but his hand stilled hers, pressing it down over the straining weight of his erection.

'Better leave them on.' He was having trouble controlling his breathing, she realised.

'No.' She shook her head and burrowed her fingers beneath his. 'I know what to do. Let me touch you, Giles.'

'You are— Oh, God.' He sank back as her determined hands pulled down his breeches and tossed them away.

'Oh.' He was…magnificent. The fight had battered and bruised his upper body, but below the waist the skin was unblemished, winter-pale. The dark hair that arrowed down from his waist added emphasis to a masculinity that did not need any enhancement. Isobel realised he was holding his breath and did what instinct was clamouring at her to do. She bent and kissed him there, her hands curved over the slim hips.

Satin over teak beneath her lips, the scent of aroused male musk in her nostrils, lithe muscles in tension beneath her hands, his sharply indrawn breath—every sense was filled with him as she trailed her lips upwards.

'Isobel.' He sounded in pain, but she knew enough to realise this was not agony. 'Not yet. Let me…'

She did not fight him as he pulled her up to lie beside him. She would let him lead because it was on him that the burden of control fell. But she would help, she would be rational and—

Giles took her right nipple between his lips and tugged and all rational thought vanished. Isobel pulled his head against her breast with a sob and the knowledge that he could do what he wished with her, she had absolutely no will to stop him.

His mouth, wicked and knowing, tormented each tight, aching nipple in turn, until she was writhing against his flank, gasping his name and some incoherent plea she did not even understand herself. Her body, the flesh she had thought immune to desire for so long, ached and clamoured and, as his fingers stroked down, laced into the damp curls, slipped between the swollen lips, she simply opened to him, quivering with need as he slipped into the tight heat that clenched around his fingers.

'I love you,' she managed and was silenced by his mouth, his tongue. Against her hip she could feel his straining body and reached for him, finding the rhythm as her fingers curled around him and his thumb worked wicked, knowing magic at her core. 'I love you,' she gasped, the words lost in his kiss as her body arched, pressing up into the heel of his hand, shuddering as the bliss that was almost pain took her.

'Isobel,' she heard through the firestorm and Giles thrust into her circling fingers, shuddered and was still.

How long they held each other afterwards, she did not know. She must have drowsed, for she woke to find him gently washing away the evidence of his passion, then he pulled the covers over them, snuggled her against his side and she felt the long body relax as he slid into sleep.

There was only one candle alight now, Isobel noticed hazily. And Giles had said nothing. Her body had not betrayed her as she feared. He had not realised she had borne a child and her secret was still safe from the man she loved.

'What time is it?'

'I can't tell with you wrapped round me like this,'

Giles said, disentangling the clinging limbs that chained him so deliciously to the bed. He managed to raise himself on one elbow and lift the carriage clock that stood on the night table. It was almost completely dark and he had to bring it to his face to squint at the hands in the faint glow from the fire. 'Half past four. I must go soon.'

'Already?'

Isobel sounded peevish, he noted, amused, as she burrowed back against his side. The chuckle turned to a gasp as she slid one hand down and stroked. 'Ten minutes. Fifteen,' he amended as the caress tightened into a demanding grip.

'Only fifteen?' Isobel wriggled up to kiss his stubbled jawline. 'You are all bristles.'

'You would be amazed at what I can do in fifteen minutes with these bristles,' Giles said and burrowed down the bed, ignoring the twinges from his ribs.

'Oh, do mind your nose and the stitches,' Isobel said. Then, '*Oh*!' in quite another tone as he pressed her thighs apart and began to make love to her with mouth and tongue and, very gently, his teeth.

She was not shocked, he realised as he luxuriated in the scent and taste of warm, sleepy, aroused woman. Her fiancé must have made love to her like this as well. He half expected a twinge of jealousy, but surprised himself by feeling none, only pity for the other man. He would have married her if only he had lived, poor devil.

Then everything but the present moment and the pleasure of pleasuring Isobel was driven from his mind as she took his head in her hands and moaned, opening for him with complete trust, total abandon.

'Ten minutes,' Giles said with what even he recognised as smug masculine satisfaction when they lay panting in each other's arms, half inclined to laughter, completely relaxed.

'Fast is almost as good as slow,' Isobel murmured, kissing her way up from the tender skin just below his armpit to his collarbone. 'Giles, do you regret that your mother kept you instead of finding you a home where you would grow up with a family you thought were your own?'

'What on earth makes you ask that?' He sat up and struck a light for the candle beside them. Isobel rolled on to her back, her hair a tangled, wanton mass of shifting silk on the pillows. Giles bent and kissed her between her breasts.

'I don't know. Do you regret it? It cannot have been easy, being known as the Scarlet Widow's illegitimate son. It sounds as though you were bullied at school and there are some in society who shun you.'

'I would probably have been bullied anyway,' he

said with a shrug. 'I was far too pretty—a real little blond cherub until I started to grow and my hair darkened. And if Geraldine had tried to give me away my grandfather would have had something to say about it, so I would have ended up with him and been an illegitimate gardener's boy instead of having the education and the opportunities I have had. No, I do not regret it. I know who I am, where I came from. I am myself and there is no pretence, no lies.'

'You call your mother by her first name?'

'The last thing she wants is an almost-thirty-year-old man calling her "Mama." It makes people do the arithmetic and I doubt she'll admit to forty, let alone fifty.'

'I suppose her position protected her at the time, made it easier for her to keep you.'

'No.' At first he had assumed that, but with maturity had come understanding. 'It was anything but easy. I picked up some of the story from her, some from my grandfather, but she kept me when it would have been an obvious thing for her to have pretended she was with child by her late husband. All she had to do was to apparently suffer a miscarriage late on, then retire from sight to recover, give birth and hand me to Grandfather.

'But she brazened it out and never pretended I was anything but my true father's son. I remember that whenever she is at her most outrageous. She is a very difficult woman.'

'She must have loved him very much,' Isobel ventured. She was pale and seemed distressed. Perhaps this was bringing back memories of her fiancé's death.

'She had been in a loveless, if indulgent, marriage to a man old enough to be her father for four years. She must have needed youth, heat, strength.' Had it been love? Or, as he suspected, had Geraldine simply needed to feel the emotion as she did with every lover since? It was such an easy excuse, love. But how did you learn to feel it genuinely?

'My father was young, handsome, off to fight in his scarlet uniform. Perhaps he was a little scared under all the bravado. By all accounts it was not some wanton seduction by an experienced older woman or some village stud taking advantage of a vulnerable widow.'

'How brave she was.'

'It cut her off from her own family, from her in-laws and, for a long time, from society. But she fought her way back because I think she realised that my future depended upon it.' Giles got out of bed and began to dress. 'Not that she was ever the conventional maternal figure. And the shocking behaviour is probably a search for the love and affection she experienced for such a short time. Not that she would ever talk about it.' What had she felt when she heard of his father's death in battle? He had never wondered about that before. Now with someone to care about himself, the thought of his mother's pain was uncomfortably real.

Isobel still looked pensive. 'Giles, what are we going to do?'

'I am going to my own bed and you are going back to sleep. And check the pillow for hairs when you wake.' He rummaged under the bed for a missing slipper, determinedly practical.

'Our hair is close enough in colour for Dorothy not to notice. You have had a lot of practice at this sort of thing,' she said slowly. 'Only I presume it is suspicious husbands you need to deceive, not protective ladies' maids.'

'Complacent, neglectful husbands—a few in my time,' he confessed. 'I do not make a habit of it. Are you jealous?'

'Of course.' Isobel sat up straight and shook her hair back. It seemed her brooding mood had changed. The sight of her naked body filled him with the desire to rip his clothes off and get back into bed again.

'Yes, of course I am jealous even though I have no right to be,' she said with a half smile. 'My brain is all over the place—I am not thinking straight. When

I asked what we are going to do, I did not mean now. I meant afterwards. In the morning.'

'And for the rest of our lives?' Giles pulled on his robe and made himself meet her eyes, too shadowed to read. 'I do not know, Isobel. I honestly do not know anything, except that this has no future.'

He turned the key in the lock and eased the door ajar. 'The servants are beginning to stir, I can hear them moving about on the landing above.' He looked back at her, upright, shivering a little in the morning air, her lips red and swollen from his kisses, her eyes dark. What he wanted was to drag her from the bed, bundle her in to her clothes and flee with her, take her home to Norfolk and be damned to the consequences. Was that love? If it was, it was selfish, for nothing would more surely destroy her

'Go back to sleep,' Giles said instead and went out into the darkness.

What she wanted to do was to get up, get dressed, throw her things into a portmanteau and follow him, beg him to take her away, to his home and his grandfather and let the world say what it would. Because this was love, however much she might fight it. Love was too precious, too rare, to deny.

But it was impossible to act like that, as though she had only her own happiness to think of. Her parents would be appalled and distressed. Cousin Elizabeth and the earl would be mortified that such a scandal had occurred while she was under their roof. Giles's business, his whole future, would suffer from the scandal.

He cared for her and that was a miracle. He had shown her love, all through the night, as much by his care and restraint as by the skill of his lovemaking. Perhaps he would come to realise that he loved her, but some deep feminine instinct told her that he would be wary of admitting it, even if his upbringing, his past, the constraints upon him, allowed him to recognise it.

She had given him everything she could, except that one deep, precious secret. Annabelle. Lucas's child was being raised as a legitimate Needham, believed by all the world to be the twin of little Nathaniel, the child of her friend Jane and Jane's husband Ralph Needham, Lucas's half-brother. The two men were drowned together when their carriage overturned into a storm-swollen Welsh mountain beck late one winter's night.

No one knew except Jane, her small, devoted household in their remote manor and the family doctor. Annabelle was growing up secure and happy with all the prospects of a gentleman's daughter before her and Isobel dared not risk that future in any way.

She saw her child once or twice a year and lived, for the rest, on Jane's letters and Annabelle's messages to *Aunt Isobel*. Her parents would never know their own grandchild. She had not heard her daughter's first words nor seen her first steps.

If she married again Isobel knew her conscience would tear her apart. How could she take her marriage vows while hiding such a thing from her husband? But how could she risk telling a man when he proposed? If he spurned her and then could not be trusted with the secret it would be a disaster.

Giles had said he was glad he had stayed with his mother, that he knew who he was. No pretence, no lies, he had said and he obviously admired and loved the Dowager for the decision she had taken. He would not understand why Isobel gave her child away; he would think she did not have the courage of his own mother to keep Annabelle and defy the world.

There was a very large lump in her throat and her face was wet, Isobel realised. She dared not let Dorothy find her like this. She slid out of bed, her legs still treacherously weak at the knees from Giles's lovemaking, and splashed her cheeks in the cold water on the washstand. Then she smoothed the right-hand side of the bed, tucked it in and got back in, tossing and turning enough to account for the creases.

* * *

A clock struck six and Isobel knew she had been lying, half asleep, half waking and worrying, since Giles had left her. In an hour and a half Dorothy would bring her chocolate and hot water. She must try to sleep properly despite the warm tingling of her body and the agitation of her mind. Whatever the day brought, she would need her wits about her.

# CHAPTER FIFTEEN

THERE WAS NO sign of Giles at breakfast, nor was he with the earl, Isobel discovered after some carefully casual questions. Lizzie finally gave her a clue.

'I think it is such a pity,' she was protesting to Anne as they entered the breakfast room. 'Good morning, Cousin Isobel. Have you heard the awful news? Mr Harker is conspiring with Papa to demolish the Hill House.'

'Really, Lizzie! You are dramatising ridiculously,' Anne chided as she sat down. 'Papa has decided it is not worth reconstructing, that is all. Much better that it is safely demolished.'

'But Mr Repton said—'

'Mr Repton is not always right and it is Papa's decision. Anyway, we would not be here to use it for ages, even if it was rebuilt.'

'Well, I am very disappointed in Mr Harker,' Lizzie announced darkly. 'He had better not try to knock down my castle.'

'I believe he is going to see what can be saved of

the stonework to go to strengthening the Gothic folly,' her sister soothed. 'I expect that is what he is doing today. I heard him say something to Papa about good dressed stone not going to waste.' Lizzie subsided, somewhat mollified.

'Is Cousin Elizabeth coming down to breakfast or have I missed her?' Isobel asked. 'I was going to ask her if I might ride this morning.' If Giles was not at the Hill House, then she would ride over the entire estate to find him, if necessary.

'Oh, Mama left early to drive into Cambridge to take Caroline to the dentist,' Anne said. 'I know it is Sunday, but she woke with the most terrible tooth-ache. Mama says we can all go to evensong instead of matins. But I know she will not mind you taking her mare. Benson, please send round to the stables and have them saddle up Firefly for Lady Isobel.' As the butler bowed and crooked a finger for a footman to take the message, Anne added, 'I do not think this sunshine will last—my woman predicts a storm coming and she is a great weather prophet.'

The sky was certainly dark to the west as the groom tossed Isobel up into the saddle of the countess's pretty little chestnut mare. 'Shall I come with you, my lady? She's a lively one.'

'No, thank you. I can manage her.' She held the

mare under firm control as they crossed in front of
the house and then gave her her head up the hill towards the derelict prospect house.

Giles's big grey was tied up outside and whickered
a greeting as Isobel reined Firefly in. A movement
caught her eye and she glanced up to find Giles sitting at the window over the portico. One foot up on
the sill, his back against the frame, he turned his
head from the distant view he had been contemplating and looked down.

'Isobel. You should not be here.' But he smiled as
he said it and a tremor of remembered pleasure ran
through her.

She brought the mare up next to the grey and slid
down to the steps, managing to avoid the mud. 'But
we need to talk,' she said, tilting her face to look at
him as she tied the reins to the same makeshift hitching post.

'Come up, then.' Giles disappeared from sight and
met her at the top of the staircase.

'This feels so right. So safe,' she said and walked
into his arms without hesitation. 'I do love you so, I
know that now.'

Giles's reply was muffled in her hair, but she
heard the words and the happiness was so intense it
made her shiver. 'Last night was very special for me,
Isobel.' Then he put her away from him and the look

on his face turned the frisson into one of apprehension. 'But I have been up here for hours thinking—without any conclusion other than this is wrong and we must part.'

'No! No,' she repeated more calmly as she walked past him into the chamber. 'We are meant to be, meant for each other. I refuse to give up.'

'There is no way. We cannot change who I am and that is that.' The bruises on his face were yellowing now, the swelling subsiding. Isobel stood biting her lip and looking at his profile as Giles stared out of the window, his mouth fixed in a hard line.

'Your nose is not so very crooked,' she said after a moment. 'It is not as bad as when it was so swollen. Now it just looks interesting. Perhaps this—us—is not so bad either if we give it time and think.'

'The only thing that would make our marriage acceptable is your ruin, and you know it as well as I do. And there is no alternative for you other than marriage.'

'Then what is to become of us?' she said, her voice cracking on the edge of despair.

'We will learn to live without each other,' Giles said harshly. 'Just as you learned to live without Lucas when he died.'

'I would not call it living,' Isobel whispered. At first, despite the bitter grief, it had been bearable.

That year when she had been with Jane, their pregnancies advancing together, the month after the births when she could hold Annabelle, truly be a mother to her—that had been a time of happiness mixed with the mourning. It was only after she had returned home, doubly bereaved of both fiancé and child, that Isobel had plunged into deep sadness.

'I do not think I realised how depressed I was,' she said, looking back over the past four years. 'Even when I felt better I did not want to mix socially, look for another man to love, because I did not believe there was one. I could not see what the future held for me. Now—'

'Now you must start afresh,' Giles said and turned from the window to look at her. 'You have the courage and the strength, you know you have. And you are better off without me, even ignoring my birth. I have been—I am—a rake, Isobel. I have never courted a respectable young woman.'

'So will you forget me easily?' He had made love with her, slept with her, been thinking about her for hours—and he still did not know if he loved her, she thought, her confidence shaken.

'No.' He shook his head. 'You have marked my heart as surely as these scars will mark my face. I will never forget you, never cease to want you. You are, in some way I do not understand, mine.'

'But you will find a wife and marry and have children.' She could see it now. He would find an intelligent, socially adept daughter of some wealthy city merchant and she would love him and he would be kind to her and together they would raise a family and Isobel would see them sometimes and smile even though her heart was cracked in two...

'Yes. And you will find a husband. We will find contentment in that, Isobel.'

How the sob escaped her, she did not know; she thought she could control her grief. 'It sounds so dreary,' she said and bit her lip.

'You will make a wonderful mother,' Giles said. 'You will have your children.'

'Oh, no. Do not say that. Do not.' And then the tears did finally escape, pouring down her face as she thought of Annabelle and the children she would never have with Giles.

'Sweetheart.' Giles pulled her into his arms, kissing away the tears. 'Please don't cry. Please. I am sorry I cannot be what you want me to be.'

She turned her head, blindly seeking his mouth, tasted her own tears, salt on his lips. 'Love me again, Giles. Now and every night while we are both here.' He went so still she caught herself with a pang of guilt. 'I'm sorry, that is selfish, isn't it?' She searched his face, looking for the truth she had learned to read in his eyes. 'It isn't fair to expect you not to make love fully.'

'I would want to be with you even if all I could do was kiss your fingertips,' Giles said, his voice husky. 'You gave me so much pleasure last night, Isobel. But I have no right to let you risk everything by coming to your chamber again.'

'If that is all we have, just the time we are both here, then surely we can take that, make memories from it to last for ever? We will not be found out, not if we are careful as we were last night.' It was Sunday, so perhaps it made what she was asking even more sinful. But how could loving a man like this be a sin?

'Memories?' He held her away from him, studying her face, and then he smiled. It was a little lopsided, but perhaps that was simply because of the stitches in his cheek. 'Yes. We will make one of those memories here and now and use that little chamber one last time for the purpose for which it was intended.'

There was a rug thrown over the chair at the desk he had been using to write his notes. Giles spread it over the frame and ropes that were all that remained of the daybed in the painted chamber and while he closed the battered shutters Isobel shed her riding habit, pulled off her boots and was standing, shivering slightly in her chemise and stockings, when he turned.

'Goose bumps,' she apologised, rubbing her hands over her chilled upper arms.

'I'll warm them away. Don't take any more off, it is too cold.' He wrapped his greatcoat around her, then eased her on to the bed before stripping to the skin.

Isobel lay cocooned in the Giles-smelling warmth of the big coat and feasted her eyes on him. He would be embarrassed if she told him how beautiful his body was, she guessed, and besides, many other women had told him that, she was sure. Instead she wriggled her arms free to hold them out to him. 'Giles, come into the warm.'

'I am warm.' He wrapped her up snugly again, then parted the bottom of the coat so he could take her feet in his hands, stroking and caressing them through her stockings, teasing and warming and arousing as he worked his way up. Then he flipped the coat back over her lower legs and proceeded to kiss and lick and nibble her knees until Isobel was torn between laughter and desperation.

'Giles!'

'Impatience will be punished.' He covered her knees, then shifting up the bed, left precisely the part she wanted him to touch shrouded. He pushed up her chemise to lick his way over the slight swell of her belly, into her navel, up between her breasts without once touching the curve of them, the hard nipples that ached for his touch.

Only when he reached her chin and she was whimpering with desire and delicious frustration did he lie on the bed beside her, lower his mouth to hers and kiss her with languorous slowness while his hands caressed her, edging her to the brink, then pulling back, building the pleasure until Isobel thought every nerve must be visible as they quivered under the skin, then leaving her again teetering on the edge of the abyss.

'Oh, you wretch,' she sobbed, her fingers tight on the hard muscle of his shoulders as she arched, seeking his touch. 'You torturer.'

'Touch me,' Giles said, bringing her hand to clasp around him. 'Take me with you.' Then he held nothing back, his body at her mercy, his hands demanding, demanding, until Isobel lost all sense of what was her and what was Giles and surrendered to the mindless oblivion of pleasure.

She came to herself to find him slumped across her, relaxed into sleep. 'Giles?'

'Mmm.' His lids fluttered, the dark lashes tickling her cheek, then he was still again.

Isobel tugged the greatcoat more securely over them, curled her arms around him and lay, cheek to cheek, thinking. Nothing lasted for ever. She had him now and for a few days and precious nights even though she did not have his words of love. She would not waste those moments by anticipating the inevitable parting; she would live them and revel in them and then do her best to live without him. *I will not pine. I will find some purpose, some joy in life. I will not allow something so precious to destroy me.* In the distance thunder rumbled.

An hour later they approached the house from different directions, Giles from the western drive, Isobel retracing her route, bringing Firefly across the wide sweep of gravel before the house to the stables. They met, as if by chance, outside the stable arch.

'Mr Harker! Good morning.' Isobel let the groom help her dismount and waited while Giles swung down from the grey. The sound of bustling activity made her look through into the inner yard where the back of a chaise was just visible.

'Visitors,' Giles observed. 'Have you had a pleasant ride, Lady Isobel?'

'Very stimulating, thank you. But I fear it is about to rain.' She caught up the long skirt of her habit and walked with him across to the front door. Benson opened it as they approached and Isobel stepped into the hall to find the callers had only just been admitted. A grey-haired man of medium height with a commanding nose turned at the sound of their entrance, leaning heavily on a stick. Beside him a thin lady in an exquisitely fashionable bonnet started forwards.

'Isobel, my darling! What good news! We had to come at once even if it did mean travelling on a Sunday.'

She stopped dead on the threshold. 'Mama. Papa.' Her mother caught her in her arms as Isobel felt the room begin to spin. There was a crash of thunder and behind her the footman slammed the door closed on the downpour. *No escape.*

'Darling! Are you ill? You have gone so pale—sit down immediately.'

'I…I am all right. It was just the shock of seeing you, Mama. Thank you, Mr Harker.'

Giles slid a hall chair behind her knees and Isobel sat down with an undignified thump. 'Lord Bythorn, Lady Bythorn.' He bowed and stepped away towards the foot of the steps.

'Wait—you are Harker?'

'My lord.' Giles turned. His face had gone pale and the bruises stood out in painful contrast.

'Lord James Albright tells me that you were injured standing with him to bring to account those scum who compromised my daughter. And I hear from her own letters that you rescued Isobel and young Lizzie from the lake.'

'The lake was nothing—anyone passing would

have done the same. And Lord James is an old friend, my lord. I merely did what I could to assist him.' Giles made no move to offer his hand or to come closer. Isobel realised her mother had not addressed him and she was looking a trifle flustered now. Of course, they knew who he was, what he was, and Giles had expected that, should he ever meet them, he would receive this reaction.

'You have my heartfelt thanks.' The earl paused, a frown creasing his brow. 'You are a resident in this house?'

'I am undertaking architectural work for the earl. Excuse me, my lord. Ladies.' He bowed and was gone.

'Well, I'm glad to have the opportunity to thank the fellow in person,' her father said, wincing from his gout as he shifted back to face her. 'But I must say I'm surprised to find him a guest in the house.'

'Lady Hardwicke always gives rooms to the architects and landscape designers,' Isobel said indifferently. 'The earl works so closely with them, I believe he finds it more convenient. I met Mr Soane when I arrived, but I have not yet met Mr Repton.'

'Soane? Well, he's a gentleman, at least. I hear rumours of a knighthood,' her father said. Isobel opened her mouth to retort that Giles was a gentleman, and a brave and gallant one at that, then shut it with a snap. To defend him would only arouse suspicion.

'The man looks a complete brigand with his face in that state,' her mother remarked with distaste.

'He was injured in the fight defending Lord James and, by extension, me.'

'Well, he might be less of a menace to women now he has lost his looks. The man was a positive Adonis, so I hear—and there are enough foolish ladies with the instincts of lightskirts to encourage men like that,' Lady Bythorn added with a sniff.

'Perhaps he is only a menace to married ladies,' Isobel said sweetly, her hands clenched so tightly that a seam in her glove split. 'Cousin Elizabeth has no qualms about allowing him to socialise with her daughters or myself. Suitably chaperoned, of course.'

'I am glad to hear about the chaperonage, at least! But that is all academic—I expect your woman can have your things all packed by the time we have finished luncheon.'

'Packed?

'Well, of course.' Her mother beamed at her fondly. 'Now everyone knows the truth of what happened, there is no reason for you to be hiding in the country. You can come home and do the Season just as we planned.'

'But—' Isobel could hear Cousin Elizabeth's voice

coming closer. And the butler and footmen were still standing in the background, having stood to attention with blank faces throughout Lady Bythorn's opinions on Giles's morals. This was no place to start arguing with her parents about her future.

'Margaret! Bythorn! What a pleasant surprise.' The countess sailed into the hall, beaming. 'You've come to collect dear Isobel, of course. We are going to miss her sadly.' She ushered them towards the Yellow Drawing Room. 'Margaret, would you like to go up with Isobel to her room? I will ring for her woman to bring you whatever you need after your journey. You must have set out at the crack of dawn to make such good time.'

'I will go up in a moment, Elizabeth—it is so good just to see Isobel again! We left as soon as we received Lord James's letter and put up overnight at the Bell at Buntingford. I could not wait to get my dear girl home again. Thank heavens we have not missed anything of the Season.'

'I imagine Isobel is more glad about the restoration of her reputation than the opportunity to take part in social events,' Cousin Elizabeth said with a glance at Isobel. There was understanding in the look and a kind of rueful sympathy. She, at least, had some inkling of how reluctant Isobel was to plunge back into the social whirl that she so disliked and the imagination to understand what gossip and snide remarks would still follow her.

'I would prefer to stay here, Mama,' Isobel said. She folded her hands on her lap and sat up straight, as though perfect deportment would somehow be a barricade against this disaster. If she let her shoulders droop, if she relaxed in the slightest, she did not think she would be able to stop herself either sobbing in despair or running to find Giles.

# CHAPTER SIXTEEN

'STAY HERE?' SAID Lady Bythorn, turning her gaze on Isobel. For a moment she thought there was hope, then her mother shook her head. 'But you cannot impose on Lady Hardwicke's hospitality now it is not necessary. Really, Isobel, it is about time you shook off this pose of indifference to society. We should never have allowed you to stay with Mrs Needham for over a year in that remote place as we did. I declare you came back a positive stranger to us.'

'I am sorry, Mama.'

'It would be best for you to go back to London, Isobel,' Cousin Elizabeth said. 'We will miss you, but there is the risk that rumours may begin again if you do not make an appearance. It might seem that you have something to hide after all.'

So there was no help there. Where else could she go? If she ran away to Jane and Annabelle, then Papa would fetch her back and she did not think she could face him meeting his granddaughter all unawares. Without her allowance she had no money. To throw herself into Giles's arms would be to embroil him in a scandal that might wreck his career.

It seemed very hard to think coherently. Isobel felt she was running through a darkened house, banging on doors that all proved to be locked, twisting and turning in a maze of corridors.

She had thought she had a few more precious days with Giles—now those had been snatched away from her. She had to speak to him. When he left the hall he had turned towards the stairs. He must have gone up to his chamber to change.

'Mama, shall I show you to my rooms? I can set Dorothy to packing.' From somewhere she dredged up the courage to smile and stand and pretend composure.

'Of course.' Her mother linked arms with her as they went up the stairs. 'Now, you only have to overcome this indifferent shyness you seem to feel and all will be well. The country air has done you good—your cheeks are rosy, your lips look fuller and there is such a sparkle in your eyes.'

All the consequence of Giles's lovemaking, if her mother did but know it. It seemed she had no suspicion that anything untoward had occurred, even though they had entered the house together. Perhaps it seemed impossible to Mama that her daughter would even think of flirting with someone in his position, let alone anything else.

'Here we are. It is a lovely view, is it not? Dorothy, please can you pack all my things as soon as possible—I am sure you can ask for help if you need it. We will be leaving after luncheon, so do not neglect your own meal. But first, please fetch hot water for her ladyship.'

'Yes, my lady.' The maid bobbed a curtsy to the countess. 'I am so glad Lady Isobel is going home, my lady, if I may be so bold.'

'Thank you, Dorothy. We are all delighted,' Lady Bythorn said and the maid hurried out.

'Mama, would you excuse me while I run up to the nursery and schoolroom and say goodbye to the children? I have become very fond of them.'

'Of course. I will just sit here and admire the prospect from the window and rest a little.'

Isobel dropped a kiss on her mother's cheek and went out of the door leading to the back stairs. As soon as she was out of sight she ran up to the attics and into the schoolroom.

'Cousin Isobel!' Lizzie jumped up beaming from her seat beside Caroline, who had her head wrapped in a shawl and was looking very woebegone.

'Excuse me, Miss Henderson, for interrupting your

lesson, but I have to say goodbye to the children. My mama and papa have come to collect me, Lizzie.'

'Oh.' Her face fell. 'Can you not stay a little longer?'

'No, I am sorry. I promise I will write to you all. Is Charles in the nursery? I must kiss him as well,' she said as she disentangled herself from the children's hugs.

'If you are all very good, we will wrap up warmly and go out on the leads to wave Lady Isobel goodbye,' the governess suggested.

'That will be lovely. Thank you. Now, I will be going to London, so I will send you all a present. Would you like that?'

She left them agog at the thought of gifts arriving when it was not even their birthdays or Christmas and whisked down the stairs and along the passage leading to Giles's bedchamber. There would be just time, if he was only still there.

Isobel pressed her ear to the panels, but she could hear no voices, so the valet was not with him. Without knocking she opened the door and slipped inside.

'Isobel!' Giles strode out of his dressing room and shut the door behind her.

'Your face—why have you taken the dressing off? The doctor hasn't even removed the stitches. Oh, it looks so sore!'

'It looks thoroughly unsightly and will, I hope, convince your parents that no daughter of theirs would look twice at its owner.' He gave her a little shake. 'What on earth are you doing here? There will be hell to pay if you are found with me.'

'I had to talk to you,' she protested. 'And I do not know when we could have snatched even a moment alone. Papa intends to return home immediately after luncheon. Giles, what are we going to do?'

'Nothing, except come to our senses,' he said, his face harsh. 'This is a blessing in disguise—the longer we were together, the more chance there was of this being discovered.'

'But we have no chance to plan now—'

'There is nothing to plan for. You are not a romantic young girl, Isobel. You knew this was hopeless, just as I did, but we let ourselves daydream and now it is time to wake up.'

'Just like that?' She stared at him. The cold, aloof man of their first meeting was back and her tender lover was quite vanished. 'No regrets, no sadness, just a *blessing in disguise*? I love you, Giles.'

'And I let myself think I could dally with an earl's daughter.' He cupped his hand around her cheek. 'Sunshine in February. I should have known there would be a frost to follow. *Wake up*, Isobel—it is over.'

'So you really do not love me?' she asked painfully. He thought of what had happened as just a dalliance? The rain drumming on the window echoed the frantic beating of her heart.

'I told you that. And you have not fallen in love with me, if you will only be honest with yourself. You had been hurt and rejected by people you thought were your friends. You wanted affection and you wanted to rebel, too.'

'You think so? After we made love as we have, you can still say it was all a delusion, an act of rebellion? It must have been, because I thought I knew you and now I do not think I do, not at all.'

She turned away, unable to bear his touch any longer, then swung back. 'Why did you fight for me if I was not important to you?'

'It was the right thing to do, for my friends and for any lady who had been betrayed in that way.'

'Gallantry, in effect. Just like rescuing two drowning people from the lake. I thought I was your friend.' It sounded forlorn, but however much it hurt her pride, she could not help herself. 'You said I belonged to you.'

'It was wrong of me to think I could make a friend of an unmarried lady and what I said about you being mine was foolish sentimentality.'

'So there is nothing between us?' It was like sticking pins into her flesh, but she had to have the truth from him. 'You were gallant and then deluded. We made love, but that was merely lust.'

'I admire your courage and your generosity, your wit and your elegance. I was privileged to share your bed, and my lips will be for ever sealed about that. You need have no fear I would ever give the slightest hint that so much as a kiss had passed between us.'

Isobel stared up at the scarred, battered face and tried to find her friend, her lover, her love, somewhere behind the hard mask. But there was nothing, just a faint pity, the hint of a smile. 'I trusted you, Giles.'

'I never lied to you. I never told you I loved you. I am sorry it went as far as it did.'

'But not as sorry as I am, Giles.' Isobel turned on her heel and walked out. She wanted to hesitate at the threshold, to stand there a moment, for surely he would call her back, but she made her feet keep walking, closed the door behind her with care and went back to her own room. He did not speak.

Her mother, hair tidied and complexion restored with the judicious use of rice powder, was sitting with her feet on a stool while Dorothy bustled about packing.

'Isobel dear—have you been crying?' Her mother sat up straighter and stared at her.

'No… Well, a little. I was upset at leaving the children, they are very sweet. I suppose it has made my eyes a trifle watery, that is all. There is the gong—shall we go down?'

They descended the stairs arm in arm again. Her mother had relaxed now, Isobel sensed. Her unaccountable daughter had yielded, the Season could be exploited in every possible way and, by the end of it she, Isobel, would have come to her senses and be betrothed to a well-connected, wealthy man who would father a brood of admirable children. All would be well.

Cousin Elizabeth and her three eldest children were already in the dining room. Lord Hardwicke and her father followed them in and then, on their heels, Giles entered.

Lady Bythorn took one look at his face, gasped audibly and plunged into conversation with Lady Anne. Cousin Elizabeth frowned, more in anxiety about the effects of leaving off the dressing than from any revulsion at the scar, Isobel thought. Her father stared, then resumed his discussion of tenancy issues with the earl. Giles, apparently oblivious, thanked Lady Caroline for the bread, passed her the butter and addressed himself to his meal.

'Some brawn, my lady?' Benson produced the platter. Isobel stared at it quivering gently in its jelly and lost what little appetite she had left.

'Thank you, no, Benson. Just some bread and butter, if you please.'

It was strange, she thought as she nibbled stoically through two slices of bread and butter and, to stem her mother's urgings, a sliver of cheese. She had not expected a broken heart to feel like this. She was numb, almost as if she no longer cared. Perhaps it was shock; they said that people in shock did not feel pain despite dreadful injuries.

Over the rim of her glass she watched Giles and felt nothing, just a huge emptiness where only a few hours ago there had been a turmoil of feelings and emotions. Hope, love, desire, fear, uncertainty, happiness, confusion, tenderness, worry—they had all been there. Now, nothing.

She found she could smile, shake her head over Cousin Elizabeth's praise of her courage in rescuing Lizzie, tell her mother of the interesting recipe for plum jam the vicar's wife had given her. When her eyes met Giles's down the length of the table she could keep her expression politely neutral, even smile a bright, social smile.

It was only as they were gathered in the formal elegance of the Yellow Drawing Room to make their final farewells that Isobel realised what she felt like.

She had visited Merlin's Mechanical Museum in Princes Street once and had marvelled over the automata jerkily going about their business with every appearance of life and yet with nothing inside them but cogs and wheels where there should have been a brain and a heart and soul.

She shook hands, and exchanged kisses, and smiled and said everything that was proper in thanks and when she saw a shadow fall across the threshold, and Giles stood there for a moment looking in, she inclined her head graciously. 'Goodbye, Mr Harker.'

But when her parents turned to look he was gone. Like a dream, she thought. Just like a daydream. Not a memory at all.

# CHAPTER SEVENTEEN

'I HAVE ABSOLUTELY no expectation of finding any-one I wish to marry, Mama,' Isobel said, striving for an acceptable mixture of firmness and reasonable-ness in her tone. 'I fear it is a sad waste of money to equip me for yet another Season.' For four days she had tacitly accepted all her mother's plans, now she felt she had to say something to make her understand how she really felt.

Lady Bythorn turned back from her scrutiny of Old Bond Street as the carriage made its slow way past the shops. 'Why ever not?' she demanded with what Isobel knew was quite justified annoyance. She was doing her best to see her second daughter suit-ably established and any dutiful daughter would be co-operating to the full and be suitably grateful. 'You are not, surely, still pining for young Needham?'

'No, Mama.'

'Then there is no reason in the world—' She broke off and eyed Isobel closely. 'You have not lost your heart to someone unsuitable, have you?'

'Mama—'

'Never tell me that frightful Harker man has inveigled his way into your affections!'

'Very well, Mama.'

'Very well what?'

'I will not tell you that Mr Harker has inveigled in any way.'

'Do not be pert, Isobel. It ill becomes a young woman of your age.'

'Yes, Mama. There is no illicit romance for you to worry about.' *Not now.*

'We are at Madame le Clare's. Now kindly do not make an exhibition of yourself complaining about fittings.'

'No, Mama. I will co-operate and I will enter into this Season, fully. But this is the last time. After this summer, if I am not betrothed, I will not undertake another.'

'Oh!' Lady Bythorn threw up her hands in exasperation. 'Ungrateful girl! Do you expect me to wait for grandchildren until Frederick is finally old enough to marry?'

The guilt clutched like a hand around her heart. Mama would be a perfect grandmother, she loved small children. She would adore Annabelle and Annabelle would love her. 'I am afraid so, Mama. Thank you, Travis,' she added to the groom who was putting the steps down and remaining impassive in the face of his mistress's indiscreet complaints.

Isobel followed her mother into the dress shop, sat down and proceeded to show every interest in the fashion plates laid out in front of her, the swatches fanned out on the table and the lists of essential gowns her mother had drawn up.

'You have lost weight, my lady,' Madame declared with the licence of someone who had been measuring the Jarvis ladies for almost ten years.

'Then make everything with ample seams and I will do my best to eat my fill at all the dinner parties,' Isobel said lightly. 'Do you think three is a sufficient number of ballgowns, Mama?'

'I thought you were not—that is, order more if you like, my dear.' Her mother blinked at her, obviously confused by this sudden change of heart.

One way or another it would be her last Season— either a miracle would occur and she would be courted by a man who proved to be outstandingly tolerant, deeply understanding *and* eligible enough to please her parents or she would be lying in a stock of gowns she could adapt for the years of spinsterhood to come.

'Aha! All is explained! Lady Isobel is in love,' the Frenchwoman cried, delighted with this deduction.

Isobel simply said, 'And two riding habits.' She

felt empty of emotion. That had to be a good thing. It meant she could lead a hollow life and indulge in all its superficial pleasures for a few months: clothes, entertainment, flirtation. It would satisfy Mama, at least for a while, and it would be something to do, something to fill the void that opened in front of her.

'I am not certain I quite approve of Lady Leamington,' Lady Bythorn remarked two weeks later as the queue of carriages inched a few feet closer to the red carpet on the pavement outside the large mansion in Cavendish Square. 'She strikes me as being altogether too lax in the people she invites to her balls, but, on the other hand, there is no doubt it will be a squeeze and all the most fashionable gentlemen will be there.'

Isobel contented herself with smoothing the silver net that draped her pale blue silk skirts. A shocking squeeze would mean plenty of partners to dance with, many fleeting opportunities for superficial, meaning-less flirtation to give the illusion of obedience to her mother. In large, crowded events she felt safe, hidden in the multitude like one minnow in a school of fish.

Following the scandal of Lord Andrew's arrest and subsequent disappearance to his country estates, she found herself of interest to virtually everyone she met. Men she had snubbed before seemed eager to try their luck with her again, young ladies gasped and fluttered and wanted to know all about how *ghastly* it had been. The matrons nodded wisely over the sins of modern young men and how well dear Lady Isobel was bearing up.

'I do not care any more, so I have suddenly become attractive,' she said wryly to Pamela Monsom who stopped for a gossip when they met in the ladies' retiring room. Pamela had been one of the few friends who had stood by her in the aftermath of the scandal, writing fiercely to say that she did not believe a word of it and that men were beasts.

'It is not just that,' Pamela said as she studied her, head on one side. 'Although you are thinner you also look more… I don't know. More grown up. Sophisticated.'

'Older,' Isobel countered.

'Oh, look.' Pamela dropped her voice to a whisper. 'See who has just come in!'

'Who?' Isobel pretended to check her hem so she could turn a little and observe the doorway. 'Who is that?'

The lady who had just entered was exceedingly beautiful in a manner that Isobel could only describe as *well preserved*. She might have been any age above thirty-five at that distance—tall, magnificently proportioned, with a mass of golden-brown hair caught up with diamond pins to match the necklace that lay on her creamy bosom.

She swept round, catching up the skirts of her black gown, and surveyed the room. The colour was funereal, but Isobel had never seen anything less like mourning. The satin was figured with a subtle pattern and shimmered like the night sky with the diamonds its stars.

'That, my dear, is the Scarlet Widow,' Miss Monsom hissed. 'I have never been this close before—Mama always rushes off in the opposite direction whenever she is sighted. I think she must have had a fling with Papa at some point.' She narrowed her eyes speculatively. 'One can quite see what he saw in her.'

For the first time in days Isobel felt something: recognition, apprehension and a flutter very like fear. The wide green eyes found her and she knew Pamela was right: this was the Dowager Marchioness of Faversham, Giles's mother.

The lush crimson lips set into a hard line and the Widow stalked into the room.

'She is coming over here!' Pamela squeaked. 'Mama will have kittens!'

Isobel found she was on her feet. Her own mother would be the one needing the smelling bottle when she heard about this. 'Lady Faversham.' She dropped a curtsy suitable for the widow's rank.

'Are you Lady Isobel Jarvis?' The older woman kept her voice low. It throbbed with emotion and Isobel felt every eye in the retiring room turn in their direction as ladies strained to hear.

'I am.'

'Then you are the little hussy responsible for the damage to my son's face.'

'I shall ignore your insulting words, ma'am,' Isobel said, clasping her hands together tightly so they could not shake. 'But Mr Harker was injured in the course of assisting Lord James Albright to deal with his sister's errant fiancé who had assaulted me.'

'You got your claws into him, you convinced him that he must defend your honour and look what happened!' The Widow leaned closer, the magnificent green eyes so like Giles's that a stab of longing for him lanced through Isobel. 'He was *beautiful* and you have scarred him. You foolish little virgin—you are playing with fire and I'll not have him embroiled in some scandal because of you.'

*No, I do not want to feel, I do not want to remember...* 'I should imagine that Mr Harker has far more likelihood of encountering scandal in your company than in mine, ma'am,' Isobel said, putting up her chin. 'If a gentleman obeys an honourable impulse on my behalf I am very grateful, but as I did not request that he act for me, I fail to see how I am responsible.'

'You scheming jade—'

'The pot calling the kettle black,' Isobel murmured. Her knees were knocking, but at least her voice was steady. She had never been so rude to anyone in her entire life.

'I am warning you—keep your hands off my son.' By a miracle the Widow was still hissing her insults; except for Pamela beside her, no one else could hear what they were talking about.

'I have no intention of so much as setting eyes on your son, ma'am, let alone laying a finger on him,' Isobel retorted.

'See that is the truth or I can assure you, you will suffer for it.' Lady Faversham swept round and out of the room, leaving a stunned silence behind her.

'What dramatics,' Isobel said with a light laugh. 'I have never met Lady Faversham before and I cannot say I wish to keep up the acquaintance!'

That produced a ripple of amusement from the handful of ladies who had been staring agog from the other end of the room. 'What on earth is the matter with her?' Lady Mountstead demanded as she came across to join them.

'Her son was injured assisting Lord James Albright to put right an unpleasant situation—I am sure you know to what I refer. The Dowager blames me for some reason.' But not as much as she blamed herself.

Isobel lingered, working to dampen down the speculation, turn it towards gossip about the scandalous Widow and away from her own affairs. She felt reasonably confident she had succeeded when she left the retiring room, but her mother would be aghast, she knew it.

'I had best go and find Mama and warn her of that little incident,' she said to Pamela. 'If we do not see each other again tonight, you must call, very soon.'

'I will most certainly do that.' Pamela was still wide-eyed with speculation. 'And I expect to hear all about the shocking Mr Harker. But now I suppose I had better go and rejoin my party in the supper room.' She hurried off.

Thoroughly flustered, Isobel took the other right-hand corridor. It was deserted, badly lit, but she thought it might lead to the end of the ballroom where she had last seen her mother. The temptation to tell her nothing at all was strong, but the gossip would be certain to reach her ears, so she had no choice but to warn her.

She hurried on, head down, trying to think of a way to break the news that she had been accosted, in public, by the Scarlet Widow. 'Ough!' The man she had walked right into caught her by both arms to steady her, then, as she looked up, the grip tightened. 'You!'

'Me,' Giles agreed. He did not release her and she stood still in his grasp, not knowing whether that was because she wanted to have his hands on her or because struggling would be undignified.

'Your face is healing well.' It was the first thing that came into her head that she dared say out loud. *I love you* or *You abandoned me* or *Take me away with you* or *I hate you* were all impossible. 'How long have the stitches been out?' The scars were still red, but the swelling and bruising had gone—soon they would begin to fade.

'Two weeks.'

'You look…it makes you look dangerous.'

'So I have been told.' Something in his tone suggested that whoever had said so had been female. 'You appear to be enjoying yourself, Isobel.'

'Do I? You have been watching me?'

'You are hard to miss in that gown and when you are so ubiquitous. Dancing every dance, flirting with so many gentlemen. Your heart has quite recovered, I see.'

'And also whatever of yours was engaged.' Isobel twisted her right hand out of his light grip and flicked at the trace of face powder on his lapel. 'The lady favours Attar of Roses, I think.'

'One of them, as I recall, yes.' He sounded bored, like a tomcat who could hardly be bothered with the hunt. With his newly broken nose and the scars above the immaculate white linen and complicated neck-cloth, he looked like a pirate playing at being a gentleman.

'Such a bore for you, all these women throwing themselves at you,' Isobel said, her voice dripping with false sympathy. 'Still, I suppose you can hardly afford to neglect your admirers—who knows, one of them might be about to persuade her complaisant spouse that she needs her boudoir remodelled.'

'The lady with the Attar of Roses wants a new library as a present for her husband.'

'And I am sure she will be at home the entire time to supervise.'

'Probably.' He was angry at her jibes. The colour was touching his cheekbones and the green eyes were cold, but the drawl was as casual and as insolent as before. 'What are you doing in town, Isobel?'

'The Season. What else?' She shrugged.

'I thought that was the last thing you wanted.'

'That was before a certain gentleman reminded me about the pleasures of the flesh,' she said, smiling at him when his brows snapped together in a frown. A demon seemed to have taken control of her tongue.

'I thought perhaps I might be…entertained if I came to London.'

'And I thought you did not want to marry again.'

'Were we discussing marriage, Giles?'

'You little witch. If it is fleshly pleasure you want—' He tugged on the wrist he still held captive, pulling her against his exquisite silk waistcoat. The lingering scent of roses warred with his citrus cologne in her nostrils and under it was the faint musk of a man who was hot with temper.

And lust, she realised as his mouth came down and his hands trapped her and his lips punished her for defiance. She knew his body and he knew hers. She found she had clenched one hand on his buttock, holding him tight against her. The pressure of his erection sent tongues of flame to the core of her as his mouth left hers and he began to pull at the neckline of her gown, his lips seeking the nipple, his tongue and teeth wreaking havoc with her senses.

They were crushed into a corner now, his hand under her skirts as she lifted her leg to hook it around his hip to give him access. It was mad, insane, they were both so angry, both so—

The sharp clip of heels on marble was like a bucket of cold water thrown in her face. Isobel gasped, found her feet, pushed at Giles even as he spun round instinctively to shield her.

'Geraldine,' Giles said. His mother.

From behind him Isobel could see the dark sheen of black satin, the glitter of diamonds. She pushed her way free to stand at his side and confront the other woman, her chin up.

'You little fool,' the Dowager hissed. 'So you lied to me. You will be sorry for this. Very sorry.'

Isobel simply turned on her heel and walked away. Neither of them made the slightest attempt to stop her.

The passage turned and she jumped at the sight of someone coming towards her, then she saw it was her own reflection in a long glass. Her bodice was awry, her hair half-down, her skirts crumpled. With hands that shook Isobel righted her gown, twisted the loose ringlets back into order, fanned her face with her hands until the hectic colour began to subside, then went out into the ballroom before she had time to think about what had just happened.

'Mama.' Lady Bythorn was deep in conversation with the Dowager Lady Darvil, but she turned with a smile that became rigid when she saw Isobel's face.

'Are you unwell, my dear? You look quite—'

'Flustered,' Isobel hissed. 'I know. Mama, I must speak with you alone. Urgently.'

'You have the migraine?' Lady Bythorn said clearly as she got to her feet. 'Do excuse us, Georgiana, I fear Isobel is suffering from the heat—we had best go home. Come, dear.'

With a suitably wan smile for Lady Darvil, Isobel let herself be led to the hallway and fanned while their cloaks were found and the carriage called.

'What is it?' her mother demanded the moment they were inside. 'Has someone been referring to the scandal?'

'No. Mama, the Dowager Lady Faversham found me in the retiring room and said the most horrible things. She blames me for the injuries Mr Harker suffered.'

'Oh, my heavens! That frightful creature. I knew Frederica Leamington could not be trusted not to invite the wrong sort of people. Did anyone hear her?'

'Only Pamela Monsom and she is very discreet. There were other people in the room, but they did not hear exactly what she said and when she left I explained that she was upset about Mr Harker's scars and they were very sympathetic. But they are sure to gossip.'

'And now your name will be linked with his,' her mother observed grimly. 'There is nothing to be done but brazen it out—thank goodness he was not there tonight!'

Isobel bit her lower lip. She did not feel capable of confessing to her mother that Giles Harker had indeed been at the ball. Her body still quivered from his touch and from the anger that had flashed between them.

'There, there.' Her mother leaned over in the shadowed interior to pat her hand. 'It will be all right. That woman has such a dreadful reputation that no respectable person would believe a word she has to say.'

*But I do. She said I would be sorry, and she meant it.*

# CHAPTER EIGHTEEN

'WHAT THE DEVIL are you about?' Giles planted himself squarely in the corridor to block his mother's furious, impetuous path. She was quite capable of sweeping out into the ballroom on Isobel's heels and continuing this scene there.

'You fool,' she snapped at him, eyes flashing. 'You aren't content with having your face ruined for the sake of that little madam, but now you are getting yourself entangled with her. She'll be the ruin of you! She's an earl's daughter—Bythorn won't stand for it and he has influence.'

'And he never slept with you, so you can't play that card,' Giles drawled, hanging on to his temper by a hair's breadth. 'I am not entangled with Isobel Jarvis—'

'Hah!'

'We were merely continuing an argument.'

'An argument? I have heard it called many things, Giles, but never that!'

'I am not having an affair with the girl.'

'No,' the Widow said grimly. 'You fancy yourself in love with her.'

'I am not in love with her. I am considering strangling her.'

'Listen to me! I have found you the perfect wife, Giles,' she said as he turned on his heel.

'Really?' he threw back over his shoulder. 'Some plain daughter of a Cit?'

'No. Caroline Holt, the daughter of Sir Joshua Holt.'

'And what is wrong with her? Or the family, that they should consider allying themselves with us?'

'There is absolutely nothing wrong with Miss Holt who is tolerably pretty, intelligent and twenty-three years old. What is wrong with her father is a series of investments that have gone badly wrong, an estate mortgaged to the hilt and four unmarried daughters on his hands.'

Giles turned round fully to face his mother. 'So Caroline is the sacrificial lamb. You buy her for me, Holt pays off the debts and the other girls can enter the Marriage Mart with some hope of attracting respectable husbands. Provided they aren't seen with their brother-in law, that is.'

'Exactly. And you get a well-bred wife who will be grateful for all we have done for her family.'

'How did you find her?' he asked even as he wondered how he was managing to keep his temper, and the urge to storm into the ballroom and drag Isobel out of it, under control.

'I have excellent enquiry agents.'

Of course, Geraldine had always prided herself on being able to find out anything about anyone. It was how she made such good choices in her lovers, avoided blackmailers, kept away from men with wives who had connections that would be dangerous to her and always found the right place to invest her money.

'I hope you have not made the Holts any promises.' His body was throbbing with frustrated desire. He felt as though he had been kicked in the gut and he had an overwhelming need to break something. 'Because I am not marrying the girl, for which she should be profoundly grateful. I have told you before, there is nothing you can buy me, least of all a wife.'

A dismissive flick of Geraldine's hand was all the acknowledgement she gave that she had heard him. 'Caroline Holt is not going anywhere far from her home in the wilds of Suffolk,' the Widow said with a thin smile. 'She will wait until you come to your senses about the Jervis chit.'

'My senses are perfectly in order, ma'am. My refusal to marry Miss Holt has nothing to do with Lady Isobel.'

'Liar!' she threw at him. 'She ruined your looks and yet you lust after her like a—'

'Mother,' Giles said. It stopped her in midrant. He never called her that unless he was deeply angered and she knew it. 'I have it on good authority that a broken nose and a couple of scars gives me an interesting air of danger. Really, I should thank Lady Isobel.'

The Widow took a deep breath. 'I would sacrifice everything for you, Giles. I would do anything to ensure your future.'

It was guilt, he knew, although she would never admit it, or probably even recognise it. Her actions had made him a bastard—now she would fight tooth and nail to force society to accept him.

'I can look after my own future,' he said, not unkindly. He hated it when her voice shook like that. 'Society accepts me for who I am and I make my own way in it. Go back to Carstairs and stop plotting: I'll not have Lady Isobel insulted.' Knowing Jack Carstairs, her current youthful lover, he would be scouring the house trying to discover where Geraldine had got to, well aware that he would probably have to extricate her from some scrape or another when he did find her.

Giles walked away with the firm intention of getting drunk. Behind him he thought he heard

Geraldine repeat, 'Anything,' but he was not certain. Besides, there was no need to worry—there was nothing that she could do to harm Isobel. He was her only dark secret and Geraldine would not risk involving him in further scandal.

'Who is your letter from, Isobel?' Lady Bythorn glanced up from her own correspondence. 'You've been staring at the same page for minutes. Is the handwriting bad?'

'No. No it is from Jane Needham. I am just... thinking.'

*We are all in the best of health and the children are flourishing despite being cooped up with the dreadful weather,* Jane had written. *Nathaniel wants a puppy and Annabelle wants a kitten, so I foresee scratches all round before much longer. The oddest thing happened the other day: there was a stranger staying at the Needham Arms—we heard all about him because, as you know, we hardly ever get any strangers in the parish and the rumour was he looked like a Bow Street Runner. Which is pure fancy of course, because no one here has ever seen a Runner!*

*But he came to the house asking for you and when I saw him and told him he was mistaken, that you do not live here, he just brushed it aside and said he's heard you stayed here sometimes. I demanded to know his business and he said he had been sent by a distant relative of yours, a sea captain, who was estranged from the family and was trying to make contact again, but who did not want to go directly to your parents. It sounded the most perfect nonsense to me and I said as much and he bowed himself off. But the thing that worries me is, when Molly went out for firewood yesterday afternoon she found him talking to the children in the yard—they had gone to look at the puppies.*

*She sent him about his business and I have had young Wally Hoskins go with them everywhere since then, just in case. But if he was intending to kidnap them—why these children? We are not wealthy, he must have realised that.*

*I thought I had better tell you—because of him asking for you by name. Perhaps I am worrying too much and he is just what he said. Or slightly mad. But I must confess to being anxious.*

'Mama, do we have any relative who is, or was, a sea captain? Or any relative who is estranged from the family?'

'A sea captain? Or someone estranged? Goodness, no, I do not think so. In fact I am certain. Why?'

'Oh, Jane met someone who said something that puzzled her. She must have misunderstood.'

'No doubt she did. I cannot help but think that living so secluded as she does cannot be good for her.'

Isobel folded the letter, then opened it again. The mysterious man had been asking for her and then he was found with the children. *Annabelle.* Lady Faversham's words came back to her like a curse, even though it had been almost a month since they were uttered. *You will be sorry for this. Very sorry.*

She could not possibly know and Isobel had seen neither her nor Giles since that night. And yet Annabelle was Isobel's only weak spot, the only secret she was desperate to keep. She tried to tell herself it was pure fancy, yet she could not be easy in her mind.

Three days later there was another letter. It began, *Do not leave this lying around, for I cannot write in such a way that would disarm suspicion if your mother reads it and yet convey my anxiety adequately. The strange man is still hanging around the neighbourhood—and still asking questions about us. When you were here, how long you stayed, what happened to Ralph, how old the children are—he has looked at the parish registers, I am certain, for Mr Arnold found him right by the cupboard where they are stored and it was not locked.*

*He is very subtle about it, which, I confess, wor-*

*ries me most of all, for it seems* professional *some-how. It is only by piecing together bits of gossip that I can see a pattern in his questions, for he never in-terrogates the same person for long. I have spoken to the few servants who were with us that year and who know the truth so they are on the alert. I can-not see how he would approach Dr Jameson, who, besides, would never say anything.*

*Can you make any sense of this, dearest Isobel? I vow I cannot. I have hired two of the Foster brothers—you recall what a size they are—and they patrol the house and yard at night and one of them is always with the children by day. It is doing dreadful things to Nathaniel's vocabulary!*

It would not take much effort for anyone to find out where she had spent that year after Lucas's death—they had made no secret of it at the time, quite de-liberately. Isobel's refusal to allow any friends or relatives to visit had been lamented by Lady Bythorn to all her circle and had been attributed to hysterical grief followed by a sad decline. The very openness of her mother's complaints seemed to disarm all sus-picion that there was anything to hide and Isobel's reluctance to socialise since her return had contrib-uted to the diagnosis of a melancholic temperament.

'Jane is unwell,' she said to her parents, the letter tight in her hand. 'I must go to Hereford.'

'Now?' Her father put down the copy of *The Times* he had been muttering over and frowned at her. 'In the middle of the Season? All that way?'

'It would take me only twenty-four hours, even if I go by the Mail, but if I might take a chaise, Papa, I could do it in less time and more comfortably.'

'Certainly not the Mail,' her mother said firmly. 'And a chaise? Oh, dear, you know how those things bring on my migraine and they do your father's gout no good at all.'

'I can go with Dorothy, Mama, there is no need for either of you to disturb yourselves. If we leave before luncheon and take a basket with some food we can go right through to Oxford for the night with only stops for changes—and there are any number of most respectable inns where I could find a private parlour.'

It took almost an hour of wrangling to convince her parents that she could not possibly abandon her friend when she was unwell and worried about the children. That, yes, of course she would come home just as soon as she could and not miss the Lavenhams' ridotto which promised to be the event of the Season. And yes, she would take the greatest care on the road and not speak to anyone unless absolutely necessary and certainly no gentlemen.

It was only then, as she organised her packing, that

the apprehension churning in her stomach turned to real fear. If she was ruined, then that was just too bad, although she was very sorry that the disgrace would distress her parents. But for Annabelle to be exposed as an illegitimate child would destroy all her prospects as well. And what of Jane? There might be penalties for allowing a false record to be entered in the registers. Would it even cast a shadow over little Nathaniel's legitimacy?

It had to be Lady Faversham behind this, for surely Giles would not do anything to hurt her, however angry she made him. It was only as she climbed into the chaise and waved goodbye that she realised she had no idea what she could do when she reached Hereford. But she could not sit in London while her child was in peril and leave Jane to face whatever this was alone.

'You were right—Geraldine's up to something and she's planning to go to Hereford of all places.'

'Are you certain?' *Hereford.* Giles put down his knife and fork and stared at Jack Carstairs over his half-eaten breakfast. His mother's lover had arrived at his Albany chambers without warning and seemed decidedly put out.

Since the confrontation at the Leamingtons' ball Giles had been at pains to avoid Isobel. It would do her reputation no good to be seen with him and it seemed he could not trust himself to keep his hands off her. There were two things he could do to protect her: stay out of her way and make certain his mother did her no harm.

Before Jack's arrival, it had occurred to him after a night of tossing and turning that the best way to circumvent Geraldine was to discover where Isobel was vulnerable. He was certain there was something, something more to her past than the simple loss of her virginity to her fiancé.

Unable to sleep, his remedies had been either a cold bath or distraction. Shrugging into his robe he had taken a candle and pulled the *Peerage* off the shelves. He might as well start by getting the family straight: Isobel's family, the Jervises—no, after ten minutes he could see nothing out of the ordinary there.

Then, on impulse, he looked under Needham. The current viscount was a half-brother of Lucas who had drowned in January 1797. He looked at the other entries for the same name. *The Hon. Ralph Needham decd.* Lucas's other half-brother, he worked out. And he had died on the same day as Lucas, Giles realised, flicking back to check. *Married Miss Jane Barrymore, by whom issue Nathaniel and Annabelle.* Twins born posthumously in September 1797. *Longmere Manor, Gaston, Hereford.*

Hereford rang a bell. Isobel had mentioned it with a note of longing in her voice and then, when he would have questioned her about it, for the area was unknown to him, she had abruptly changed the subject.

Giles had stared at the entry, working out the relationships. Ralph was Lucas's younger half-brother. That was a close connection to Isobel, but what did it signify and how could it harm her? *Lucas and I were lovers*, she had confessed. But what of it? She had been betrothed to the man. He ran a finger over the close-packed black lines of type, half-formed ideas worrying at the edges of his mind.

Giles dragged himself back to the present and the other man. He had taken Carstairs into his confidence to a degree, putting it to him that it was in Geraldine's interests if they could stop her embarking on a destructive feud with Lady Isobel.

'I'm certain. But I've no idea why, she won't tell me. Threw the coffee pot at my head when I wouldn't go with her. Damn it, Harker,' Carstairs said, pulling out a chair and sitting down, 'I'm not trailing half across the country in support of one of her vendettas and I told her so. Told her you wouldn't like it, either. Is there any fresh coffee?'

'Hicks! Coffee for Mr Carstairs.' Giles picked up

his own cup and frowned into the dregs. They held no answers. 'Any more letters?'

The other man nodded. 'She's been getting letters daily that have been pleasing her inordinately, as I told you, and then this one arrived and she said, *Hah! I've got the little hussy now* and ordered her woman to pack and sent her footman out to hire a chaise.

'Thought you ought to know, because I'm pretty certain it has some connection with Lady Isobel. Or, at least, something to do with you. When she got these letters she'd stare at that portrait of you over the fireplace with such a look in her eyes. Brrr.' He shuddered theatrically and peered at Giles more closely.

'How's the face? Looks as though it is healing well. Thought they'd carved half of it off, the way Geraldine was carrying on at first.'

Giles shrugged. 'Healing. There will always be scars. Geraldine attaches too much importance to looks.' What the devil had the woman discovered about Isobel?

He was prepared to go to any lengths to protect her, he realised, even though he was not willing to put a name to his feelings. Her hints at the ball that she might take a lover had made him jealous, furiously jealous, even while he knew she was deliberately provoking him and would no more do such a thing than fly. With disastrous honesty she had told him she loved him and she had meant it. His attempts to reject her for her own good had made her angry, but it had not changed her love for him, he sensed that.

'I'm going to Herefordshire to find out what is going on. But I'll see Geraldine first and make damned certain she stops this nonsense.'

'The best of luck, old chap,' Carstairs said with a rueful grin.

Isobel got down from the chaise at the Bell in Oxford at seven in the evening, nine hours after she had finished reading Jane's letter at breakfast that morning. They had made better time than she had expected, but even so she felt exhausted already and there were another fourteen or fifteen hours travelling ahead of her.

'Looks a decent enough place,' Dorothy conceded with a sniff as one of the porters came forward, touched his forelock and took their bags.

'We will require two adjoining bedchambers and a private parlour,' Isobel said. 'The quieter the better.'

'Yes, ma'am, there's just the thing free, if you'll come this way.'

'And hot water and tea and a good supper,' Dorothy chimed in, clutching the dressing case that she insisted on keeping with her even though Isobel had brought no jewellery.

'We're famous for our suppers, at the Bell.' The man halted. 'Just mind this chaise coming in, ma'am.'

The vehicle with four horses sweating in the traces swept into the yard and pulled up in front of them. Isobel stepped back to take a new path to the inn entrance.

The door opened in her face, the porter hurried forwards. 'Here, mind the lady!' Dorothy took her arm and a tall figure dropped down onto the cobbles.

'Giles!'

'What the devil are you doing here?' He slammed the carriage door shut and confronted her, for all the world as if he had a right to know of her movements, she thought, feeding her temper to keep the treacherous delight at seeing him at bay.

'Never you mind my lady's business and watch your tongue, you rogue.' Dorothy planted her hands on her hips and confronted him, bristling. 'A respectable lady ought to be able to travel the country without being accosted in inn yards by the likes of you!'

Heads were turning, more carriages were pulling in. 'I think we would draw less attention if we go inside,' Isobel said, tugging at her stalwart defender's arm. 'Come, Dorothy.'

'I'll have them fetch the parish constable, I will,'

the maid scolded as she marched into the inn on
Isobel's heels. 'I told you he was no gentleman.
What's he doing here, I'd like to know!'

# CHAPTER NINETEEN

'I, TOO, WOULD like to know what Giles Harker is doing in Oxford,' Isobel said with feeling. She felt queasy with surprise and nerves, her pulse was all over the place and her thoughts were in turmoil. After that initial shock, the delight of thinking that, somehow, he had come for her, common sense reasserted itself.

What *was* Giles doing here? It was too much of a coincidence that they should both find themselves in an Oxford inn. Had she been wrong and he was the one behind the mysterious stranger who was probing the secrets of Longmere? But if that was the case it could only be out of some twisted desire to hurt her, to expose her secrets, and surely she had done nothing to deserve that? It was hard to believe she had been so far awry in her assessment of his character.

'Welcome, my lady.' The landlord appeared and ushered them farther in. 'If a nice pair of rooms with a parlour on the quiet side of the house is what is wanted, we have just the thing. If you will follow me, ma'am.

'I'll have hot water sent up directly, my lady, and supper will be on the table within the half hour. Here you are, ma'am.'

'That looks very satisfactory, thank you.' He could have shown them into a prison cell for all Isobel cared, or noticed. The man bowed himself out and Dorothy threw herself dramatically in front of the door, her back pressed to the panels.

'He'll not get in here, the vile seducer!'

'Oh, for goodness' sake, Dorothy, Mr Harker is no such thing, although what he is doing here I have no idea.' A rap on the door made Dorothy jump. She emitted a small scream and flung it open to reveal a startled maid with a jug. 'Your hot water, ma'am.'

'Thank you.' Isobel waited until the girl had gone before she turned back to Dorothy. 'There is no need for alarm. Please be less melodramatic! There is absolutely no call for all this shrieking—oh!' She pressed her hand to her thudding heart as the door swung open on the knock and Giles stepped into the room.

'Lady Isobel. Will you join me for supper?'

'Certainly not. I have no intention of dining with a man in an inn, and most definitely not with you.' She looked at him with painful intensity. The scars were paler and thinner now. His expression was politely neutral, but his eyes were wary. *As well they might be*, she thought as she strove to settle her breathing.

'The middle of the Season seems an unusual time to be taking a long coach journey, Lady Isobel,' Giles observed. 'Your admirers will be missing you.'

She did not attempt to cover her snort of derision. 'I hardly think so. A friend needs me for a few days, then I will be returning.'

'A friend in Oxford?' He leant a shoulder against the door frame and frowned at her.

'No. If that was the case I would hardly be staying in an inn.'

'Where my lady is going is none of your business,' Dorothy interjected. 'Shall I go and get a couple of pot boys and have him thrown out, ma'am?'

'I do not think that is necessary, thank you, Dorothy.' Isobel doubted two lads would be capable of ejecting Giles in any case. She knew he was strong and fit, but now he looked leaner—and tougher with those scars and his dark brows drawn together into a frown. 'Mr Harker will be leaving immediately, I am certain.'

'If I might have a word with you first—alone.' He straightened up and held the door open for Dorothy.

Isobel opened her mouth to protest, then thought better of it. If five minutes of painful intimacy meant she discovered what he was about, then it would be worth it. 'Dorothy, go downstairs, please. No,' she said as the maid began to launch into a protest. 'Either you go or Mr Harker and I will have to. I wish to speak to him confidentially.'

'But, my lady—'

Giles bundled the maid out of the room, closed the door and locked it before she could get another word out.

'It is a strange thing if a lady may not visit a friend without being waylaid and interrogated,' Isobel snapped.

'Yes. I wonder that you stand for it,' he said musingly, his eyes focused on her face. 'I would have expected a cool *good evening* on seeing me and then for you to refuse to receive me. It is very shocking for us to be alone like this.'

'I am well aware of that, Mr Harker! I want to know why you are here.'

'In Oxford? Why should I not be?'

'In Oxford, in this inn, at this time? I was foolish enough to fall in love with you, Giles Harker. Even more foolish to trust you. This is too much of a coincidence for my liking.'

'That trust certainly appears to have vanished. Isobel, you know full well you could trust me to take only what was offered to me.'

'I am not talking about—' She could feel herself

growing pink, whether from anger, embarrassment or sheer anxiety she could not tell.

'Sex?'

'Yes, *sex*.' She was blushing, she knew it, and it was more from desire and anger at herself than embarrassment. 'I am talking about the way you abandoned me, washed your hands of me the moment my parents appeared.'

His eyebrows rose. 'You wanted me to treat you as a friend in front of your parents? You wanted to risk your reputation by acknowledging a liaison with me?'

'No, I did not want that and you know it! But there was no word of affection or regret, no acknowledgement that I was distressed or of what we had shared. You had your amusement—and yes, I am aware of your self-control, I thank you—and then, when it all became difficult, you shrug me and my feelings aside.'

Giles pushed away from the door, all pretence of casualness gone. 'Isobel, I only did what was practical. It would not have helped to have drawn out our parting, merely added to your unhappiness.'

'Practical? Giles, there was nothing practical about my feelings for you.'

'Was? Past tense?' He came so close that the hem of her skirts brushed his boots, but she would not retreat. 'I thought that when you loved, you would love for ever.'

'Then I cannot have been in love with you, can I? Just another foolish woman fascinated by your handsome face.'

'We did not make love until after this.' He gestured towards his scarred cheek.

'Guilt, then. Gratitude. Lust. Call it what you like. It was certainly lust, those few mad moments in the passageway at the Leamingtons' ball!' Only her anxiety for Annabelle and Jane, only the price of misplaced trust, kept her from falling into his arms. 'What do my feelings for you matter? I want to know why you are here. Are you following me?'

'No,' Giles said. 'I am not following you and our meeting here is a genuine coincidence.' Truth? Lies? How could she tell? She had thought he had fallen in love with her and he had not. Obviously she could not understand him at all.

If she did not love him, he would not make her so angry. If she only dared trust him—but he would be disgusted when he realised she had given away her child, had not had the courage to raise her as his own mother had raised him. Whatever she thought of the Scarlet Widow, the woman's fierce love for her son could not be mistaken.

'You are very agitated for a woman who is merely

going to visit a friend for a few days,' he remarked, cutting through her thoughts and sending her tumbling into unconsidered speech.

'If I am agitated, then it is because I cannot get free from you. It seems I cannot keep even my secrets—' She stumbled to a halt.

'So,' Giles said slowly, his eyes never leaving her face with its betraying colour, 'I am right. You have a secret, one greater than the loss of your virginity, one that you would not trust to me even though you tell me you loved me, even though then you had no reason to mistrust me. You are afraid. Is it a secret that lays you open to blackmail, perhaps?'

'Blackmail?' Isobel went cold. 'No, of course not.' Was that what the prying stranger was about? But who had sent him? 'You may leap to whatever conclusions you wish, Giles Harker. You have made me so angry I scarce know what I am saying.'

'No, you are not angry.' He caught her hands in his and held them even when she tugged. 'Or, rather, anger is not the main emotion here. You are afraid.'

Unable to free herself without a struggle, Isobel turned her face away. What she was going to do when he left her alone—if he ever did—she had no idea. She dared not let him know where she was going or she might lead him to Annabelle. All she could do was to get to Jane and try, somehow, to work out how to protect her daughter and her friend.

'Of course I am afraid—I am locked in a room and being manhandled. Am I your prisoner while you interrogate me?' she demanded. Defiance was the only weapon she had against the fear and the awful weakness of her love for him. And that love would betray Annabelle.

Giles released her wrists and she stood rubbing them, although he had not held her tight enough to hurt. The touch of his hands, the fingers that had orchestrated such pleasure in her, seemed to burn like ice. 'This has gone too far for me to walk away from it now, Isobel, whether you want me or trust me or not. You are in trouble, more trouble than you know.'

He turned the key in the lock and walked out, letting the door slam behind him. Isobel sank down in the chair behind her, her knees suddenly like warm wax.

'My lady? I passed him on the stairs and he looked like thunder—are you all right, my lady? I should never have left you alone with him.'

'I am perfectly fine, Dorothy,' Isobel said with a calm that was intended to steady herself as much as the maid. 'Mr Harker and I had unfinished business, that is all. I did not have the opportunity to say everything I wanted to when we left Wimpole.'

She had not convinced her, but there was nothing to be done about it now. 'Dinner will be here soon and neither of us have so much as washed our hands.'

But what had those parting words meant? How did he know she was in trouble?

'Just you stop right there, my bullies.'

The chaise juddered to a halt and Isobel let down the window. 'Ned! Ned Foster, it is I, Lady Isobel. Please open the gate.'

'Yes, my lady!' the big man called back and swung open the heavy gate that barred the entrance into the manor courtyard. Chickens ran flapping in panic as the postilions brought the chaise in and Isobel heard the clang of the gate thudding back into its catches. It felt as though she was in a besieged castle. Isobel fought back the melodramatic image and gathered her things.

She was paying off the men and Dorothy was carrying the bags around to the back entrance as Jane came running down the steps, a big shawl bundled around her shoulders against the raw air. 'Isobel! I did not dare hope you'd come. How long can you stay?'

'For as long as it takes,' Isobel said grimly as she hugged her friend. 'I am so glad to be here. The weather was bad after Oxford and there was a land-slip about sixty miles from Oxford so we had to spend another day on the road. Oh, Jane,' she confessed as they entered the hallway, out of earshot of the servants. 'I do not know what is going on here, or who is to blame for it, but I have been so foolish. I fell in love with the most impossible man and I think this is a consequence. I am so sorry.'

'Foolish to fall in love?' Jane smiled. 'That is never foolish.'

'It is when the man in question is the illegitimate son of the Scarlet Widow.'

Her friend's eyes widened. 'Oh, my, I have heard of her. But how on earth did you meet him? Does he know you love him?'

'Unfortunately, yes. We made love, Jane,' she added as the drawing-room door shut safely behind them. Best to get the entire confession over as quickly as possible.

'You aren't—'

'No. But it all ended badly—I thought he felt the same for me, but it is quite obvious that he does not, and, in any case, there is no way we can ever be together. His mother sees me as a threat to him and I think she must be behind whatever is going on here. But how she ever found out, I do not know.'

'You did not tell him?'

'That I had a child? No. He knows that Lucas and I anticipated our marriage, but that is all.' Isobel paced to the window and stood staring out at the darkening gardens. 'Perhaps I am worrying unduly after all, for unless one of your people betrays us, there is no reason anyone might suspect Annabelle is not exactly who you say she is.'

'And I trust them implicitly,' Jane said, nodding. 'There might be a danger if she resembled you closely, but as it is, she is very obviously a Needham. It is seven months since you saw her, isn't it? She is growing.'

'Yes.' It seemed like seven years. 'May I see her now? I did not want to speak of this unless we were alone, but now, I cannot wait. Is she much changed?'

'I think she is perfect, but you will judge for yourself.' Her friend's smile was warm and once again Isobel was filled with gratitude that Jane had taken her child, loved her like her own and yet was prepared to share her so unselfishly. 'She is bright, quick and very lovely. Come and see—they are in the kitchen with old Rosemary, hindering her efforts to make cakes.'

Isobel almost ran down the stone-flagged passageway and into the kitchen. Two small children were perched on the edge of the big table, legs dangling, their eyes glued to the big bowl of fruit cake mixture the cook was stirring.

'More plums,' Nathanial demanded, but Isobel could only focus on the little girl.

She scooped her up, warm and sweet and slightly sticky around the mouth from stealing batter. 'Surprise!'

'Aunt Ishbel,' Annabelle said with a crow of delight and a kiss. She had never been able to get her tongue around Isobel's name.

'How pretty you look—and how sticky you are.' Isobel whirled her round in her arms and everything in the world was right again. Then she stopped at the sight of their reflection in the battered mirror propped at one end of the dresser. Annabelle, female to her chubby fingertips, examined her own image with interest. Two heads of tumbled hair, soft and slippery, sliding out of its pins, but Annabelle's was blonde while Isobel's was brown. Two rather determined little chins, but very different noses. Two pairs of wide grey eyes.

'Pretty,' Annabelle said with a crow of delight.

'Pretty,' Isobel agreed. *Oh, thank you, Lucas, for giving me this child.* And anyone who saw them together would not pick up any significant likeness, she was sure. She turned to see Jane smiling as she watched them.

'She grew so quickly,' Jane said. 'One minute she was still a chubby little baby and the next, there she is—a little girl. Now I think we can see what they will be like when they grow up. They are both going to have the Needham height, don't you think?'

'Yes,' Isobel agreed, swallowing the tears that threatened to well up. It was ridiculous to weep because she was so happy to be here and it would frighten Annabelle. 'I cannot believe how she has grown.'

She had dreamed of the experiences she and her 'niece' would share as Annabelle grew up. They would go shopping together, she would be there at her first parties, her first dance. She would hear her whispered confidences about first love.

'Isn't it bath time?' she asked, grinning at little Nathaniel as he stuck out his lower lip mutinously. 'Come along, I'll tell you stories about Wimpole Hall where I have been staying and about London and I'll tuck you up in bed.'

'Cake,' Annabelle said. 'Cake and bath and stories and bed.'

'Bath and bed and stories now, cake in the morning,' Isobel countered, holding out her hand to the little boy. 'How many stairs is it up to bed? I'll wager you cannot count them yet.'

'I can!' He was off at a run and Isobel followed him, her cheek pressed against Annabelle's soft one.

*Oh, Lucas, what a lovely child we made. I'll protect her, I promise.* Even if the danger was from the man she now loved.

'Come and see the kittens.' Annabelle stood beside the breakfast table and hopped from one foot to the other while Isobel spread honey on her last piece of toast. 'Mama says I may have a kitten.'

'A puppy,' Nathaniel contradicted.

'Both,' Jane said, rolling her eyes. 'But by the time they decide which they are going to have they'll be grown cats and dogs.'

'Shall I help choose?' Both heads nodded as one— this was obviously the solution to an intractable problem.

'Come along, then.' Isobel put down her napkin. 'And wrap up warmly.'

The farmyard was enclosed, with high arches in the walls to east and west. The walls kept out the wind and the stall-fed cattle and the horses kept the barns and stables surprisingly warm, so it was no hardship to sit on a bale outside the cowshed while the children brought out the kittens and puppies for inspection.

'I think the little boy with the white tip to his tail,' she said to Nathaniel. The pup was big and bold and looked as though he would cope well with the rough and tumble of life with Nathaniel. 'And the black-and-white kitten with the white tip for Annabelle—and then they will match.'

Delighted, the children reached for their new pets and Annabelle promptly had her knuckles swiped by the mother cat who had stalked out to see what was going on. Isobel hauled the crying child onto her lap and hugged her and the kitten equally while she wrapped a handkerchief around the scratched hand. 'It is all right, she was only cross because—'

'What a charming picture. Maternal love. I thought that must be the secret, from the timing of things.' The deep, familiar voice cut through the sounds of the farmyard, the child's sobs, the barking of the sheepdog on its chain.

# CHAPTER TWENTY

ISOBEL FROZE AND Annabelle stopped wailing to inspect the new arrival.

'Go—' With an effort Isobel moderated her tone so as not to frighten the children. 'Nathaniel, Annabelle, go inside and ask Cook to find a proper bandage for Annabelle's hand and tell her I said you may have a slice of cake each.'

They ran, tears and strange men forgotten, before she changed her mind about cake directly after breakfast. Isobel stood up, the kitten unregarded in her hands. 'You are not welcome here, Giles. How did you get in?'

'The brawny yokel outside is guarding the front gate, but he does not appear to have the wit to work out that there is a perfectly obvious track leading to this one.' Giles strode across the straw-strewn yard and stopped by the mounting block.

'What do you want?' Isobel demanded.

'To discover if what I suspect, what my mother believes she has discovered, is true.'

'Your mother discovered? So this is blackmail?' *Is it a secret that lays you open to blackmail, perhaps?* Giles had asked. *He knows*, she thought, a sort of bleak misery settling over her, eclipsing even the fear.

'It would have been if I had not caught Geraldine in time and made her tell me exactly what she had discovered about you. She's as protective as that mother cat and has about as many scruples.'

'What do you think you know?' Isobel asked. Her lips felt stiff, the question almost choked her, but she had to know what she was fighting.

'That you have a love child whom you gave away to your friend to raise as her own.'

'I did not want to let her go!' The kitten gave a squeak of protest and Isobel set it down next to its mother who promptly began to wash it. 'It was the only thing to do. I suppose you think I have no courage because your mother kept you.'

'I have to thank her for that,' Giles said.

'It seems she had no scruples about shaming her family or taking you from your grandfather's care. You grew up with a mother who had a scandalous reputation, and, apparently, she had no concerns about bringing you up to have to fight every day of your life because of who you are.'

'She gave me life and she gave me, I hope, some of her courage. But she had to fight for so long that she does not know how to stop. When I discovered that she had found out something to your detriment and was coming here to threaten you with it, I stopped her.'

'How? Are you telling me you can control that woman?'

'Oh, yes. She believed me when I told her that if she tried to hurt you I would take her back to the Dower House, lock her in and keep the key. I have done it before when she went beyond the limit and I'll do it again if I have to.'

'Then I must thank you for that, at least,' she threw at him. 'But if you have the situation under control, what are you doing here?'

'I wanted to make sure you were safe here, that her agents had gone. I knew you had a secret before she discovered what it was.'

'How?' She had been so careful...

'Just putting together things that you said. I realised it was something here, in Herefordshire, something to do with Needham.' He took a step towards her, then shook his head and turned back to hitch one hip on the mounting block. 'I must have gone over every word you have said to me, Isobel. Every silence, every moment when there was such sadness in your eyes. Until I realised she was on your trail all I wanted to do was protect you by keeping away.'

'Why, Giles? Why did you care so much? Are you—?' Isobel broke off, her courage almost failing. But she had to know. 'Are you telling me you love me after all?' she asked flatly.

'No,' he said, his face tight and stark. 'Nothing has changed, Isobel. I care for you, I want to keep you safe. And I am every bit as ineligible for you as I ever was.'

Her pride would not let her weep or plead. 'What a good thing,' she said. 'Of course, I have realised that I do not love you—it was a foolish infatuation when I was lonely and miserable. Now I am doing the Season and looking for a husband—I will be delighted if I never see you again.'

'I was a foolish infatuation, was I, Isobel? In that case either your acting skill is incredible or you have equally good powers of self-deception. You fell in love with me and I believe your current protestations as much as I did those at Oxford or at the ball.'

'I am not a good actress, merely someone telling the truth,' she said forcing the words out between numb lips. 'I needed what you could give me at Wimpole. I needed heat and warmth and…affection.' One brow slanted up satirically at the euphemism. She felt her cheeks burn red. 'You do not care for me now, so why are you concerning yourself? I told you at Oxford that I did not want you.'

'On the contrary, at Oxford you told me I had betrayed your trust and your feelings.' He stood up and took one step towards her before her upflung hand stopped him.

'I would say anything to get rid of you,' she threw at him, desperate to hang on to the last shreds of her self-control. 'I do not want you, I do not need you—all I need is your silence and for you to keep your blackmailing mother silent also.'

'So the little girl is your daughter and your friend is raising her as the twin of her son.' He glanced down at the Border Collie puppy that was attempting to chew the heel of his boot, picked it up by the scruff and handed it to Isobel. She caught it up without taking her eyes from his face and clutched the warm squirming bundle to her bosom like a shield. 'She has your eyes. May I see her?'

'No! I have told you, I do not want anything more to do with you. Go back to London and marry a wife your mama will buy you. She will purchase your heirs in the same way as she bought your accent and your education and your smooth society manners.'

'No one controls my life.' There was anger in his voice. 'Not since I was a child. Do you condemn my mother for wanting the best upbringing she could get for me? What do you buy for your child, Isobel? Do you pay for her clothes and her nurse? Will you pay for her governess? Will you search for the right husband for her when she is old enough to make her come-out, even if you do it from behind the walls of your own home? Or will you wash your hands of her and leave it all to Mrs Needham so you can walk away and find this husband you seek?'

'Between us Jane and I will do everything we can for the children. I thought this would be best for Annabelle. I did not want her to grow up as...'

'A bastard?' Giles enquired in a tone that made her wince. 'I manage.'

'I do not want her to have to *manage*. And it is different for a woman and you know it,' she threw at him.

'Isobel, are you all right?' She turned and there was Jane, a shotgun in the crook of her arm. 'Don't you dare lay a finger on her,' she said fiercely to Giles.

Giles took a reckless step towards the woman with the gun. A woman who Isobel knew was perfectly capable of taking a shot at a cattle thief. And now it was the children under threat. 'There is no call to shoot anyone.'

'None at all if you leave,' Jane agreed. 'And are silent about this.'

'I will tell no one,' Giles said. Then, ignoring both Jane and the gun, he went to stand in front of Isobel. He lifted the puppy from her arms and set it down before catching her hands in his. 'Isobel, I thought you loved me.' He spoke directly to her as though they were alone, so close she could feel his warmth, smell his familiar scent of clean linen and citrus and something that was simply Giles.

'I—' She stared into the green eyes and the farmyard seemed to vanish. Jane, the animals, everything faded away and there was only the two of them, handfast. She could not lie to him, not about this. 'Yes, I love you. I try not to, but I cannot lie to you about it.' And in his eyes she thought she read an answering love and all the doubt and fear vanished. 'I love you, I trust you and I am sorry that my faith in you wavered for a while.'

She waited for the words, but they did not come, only a shadow that clouded the clear green eyes and a twist of the mouth that she so much wanted to kiss. 'Do you truly not love me?' she had to ask at last when he did not speak. 'Can I be so wrong in what I feel from you?'

'I cannot allow myself to love you, Isobel. There is no future for us. Nothing has changed except that now I know you are too vulnerable with this secret to risk the slightest breath of scandal. The secret is safe, I promise you. There will be no risk, Isobel, because this ends here. This is where we part.'

'I know.' She had faced that finally on the long drive. There had never been any hope because a scandal would ruin him, would break her parents' hearts, might even compromise Annabelle's future in ways she could not foresee. 'I know that. I give up.' Her voice cracked and she controlled it somehow. 'I just need you to tell me how you feel, Giles.'

'No.' His face was stark as he bent his head. 'No, I will not say I love you, Isobel. Only that I care too much to make this worse than it already is.' The kiss was gentle, achingly tender. His lips lingered on hers and she could taste the heat and the passion that he was holding in check, feel the tremor that ran through him when she raised her arms and curled them around his neck to hold him for just a moment longer.

'Goodbye, Isobel.' He turned and strode out of the yard and when she sank down onto the bale, her legs too weak to hold her, and looked around, she was alone. Jane had gone. Distantly there was the sound of carriage wheels, then silence.

Something wet touched her hand and she looked down. The puppy that had been chewing Giles's boot was licking her hand. It wasn't the pup Nathaniel had chosen, but a skinny little female with a comical white patch over one eye. Isobel scooped her up and the puppy licked her nose.

'Hello,' Isobel said, her voice sounding thready in her own ears. Then she got up and walked inside with the dog in her arms. 'One more day and then we are going to London,' she said to it as it wriggled.

'Isobel.' Jane stood just inside the empty kitchen and hugged her and the pup together. 'Oh, my dear.' When Isobel just shook her head she said, 'I would not have shot him, you know. Not the man you love.'

'Thank you,' Isobel said, her smile hurting. 'I will go home tomorrow. May I take the puppy? I don't expect trying to housetrain a dog in a post-chaise is easy, but I will manage. We will be fine.'

'Of course you will,' Jane said and her face showed that she knew it was not the puppy that Isobel was talking about. 'Come and let Annabelle choose a name for it.'

A puppy in a post-chaise was certainly an excellent distraction. Maude, as Annabelle inexplicably named the black-and-white bundle, proved to be ravenously hungry and ate and drank everything put in the dishes on the floor for her—with inevitable consequences. Jane had the foresight to give them a small sack of sawdust and a large roasting dish, so Dorothy climbed out to empty it at every stop, complaining vociferously.

But Isobel would not let her chastise Maude, even

when she started to chew shoes and the edge of the carriage rug. 'She's only a baby, Dorothy,' she said, picking up the puppy and receiving a wet slurp on the nose for her pains. With a contented sigh the little dog went to sleep on her lap, worn out by her adventure.

Which left all the stages from Gloucester still to sit through. They would not arrive in London until past ten that night after a six o'clock start in the morning. Dorothy started to doze, wedged in one corner against the jolting, but Isobel sat upright, cradled the puppy on her lap and let her mind wander where it might. She was too tired and too hurt to try to think sensibly. And besides, what was there to think about?

Other than Annabelle, she realised with a smile that faded as the guilt took over once more. Her parents would adore her and yet they would never know they had a granddaughter.

She realised she was about to drift off, and did not fight it. It would bring dreams, she supposed, but dreams were all she had left now.

*Trust...I trust you.* The words she had said to Giles. But it was not his face in the dream, it was her parents, watching her anxiously. She woke, but the image did not fade. They had trusted her when she had fled to Hereford, loved her enough to leave her there a year when she wrote and begged not to be asked to come home. They had believed her when she was sent home in disgrace after the house party when virtually no one else had. If she could trust anyone, she could trust her parents, she realised. Perhaps, after all, some good could come of this unhappiness.

Isobel curled into the corner of the chaise and went back to sleep.

'God, she has courage, my Isobel,' Giles said to himself as he sat at the writing table in his inn bedchamber.

Isobel, so frank, so brave, so direct with the truth and with her love. She had known he would never act on his true feelings, never show her what was in his heart. The most she could hope for was his flirtation and his idle, thoughtless kisses. So she had shown him what love was.

He screwed up what he had been writing and threw the paper on the fire. A letter would only do more damage. He had written the words he had wanted to say, the true words. But they were better as ashes—it would do Isobel no good to tell her he loved her.

What was he going to do now? He was not going to marry Miss Holt, that was certain. Somehow he would have to make Geraldine accept that. She only wanted him to be happy and she found his independence infuriating. She wanted to arrange everything to her satisfaction, including his happiness.

He would be happy again, one day, he supposed. One day.

# CHAPTER TWENTY-ONE

'MAMA. PAPA. MAY I speak with you?'

'We have been speaking to each other for the last
half hour,' Lord Bythorn pointed out. But he folded
his copy of the *Morning Chronicle*, laid it beside his
breakfast plate and waited.

'I mean, in private. In your study.' Isobel's chest felt
tight, her breakfast—what little of it she had managed
to eat—was sitting uneasily in her stomach and she
was all too aware of her parents' anxious attention.

'Very well, if you can keep that confounded puppy
of yours out of it. It has already destroyed my slippers and it has only been in the house twelve hours.'

'Thank you, Papa.' He was making a joke out of
it, bless him.

'Now, what is this about, eh, Isobel?' He sat behind his big desk, Isobel and her mother in the two
wing chairs in front of it. 'This looks uncommonly
like a confession.'

'It is.' *Trust*, she reminded herself. *Too late to back*

*out now. Just trust them, they love you.* 'In the last few weeks before Lucas was killed, we were lovers.'

She heard her mother's sharply indrawn breath. Her father's face went blank, then, to her surprise, he said, 'Shocking, but not so very unusual.' There was the very faintest suspicion of a smile in the fleeting look he sent her mother. Isobel opened her mouth to blurt out a question and shut it hurriedly.

'After he died, I discovered I was pregnant.' This time the breath was a gasp and her father's face lost its smile as the colour ebbed out of his cheeks. 'That was why I stayed with Jane. She is not the mother of twins: her daughter is mine. Your grandchild.'

The silence was broken only by her mother's sob, quickly stifled with her hand. Isobel reached out her own hand, hesitated, then withdrew it.

'You could not trust us to look after you?' her father asked with a gentleness that warned her he was keeping a tight rein on his emotions.

'No,' Isobel admitted. Only the truth would serve now. 'I was not thinking very clearly. I wanted Lucas and he was gone—I was frightened that the child would be taken from me. I could not trust anyone except Jane.' The tears were running down her mother's face now. This was as bad as she feared it would be—she had hurt them dreadfully. 'I am so sorry. I did it for the best.'

She turned and this time took her mother's hand. It stayed in hers and, after a moment, the fingers curled around her own. 'Her name is Annabelle.' It was her grandmother's name.

'Why now? Why are you telling us now? Is something wrong with her?' Her mother clutched her hand with a desperate urgency.

'She is perfect and she is well. No, it is not that. I realised I am never going to marry and have a family. And I saw that I was depriving you of your grandchild and that was wrong. And I have been thinking a lot about trust, these past few days—and I knew I should have trusted you from the beginning.'

'Who knows about the child?' her father asked.

'Jane's old family retainers, but they would never betray her secrets and they adore Annabelle. The doctor, and he is a family friend.' She saw their relief and knew she had to shatter it. 'And the Dowager Marchioness of Faversham and her son, Giles Harker.'

'What! That wanton creature? How in blazes did she discover this?'

'She feared I would marry Giles and that there would be a great scandal which would harm him. She uses enquiry agents all the time, it seems, so she set a man to find what secrets I might have. Her intention was to blackmail me into giving up Giles.'

'Marry him? Give him up?' Her mother stared, aghast. 'You are not having a liaison with that man?'

'I am in love with that man,' Isobel corrected gently. 'But, no, we are not lovers and I will not marry him— she is quite right, the scandal would ruin him. He will not admit he loves me because he thinks it would ruin *me*.'

'You love him? He is a—'

'So is our granddaughter,' Lord Bythorn said and her mother gave a gasp of dismay. 'Will he and that woman hold their tongues?'

'Oh, yes. She had no other motive than to protect her son, she will wish me no harm once Giles has convinced her I am no threat to his standing or his career.'

'Hah!' Lady Bythorn said, swiping ineffectually at her eyes with a tiny scrap of lace.

'Mama, he saved my life when I would have drowned. He was scarred defending my honour.'

'True enough,' her father admitted. 'Can we see Annabelle? Or must you keep her from us?'

'No! Of course I will not. But we cannot acknowledge who she is, you must see that. Her prospects are good now—her birth seems perfectly respectable, she will grow up without any stain, a Needham. And her supposed father was Lucas's half-brother, after all.

'But we can visit. She calls me "Aunt," so it is only

natural that you should take an interest in her. Jane can visit us here and bring the children.'

'Oh, yes.' Lady Bythorn brightened, sat up and rubbed her palms over her wet cheeks. 'My *grand-daughter*! Oh, my goodness.'

'And what of you, Isobel?' her father asked.

She shook her head. 'I cannot marry. I cannot hide this from my husband and even if I did find someone, I dare not risk Annabelle's reputation by telling him before I am wed.' She added, 'I will finish this Season, I do not wish to cause any further talk.'

'Oh, my dear.' He sighed and shook his head, but when he looked at her there was a smile lurking under the heavy dark brows. 'But thank you for my grand-child.' As she got up he rose too and came round the desk to embrace her. 'I had hoped, after Needham's death, you could have found a good man who would love you.'

'I did, Papa,' she said. 'But it seems I cannot have him. I must write to Jane.'

The Season was in full swing now. Isobel hurled herself into it as though the sea of frivolity and pleasure could wash away the pain and the longing. Only her parents' delight in hearing about Annabelle kept her spirits up and the arrival of some portrait sketches that Jane had asked the village schoolmaster to make had them in a frenzy of planning for a visit just as soon as the summer came.

Taking tea after dinner a week after her return, Isobel overheard her father in conversation with their host. '…remodelling the entire West Wing of the Priory,' Lord Roehampton said. 'Got a very promising young architect working on it—Harker. But I was forgetting,' he added, lowering his voice. 'He's the man who stood up for Albright over that wretched business your daughter fell victim to. Good show, that. His mother's a menace in society, but he can't help that and, to do him credit, he stands by her. Loyal, as I said to Lady Roehampton when she was cavilling about employing him. The man's got the instincts of a gentleman.'

'Yes,' Lord Bythorn said slowly. 'It seems he has.'

Isobel stared at her father, a hope forming in her mind so improbable, she hardly dared try to think it through. As the three of them sat in the carriage on the short ride home through the streets of Mayfair she said abruptly, before she could give herself time to lose courage, 'Papa, if Giles Harker came to you now and asked for my hand in marriage, what would you say?'

'My love, he would not do such a thing. He knows it would cause a scandal. I think I've discovered enough about the man by now to know he won't hurt you,' her father said gruffly.

'But if he did, would it cause a scandal if you said *yes*?' she asked. 'I know it would if you forbade the match and we ran away together. But if it was seen that you approved, would that not make all the difference?'

'Isobel!' her mother interjected. 'You cannot marry a man born out of wedlock.'

'Why not? I am not going to marry any other man and it seems to me that if it does not hurt anyone else, then I may as well be happy as not! It is not as though I wish to be received at court again or spend my time at Almack's. Papa—if you gave us your blessing, *would* there be a scandal? One that would hurt you and Mama, be difficult for Frederick at school? One that would ruin Giles's business?'

Her mother moaned again at the word *business*, but her father said, after a pause, 'You heard me talking to Roehampton? I must confess, I see Harker in a different light now, with all that has happened. No, I do not think it would cause more than a seven-day wonder, not if I gave it my blessing and your mother received him. You have enough of a reputation for eccentricity already, my dear.'

'Oh, Papa!' She launched herself across the carriage and hugged him, squashing his silk hat. 'Thank you!'

'But he will not ask me, will he?' Lord Bythorn said gently, setting her back on her seat. 'The more he cares for you, the less likely he is to approach you again.'

'No,' Isobel agreed. 'So I will just have to ask him.'

Her mother subsided against the squabs with a moan. 'I knew I should have brought my smelling bottle!'

The first thing was to find out where Giles was, Isobel decided as she sat up in bed the next morning nursing a cup of chocolate in her hands. The work at Wimpole could not have been completed yet, but she assumed that, like Mr Soane, he would have several commissions in hand at any one time. Some she knew about, such as Lord Roehampton's West Wing, but Giles could be anywhere.

There was only one person in London who might know, and Mama would have the vapours if she thought her daughter was going anywhere near her. It did not seem to have occurred to her parents that if she married Giles then the Scarlet Widow would be her mother-in-law, which was probably a sign that they believed there was little chance that such a thing would ever happen. Well, time to worry about that later, she thought philosophically. Just at the moment it was the least of her worries.

'Will you fetch me a London directory please, Dorothy?' she called.

'Yes, my lady. Just one moment. This dratted dog has chewed the tassel on the curtain tie.' The maid sounded exasperated, but Isobel knew full well that she doted on Maude and sneaked biscuits to her in her basket.

'Here we are.' Dorothy bustled out of the dressing room with the book in her hands. 'Heard about an interesting shop, have you, my lady?'

'Er...no. I am just looking up the address of a new acquaintance.'

Lady Faversham lived not so very far away in Bruton Street. Close enough, in fact, not to need the carriage. 'My blue walking dress and the dark blue pelisse and the velvet hat this morning, Dorothy. I have some calls to make, but I can take one of the footmen with me, so you can carry on with those alterations.'

An hour and a half later, at an unconscionably early hour to be making a call, Isobel was admitted to Lady Faversham's elegant hall by her equally elegant butler.

'I am sure that if it is a matter concerning Mr Harker her ladyship will wish to receive you,' he said, admirably concealing any trace of speculation. 'If you would care to wait in here, my lady, I will enquire.'

Giles's name did indeed open doors. Isobel was received by her ladyship who was reclining on a chaise in her boudoir in a confection of lace and sea-green gauze that roused a pang of envy in Isobel's breast.

'What do you want with my son now?' the Widow demanded, narrowing ice-green eyes at her.

There did not seem to be any point beating about the bush. Isobel took a deep breath and said, 'To tell him that if he asks for my hand my father will give it to him willingly. There will be no scandal, he will be welcomed into the family.'

'*What?*' The Widow stared at her.

'My parents have accepted that I will never marry anyone else. They are grateful to Giles for what he has done for me. And,' she added as the Widow opened her mouth, 'they know about my daughter.

'And also—' she slipped in before Lady Faversham could speak. 'I am well dowered, well connected and perfectly placed to help Giles's career. All I need to know is where he is and I will go and propose to him.'

'Propose? You have courage, I will say that for you. And if I object?'

'Why should you be so spiteful?' A hint of colour touched the older woman's cheekbones under the powder. 'If he does not want me, he can always refuse. If this is some sort of trick, you have the instrument of revenge in your own hands.'

'I only want him to be happy,' Lady Faversham said and to her horror Isobel saw one tear roll down her cheek. 'And he is so stubbornly independent. Will you make him happy?'

'Oh, yes,' Isobel said. 'I promise.'

'Excellent.' With a dab of lace the tear was gone, taking the momentary weakness with it, and the green eyes defied Isobel to ever recall she had seen it. 'He is at Wimpole Hall.'

'Thank you.' She turned to go, then on an impulse swung round. 'Where did you purchase that exquisite robe?'

'Mirabelle's,' the Widow said and, to her amazement, smiled. 'Buy blue, not green. Blue and silver.'

Giles floated on his back in the plunge pool, ears below water, the steam coiling and rising around him. It had been a long, hard, damp day up at the Hill House supervising the demolition and the salvaging of the best stone and he had become chilled to the marrow.

The heat soothed his body, but the more he relaxed physically, the more his imagination could work and the worse the pain in his heart was. The gentle lap of the water made him think of Isobel's caressing fingers, the silence gave her voice space to echo in his mind. *I love you, Giles.*

He had done the only thing he could for her and her daughter, he told himself for the thousandth time. He had left her, he had silenced his mother and he had refused to tell Isobel what was in his heart. *Cruel to be kind*. The easy cliché mocked him. Cruel to be perhaps less cruel in the long run, that was the best he could hope for.

Before Isobel had come into his life he had never felt lonely. Now he ached with it. Here at Wimpole, as the bustle of the family's preparations for their departure to Ireland gathered momentum, he could have company every hour of the day and evening if he chose. But he knew he would feel this alone in the midst of thousands without Isobel.

It seemed that to deny love, the emotion he had never believed he could feel, required as much courage and resolution as facing a fellow duellist. The pain certainly lasted longer, bad enough to force him to admit that the emotion was true and would never leave him. He loved her. He could admit it now he was no longer a danger to her, now he would never see her again, except, perhaps, across a crowded ballroom.

He wanted to write to her, tell her how he felt, tell her why this was so impossible. He wrote the letters every night and every morning burned them. How long was it going to be before he could shake off this sensation that without her he was merely a hollow shell, going through the actions of life? Or perhaps he never would be free of it. Perhaps the heart could not heal as the body did.

But doing the honourable thing, the right thing, was never going to be easy. He was not a gentleman, but, for Isobel's sake, he was going to behave like one. He could cope with physical pain, he just had to learn to deal with mental torment, too, or go mad.

A ripple of water splashed his face and his floating body rocked. Someone else had got into the pool. Lord Hardwicke or young Philip, he supposed, opening his eyes and staring up at the vault of the ceiling, wishing they would go away. The other bather said nothing. Giles raised his head and saw something on the curving edge at the end of the pool.

A small black-and-white puppy was sitting on its haunches watching him. Its tongue lolled out, its tail thrashed back and forth—it was obviously delighted to see him. A long blue leash curled onto the damp brown marble where it had been dropped.

Giles surged to his feet, turned and found Isobel, as naked as a water nymph, her wet hair on her shoulders, standing behind him.

'Isobel.' She smiled, that warm, open trusting smile. 'No! No, go away, damn it! I do not want you.' And he turned to forge his way through the water to the steps.

# CHAPTER TWENTY-TWO

'GILES.' HER VOICE stopped him for a second, two, three, then he summoned up all his will and began to walk away again. 'Giles. Please. If you feel anything at all for me, answer one question.'

He should keep going, deny his feelings for her sake, but he found he could not lie to her. 'What is it?' He did not turn around: to see her face, those wide eyes, would be too much to bear.

'If you had not only my father's agreement, but his blessing, his public acceptance, would you marry me?'

'If wishes were horses, beggars might ride,' he said, still looking at the steps that rose out of the water, then twisted steeply to the changing area. Escape. His voice was choked in his throat.

'It is not a wish, it is a fact.'

It could not be. It was impossible. He was dreaming.

'Giles,' the voice from his dreams persisted, 'I

wish you would turn around. I am trying to propose to you and it is very difficult talking to the back of your head.'

That brought him round in a spin that created waves. The puppy retreated with a yap of alarm as water sloshed over the sides. The naked nymph was still there, her wet hair almost black, plastered over the curves of her breast. Not a dream, not an hallucination. The real woman.

'Isobel…' He sank his pride and tried an appeal. 'This is not fair. Not to you, not to me, to pretend this is possible.'

'I have only ever lied to you to protect my daughter,' she said, her gaze locked with his. 'I swear on her life that I am not lying to you now. I am not delusional. My father accepts I will marry no one else, ever. I told my parents all about Annabelle, you see, so finally they understand. And once my father thought about it, once he began to hear about you from other people, he realised that he respected you.'

She made no move to come closer to him, only waited patiently, watching his face as he worked painfully through what she was telling him. 'You told them about Annabelle—risked that, for me?'

'No.' She shook her head, painfully honest as ever. 'But it is because of you that I told them. You made me think about trust and honour and what I was with-holding from them because I dared not take a chance on their love. So I told them. It was later that I re-alised that, now they have given up all hope of me making a conventional match, they might consent if they thought you would make me happy.'

'There is a lesson for me in that, you do not have to spell it out,' Giles said. *Trust and the withholding of love.* He had not trusted her to be strong enough to cope with his impossible love as well as her own. 'I thought I was doing the right thing, making the right sacrifice.'

'So it was a sacrifice?' For the first time he saw her fear and her uncertainty in the wide grey eyes and the way she had caught her lower lip between her teeth.

Still the words would not come. How could he risk her regretting it as soon as the knot was tied? So much of her life that she took completely for granted would be lost to her. But if Isobel could trust him, then he must trust her. 'Yes, it was a sacrifice,' Giles admitted.

Her smile was radiant. 'Oh, thank goodness.' It was an ungainly business, splashing towards each other through water that was more than waist-deep. Giles found he was laughing when he finally had Isobel in his arms and so was she, and crying, and the puppy was yapping.

'This is so bizarre it has to be true,' Giles said, his arms full of wet woman. His pulse was racing, he felt dizzy. 'I thought I was dreaming. How on earth did you get here?'

'Never mind that! Will you marry me?' Isobel demanded, her arms twined round his waist.

'Are you sure?' This time he knew she saw his hesitation clearly, realised he had not said those words that mattered to her so much.

'Not if you are not.' All the animation drained away, leaving her naked and vulnerable. 'I am sorry if I misunderstood. I thought it was only the fear of scandal that stopped you and if that was no longer there, it would be all right.' Isobel pushed away from him and splashed to the steps. She climbed out, dripping and naked, the puppy gambolling around her feet until it sensed her unhappiness and crouched, whining.

'Isobel!' Giles took three long strokes and climbed the steps beside her. 'You do not realise what it would mean to be married to me.' He caught her, blocked her escape up the narrow twist of steps that led to the changing area.

'You are used to a great house, a London home,

dozens of servants. You are received at Court, you are invited to the most fashionable functions.

'I cannot give you that. You won't be received at Court any longer, there will be people who will snub us, my country home is a tenth the size of this and if we want to live in London we must rent, at least at first. I don't own a carriage. I—'

'Is that all?' she demanded. 'What do you think I want, Giles?' When he just stood and looked at her, she prodded him in the ribs.

'Me?' Isobel nodded. 'Our children?' Another nod.

'That is all and that is everything. I have a perfectly good dowry which will keep me in all the fashionable frivolity I want—if I want it. The rest can go to the children if you are too stiff-necked to take it to buy a town house or a carriage or whatever you want to improve the estate.'

'Truly?'

'Truly. Now, tell me why you will not marry me, because the only reason that I am prepared to accept is that you do not love me.'

It was like shackles breaking or a dam bursting inside. There was only one thing between him and having the woman he loved and that was his stubborn fear of believing what Isobel was telling him.

Giles took a deep breath. 'I love you.' He found he

was grinning. 'I love you. I never thought I would be able to say it to you.' He picked her up, slippery as a fish, and started to climb as she wrapped her arms around his neck and buried her face against him. Apparently his love had run out of words.

Giles stood her on her feet when they reached the little changing room. His brocade robe hung neatly on one of the hooks on the wall that was warmed by the boiler. His slippers equally tidy below. 'My dear love,' he said mildly as he surveyed the scattered feminine clothing that strewed the floor. 'Am I to expect our home to be in this much of a muddle?'

'I was in a hurry,' Isobel said with dignity. She ran her hands over his body. 'I still am. You love me,' she murmured, as if she could still not quite believe it.

Giles caught her wrists as her fingers descended lower. 'And I will prove it to you. But I refuse to make love to you on the floor.' *Not here and not now, anyway.* There was a large bearskin rug in front of his dressing-room fire at home that had fed a particularly delicious and tormenting fantasy about Isobel.

'In my bedchamber, then. Or yours?'

'Neither.' Reluctantly he let her go and pulled on his robe, stuffed his feet into his slippers. There was something respectable about slippers. Wicked rakes did not make passionate love in slippers.

'Why not? You want me.' She slanted a look that was pure provocation from beneath her wet lashes.

'Of course I want you, you witch. I love you. But I am going to marry you.' *Marry you.* He repeated the words in his head, trying to convince himself that this was really going to happen. 'So I am going to do this properly. Respectably.' Isobel opened her mouth to protest. 'I am going to go and get dressed. So are you and you will then find Lady Hardwicke.

'I will ask the earl if he can spare me for a few days. We will drive back to London, in separate chaises, where I will formally ask your father for your hand. We will then proceed to do whatever it is that respectable people do for the duration of a respectable betrothal before they are respectably married.'

'Giles, that will take *weeks.*' Isobel rescued a stocking from the puppy and began to pull it on. Giles studied the way the walls had been painted with minute attention while the rustling and flapping of her dressing went on.

'Precisely. Our wedding is going to be the exact opposite of an elopement.'

'I am dressed. You may stop looking at the architraves or whatever it is you are pretending such interest in.'

'Soffits,' he said vaguely. 'God, you are beautiful.'

'No, I am not. I am—'

'Beautiful. I love you.'

'Then kiss me, Giles. You haven't kissed me since you told me you loved me.'

'Not here.' He watched as she wrapped her wet hair into a towel. 'I will walk you to your room and I will kiss you at your door because I cannot trust myself to touch you here.' He looked down. 'Why is there a puppy chewing my slipper?'

'It is the same one from the farmyard. You gave her to me to hold. She is the only thing you ever gave me—except my life and my honour and a broken heart—so I had to keep her.'

'Oh, hell,' he said, appalled to find his vision blurring. 'Come here.'

Isobel melted into his arms and Giles wondered why he had not realised from the first moment that he touched her that this was where she belonged. Her body was slender and strong in his embrace and her mouth hesitant, soft, as though she was shy and this was the first time.

So he kissed her as though it was, as though this was new for both of them. And it was true, he realised, because this was love and he had never loved before. So he did not demand or plunder, only explored and tasted gently, leisurely, until she was sighing, melting in his arms and he realised that he was more simply happy than he had ever been in his life.

'What was your favourite thing about the wedding breakfast?' Giles asked Isobel as she curled up against him on the wide and opulent seat of the carriage that had been his mother's wedding present to them.

'My father plotting a new shrubbery with your grandfather's advice and your mother and mine circling each other like wary cats and then deciding their mutual curiosity about each other's gowns was too much to resist. I have to say, it does help that Papa never had an affaire with her. Did you notice Pamela Monsom's father dodging about the room to avoid her? Pamela is convinced there was something between them.'

'Oh, Lord,' Giles groaned.

'It doesn't matter. Or rather, it does to Lady Monsom, of course, but we can't help that now. I like your mama—she says what she thinks and she is very kind to me now she doesn't regard me as a menace to your well-being.'

'She has had eight weeks to get used to the fact,' Giles said.

'And we have had eight weeks of blameless respectability.' She snuggled closer and nibbled his earlobe.

'I am not going to make love to you in the carriage,' he ground out. 'There is a big bed waiting for us. After that you may assault me where and when you please.' She curled her tongue-tip into his ear. 'Within reason!'

'Very well.' With an effort Isobel stopped teasing him, sat back and watched the countryside rolling past in the sunshine of the late afternoon. 'Wasn't Annabelle lovely? The children were so well behaved. I am so glad Jane brought them down.'

'We will have them to stay whenever she can come,' Giles promised. Isobel had watched him, seen how he was with both the children, how careful he was not to single Annabelle out. He would make a wonderful father.

'We are here.'

She craned to look at the grounds as they rolled up the carriage drive. The house when they reached it was perfect, the brick and dressed stone still crisp with newness, but the garden already embraced it, softened it. 'I love it,' she said and felt his pleasure at hers. 'Where is the room with the big bed?'

'At the back, overlooking the lake. Don't you want to eat first?'

'No, I want to make love,' she whispered in his ear as he swung her down from the carriage. 'Where is everyone?'

'I told them you would meet them in the morning. You see, I guessed you might want to inspect the bedchamber first—there should be a cold meal laid out.'

The front door opened as if by magic as he swept her up into his arms and carried her up the steps, but there was no one to be seen in the hall with its wide staircase. Giles carried on up to the first floor to where double doors stood open on to a room decorated all in palest grey and in blue silk with a wide Venetian window framing the landscape and, as he had promised her, a very big bed.

'Lady Isobel Harker,' Giles said as he set her on her feet. 'There is something in the marriage service about worshipping you with my body and I take promises very seriously.'

'I hope so, Mr Harker,' she murmured as he began to unfasten her gown. Silk and lawn whispered to the ground, her stays followed with a facility that she would tease him about later. But now this felt too important for levity, only for deep happiness.

Giles carried her to the bed and stripped off his own clothing. 'I have never seen you without all those bruises,' she murmured, running her hands over the

flat planes of his chest, the ridged muscle of his stomach. 'I was too nervous to notice in the pool that they
had gone.'

He lowered himself over her, his scarred cheek
resting next to her smooth one and she twisted so
she could kiss it, then his nose with its new bump.

'I love you,' he told her as his hands began to caress
her. Every time he said the words it seemed to her
that it was never just a phrase. Each time he seemed
to find it wonderful and new, a surprise to love and
be loved.

'Show me,' she whispered back, curling her legs
around his waist, cradling him between her thighs
where she had wanted him for so long.

'Eight weeks of respectability is all very well,'
Giles said, his voice husky. 'But it makes a man very,
very impatient.'

'So am I,' Isobel told him, and lifted her hips to
press against him, took his mouth and thrust with
her tongue to tell him it was all right to be urgent,
to take her. It had been a long time since Lucas, but
for all his scarce-controlled desire Giles was gentle.
She opened to him when he entered her, as he slid
home deep and sure to make her his, and then she
lost every trace of apprehension in the heat and the
joy of their merging and the pleasure that he spun

out of caresses and kisses to send her wild and desperate for release.

They cried out together and sank into sleep together. When she woke Giles was watching her and lifted his hand to trace where his eyes had been roaming, across her brow, down her cheek, softly over her lips.

'You were meant for me,' Isobel told him.

'I know. I think I knew from the moment I caught your hand in the lake and feared I was too late. Mine,' Giles said. 'Mine for ever.' And he began to prove it all over again.

\* \* \* \* \*

# TARNISHED
# AMONGST
# THE TON

With love for AJH—and thanks
for all the London walking!

# Chapter One

 ᘒᘒᘒᘒᘒᘒᘒ

*3 March 1816—the Pool of London*

'It is grey, just as everyone said it would be.' Ashe
Herriard leaned on the ship's rail and contemplated the
wide stretch of the River Thames before him through
narrowed eyes. It was jammed with craft from tiny
skiffs and rowing boats to those that dwarfed even their
four-masted East Indiaman. 'More shades of grey than
I had realised existed. And brown and beige and green.
But mostly grey.'

He had expected to hate London, to find it alien, but
it looked old and prosperous and strangely familiar,
even though every bone in his body wanted to resent it
and all it represented.

'But it is not raining and Mrs Mackenzie said it rains
all the time in England.' Sara stood beside him, huddled
in a heavy cloak. She sounded cheerful and excited although her teeth were chattering. 'It is like the Garden
Reach in Calcutta, only far busier. And much colder.'
She pointed. 'There is even a fort. See?'

'That's the Tower of London.' Ashe grinned, unwilling to infect his sister with his own brooding mood. 'You see, I have remembered my reading.'

'I am very impressed, brother dear,' she agreed with a twinkle that faded as she glanced further along the rail. '*Mata* is being very brave.'

Ashe followed her gaze. 'Smiling brightly, you mean? They are both being brave, I suspect.' His father had his arm around his mother and was holding her tight to his side. That was not unusual—they were unfashionably demonstrative, even by the standards of Calcutta's easy-going European society, but he could read his father and knew what the calm expression combined with a set jaw meant. The Marquess of Eldonstone was braced for a fight.

The fact that it was a fight against his own memories of a country that he had left over forty years ago did not make it any less real, Ashe knew. Estranged from his own father, married to a half-Indian wife who was appalled when she discovered her husband was heir to an English title and would one day have to return, Colonel Nicholas Herriard had held out until the last possible moment before leaving India. But marquesses did not hold posts as military diplomats in the East India Company. And he had known it was inevitable that one day he would inherit the title and have to return to England and do his duty.

*And so did his own son*, Ashe thought as he walked to his father's side. He was damned if he was going to let it defeat them and he'd be damned, too, if he couldn't take some of the burden off their shoulders even if that meant turning himself into that alien species, the perfect English aristocrat. 'I'll take Perrott, go ashore and make certain Tompkins is here to meet us.'

'Thank you. I don't want your mother and sister standing around on the dockside.' The marquess pointed. 'Signal from there if he's arrived with a carriage.'

'Sir.' Ashe strode off in search of a sailor and a rowing boat and to set foot on dry land. *A new country, a new destiny. A new world*, he told himself, *a new fight.* New worlds were there to conquer, after all. Already memories of the heat and the colour and the vivid life of the palace of Kalatwah were becoming like a dream, slipping though his fingers when he would have grasped and held them. All of them, even the pain and the guilt. *Reshmi*, he thought and pushed away the memory with an almost physical effort. Nothing, not even love, could bring back the dead.

*There must be reliable, conscientious, thoughtful men somewhere in creation.* Phyllida stood back from the entrance to the narrow alleyway and scanned the bustling Customs House quay. *Unfortunately my dear brother is not one of them.* Which should be no surprise as their sire had not had a reliable, conscientious bone in his body and, his undutiful daughter strongly suspected, not many thoughts in his head either beyond gaming, whoring and spending money.

And now Gregory had been gone for twenty-four hours with the rent money and, according to his friends, had found a new hell somewhere between the Tower and London Bridge.

Something tugged at the laces of her half-boots. Expecting a cat, Phyllida looked down to find herself staring into the black boot-button eyes of the biggest crow she had ever seen. Or perhaps it was a raven escaped from the Tower? But it had a strange greyish head and neck, which set off a massive beak. Not a raven, then. It shot her an insolent look and went back to tugging at her bootlaces.

'Go away!' Phyllida jerked back her foot and it let go with a squawk and went for the other foot.

'Lucifer, put the lady down.' The bird made a harsh noise, flapped up and settled on the shoulder of the tall, bare-headed man standing in front of her. 'I do apologise. He is fascinated by laces, string, anything long and thin. Unfortunately, he is a complete coward with snakes.'

She found her voice. 'That is unlikely to be a handicap in London.' Where had this beautiful, exotic man with his devilish familiar materialised from? Phyllida took in thick dark brown hair, green eyes, a straight nose—down which he was currently studying her—and golden skin. *Tanned skin in March?* No, it was his natural colour. She would not have been surprised to smell a hint of brimstone.

'So I understand.' He reached up and tossed the bird into the air. 'Go and find Sara, you feathered menace. He swears if he's confined to a cage,' he added as it flew off towards the ships at anchor in mid-stream. 'But I suppose I will have to do it or he'll be seducing the ravens in the Tower into all kinds of wickedness. Unless they are merely a legend?'

'No, they are real.' *Definitely foreign, then.* He was well-dressed in a manner that was subtly un-English. A heavy black cloak with a lining that was two shades darker than his eyes, a dark coat, heavy silk brocade waistcoat, snowy white linen—no, the shirt was silk, too. 'Sir!'

He had dropped to one knee on the appalling cobblestones and was tying her bootlaces, allowing her to see that his hair was long—an unfashionable shoulder-length, she guessed—and tied back at the nape of his neck. 'Is something wrong?' He looked up, face serious and questioning, green eyes amused. He knew perfectly well what was wrong, the wretch.

'You are touching my foot, sir!'

The gentleman finished the bow with a brisk tug and stood up. 'Difficult to tie a shoelace without, I'm afraid. Now, where are you going? I assure you, neither I nor Lucifer have any further designs upon your footwear.' His smile suggested there might be other things in danger.

Phyllida took another step back, but not away from assaults on her ankles or her equilibrium. Harry Buck was swaggering along the quayside towards them, one of his bullies a pace behind. Her stomach lurched as she looked around for somewhere to hide from Wapping's most notorious low-life. Nausea almost overcame her. If, somehow, he remembered her from nine years ago...

'That man.' She ducked her head in Buck's direction. 'I do not want to be seen by him.' The breath caught in her throat. 'And he is coming this way.' Running was out of the question. To run would be like dragging a ball of wool in front of a cat and Buck would chase out of sheer instinct. She hadn't even got a bonnet with a decent, concealing brim on it, just a simple flat straw tied on top of a net with her hair bundled up. *Stupid, stupid to have just walked into his territory like this, undisguised and unprepared.*

'In that case we should become better acquainted.' The exotic stranger took a step forwards, pressed her against the wall, raised one cloak-draped arm to shield her from the dockside and bent his head.

'What are you doing—?'

'Kissing you,' he said. And did. His free hand gathered her efficiently against his long, hard body, the impudent green eyes laughed down into hers and his mouth sealed her gasp of outrage.

Behind them there was the sound of heavy footsteps, the light was suddenly reduced as big bodies filled the entrance to the alleyway and a coarse voice said, 'You're on my patch, mate, so that'll be one of my doxies and you owe me.' *One of my doxies. Oh God. I can't be ill, not now, not like this.*

The man lifted his head, his hand pressing her face into the soft silk of his shirt. 'I brought this one with me. I don't share. And I don't pay men for sex.' Phyllida heard Buck's bully give a snort of laughter. Her protector sounded confident, amused and about as meek and mild as a pit bull.

There was a moment's silence, then Buck laughed, the remembered hoarse chuckle that still surfaced sometimes in her worst dreams. 'I like your style. Come and find my place if you want to play deep. Or find a willing girl. Ask anyone in Wapping for Harry Buck's.' And the feet thudded off down the alleyway, faded away.

Phyllida wriggled, furious with the one man she could vent her feelings on. 'Let me go.'

'Hmm?' His nose was buried in the angle of her neck, apparently sniffing. It tickled. So did his lips a moment later, a lingering, almost tender caress. 'Jasmine. Very nice.' He released her and stepped back, although not far enough for her peace of mind.

She usually hated being kissed, it was revolting. It

led to other things even worse. But that had been…surprising. And not at all revolting. It must depend on the man doing the kissing, even if one was not in love with him, which was all Phyllida had ever imagined would make it tolerable.

She took a deep breath and realised that far from being tinged with brimstone he actually smelled very pleasant. 'Sandalwood,' she said out loud rather than any of the other things that were jostling to be uttered like, *Insolent opportunist, outrageous rake. Who are you?* Even the words she thought would never enter her head—*Kiss me again.*

'Yes, and spikenard, just a touch. You know about scents?' He was still far too close, his arm penning her against the wall.

'I do not want to stand here discussing perfumery! Thank you for hiding me from Buck just now, but I wish you would leave now. Really, sir, you cannot go about kissing strange women as you please.' She ducked under his arm and out onto the quayside.

He turned and smiled and something inside her did a little flip. He had made no move to detain her and yet she could feel his hand on her as though it was a physical reality. No one would ever hold her against her will, ever again, and yet she had felt no fear of him. *Foolish. Just because he has charm it does not make him less dangerous.*

'*Are* you strange?' he asked, throwing her words back to her.

There were a range of answers to that question, none of them ladylike. 'The only strange thing about me is that I did not box your ears just now,' Phyllida said. And why she had not, once Buck had gone, she had no idea. 'Good day, sir,' she threw over her shoulder as she walked away. He was smiling, a lazy, heavy-lidded smile. Phyllida resisted the urge to take to her heels and run.

She had tasted of vanilla, coffee and woman and she had smelt like a summer evening in the raja's garden. Ashe ran his tongue over his lower lip in appreciative recollection as he looked around for his father's English lawyer.

*I will send the family coach for you, my lord,* Tompkins had written in that last letter that had been delivered to the marquess along with an English lady's maid for *Mata* and Sara, a valet for his father and himself. The most useful delivery of all was Perrott, a confidential clerk armed with every fact, figure and detail of the Eldonstone affairs and estates.

*Given that your father's rapid decline and unfortunate death have taken us by surprise, I felt it advisable to waste no time in further correspondence but to send you English staff and my most able assistant.*

His father had moved fast on receiving the inevitable, unwelcome news. Ashe was recalled from the Principality of Kalatwah where he had been acting as aide-de-camp to his great-uncle, the Raja Kirat Jaswan; possessions were sold, given away or packed and the four of them, along with their retinue, had embarked on the next East Indiaman bound for England.

'My lord, the coach is just along here. I have signalled to his lordship and sent the skiff back.'

'The end of your responsibilities, Perrott,' Ashe said with a grin as he strode along the quayside beside the earnest, red-headed clerk. 'After seventeen weeks of being cooped up on board attempting to teach us everything from tenancy law to entails by way of investments and the more obscure byways of the family tree, you must be delighted to be home again.'

'It is, of course, gratifying to be back in England, my lord, and my mother will be glad to see me. However, it has been a privilege and a pleasure to assist the marquess and yourself.'

*And the poor man has a hopeless* tendre *for Sara, so it will probably be a relief for both to have some distance between them.* It was the only foolish thing Ashe had discovered about Thomas Perrott. Falling in love was for servants, romantics, poets and women. And fools, which he was not. Not any longer.

His father had done it and had recklessly married for love, which was fortunate or he, Ashe, wouldn't be here now. But then his father was a law unto himself. In any case, a soldier of fortune, which is what he had been at the time, could do what he liked. His son—*the Viscount Clere*, he reminded himself with an inward wince—must marry for entirely different reasons.

'My lord.' Perrott stopped beside a fine black coach with the crest on the side that had become familiar from numerous legal documents and the imposing family tree. It was on the heavy seal ring his father now wore.

Liveried grooms climbed down from the back to stand at attention and two plainer coaches were waiting in line behind. 'For your staff and the small baggage, my lord. The hold luggage will come by carrier as soon as it is unloaded. I trust that is satisfactory?'

'No bullock carts and a distinct absence of elephants,' Ashe observed with a grin. 'We should move with unaccustomed speed.'

'The fodder bills must be smaller, certainly,' Perrott countered, straight-faced, and they walked back to the steps to await the skiff.

'There you are!' Phyllida dumped her hat and reticule on the table and confronted the sprawled figure of her brother, who occupied the sofa like a puppet with its strings cut.

'Here I am,' Gregory agreed, dragging open one eye. 'With the very devil of a thick head, sister dear, so kindly do not nag me.'

'I will do more than nag,' she promised as she tossed her pelisse onto a chair. 'Where is the rent money?'

'Ah. You missed it.' He heaved himself into a sitting position and began to rummage in his pockets. Bank notes spilled out in a crumpled heap on the floor. 'There you are.'

'Gregory! Where on earth did this all come from?' Phyllida dropped to her knees and gathered them up, smoothing and counting. 'Why, there is upwards of three hundred pounds here.'

'Hazard,' he said concisely, sinking back.

'You always lose at hazard.'

'I know. But you have been nagging me about the need for prudence and economy and I took your words to heart. You were quite right, Phyll, and I haven't been much help to you, have I? I even call your common sense *nagging*. But behold my cunning—I went to a new hell and they always want you to win at first, don't they?'

'So I have heard.' It was just that she hadn't believed that he would ever work that sort of thing out for himself.

'Therefore they saw to it that I *did* win and then when they smiled, all pleasant and shark-like, and proposed a double-or-nothing throw, I decided to hold my hand for the night.' He looked positively smug.

'And they let you out with no problem?' The memory of Harry Buck sent shivers down her spine. He would never let a winner escape unscathed from one of his hells. Nor a virgin, either. She blanked the thought as though slamming a lid on a mental box.

'Oh, yes. Told them I'd be back tomorrow with friends to continue my run of luck.'

'But they'll fleece you the second time.'

Gregory closed his eyes again with a sigh that held more weariness than a simple hangover caused. 'I lied to them. Told you, I'm turning over a new leaf, Phyll. I took a long hard look in the mirror yesterday morning and I'm not getting any younger. Made me think about the things you've been saying and I knew you were right. I'm sick of scrimping for every penny and knowing you are working so hard. We need me to attach a rich wife and I won't find one of those in a Wapping hell. And we need to save the readies to finance a courtship, just as you planned.'

'You are a saint amongst brothers.' Which was an outrageous untruth, and this attack of virtue might only last so long, but she did love him despite everything. Perhaps he really had matured as she said. 'You promised me we could go to the Richmonds' ball tomorrow night, don't forget.'

'Not the most exclusive of events, the Richmonds' ball,' Gregory observed, sitting up and taking notice.

'It would hardly answer our purpose if it was,' Phyllida retorted. 'Fenella Richmond enjoys being toadied to, which means she invites those who will do that, as well as the cream of society. We may be sure of finding her rooms supplied with any number of parents looking to buy a titled husband in return for their guineas.'

'Merchants. Mill owners. Manufacturers.' He sounded thoughtful, not critical, but even so, she felt defensive.

'Your sister is a shopkeeper, if the *ton* did but know it. But, yes, they will all be there and all set on insinuating themselves into society. If they think that Lady Richmond is wonderful, just imagine how they are going to enjoy meeting a handsome, single earl with a country house and a large estate. So be your most charming self, brother dear.'

Gregory snorted. 'I am always *charming*. That I have no trouble with. It is being good and responsible that is the challenge. Where have you been all day, Phyll?'

Best not to reveal that she had been looking for him. 'I was in Wapping, too, buying fans from the crew of an Indiaman just in from China.' *And being attacked by a weird crow and kissed by a beautiful man.* As she had all afternoon she resisted the urge to touch her mouth. 'I'll go and put this money in the safe and let Peggy know we're both in for dinner.'

Phyllida scooped up her things and retied her hat strings as she ran downstairs into the basement. 'Peggy?'

'Aye, Miss Phyllida?' Their cook-housekeeper emerged from the kitchen, wiping her hands. 'His lordship's home with a hangover, I see. Drink is a snare and an abomination.'

'We will both be in for dinner, if you please.' Phyllida was used to Peggy's dire pronouncements upon almost any form of enjoyment. 'And Gregory has brought both the rent and the wages home with him.' She counted money out onto the scrubbed pine table. 'There. That's yours for last month and this month and Jane's, too. I'll pay Anna myself.' Jane was the skinny maid of all work, Anna was Phyllida's abigail.

'Praise be,' Peggy pronounced as she counted coins into piles. 'Thank you, Miss Phyllida. And you'll be putting the rest of it away safe, I'm hoping.'

'I will. I'm just going to the shop, I'll be back in half an hour.'

'Rabbit stew,' Peggy called after her as she ran back upstairs. 'And cheesecakes.'

The day that had started so badly was turning out surprisingly well, she decided as she closed the front door, turned left along Great Ryder Street, diagonally across Duke Street and into Mason's Yard. The rent and the wages were paid, Gregory was finally behaving himself over the campaign to find him a rich wife and there were cheesecakes for dinner.

No one was around as she unlocked the back door of the shop, secured it behind her and made her way through into the front. The shutters were closed and the interior of the shop in shadow, but she could see the flicker of movement as carriages and horses passed along Jermyn Street. She would open tomorrow, Phyllida decided as she knelt before the cupboard, moved a stack of wrapping paper and lifted the false bottom. The safe was concealed beneath it, secure from intruders and her brother's 'borrowings' alike, and the roll of notes made a welcome addition to the savings that she secretly thought of as the Marriage Fund.

Gregory's marriage, not hers, of course. Phyllida secured the cupboard and, on a sudden impulse, opened a drawer and drew out a package. Indian incense sticks rolled out, each small bundle labelled in a script she could not read, along with a pencilled scribble in English.

*Rose, patchouli, lily, whitemusk, champa, frankincense... jasmine and sandalwood.* She pulled one of the sticks from the bundle and held it to her nose with a little shiver of recollection. It smelled clean and woody and exotic, just as he had. Dangerous and unsettling, for some inexplicable reason. Or perhaps that had been the scent of his skin, that beautiful golden skin.

It was nonsense, of course. He had kissed her, protected her—while taking his own amusement from the situation—and that was enough to unsettle anyone. There was no mystery to it.

Phyllida let herself out, locked up and hurried home.

It was not until she was changing in her bedchamber that she realised she had slipped the incense stick into her reticule.

It was a while since she had bought the bundle, so it was as well to test the quality of them, she supposed. The coating spluttered, then began to smoulder as she touched the tip of the stick to the flame and she wedged it into the wax at the base of the candle to hold it steady. Then she sat and resolutely did not think of amused green eyes while Anna, her maid, brushed out her hair.

She would act the shopkeeper tomorrow and then become someone else entirely for a few hours at Lady Richmond's ball. She was looking forward to it, even if she would spend the evening assessing débutantes and dowries and not dancing. Dancing, like dreams of green-eyed lovers and fantasies of marriage, were for other women, not her. Coils of sandalwood-scented smoke drifted upwards, taking her dreams with them.

# Chapter Two

'May I go shopping, *Mata*? I would like to visit the bazaar.'

'There are no bazaars, Sara. It is all shops and some markets.'

'There is one called the Pantheon Bazaar, Reade told me about it.'

Ashe lifted an eyebrow at his father as he poured himself some more coffee. 'It is not like an Indian bazaar. Much more tranquil, I am certain, and no haggling. It is more like many small shops, all together.'

'I know. Reade explained it to me while she was doing my hair this morning. But may I go out, *Mata*?'

'I have too much to do today to go with you.' Their mother's swift, all-encompassing glance around the gloomy shadows of what they had been informed was the *Small* Breakfast Parlour—capital letters implied— gave a fair indication of what she would be doing. Ashe had visions of bonfires in the back garden.

He murmured to his father, 'Fifty rupees that *Mata* will have the staff eating out of her hand by this time tomorrow and one hundred that she'll start redecorating within the week.'

'I don't bet on certainties. If she makes plans for disposing of these hideous curtains while she's at it, I'll be glad. I can't take you, Sara,' the marquess added as she turned imploring eyes on the male end of the table.

'I will,' Ashe said amiably. Sara was putting a brave face on it, but he could tell she was daunted as well as excited by this strange new world. 'I could do with a walk. But window shopping only, I'm not being dragged round shops while you dither over fripperies. I was going along Jermyn Street. That's got some reasonable shops, so Bates said, and I need some shaving soap.'

An hour later Sara was complaining, 'So *I* have to be dragged around shops while *you* dither about shaving soap!'

'You bought soap, too. Three sorts,' Ashe pointed out, recalling just why he normally avoided shopping with females like the plague. 'Look, there's a fashionable milliner's.'

He had no idea whether it was in the mode or not. Several years spent almost entirely in an Indian princely court was not good preparation for judging the ludicrous things English women put on their heads and he knew that anything seen in Calcutta was a good eighteen months out of date. But it certainly diverted Sara. She stood in front of the window and sighed over a confection of lace, feathers and satin ribbon supported on a straw base the size of a tea plate.

'No, you may not go in,' Ashe said firmly, tucking her arm under his and steering her across Duke Street. 'I will not be responsible for explaining to *Mata* why you have come home wearing something suitable for a lightskirt.'

'Doesn't London smell strange?' Sara remarked. 'No spices, no flowers. Nothing dead, no food vendors on the street.'

'Not around here,' he agreed. 'But this is the smart end of town. Even so, there are drains and horse manure if you are missing the rich aromas of street life. Now that's a good piece.' He stopped in front of a small shop, just two shallow bays on either side of a green-painted door. 'See, that jade figure.'

'There are all kinds of lovely things.' Sara peered into the depths of the window display. Small carvings and jewels were set out on a swirl of fabrics, miniature paintings rubbed shoulders with what he suspected were Russian icons, ancient terracotta idols sat next to Japanese china.

Ashe stepped back to read the sign over the door. '*The Cabinet of Curiosity.* An apt name. Look at that moonstone pendant—it is just the colour of your eyes. Shall we go in and look at it?'

She gave his arm an excited squeeze and whisked into the shop as he opened the door. Above their head a bell tinkled and the curtain at the back of the shop parted.

'Good morning, *monsieur, madame.*' The shopkeeper, it seemed, was a Frenchwoman. She hesitated as though she was surprised to see them, then came forwards.

Medium height, hair hidden beneath a neat cap, tinted spectacles perched on the end of her nose. Perfectly packaged in her plain, high-necked brown gown. *Very French*, he thought.

'May I assist you?' she asked and pushed the spectacles more firmly up her nose.

'We would like to look at the moonstone pendant, if you would be so good.'

'*Certainement. Madame* would care to sit?' She gestured to a chair as she came out from behind the counter, lifting an ornate chatelaine to select a key before opening the cabinet and laying the jewel on a velvet pad in front of Sara.

Ashe watched his sister examine the pendant with the care their mother had taught her. She was as discriminating about gemstones as he was and, however pretty the trinket, she would not want it if it was flawed.

His attention drifted, caught by the edge of awareness that he had always assumed was a hunter's instinct. Something was wrong…no, out of place. He shifted, scanning the small space of the shop. No one was watching from behind the curtain, he was certain there were only the three of them there.

The *vendeuse*, he realised, was watching him. Not the pendant for safekeeping, not Sara to assess a potential customer's reactions, but, covertly, him. *Interesting.* He shifted until he could see her in the mirrored surface of a Venetian cabinet. Younger than he had first thought, he concluded, seeing smooth, unlined skin, high cheekbones, eyes shadowed behind those tinted spectacles, a pointed little chin. She caught her lower lip between her teeth and moved her hands as though to stop herself clenching them. There was something very familiar about her.

'How much is this?' Sara asked and the woman turned and bent towards her. Something in the way she moved registered in his head. *Surely not?*

Ashe strolled across and stood at her shoulder as though interested in her answer. She shifted, apparently made uncomfortable by his nearness, but she did not look at him.

She named a price, Sara automatically clicked her tongue in rejection, ready to negotiate. He leaned closer and felt the Frenchwoman stiffen like a wary animal. She had brown hair, from what he could see of the little wisps escaping from that ghastly cap. They created an enticing veil over the vulnerable, biteable, nape of her neck.

'I would want the chain included for that,' Sara said.

He inhaled deeply. Warm, tense woman and… 'Jasmine,' Ashe murmured, close to the *vendeuse*'s ear. She went very still. Oh, yes, this was just like hunting and he had found game. 'You get around, *madame*.'

'My varied stock, you mean, *monsieur*?' She spoke firmly, without a tremor. Her nerves must be excellent. 'Indeed, it comes from all over the world. And, yes, the pendant suits your wife so well that I can include the chain in that price.'

'But—' Sara began.

'You want it, my dear?' Ashe interrupted her. 'Then we will take it.' Interesting, and subtly insulting, that his acquaintance from the quayside assumed he was married. Perversely he saw no reason to enlighten her immediately, and certainly not to pursue this further with Sara sitting there.

What sort of man did she think he was, to kiss and flirt with chance-met women if he had a wife at home? Ashe knew himself to be no saint, but he had been brought up with the example of marital fidelity before him daily and he had no time for men who were unfaithful to their wives.

Which was why he intended to choose with extreme care. This was England, not India, and flouting society's rules would not be excused here. The family were different enough as it was, with their mixed blood, his maternal grandfather's links to trade and his paternal grandfather's reputation for dissipation.

Ashe had a duty to marry, to provide the next heir, to enrich the family name and title with the right connections and the estate with lands and money. He glanced down at his sister, reminded yet again that her own hopes of a suitable, good marriage depended on respectability. But he would be tied to the woman who brought those connections and that dowry with her. There had to be mutual respect or it would be intolerable. Love he did not expect.

'This is your own shop?' he asked as he peeled off his gloves in order to take banknotes from the roll Perrott had provided. He calculated currency conversions in his head, valuing the stock he could see. Even at Indian prices there was a considerable investment represented on the shelves around him.

'Yes, *monsieur*.' She was doggedly sticking to her French pretence. Used to negotiating with hostile Frenchmen in India, he could admire her accent.

'Impressive. I was surprised that the name is the Cabinet of Curiosity, not *Curiosities*.' Without the conflicting stinks of the river and the alleyway the subtle odour of jasmine on her warm skin was filling his senses. His body began to send him unmistakable signals of interest.

'My intention is to provide stimulation to the intellect,' she said, returning him his change. Her bare fingers touched the palm of his hand and he curled his fist closed, trapping her.

'As well as of the senses?' he suggested. She went very still. Her fingers were warm, slender. Under his thumb he felt her pulse hammering. He was not alone in this reaction. *Stimulation to the senses, indeed.*

'To find the treasures here one needs curiosity,' she finished, her voice suddenly breathless. Her accent had slipped a trifle.

'You may be sure you have stimulated mine,' Ashe murmured. 'All of them. I will return, with or without my...sister.'

Her hand tensed in his and as suddenly relaxed. Oh, yes, she was as aware of him as he was of her and the news that he was unmarried had struck home.

'I must wrap the pendant, *monsieur*.' She gave a little tug and he released her. There was no wedding ring on those long slender fingers with their neat oval nails. The hunting instinct stirred again and with it certain parts of his body that were better kept under control when he was supposed to be escorting his sister on a blameless shopping expedition.

Ashe slipped the flat box into his breast pocket, resumed his gloves and waited for Sara to gather up her reticule and parasol. 'You open your shop every day?'

'*Non.* I open as the whim takes me, *monsieur*,' the lady of curiosities said, a little tart now and very French again. He had flustered her and she did not forgive that easily, it seemed. 'I am often away buying stock.'

'Down by the Pool of London, perhaps?'

She shrugged, an elegant gesture that made him wonder if she was, indeed, French. But her accent when they first met had been completely English, he recalled and she had slipped up just now. 'Anywhere that I can find treasures for my clients, *monsieur*. Good day, *monsieur, mademoiselle*.'

'*Au revoir,*' Ashe returned and was amused to see her purse her lips. She suspected, quite correctly, that he was teasing her.

Phylllda shot the bolt on the door and retreated into the back room. *Him. Here.* As though she had not had enough trouble trying, and failing, to get him out of her head. She spread out her right hand, the one he had captured in his own big brown fist. She had felt overpowered, an unexpected sensation. What was most unsettling was that it was not unwelcome. A strong, decisive man after Gregory's lazy indecision was…stimulating. And dangerous. She reminded herself that for all the charm he was a man and one who probably had no hesitation in seizing what he wanted if charm alone did not work. Men had no hesitation in using their superior strength to take advantage of a woman.

He had been without his devil-bird, but with a charming sister who was, it seemed, as bright as she was pretty. The wretch, after that kiss, to let her think he was with his wife! It did not mean he did not have one at home, of course. Not that she cared in the slightest.

But who was he? He had paid in cash, which must mean he was not one of the *ton*. If he had been, he would have simply handed her his card and expected her to send him an account. Besides, she had never seen him before yesterday and she knew everyone who was anyone, by sight at least. Whoever he was, he was wealthy. His clothes were, again, superb, with that hint of foreign styling. His sister, too, was dressed impeccably and the simple pearls at her neck and ears were of high quality.

A wealthy trader? If he was with the East India Company it might explain his presence at the docks. A ship owner, perhaps.

Phyllida realised she was twisting the chain of her chatelaine into a knot and released it with an impatient flick of her wrist. He was the first person who had connected any of the elements of her complicated life. But provided he was not in a position to link Mrs Drummond, the dealer who scoured the East End and the docks for treasures for the stock of Madame Deaucourt, owner of the Cabinet of Curiosity, with Phyllida Hurst, the somewhat shady sister of the Earl of Fransham, he was no danger, surely?

*Except for your foolish fantasies*, she scolded herself. She had never enjoyed being kissed before and that caress by the Customs House had been skilled, casually delivered as it had been. The man was a flirt of the worst kind, Phyllida told herself as she jammed the tinted spectacles back on her nose and went to open up the shop again.

And he must flirt with everything and anything in skirts, she decided, catching sight of herself in a mirror. He could hardly make the excuse that he had been so stunned by her beauty he had not known what he was doing. When properly dressed and coiffed she was, she flattered herself, not exactly an eyesore. But yesterday, in a plain stuff gown with her hair scraped back and hidden in that net, she should never have merited a second glance. Which was, of course, her intention. And it had taken him a while, even with those watchful green eyes, to recognise her in today's outfit.

The problem was that she found herself wishing with a positively reckless abandon that her nameless man *would* spare her a second glance. And that kind of foolishness threatened the entire plan of campaign she had set in motion at the age of seventeen and which had cost her so dear. *Idiot*, she lectured herself. *If he looks at you seriously it will be as a mistress, a possession, not a wife.* And marriage was only a dream, not a possibility, for her.

'*Bonjour, madame.*' She opened the door and dipped a respectful curtsy to Lady Harington, who swept in with a brisk nod. She was a regular customer who obviously had no idea that she had spent quite fifteen minutes in conversation with Phyllida in her respectable guise only two evenings previously at a musicale.

'I have received a small consignment of the most elegant fans from the Orient, *madame.*' She lifted them from their silk wrappings and laid them out on the counter. 'Each is unique and quite exclusive to myself. I am showing them only to clients of discernment.' *And they are very, very expensive*, she decided, seeing the avid glint in her ladyship's eyes. Earning the money to drag them back from the edge of ruin and to bring Gregory into complete respectability was everything. Nothing must be allowed to threaten that.

'Thank you for my present, Ashe.' Sara slid her hand under his elbow as they made their way from St James's Square and turned right into Pall Mall. 'Why did you let the shopkeeper believe we were married?'

'I corrected her soon enough. It is no concern of hers.' *She was interested, though.*

'You were flirting with her.'

'And what do you know of flirting, might I ask? You are not out yet.' One of the problems with being male, single and all that implied was that Ashe was only too aware of the thoughts, desires and proclivities of the other single males who were going to come into contact with his beautiful, friendly, innocent sister. It was enough to make him want to lock her up and hide the key for at least another five years.

'I was out in Calcutta. I went to parties and picnics and dances. Everything, in fact.' She tilted her head and sent him a twinkling smile that filled him with foreboding. 'It is just that you were in Kalatwah and didn't know what I was up to.'

'That is different. It is all much more formal here. All those rules and scandal lurking if we trip up on as much as one of them. Especially for you, which is unfair, but—'

'I know. Young ladies must be beyond reproach, as innocent as babies.' Sara sighed theatrically. 'Such a pity I am not an innocent.'

'*What?*' Ashe slammed to a halt, realised where he was and carried on walking. If he had to take ship back to India to dismember whoever had got his hands on his little sister, he would. 'Sarisa Melissa Herriard, who is he?' he ground out.

'No one, silly. I meant it theoretically. You don't think *Mata* is like those idiotic women who don't tell their daughters anything and expect them to work it all out on their wedding night, do you? Or leave them to get into trouble because they don't understand what men want.'

Ashe moaned faintly. No, of course their mother, raised as an Indian princess, and presumably schooled in all the theory of the ancient erotic texts, would have passed that wisdom on to her daughter as she reached marriageable age. He just did not want to think about it.

He had been away from home too long and his baby sister had grown up too fast. On board ship he hadn't realised. She had been her old enthusiastic, curious self and there had been no young men to flirt with except the unfortunate Mr Perrott, so Ashe had carried on thinking of her as the seventeen-year-old girl he had left when he went to their great-uncle's court. But she was twenty now. A woman.

'Then pretend, very hard, that you haven't a clue,' he said.

'Of course,' his oh-so-demure little sister said. 'So, were you flirting?'

'No. I do not flirt with plain French shopkeepers.'

'Hmm. I'm not so certain she *is* plain,' Sara said. 'I think she would like to appear so. Perhaps because she has trouble with rakish gentlemen like you.' They stopped before a rambling pile of red brick with two scarlet-coated guards standing in front. 'What on earth is that?' she asked before Ashe could demand why she considered him rakish and how she would know a rake if she saw one.

He had been doing his homework. 'St James's Palace. It is very old.'

'It is a sorry excuse for a palace, in my opinion—the most junior raja can do better than that.' Sara wrinkled her nose in disapprobation.

'Come on, we'll go through to the park.' Ashe took her past the guards before they could be arrested for *lèse-majesté* or whatever crime being rude about the sovereign's palaces constituted.

'So, are you looking for a mistress?' she enquired as they went through the improbably named Milkmaids' Passage and into Green Park.

'No!' *Yes.* But he certainly was not going to discuss that with his little sister. It was far too long since he had been with a woman. There had been women after Reshmi—he was not a monk, after all—but the voyage had lasted months and the ship might as well have been a monastery.

'You will be looking for a wife, though. *Mata* said you would be. At least there are lots more women in London to fall in love with than there were in Calcutta society.'

'I have no intention of falling in love. I need to find a wife suitable for a viscount.' And one who was heir to a marquisate at that.

'But Father and *Mata* made a love match. Oh look, cows wandering about. But they aren't sacred, are they?'

'Shouldn't think so.' He spared the livestock a glance. 'Not unless the Church of England has developed some very strange practices. Look, there are milkmaids or cow herds or something.

'Our parents met and fell in love before they knew Father's uncle had died, making grandfather the heir,' he reminded her. '*Mata* even ran away when she found out before the wedding because she did not think she would make a good marchioness.'

'I know, but it is ridiculous! She is clever and beautiful and brave,' Sara said fiercely. 'What more could be needed?

'She is the illegitimate daughter of an East India Company merchant and an Indian princess—not the usual English aristocratic lady, you must agree. She only agreed to marry Father and to take it on because she loves him—why do you think he stayed in India until the last possible moment?'

'I thought it was because he and his father hated each other.'

That was one way of describing a relationship where a bitter wastrel had packed his own seventeen-year-old son off to India against his will.

'Father made his own life, his own reputation, in India. He never wanted to come back, especially with *Mata*'s anxieties, but they know it is their duty.' He shrugged. 'And one day, a long way away, I hope, it will be mine. And I'm not putting another woman through what our mother is having to deal with. So much to learn, the realisation that people are talking behind her back, assessing whether she is up to it, is well bred enough, watching for every mistake.'

'I had not realised it would be that bad. I am an innocent after all,' Sara said with a sigh. 'I will do my best not to add to their worries.' She flashed him a smile. 'I can be good if I try. And I suppose if you find the right wife she will be a help to *Mata*, won't she?'

'Yes,' Ashe agreed, wishing it did not feel so much like buying a horse. 'She can take on some of the duties of chaperon for you once we are married. And a suitable bride will have social and political connections.' He knew little about English politics as yet, but the intrigues of an Indian court seemed simple in comparison to what he had read.

'I want to find someone like *Mata* found Father. Poor Ashe.' Sara squeezed his arm companionably. 'No love match for you.'

He should have answered faster, made a joke of

it, because Sara knew him too well. 'Oh, was there someone?'

'Yes. Perhaps. I don't know.' He was mumbling. He never mumbled. Ashe got a grip on himself. 'It never got that far.'

'Who?' When he didn't answer she asked, 'At Kalatwah?'

*Reshmi. The Silken One. Great dark eyes, a mouth of sinful promise, a heart full of joy and laughter.* 'Yes.'

'You left her?'

'She died.' Two years ago. It was impossible, he had known it was doomed from the start and finally he had told her, far too abruptly because he didn't want to do it. They said it was an accident that she had trodden on a *krait* hidden in the dry grass and he tried to believe that it *was* chance, that she would never have chosen to kill herself in such a ghastly, painful way. But his conscience told him that she had been too distracted, too full of grief to be as careful as she normally was.

It was his fault. Since Reshmi he had organised his liaisons with clinical care, generously but with no misunderstandings on either side. And no attachments either.

'It was a long time ago, I don't think of her now.' He tried not to, because when he did there was still the ache of her loss, the memory of the sweetness of her lips on his. The guilt at having had so much power over another person's happiness and having failed her.

He would never find it again, that almost innocent feeling of first love. It had been cut short, like an amputation, and that, and the guilt, was why it hurt. He would never be that young, or foolish, again, which was a mercy because love seemed to hurt both parties. How would the survivor cope with the pain if one of his parents outlived the other?

Sara leaned into him and rested her head against his shoulder for a moment, too sensitive to ask more. After a moment she said, 'Look, they are milking the cows. Is that not truly incredible? Right by the palace!' She let go of his arm and ran across the grass, laughing, so he strode after her over the green grass, shaking off the heat and colours of India. That was the past

# Chapter Three

'How elegantly your daughter dances, Mrs Fogerty.' Judging by the amount of money lavished on Miss Fogerty's clothes and the almost painful correctness of her manners, *elegant* was likely to be a very acceptable compliment to her doting mama.

'Why, thank you.' The matron simpered and made room on the upholstered bench to allow Phyllida to sit down. Her efforts to recall to whom she was speaking were painfully visible, but Phyllida did not enlighten her. 'Her partner is an excellent dancer.' Mrs Fogerty watched Gregory closely.

'The Earl of Fransham? Yes, indeed. A very old family.' Phyllida waved her exquisite fan gently and allowed Mrs Fogerty a good look at the antique cameos she was wearing. All part of her stock, although now when she wanted to sell them she would have to go to another dealer or they might be recognised.

'You are related to him?' The older woman was avid for details.

'A connection.' If it came to serious courtship, Phyllida was resigned to fading completely into the background. 'Large estates, of course, and the most magnificent country house.' *With dozens of buckets under the drips, death watch beetle in the roof and pleasure gardens resembling the darkest jungle.* 'Although,' she lowered her voice, 'like so many of the really old noble families, the resources to invest are sadly lacking.'

'Indeed?' Mrs Fogerty narrowed her eyes and regarded Gregory's handsome figure and impeccable tailoring with sharpened interest. To Phyllida's delight she had picked up on the hint that the earl was in the market for a rich wife and was not in a position to be picky about bloodlines.

Mr Fogerty, a self-made Lancashire mill owner, was high on her list of wealthy parents in search of an aristocratic son-in-law and Emily Fogerty seemed bright and pleasant, although perhaps not strong-willed enough to deal with Gregory. She was not the only one under consideration, however, nor her favourite. After a few minutes of conversation Phyllida excused herself and drifted off in search of Miss Millington, the sole child of banker Sir Ralph Millington and her ideal candidate.

'Phyllida Hurst!' The Dowager Countess of Malling stood close to the main entrance of the Richmonds' ballroom.

'Ma'am.' She curtsied, smiling. The old dragon scared half the *ton* into instant flight, but she amused Phyllida, who knew the kind heart behind the abrasive exterior. 'May I say what a very handsome toque you are wearing?'

'I look a fright in it.' The old lady patted the erection on her head and smiled evilly. 'But it amuses me. Now, what are you up to these days, my dear?'

She was some kind of connection of Phyllida's

mother and had done a great deal to mitigate the damage of her parents' scandalous marriage and make the Hurst siblings acceptable to the *ton*, so Phyllida always made time to relay gossip, have her gowns criticised and enquire after the Dowager's pug dogs, Hercules and Samson.

'Shall we sit down, ma'am?'

'And miss all the arrivals? Nonsense.' Lady Malling fetched Phyllida a painful rap on the wrist with her fan. 'Give me your arm, child. Now, who is this? Oh, only Georgina Farraday with her hair even blonder than normal. Who does she think she is deceiving?' The set had just finished, the music stopped and her voice cut clearly through the chatter.

Phyllida suppressed a smile. 'I dare not comment, ma'am,' she murmured.

'Pish! Ah, this is more interesting. Now *that* is what I call a fine figure of a man.'

Phyllida had to agree. The gentleman standing just inside the entrance was in his late fifties, but she doubted he had an inch of spare flesh on his lean, broad-shouldered body. His hair was silver-gilt, his evening dress was cut with an expensive simplicity that set off his athletic frame and on his arm was a striking golden-skinned woman with a mass of dark brown hair piled in an elaborate coiffure.

'He is certainly handsome. And so is his lady—see how beautifully she moves. She must be foreign—Italian, do you think?' And indeed, the curvaceous figure in amber silk made every other woman in the room look clumsy as she came forwards, a faint smile on her lips, head high. There was something faintly familiar about the couple, although surely she would have remembered if she had seen either of them before?

'Of course,' the dowager said with a sharp nod of satisfaction as she made the connection. 'Not Italian, Indian. That, my dear, must be the Marquess and Marchioness of Eldonstone. He hasn't been in the country for forty years, I should think. At outs with his father, for which no one could blame him. Now the old reprobate is dead they have come home.

'The wife, so they say, is the child of an Indian princess and a John Company nabob. Interesting to see what society makes of her!'

'Or she of society.' The marchioness looked like a panther in a room full of domestic cats. A perfectly well-behaved panther and a collection of pedigree cats, of course, but the fur would fly if they tried to tweak her tail, Phyllida decided, admiring the lady's poise.

Then the couple came further into the room and she gasped. Behind them were the man from the dockside and his companion from the shop. His sister. No wonder the older couple had looked familiar. Their son—for surely he could be nothing else—had his father's rangy height and broad shoulders, his mother's dark brown hair and gilded skin. The daughter's hair was the gold her father's must once have been and she moved with the same alluring sway as her mother, a panther cub just grown up. The moonstone pendant she had bought from Phyllida lay glowing on her bosom.

Her shock must have been audible. Beside her the dowager chuckled richly. 'Now that will be the viscount. The heir to a marquisate and those looks to go with the title—there is a young man who will cause a flutter in the dovecotes!'

'Indeed,' Phyllida agreed. *Indeed!* 'The daughter looks delightful, do you not think?' She felt momentarily dizzy. She had dreamt about this man and here he was, in all his dangerous splendour. Dangerous to a spinster's equilibrium and even more dangerous to a spinster with secrets.

'Pretty gel. Got style. They all have. I doubt it is *London* style though, which is going to be entertaining,' the old lady pronounced. 'I shall make myself known. Coming, my dear?'

'I do not think so. Excuse me, ma'am.' Phyllida disengaged her arm and began to sidle backwards into the throng, all gaping at the newcomers while pretending not to.

*Oh, my heavens.* Phyllida sat down in the nearest empty alcove and used her fan in earnest. He—the Viscount Whatever—was a member of the *ton* after all and, with a sister obviously ready to be launched, the family would be here for the Season. He would be everywhere she went, at every social event.

Was there any hope that he might not recognise her? She strove to collect herself and think calmly. People saw what they expected to see—she had proved that over and over again as she served society ladies in the Cabinet of Curiosity. He had never seen her wearing anything other than the drabbest, most neutral day dress, and never with her hair exposed.

Phyllida studied her reflection in the nearest mirrored surface and stopped herself chewing her lower lip in agitation. That was better. There was nothing to connect the elegantly gowned and poised young lady who moved so easily in fashionable society with either the flustered woman he had kissed on the dockside or the French shopkeeper.

And going into hiding for the rest of the Season was not an option, either, there was a match to be made. Phyllida unfurled her fan with a defiant flourish and set out in search of Miss Millington and her substantial dowry.

She would circulate around the room in the same direction as the Eldonstone party and that would ensure she never came face to face with, as her *alto ego* Madame Deaucourt would doubtless call him, *Le Vicomte Dangereux*. At least he hadn't brought his devil-bird to the ball—that would have caused a stir, indeed.

'There would not appear to be any difficulty in attracting young ladies to you, Ashe,' his mother said with her wicked chuckle.

'I fear I am only getting the attention of Father's rejects,' he murmured in her ear. 'You are going to have to do something soon or he will be carried off by saucy widows and amorous matrons.'

'Nonsense, Nicholas can look after himself.' Anusha Herriard put her hand on Ashe's forearm and nodded to where Sara was the centre of an animated group of young ladies with an attendant circle of hopeful men. 'As can your sister, I think.'

Lady Richmond had begun the introductions, but the Herriards had soon found themselves absorbed into the throng with one new acquaintance introducing them to the next. 'This is a crush,' Ashe grumbled under his breath. 'At least at Kalatwah all one had to deal with was the odd assassination attempt and treacherous French diplomats.'

'You go and flirt with some young ladies, darling,' his mother said. 'That will cheer you up. I will rescue your father and keep an eye on Sara.'

Ashe grinned at her and began to stroll along the edge of the ballroom. As an unaccompanied male he was unable to approach any lady to whom he had not been introduced, which was curiously restful. There had been few ladies on their ship and he had been re-called from Kalatwah with too much urgency to reac-quaint himself with European society in Calcutta, so he was finding the presence of so many highly sociable women strange.

*Pleasantly strange*, he thought, allowing his gaze to skim over white bosoms exposed by low-cut gowns, unveiled faces, unmarried girls talking uninhibitedly to men not of their own family. He'd be used to it soon enough, he thought, making eye contact with a strik-ing blonde who held his gaze for a daring second too long before lowering demure lashes over her blue eyes.

A flash of clear green, like leaves unfurling beside a waterhole, attracted his attention. The unmarried girls were all wearing white or pastel gowns, the matrons strong jewel colours for the most part. That green gown was unusual, delightful in its freshness. Ashe propped one shoulder against a pillar and watched as its owner stood and talked with another lady.

The backs of these gowns were almost as intriguing as their low-cut fronts, he was coming to think. With their wearers' hair piled high, the columns of white necks, the vulnerable napes, the tantalising loose curls or dangling earrings all had a subtle erotic charm.

It was definitely too long since he had lain with a woman. Ashe shifted against the pillar, but did not take his eyes off that particular neck even though it made the tension in his groin worse. The lady in the green gown had a mass of shiny brown hair caught up in a knot with a single ringlet left to fall on her shoulder. He imagined curling it around one finger, feeling its caress like raw silk. He would pull each pin from her hair and the whole mass would come down, spilling over his hands, veiling her breasts as he freed her from the verdant silk...

A tall young man joined the two ladies and Ashe saw a resemblance between him and the brown-haired charmer at once. High cheekbones, straight noses, that dark hair. She seemed to be introducing the man to her companion and after a moment they walked on to the floor together to join the next set that was forming. The brunette watched as the dance struck up and then strolled away.

Ashe narrowed his eyes as she wandered along the edge of the dance floor, stopping now and then to chat. Three years in an environment where women habitually covered their faces with their *dupattas*, long semi-transparent scarves, had left him able to identify individuals by their walk, by their posture, their gestures. And he had met that woman before somewhere.

*But where?* Intrigued, Ashe began to shadow her along the opposite edge of the ballroom. Despite her fashionably languid progress she had an air of suppressed energy about her, as though she would rather run than walk, as if there was not quite enough time in the day for all she wanted to do. He was becoming fanciful, but her quick, expressive gestures when she stopped to talk, the direct way she resumed her trajectory when she parted from each acquaintance, attracted him. He liked energy and purpose.

'Clere.'

He was so caught up in his pleasantly erotic pursuit it took him a moment to recall that was him. Ashe stopped and nodded to the man who had hailed him. They had been introduced earlier. A baron… Lord Hardinge, that was it. 'Hardinge.'

'Enjoying yourself?'

'Frantically remembering names, if the truth be told,' Ashe lied to cover his hesitation. He liked the look of the other man who seemed bright, alert, with a humorous glint in his eyes.

'Stuck with anyone in particular?'

'I was wondering,' Ashe said, 'who the brunette in the pale-green gown was. She looks familiar, but I can't place her.'

'Want an introduction?' The other man was already heading in her direction. 'She's Fransham's sister.'

And who was he? The tall man she had seen on to the dance floor, presumably.

'Miss Hurst?' Hardinge said as they reached her. She turned as Ashe was working that out. *Miss*, so her brother was of the rank of a viscount or lower. That didn't narrow the field much.

'Lord Hardinge.' Her smile was immediate and genuine. Ashe registered warm brown eyes, white teeth, attractive colour on her high cheekbones… And then she turned to smile at him and went pale, as though the blood had drained out of her.

'Miss Hurst? Are you quite well?' Hardinge put out one hand, but she flicked her fan open and plied it vigorously in front of her face.

'I am so sorry, just a moment's faintness. The heat.' Her voice was low and husky. Ashe found himself instantly attracted, even as his senses grappled to make sense of what he was seeing. The fan wafted the subtle, sweet odour of jasmine to him and only yesterday those brown eyes, now shielded by lowered lids and fluttering fan, had glared indignantly into his as he lifted his mouth from hers. *That mouth.*

'Allow me to assist you to a chair, Miss Hurst.' He had his hand under her arm, neatly removed the fan from her fingers and was waving it, even before the other man could step forwards. 'There we are.' In front of them a window embrasure was shielded by an array of potted palms. The casement had been opened several inches for ventilation and there was a bench seat just big enough for two. 'It is all right, Hardinge, I have her. Perhaps you could get hold of some lemonade?' That would get rid of him for a few minutes.

Miss Hurst did not resist as he guided her through the fronds to the padded seat. For a moment he thought she was, indeed, overcome, but as he sat beside her he saw from her expression that she wanted privacy just as much as he did.

'You!' she hissed with real indignation. 'What do you think you are doing?'

Ashe raised an eyebrow in deliberate provocation. The angrier she was, the more off guard she would be. 'What was I doing when we have met?' He began to count off points on his fingers. 'Disembarking from a ship, shopping with my sister, attending a ball with my family. All perfectly innocent activities, Miss Hurst, or whatever your real name is. What is your objection to them?'

'You are following me... No, you are not, are you? It is just horrible coincidence.' She sighed, all the fight going out of her, and leaned back against the heavy brocade swags of the curtains as if suddenly weary.

'I have been called many things, but never a horrible coincidence,' Ashe said. 'Ah, here is Hardinge with the lemonade. Thank you so much. Miss Hurst is feeling a little better, I believe. I'll just wait with her a while so no one disturbs her.' He smiled the frank smile that seemed to lull most people into believing him completely straightforward.

There was patently no space in the alcove. The other man handed over the glass with good grace. 'Clere, Miss Hurst.' He took himself off, leaving them alone in their leafy shelter.

'Thank you, Lord Clere.' Miss Hurst took the glass, drank and set it down on the cill. 'If it were not for you, I would not require reviving.'

Ashe was tempted to observe that all the girls said that, but one glance at her expression warned him that perhaps humour was best avoided. 'Hardinge never got the opportunity to introduce me. How do you know my name?' Had she been asking about him?

'I know your title, that is all, and he just called you Clere. I saw you come in with your family and Lady Malling deduced who you all were. I was attempting to avoid you,' she added bitterly, apparently with the intent of flattening any self-congratulation that she might be interested in him.

'My name is Ashe Herriard, Miss Hurst. Have you any other disguises I am likely to meet with?'

'No, you have viewed them all.' She regarded him, her head tipped a little to one side. He was reminded of Lucifer assessing a strange object for its potential as food or plaything. 'Ashe. Is that an Indian name? I know a trader down at the docks called Ashok. He has been here for years and has an extensive business, but he told me he came from Bombay.' She smiled. 'A bit of a rogue.'

'No, that element of my name is from my paternal grandmother's family. If you want the lot I am George Ashbourne Talish Herriard.'

'And Talish means?'

'Lord of the earth.'

'That seems…appropriate,' Miss Hurst observed astringently. She was still leaning back, gently fanning herself, but the tension was coming off her in waves.

'It is somewhat high-flown,' Ashe agreed. 'After my great-grandfather, the Raja of Kalatwah.' He might as well get that out of the way now.

'Truly?' Miss Hurst sat up straight, dark arched brows lifting. 'Does that make you a prince? Should I be curtsying?' That last, he could tell, was sarcasm.

'It made my grandmother a princess and it made my mother, who had an English father, confused,' he explained and surprised a laugh from her. 'I am merely a viscount with a courtesy title.'

'She is very beautiful, your mother.' He nodded. 'And your father is exceedingly handsome. I imagine most of the women in the room have fallen in love with him.'

'They will have to get past my mother first and she is not the demurely serene lady she appears.' He stretched out his long legs and made himself comfortable. On the other side of their jungle screen the ball was in full, noisy swing. Cool air flowed through the gap in the window, wafting sensual puffs of jasmine scent and warm woman to him. There were considerably worse places to be.

'Demure? She makes me think of a panther,' Miss Hurst observed.

'Appropriate,' he agreed. 'What is your first name? It seems hardly fair not to tell me when you know mine.'

She studied him, her brown eyes wary. 'Indian informality, Lord Clere?'

'Brazen curiosity, Miss Hurst.'

That produced another gurgle of laughter, instantly repressed, as though she regretted letting her guard down. 'Phyllida. It is somewhat of a burden to me, I have to confess.'

'It is a pretty name. And have I met Phyllida Hurst on a quayside, in a shop and in this ballroom? Or are there two other names you have not told me?'

'I will reveal no more, Lord Clere.'

'No?' He held her gaze for a long moment, then let his eyes roam over her, from the top of her elaborate coiffure, past the handsome cameos displayed on the pale, delicious, swell of her bosom, down over the curves of her figure in the fresh green silk to the kid slippers that showed below her hem. 'That is a pity.'

# Chapter Four

Colour rose over Miss Hurst's bosom, up her throat to stain her cheeks. It was delicious, Ashe thought, like the flush of pomegranate juice over iced sherbet on a hot day. She was no wide-eyed innocent if she took the meaning of his glance and words so promptly. But then she was obviously no sheltered society miss.

How old was she? Twenty-five, twenty-six? Attractive, bright, stylish, but not married. *Why not?* he wondered. *Something to do with her secret lives, no doubt.*

'I would very much appreciate it if you did not mention that we had met before this evening, my lord.' She said it quite calmly, but Ashe suspected that it was a matter of far more importance than she was revealing and that she hated having to ask him.

'Members of the *ton* are not expected to be shop-keepers, I assume?'

'Precisely.'

'Hmm. Pity my maternal grandfather was a nabob, then.' He was unconcerned what people thought of his ancestry, but he was interested in how she reacted.

'If he was indecently rich, and is now dead, there is

absolutely nothing for the heir to a marquisate to worry about. Society is curiously accommodating in its prejudices.' Her expression was bleak. 'At least, so far as gentlemen are concerned. Ladies are another matter altogether.'

'So I could ruin you with this piece of gossip?'

'Yes, as you know perfectly well. Ladies are not shopkeepers, nor do they walk about anywhere, let alone the docks, unescorted. Did you spend much time as a boy pulling the wings off flies, Lord Clere?'

Ashe felt an unfamiliar stab of conscience. This was, quite obviously, deathly serious to Miss Hurst. But it was a mystery why a lady should be in business at all. Was she so short of pin money? 'I am sorry, I had no intention of torturing you. You have my word that I will not speak of this to anyone.'

The music stopped and dancers began to come off the floor. Another set had ended and he realised he should not be lurking behind the palms with Phyllida Hurst any longer. Someone might notice and assume they had an assignation. He could dent her reputation. 'Will you dance, Miss Hurst?'

He hoped to Heaven it was something he *could* dance. He was decidedly rusty and the waltz had not reached Calcutta by the time they left. He was going to have to join in Sara's lessons.

'I do not dance,' Miss Hurst said. 'Please, do not let me detain you.'

'I was going in any case. It would be more discreet. But you mean you *never* dance?'

'I do not enjoy it,' she said.

*Liar.* All the time they had been together on the window seat her foot had been tapping along with the music without her realising. She wanted to dance and for some reason would not. *Interesting.* Ashe stood up. 'Then I will wish you good evening, Miss Hurst. Perhaps we will meet window shopping in Jermyn Street one day.'

'I fear not. It is not a street where I can afford to pay the prices asked. Good evening, Lord Clere.'

He bowed and took himself off, well clear of her hiding place. He watched the couples whirling in the waltz, concluding that professional tuition was most definitely called for before he ventured on to the floor. After an interval Miss Hurst emerged and strolled off in the opposite direction.

Ashe wondered if there were any more unmarried ladies around with that combination of looks, style, spirit and wit. He had expected all the eligible young women to be cut from the same pattern: pretty, simpering, dull. Perhaps hunting for a wife would be more interesting than he had imagined. Miss Hurst had her scandalous secrets, and she was a little older than most of the unmarried girls. But she was certainly still well within her childbearing years and a shop was easy enough to dispose of.

He found his parents, who were watching Sara talk to a group of just the kind of girls he was thinking of so disparagingly. 'There you are.' His mother put her hand on his arm to detain him. 'Lady Malling, may I introduce my son, Viscount Clere. Ashe, this is the Dowager Countess of Malling.'

He shook hands and exchanged pleasantries. This was the lady who had been with Phyllida when they had arrived at the ball. As he thought it he saw her again, talking to the young man he had guessed was her brother.

'Perhaps you can tell me who that is, ma'am. The tall man with the dark brown hair just to the left of the arrangement of lilies.'

'Gregory Hurst, Earl of Fransham,' the dowager said promptly. 'A good-looking rogue.'

Had his study of the *Peerage* been so awry? 'I am a trifle confused. I thought the lady with him was his sister, but she was introduced to me as Miss Hurst and if he is an earl…'

'Ah.' Lady Malling lowered her voice. 'She *is* his full, elder, sister. However, I regret to say their parents neglected to marry until after her birth. Such a scandal at the time! It makes her, unfortunately, baseborn.'

'But she is received?'

'Oh, yes, in most places except court, of course. Or Almack's. Charming girl. But she won't make much of a marriage, if any. Even leaving aside the accident of birth, she has not a penny piece for a dowry—goodness knows how she manages to dress so well or where those cameos came from—and Fransham is wild to a fault and no catch as a son-in-law. Except for the title, of course. He may attach a rich cit's daughter with that.'

*Hell and damnation.* Eccentricity was one thing, but illegitimacy and no dowry on top of dubious commercial activities were all the complete opposites of what he had set out as essential qualities for a wife. Suddenly doing his duty seemed considerably less appealing.

Even as he thought it Phyllida turned and caught his eye. Her mouth curled in a slight smile and she put her hand on her brother's arm as though to draw attention to the Herriard party.

Still wrestling with that revelation, Ashe raised one brow, unsmiling, and inclined his head a fraction.

The smile vanished as she glanced from him to Lady Malling, then her chin came up and she turned away. Even at that distance he could see the flags of angry colour on her cheeks.

*You clumsy fool.* That had been ungentlemanly, even if it had been unintentional. He had been surprised and disappointed and… *No excuses. You were a bloody idiot*, he told himself. Now what? He could hardly go over and apologise, he had already dug himself into a deep enough hole and what could he say? *So sorry, I have just realised you are illegitimate and poor as a church mouse and absolutely no use to me as a wife, but I didn't mean to snub you.*

And then he stopped thinking about himself and looked at his mother, the offspring of an Indian princess and a John Company trader with an estranged English wife.

'Illegitimacy is not a barrier to being received, then,' she observed as though reading his mind.

One glance at Lady Malling told him she knew exactly what the marchioness's parentage was. 'Goodness, no,' the older woman said. 'It all depends on the parents and the deportment of the person concerned. And rank.'

'And money,' his mother observed coolly.

'Oh, indeed.' The dowager chuckled. Her eyes barely flickered in the direction of the suite of stunning Burmese sapphires his mother was wearing. 'Society can always make rules and bend them to suit itself. Do tell me, which are your days for receiving, Lady Eldonstone?'

'Tuesday, Wednesday and Friday,' *Mata* said. Only her family would know she had made that up on the spur of the moment. 'I do hope we will see you soon in Berkeley Square, Lady Malling.'

'Be sure I will call.'

Ashe looked back across the room. Phyllida Hurst had vanished.

*The bigoted beast.* Phyllida slipped through the crowd and into the ladies' retiring room before she betrayed her humiliation by marching straight over and slapping Ashe Herriard's beautiful face for him.

He had flirted—worse than flirted on the quayside— he had joked with her this evening, promised to keep her secret and then, the moment he discovered who she was, snubbed her with a cut direct.

She flung herself down on a stool in front of a mirror and glared at her own flushed expression. *Stupid to let myself dream for a moment that I was a débutante flirting with a man who might offer marriage. Stupid to dream of marriage at all.* What had come over her to forget the anguish of that struggle to resign herself when she had faced the fact that she would never marry? *I will not cry.*

'Is anything wrong?' She had not noticed it was Miss Millington on the next stool.

'Men,' Phyllida responded bitterly as she jabbed pins into her hair.

'Oh dear. One in particular or all of them? Only I liked your brother very much, Miss Hurst, he is such a good dancer and so amusing. He has not made you angry, surely?'

'Gregory? No, not at all.' Gregory was being a positive paragon this evening. 'No, just some tactless, top-lofty buck. I hope,' she added vengefully, 'that his too-tight silk breeches split.'

Miss Millington collapsed in giggles. 'Wouldn't that be wonderful? I believe the gentlemen wear nothing beneath them, they are made of such thin knitted silk. What a shocking revelation!'

Phyllida imagined a half-naked Lord Clere for a moment, visualised those long legs and taut buttocks, then caught Miss Millington's eye in the glass and succumbed to laughter, too. 'Oh dear. He is very good-looking and has a fine figure, but I suppose it is too much to hope for.'

The other young woman hesitated. 'I wonder if you might care to call on Mama, Miss Hurst. Perhaps it is forward of me, but I think we could be friends.'

Phyllida cast a hasty glance around the room, but they were alone at one end. 'United in our desire to study Classical statuary, or perhaps anatomy?' she asked wickedly. 'I would like that very much. Will you not call me Phyllida?'

'And I am Harriet.' Miss Millington fished in her reticule. 'Here is Mama's card. She receives on Tuesdays and Thursdays.'

'Thank you, I look forward to it.' Feeling considerably soothed, Phyllida dusted rice powder lightly over her flushed cheeks and went out to look for Gregory.

They found each other almost immediately, both, it seemed, ready to go home. 'I have done my duty by all six of the young ladies you listed for me,' he said as he helped her with her cloak in the lobby. 'If I stay any longer I will get confused between bankers' daughters, mill-owners' heiresses and the offspring of naval captains awash with prize money.'

'Did you like Miss Millington?' Phyllida asked as he handed her into a hackney.

'Miss Millington? She's the tall brunette with a nice laugh and good teeth. She has a certain style about her.'

'I have good news. She thinks you are a fine dancer, has invited me to call and we are now on first-name terms. I really like her, Gregory.'

'I did, too,' he admitted.

'Now all we have to do is to make sure she falls in love with you and that you do not fall into any scandals that will alarm her fond papa.'

'And we will do the difficult things after breakfast, will we?' he asked with a chuckle. 'I'll do my best to be a good lad, Phyll.'

*Please*, she thought. *And fall in love, for Harriet's sake*. And then she could retreat to the little dower house in the park and spend her time finding items for her shop, for which she would employ a manager. She would be independent, removed enough not to cause a newly respectable, and wealthy, Earl of Fransham any embarrassment and free from the deceits and dangers of her current situation.

It all seemed so simple. *Too simple? No, we can do it*.

Phyllida managed to maintain her mood of optimism through the short journey home, a cup of tea by her bedchamber fire and the rituals of undressing and hair brushing.

But when she blew out the candle, lay back and shut her eyes, the image against her closed lids was not of a happy bridal couple in a cloud of orange blossom, but Ashe Herriard's disdainful face as he watched her across the ballroom floor.

*Bigoted, arrogant beast*, she thought as she punched the pillow. *Your opinion isn't worth losing a wink of sleep over and so I shall tell you if I am ever unfortunate to meet you again*.

* * *

At five o'clock the next morning Phyllida was not certain how many winks of sleep she had lost, but it was far too many and lost not to constructive thoughts or pleasant half-dreams, but a miserable mixture of embarrassment and desire. She pushed herself up against the piled pillows to peer at the little bedside clock in the dim light. Quarter past five.

It was hopeless to try to get back to sleep. The best she might hope for was to toss restlessly, remembering the heat of Ashe Herriard's mouth on hers, his long-limbed elegance as he sat on the window seat. It was bad enough to have thoughts like that without entertaining them for a man who despised her for an accident of birth.

Phyllida threw back the covers and got out of bed to look through the gap in the curtains. It was going to be a nice day. If she could not sleep, at least she could get some fresh air and exercise. A walk in Green Park would relax her and put her in a positive frame of mind for the morning.

The water in the ewer was cold, of course, but that did not matter. She scrambled into a plain walking dress and half-boots, tucked her hair into a net, took her bonnet by its ribbons and threw a shawl around her shoulders.

Anna would be stirring soon, making herself breakfast down in the basement kitchen. Her maid liked to start the day well ahead of herself, as she put it. They could have breakfast together and then go out.

Anna was already halfway down the stairs. 'What are you doing up and about, Miss Phyllida?'

'Joining you for breakfast. Then I want to go for a walk.'

'Not by yourself, I'm hoping!' The maid went to the pump and filled the big kettle. She was in her forties, plain, down to earth and with a past she never spoke of.

'No, even at this hour someone might see me, I suppose, and that would be a black mark against my impeccable reputation.' Phyllida lifted half a loaf from the bread crock and looked for the knife.

'We wouldn't want to be risking that, now would we?' Anna enquired sardonically. She had been with Phyllida for six years now, knew about the shop and was not afraid to say what she thought about her mistress's life.

'No, we wouldn't,' Phyllida agreed, equally straight-faced. 'So I'll have a nice brisk walk and you can take a rug and a journal and sit on one of the benches beside the reservoir so the proprieties will be observed.'

It was just after six when they set out, weaving through the grid of streets that would take them into Green Park. Around them the St James's area was waking up. Maids swept front steps, others, yawning, set out with empty baskets to do the early marketing. Delivery carts were pulling up at the back entrances for the numerous clubs, hells and shops that served this antheap of aristocrats, rakehells, high-class mistresses and respectable households. The sprawl covered the gentle slopes down to the old brick Tudor palace of St James and, beyond it, St James's Park.

That would be too risky for an early-morning walk, Phyllida knew. Dolly mops and all their sisters of the night would be emerging from their places of business in the shrubberies, along with the occasional guardsman hurrying back to barracks having served a different kind of clientele altogether.

The early riders would make for the long tracks of Hyde Park, leaving Green Park as a quiet backwater until at least nine. 'You can sit and read while I go past the lodge and the small pond down to Constitution Hill and back,' Phyllida suggested as they turned up the Queen's Walk towards Piccadilly. 'Unless you want to come with me?'

'You look in the mood for walking out a snit,' Anna observed. 'You'll do that better alone. Who upset you?'

'Oh, just some wretched lordling newly arrived in town and shocked to the core to discover he's been flirting all unwittingly with a baseborn woman.'

'More fool he. You shouldn't let him upset you.' There was nothing to say to that, but Anna seemed to read plenty into Phyllida's silence. 'I suppose you were liking him up to then.'

'Well enough.' She shrugged.

'Handsome, is he?'

'Oh, to die for and well he knows it.' And he had seemed kind. He had a sense of humour, he loved his sister, he was eminently eligible. If she had not been who she was, then this morning she would have woken hoping for a bouquet from him by luncheon. What would it be like to be courted by a man like that, to hope for a proposal of marriage, to look forward to a future of happiness and children?

'A good brisk walk, then, and some stones to kick instead of his foolish head.' Anna surveyed the benches. 'That one will do me, right in the sun.'

'Thank you, Anna.' The maid's brisk common sense

shook her out of her self-indulgent wonderings. 'If you get chilled, come and meet me.'

She waved and set off diagonally along the path towards the Queen's House on the far side of the Park. The early sunlight glinted off the white stone in the distance and the standard hung limp against the flagstaff in the still air. Phyllida breathed in the scents of green things breaking their winter sleep to thrust through the earth. That was better. When she was fully awake, feeling strong and resolved, then the weakening dreams could be shut safely away.

Rooks wheeled up from the high trees where they were building nests, jackdaws tumbled like acrobats through the air, courting or playing. Ahead of her the magpies had found something that had died during the night, a rat or a rabbit, she supposed, eyeing their squabbles with distaste as they fought for unsavoury scraps. She would have to detour off the path to avoid the mess.

As though a stone had been thrown into the midst of them the birds erupted up into the air, flapping and screeching at something that landed right next to their prize. For a second she thought it must be a bird of prey, then it turned its grey head and huge black beak in her direction, assessing her with intelligent eyes.

'Lucifer!' Surely the city had not been invaded by these grey-hooded crows? It stopped sidling up to the food and began to hop towards her. 'No, go away! I don't want you, you horrible bird. Shoo!'

As she spoke she heard the thud of hooves on turf coming up fast behind. The big bay horse thundered past, then circled and slowed as its rider reined it in and brought it back towards her at a walk. 'Lucifer, come here.' The crow flapped up to perch on the rider's shoulder, sending the horse skittering with nerves. The man on its back controlled it one-handed and lifted his hat to her with the other.

'Miss Hurst. I apologise for Lucifer, but he seems to like you.'

Of course, it had to be Lord Clere.

## Chapter Five

Phyllida looked from bird to master. 'The liking is not mutual, I assure you.' Why couldn't Lord Clere ride in Hyde Park like everyone else? Why couldn't he ride with the fashionable crowd in the afternoon? Why couldn't he leave the country altogether?

'I imagine the dislike applies to me as well,' he said. 'May I walk with you?'

'I can hardly stop you. This is a public park.' It was ungracious and she did not much care. Phyllida started walking again, the crow flapped down to claim its prize on the grass and Ashe Herriard swung out of the saddle.

'Is it? Public, I mean? I assumed it was, but there are no other riders. I was beginning to wonder if I had broken some dire rule of etiquette.' He did not sound as though he cared a toss for such rules.

'The fashionable place to ride is Hyde Park,' she informed him. 'Even at this time of day those who wish for some solitude and a long gallop go there, leaving walkers in peace. I suggest you try it.' *Now.*

He did not take the hint, but strolled beside her at a perfectly respectable distance, whip tucked under one elbow, the horse's reins in the other hand. She could not have been more aware of him if he had taken her arm. What did he want? Probably, Phyllida thought, bracing herself, he was going to make some insulting suggestion now that he knew about her birth. He had kissed her by the river, flirted in the ballroom. What would the next thing be?

'Hyde Park was where I was going, but on the map this looked a more pleasant route than finding my way through the streets. I did not hope to see you.'

'Why should you?' Phyllida enquired with a touch of acid.

'To apologise.'

That brought her to a halt. 'Apologise?' It was the last thing she expected him to do. She stared up at him and he met her eyes straight on, his own green and shadowed by thick black lashes. Even in the conventional uniform of a gentleman—riding dress, severe neckcloth, smart beaver hat—he seemed faintly exotic and disturbing. But more disturbing was the expression on his face. He was not teasing her, or mocking her. She could have dealt with that, but he appeared quite serious.

'For my rudeness last night. I have no excuse. I had just discovered who your brother is, so I was confused by your lack of a title, then I was surprised when Lady Malling explained. Your smile caught me in the middle of those emotions with my thoughts...unsorted.'

'Do you have to sort your thoughts, my lord?' It was such a direct explanation with no attempt to excuse himself that Phyllida felt herself thawing a trifle. *Dangerous.* Little alarm bells were jangling along her nerves. *He cannot be anything to you and you do not want him to be, either.*

'My brain feels like a desk that has been ransacked by burglars,' he admitted and her mouth twitched despite everything. 'Or one where all the files have been overstuffed and have burst. I am still, even after three months at sea, having to remember to think in English all the time. There are all the rules of etiquette that are different enough to European society in Calcutta to be decidedly confusing and so removed from my great-uncle's court where I have spent the past few years that they might be from a different planet.

'Then there is all the family stuff to learn, the estate, the... But never mind that, it sounds as though I am excusing myself after all and that was not my intention.'

'You did not want to come back, did you?' Phyllida asked. It was not a lack of intellectual capacity to cope with all those things that she heard in his voice, but the irritation of a man who did not want to be bothered by them, yet was making himself care. How interesting. Most of London society assumed that there was no greater delight and privilege than to be part of it and absorbed in every petty detail.

'The only one for whom England is *back* is my father. For my mother and sister it is as strange as it is for me. But I offended you and I apologise.'

'You are forgiven.' And he was, she realised. It had not just been good manners that made her say it. *Why? Because you have beautiful green eyes? Because you have been honest with me? Because I am deluding myself?* 'So, what do you intend to do with yourself now, Lord Clere?'

'We will stay in London for the Season and see my sister launched. We all need to outfit ourselves, the town house must be resurrected from fifteen years of neglect. I must learn to be a viscount, the heir and an English gentleman. Dancing lessons,' he added grimly, surprising a laugh from her.

At some point they had veered from the path towards the Queen's House. Phyllida looked round and found they had reached the edge of the park close to the point where Constitution Hill met the Knightsbridge Road. 'You cross here to Hyde Park.' She pointed. 'That is the Knightsbridge Turnpike.'

'Then Tattersalls is near here. I was intending to find it after I had ridden.' He whistled. The big crow flapped up and perched on the fence, eyeing her bonnet trimmings with malevolent intent.

'That is not something a young lady knows about, my lord.' She attempted to look demure. 'But, yes, it is just around the corner behind St George's Hospital.'

'Thank you.' Ashe swung himself up into the saddle, all long legs, tight breeches, exquisite control. 'I hope we will meet again, Miss Hurst. Now we know each other better.'

*The stuff of every maiden's dreams.* Phyllida suppressed a wince at her choice of words and lifted a hand in farewell as he took the horse out into the traffic and across to the other park. Ashe had been surprised and taken aback at what he had discovered about her and confessed as much, she thought as she made her way back to Anna. It was honest of him to admit it so freely.

And yet, thinking about it without his distracting presence looming over her, she had the uneasy feeling there was more than that in the blank look he had sent her last night, if only she could put her finger on it. He had apologised with disarming frankness, but he had not told her the whole truth. It would be as well to be wary of Lord Clere, however decorative and amusing he might be. *Now we know each other better.*

That had been a stroke of luck. Ashe turned his hired hack's head towards what he guessed was the famous Rotten Row and pressed the horse into a canter. He had not wanted to enquire about the Hursts' address and risk drawing attention to his interest in Phyllida, nor had he wanted to disconcert her by turning up in her shop. This encounter had been ideal, without even a passer-by as witness if she had done what he deserved and cut him dead in her turn.

But she had not. She had been gracious, ladylike with an edge of acid humour that he enjoyed. She had poise, intelligence, looks and enough maturity not to be expecting hearts and flowers and hypocritical pro-testations of love. *Damn it, she is perfect.* He liked her, he was attracted to her and she bore not the slightest re-semblance to Reshmi, his dead love. In fact, he would have no objection to marrying her tomorrow and cut-ting short this tiresome search for a wife.

Except that Phyllida Hurst was baseborn and, as if that was not enough, had a secret life that would ruin her if it was exposed and a brother who was, apparently, no catch as a relative. That old harridan Lady Malling had made it quite clear how ineligible she was.

Phyllida would not be received at court and she was not the sister-in-law for a young lady making her come-out and who deserved to be launched into the highest echelons of society.

Ashe guided his mount on to a smaller track, away from a group of riders in the distance, and gave it its head. She was twenty-six, he had discovered last night.

Unmarried, ineligible, old enough to have forgotten girlish fantasies about love. Might she find the prospect of a liaison interesting? His body tightened at the thought and he knew it had been in the back of his mind, unacknowledged, since he had discovered the truth about her.

He explored the idea. For three years he had been in an environment where encounters with respectable women were formalised, distant and impersonal. The women one knew, in all senses of the word, were *not* respectable, they were courtesans like Reshmi. He had no model for a sexual relationship with a lady in this world. How did one manage a liaison in this chilly, alien, new society? He had no wish to ruin her in its eyes, but he could be very, very discreet and with her two secret identities she had already proved she could be, too.

He would think about it. But first, before anything, he had to get a decent horse because this slug was useless. Tattersalls, his objective this morning, might be open by now and there, at least, he could get what he wanted, simply by exercising good taste and expending money. Horses were much less trouble than women.

'I've been talking to that Indian chap.' Gregory strolled into the sitting room and collapsed on to the sofa with his usual indolence.

'Ashe...I mean, Lord Clere?' Phyllida dropped a handful of paste jewellery she had bought from a dealer in Seven Dials back into its box and hoped she was not blushing.

It seemed her brother did not possess the instincts of a natural chaperon. 'Oh, you know him, do you? Interesting fellow. Great eye for a horse and the money to back his judgement.'

'You haven't been betting again?' Her heart sank. Had Gregory's virtuous resolutions been too good to last after all?

'No!' He looked wounded. 'I was round at Tatts, just looking, blowing a cloud, chatting. You know. Clere bought two riding horses for himself, a pretty little mare for his sister and a carriage pair.'

'Good lord.' She pushed away the jewellery and tried some mental arithmetic. 'That is a huge amount of money, all in one go.'

'I know. And they were all good buys. No gulling him. They've got that pair of greys that Feldshore had to sell to meet his gaming debts, you remember them? Showy as they come. Clere just walked round them, had them trotted out and said, "Weak pasterns." What do you think of that?'

'Amazing,' Phyllida agreed, trying to recall what a pastern was. 'I hope he can pay for all this.' She could just see Ashe surveying the bloodstock down that straight nose of his, rejecting the inadequate with a word. It took no leap of imagination to see him as a raja in his palace, waving a dismissive hand as slave girls were paraded in front of him, or crooking a long finger in summons if one pleased him.

'Grandfather was a nabob. Father's a marquess, he's the only son. Must be rolling in it,' Gregory said with amiable envy.

'And his grandmother was an Indian princess,' Phyllida could not resist adding.

'You've really been talking to him by the sound of it.'

'Mmm.' Phyllida tried to focus on the clasp of a rather pretty necklace of polished Scottish pebbles.

'You'll be pleased that I've invited him for dinner, then.'

'*What?*' The necklace ran through her suddenly nerveless fingers and back into the box with a rattle.

'You're *not* pleased?' Gregory's normally cheerful expression became a scowl. 'Has he acted in some way you did not like? Or said something out of turn? Because if so...'

'No, nothing like that.' The last thing she wanted was her brother charging off issuing a challenge. 'He did not realise about our parents' marriage and then, when he did find out, he allowed his...surprise to show. That was all. He apologised.'

The scowl was still in place. 'You liked him, didn't you, Phyll?'

She managed a rueful smile and a shrug. 'He is intelligent and attractive. I found him amusing to talk to.'

'He'll be looking for a wife,' Gregory said cautiously.

'I know, that is only to be expected.' Her stomach took a sickening swoop. *That* was what he was skirting around when he apologised. He had mentally assigned her to the ranks of eligible young women—despite what he had seen of her business—and he was inclined to like her. And then he had discovered that she was completely unsuitable...

'And if he liked you he might have been interested and then he discovered—' Gregory ploughed on, in unwitting echo of her thoughts.

'That I am baseborn. Quite. Don't look so tragic, Gregory. Lord Clere and I had a conversation, that is all. It is not as though we had been meeting for weeks and formed an attraction and then he found out. He is no different from all the rest of the gentlemen we socialise with. I really do not regard it.'

*But I do*, she realised, even as she spoke. Everyone was perfectly civilised about her status, she was invited to many events, received by all but the highest sticklers. She would never get vouchers for Almack's, of course, never be presented at court. Her marriage prospects were non-existent, at least amongst the *ton*, who would object to her birth in an alliance with one of their sons, or amongst the rich middle class families who wanted impeccable bloodlines for their money.

It had never mattered so much before, Phyllida realised. She could not recall the time when she was ignorant of her status, of the oddity of her parents' marriage and what it meant for her. She had her own interests, her business, her friends and her ambitions for Gregory and that was enough. It had to be. There were daydreams, of course, moments of sadness. Of more than sadness when she had held friends' babies in her arms, but she had learned to control those foolish hopes.

But Ashe Herriard had shaken her. She liked him and she was attracted to him. It would always have been impossible, of course. The consequences of the choice she had made when she was seventeen meant marriage was out of the question anyway.

Yet somehow, with this man, it hurt. They had only just met and she might yet come to find she only felt mild attraction to him, or she might discover something to dislike in him. He could well have paid her no more attention after the ball. But it was as though someone had just told her for the very first time that she was un-

marriageable: shock, a sense of loss, a dull pain somewhere under her breastbone.

*Foolishness*, she scolded herself. *A kiss, a pair of
green eyes, a sense of strength and virility, that is all it
takes to fill you full of pointless yearnings.* It was useless to repine and wish that things were different. They
were not and that was that.

The thoughts had run through her mind in seconds
and Gregory was still watching her with trouble in his
brown eyes. 'I will tell him we've a crisis in the kitchen
or something and take him to White's,' he offered.

'No, don't be silly.' Where the bright smile came
from she had no idea. 'We will have a dinner party, it
will be a pleasure. Now, who else can we invite? I think
we must stick at eight of us, otherwise we will be uncomfortably cramped. Shall I see if Miss Millington's
parents will allow her to come? If we invite a married
couple, then I cannot see they will have any objection.
Lucy and Cousin Peter would be ideal—I am sure Mrs
Millington would find a baronet who is a Member of
Parliament respectable company for her daughter.'

'That's six, including us. I'll invite the Hardinges
as well, shall I?'

'Mrs Millington will be in a second heaven! An earl,
a baronet, a viscount and a baron. I cannot believe she
can refuse to allow Harriet to come. I will call tomorrow. What day did you tell Lord Clere?'

'I said I must check dates with you and would get
back to him. He seemed pleased.' Gregory frowned
again. 'He had better not be trifling with you, Phyll.'

'No, of course he is not. No one trifles with me. Now,
shall we see if Wednesday will suit everyone?'

\* \* \*

'A letter for you, my lord.' Herring proffered a silver salver.

Ashe ran his finger under the red-wax seal and scanned the single page. 'My first dinner invitation,' he remarked to his father who was seated in the chair opposite him, long legs outstretched as he studied the surveyor's account of the state of Eldonstone, the Hertfordshire country house.

'Bachelor affair?'

'Apparently not. It's from Fransham. I met him at Tattersalls today. He says he's invited Lord and Lady Hardinge—he was at the ball yesterday—and a Sir Peter Blackett who is an MP, with his wife, and a Miss Millington, whoever she is.'

'Your mother is threatening a dinner party.' Lord Eldonstone made a note against a column of figures and tossed the bundle on to a side table. 'I suspect we won't get away with only seven sitting down to eat.'

'Eight, if Fransham's sister is acting as hostess.'

Ashe could have sworn he kept his voice neutral, but his father arched an eyebrow. 'Miss Hurst? She looked an intelligent and refined young woman. Unfortunate for the poor girl to have had such a careless father.'

'Yes,' Ashe agreed. *And she is mysterious, and smells of jasmine and has an edge to her tongue. And I cannot get her out of my head.* 'Is that report making depressing reading?'

His father grimaced. 'About what I expected. You neglect a place that size for as long as my father did, and screw every penny out of the land while you are at it, and the results are never going to be good.'

'Sounds expensive. Should I have taken more care with the amount I have just spent on horseflesh?'

The marquess shook his head. 'We can cope easily enough with this, and when we get the estate turned around and the income recovers it will look after itself. I was thinking of going down there next week for a few days—do you want to come?'

They had agreed on board ship that Tompkins would organise the essential cleaning and restocking of the house, engage more servants and generally get it habitable before the family visited. Establishing themselves in society, launching Sara and holding endless meetings with lawyers and bankers had to take priority over the country estate.

'So soon?' Ashe acknowledged to himself that he was ambivalent about the Hertfordshire house. London was a city and he felt comfortable in cities. But rural England was a foreign country. Green and lush as though there was a monsoon every day of the year, foxes to hunt, not tigers. Tenants to get to know, not hundreds of subsistence peasants totally at their raja's beck and call. And part of him knew that it was the country estates that defined the English nobleman: the unknown house was his fate and his responsibility.

Ashe smiled grimly to himself. He had been trained to fight—this was simply another battlefield, a more subtle one that would require all his diplomatic skills.

'Just a flying visit. We'll leave your mother and sister here.'

'I'll come, with pleasure.' His father wanted his support, although he would never admit it, and the sooner they got this over with, the better. 'After all, there is no waltzing in the countryside.' *And no distracting Miss Hurst, either.*

# Chapter Six

By the time Wednesday came around Ashe, like the rest of his family, had an array of gilt-edged cards to sift through and they were all keeping Edwards, the marquess's new secretary, busy with acceptances and the occasional regret.

But this dinner party would be a modest beginning to his London social life, he supposed, eyeing the narrow house in Great Ryder Street. When he mounted the steps and knocked, only to have the door answered by a maid, he realised just how modest. Male staff only above stairs in the afternoon and evening was the rule, Perrott had explained, although to find female staff anywhere but in the ladies' bedchambers was a novelty to Ashe.

Inside there was none of the oppressive splendour of the Herriard town house, for which he envied them. But it was elegantly, if simply, decorated and furnished and he suspected Phyllida's eye for style and her nose for a bargain had contributed to that.

'Clere! Glad you could come. Welcome.' Fransham came forwards with outstretched hand and began to introduce him. Hardinge greeted him as an old acquaintance and Ashe liked the direct friendliness of his wife. The Parliamentary baronet, Blackett, was thin and serious, but his wife made up for it with plump joviality and then there was a Miss Millington, who was introduced as 'My sister's friend.' From the shy glance she directed at Fransham, Ashe suspected there was something more to her presence than that.

Phyllida came in as he was agreeing with Miss Millington that the sunshine that morning had been very pleasant. 'Lord Clere will consider it the depths of winter, I imagine,' she said as she smiled in greeting. 'Good evening, Lord Clere. Confess, you do not consider our feeble spring sunshine worthy of the name.'

'I will admit to not having been warm since about Gibraltar,' he countered. 'But I have high hopes that the summer may reach the temperature of an Indian winter, Miss Hurst. Meanwhile, I am thawing in the kind welcome I have received in London.'

Hardinge chuckled. 'A diplomat, forsooth.'

'I was, after a fashion. I acted as an aide for several years to my great-uncle, the Raja of Kalatwah, and that involved some diplomacy.'

'In which languages?' Sir Peter enquired.

'Hindi and Persian. I speak some native dialects with rather less facility,' Ashe admitted.

'We shall have to enlist you to the Foreign Office.' How serious he was, Ashe could not tell.

'It would be most interesting, I am sure, but I will be much engaged with our estates for some time. My grandfather was not able to give them the attention they required.' Which was code for, *Spent all his time and money drinking, gaming and wenching while the place crumbled about him.* By the look of it the other men understood exactly. They had probably known the old devil, Ashe thought.

'Dinner is served, ma'am.'

The maid must be their only upstairs servant, Ashe concluded as the party paired up to go through. He was the highest-ranking male guest so Phyllida took his arm and showed him to the seat at her right hand. He was flanked by Lady Hardinge, but with such a small party it was easy to talk to everyone and no one seemed to have any inhibitions about conversing across the dining table.

'You are in town for the Season, Lord Clere?' Lady Hardinge enquired.

'My mother wished my sister to come out this year and, arriving from India as we have, there is much to arrange as you may imagine. Staying in London for the Season seemed sensible. But I am merely an appendage to the ladies of the household, I can hardly be said to be doing the Season.'

'I think you will find you are, whatever your intentions,' Lady Blackett said with a chuckle. 'What a fortunate thing that with the sea voyage and so forth you are out of mourning. I imagine that you too will have matrimonial ambitions, Lord Clere. From what I hear, the gossip is all about the dashing new bachelor who has joined the Marriage Mart.'

'I have certainly not done that, ma'am. It sounds quite alarming.' He must find himself a wife, true, but he had no intention of making himself a target.

'Terrifying,' Hardinge agreed in a stage whisper, causing general laughter. 'Avoid Almack's like the plague, is my advice,' he added.

'But have you not read *Pride and Prejudice*, Lord Clere?' Phyllida enquired. When he shook his head she quoted, ' "*It is a truth universally acknowledged, that a single man in possession of a good fortune must be in want of a wife.*" All the matchmaking mamas will have you in their sights already, I fear.'

'That sounds decidedly dangerous and I will have to take evasive action,' he said. 'I have been stalked by tigers before now, so hopefully my skills will enable me to escape.'

'You will have to succumb sooner or later, Clere,' Fransham observed with a grin. 'I used to be just as skittish myself, but now I am beginning to see the benefits of matrimony.' He did not glance at Miss Millington as he spoke, but she coloured faintly.

'I expect I shall, too,' Ashe agreed. 'But I prefer to make my own choices and not to be hunted down by terrifying matrons in search of a son-in-law with a title and all his own teeth.'

'We must stop teasing poor Lord Clere,' Phyllida said amid the general laughter. 'He has come to London expecting stately banquets and refined conversation and finds himself at a small dinner party with frivolous friends.'

'But charming frivolous friends,' Ashe corrected her. He caught her eye as he spoke and smiled, thinking how warm her brown eyes were and how delightful she looked when she was happy.

She became serious as he looked at her. Her eyes widened and he had a sudden fantasy of her lying beneath him, looking up with fathomless eyes and parted lips. *Oh, yes. Spread on a coverlet of green silk, gasping her pleasure as I lick every inch of those pale curves.*

The thought of her skin against his, ivory against gold, was an erotic provocation all of its own. Why had he been undecided for a moment about his intentions towards her?

His thoughts must have heated his gaze, for Phyllida blushed and turned to the maid. 'That will be all for the moment, Jane. I will ring when I need you.'

She spoke to Lord Hardinge on her left about an opera he had missed the previous week and conversation turned to the theatre and the arts. Ashe joined in the ebb and flow of talk, but mainly listened, absorbing information with the same focus he had employed when on a mission for his great-uncle.

Anything about this new world was useful, but he found himself listening more and more to Phyllida as the meal progressed. She was an excellent hostess, keeping conversation flowing and drawing everyone in with the skill of an accomplished matron. Her own contributions revealed an interest in cultural matters that seemed far reaching and well informed. One would not be bored after the lovemaking. She would not be a mistress from whose bed one hurried.

There, he had thought the word. *Mistress.* A longterm relationship, not the brief liaisons he had been making do with since Reshmi died. And this time he was forewarned not to become emotionally involved, nor to let his partner in passion become so, either. Reshmi had been his first, his only, love and that had hit him hard. Now he was more experienced, was on his guard against that kind of devastation to his heart, and it would not happen again.

'They say there is a consignment of remarkable Chinese porcelain just arrived,' Sir Peter said, cutting into his musings. 'But whether that is rumour or fact I cannot establish. Perhaps it will be offered at auction, but as far as I can tell none of the big houses are handling it.'

'It does exist and is very fine, but the shippers are intending to sell direct to dealers from the warehouse,' Phyllida said. Everyone looked at her with polite astonishment. 'That is…I heard someone discussing it at the Trenshaws' musicale the other day and complaining that by the time the public sees the items they will have increased in price considerably.'

'Just for a moment I had visions of you inspecting the goods in some ghastly warehouse down at the docks, Phyllida dear,' Lady Blackett said with a chuckle. 'I know how much you like fine porcelain, but wouldn't that be a scandal!' She laughed and everyone joined in. Ashe thought Phyllida's amusement was forced and her brother's smile was tight, but no one else seemed to notice.

'And dangerous,' Ashe said. 'From what little I saw of the docks area, it is no place for a lady.'

This time the look Phyllida directed at him aroused no fantasies of lovemaking. She looked as if she wished she had a hatpin to apply to his anatomy. 'Some unfortunate women must carry on their business in that area, Lord Clere. If it is dangerous for them, it is because they are at the mercy of the men who lurk there and who try to take advantage of them.'

'Yes, but *working* women,' Sir Peter said. 'Many of them no better than…' He seemed to recollect that he was in mixed company and not making a speech in the House. 'Not refined ladies, is what I meant. What a scandal it would be, to find a gentlewoman in such an area.'

There was a general murmur of agreement before, to Ashe's surprise, Miss Millington said, 'I believe many ladies support charities in the East End of London and go there themselves to give succour, even to the unfortunate women to whom Sir Peter referred.'

That turned the conversation to a discussion of charities and the best way to support the deserving poor. Ashe aroused considerable interest by describing the *sadhus* who, clad only in a sacred thread and a thick smearing of ashes, lived on the offerings of passers-by.

'Naked? But surely ladies cannot avoid encountering such men? Is it not a public outrage?' Lady Hardinge asked.

'In India nudity may be considered shocking, erotic, aesthetic, practical or religious, depending entirely on context,' Ashe explained. 'My mother or sister would think nothing of dropping a few coins into the begging bowl of a naked *sadhu*, but they would be shocked to find a member of the household walking about without a shirt, for example.' They still looked dubious. 'Have the ladies here never viewed naked Classical statuary and admired it for its aesthetic qualities?'

That made them laugh in rueful acknowledgement that he had scored a point. 'But cold white marble is quite another thing from real live flesh,' Phyllida objected. 'If I came upon the figures from Lord Elgin's marbles walking in Green Park, coloured as in life, as I believe they once were, I would be shocked.' Ashe caught her glance at Miss Millington who was obviously suppressing a smile at some secret joke they shared.

The unmarried ladies were not as uncurious about men as they were supposed to be, he concluded. Ashe

imagined Phyllida viewing the erotic carvings that decorated some of the rooms in the palace at Kalatwah. She
would be shy, perhaps, but also intrigued and aroused.
He found the thought more than arousing himself, his
intent hardening along with his body.

There was that amused, appreciative look in Lord
Clere's eyes that made her want to blush. Phyllida felt
as though he could read her mind and see her memory
of telling Harriet Millington that she wished his tight
evening breeches would split. Provoking man, he was
able to flirt without a word spoken.

She caught the attention of her female guests.
'Ladies, shall we?'

When they reached the drawing room the door was
hardly closed behind them when Lucy Blackett exclaimed, 'What an attractive man! So exotic with those
golden good looks. You are a dark horse, Cousin Phyllida, keeping him a secret.'

'Not at all,' she protested. 'He is Gregory's friend.
He met him at Tattersalls the other day and invited him.
I feel sorry for the whole family, don't you? It must be
so strange finding themselves in England for the first
time with such a vast, neglected inheritance and everything so strange.'

The other women looked disappointed that she was
not admitting to an ulterior motive in inviting Ashe, but
Phyllida turned the conversation and they were discussing Harriet's plans to visit the Lake District with her
parents in the summer when the men rejoined them.

The rest of the evening passed pleasantly. At length
Jane came in to announce that the carriages had arrived

and there was a general move to depart before the three equipages completely jammed the narrow street.

Harriet's maid came up from the kitchen and Gregory offered to escort Miss Millington home. 'I can get a hackney back,' he explained, running down the steps, hat and gloves in hand.

'Am I right in assuming your brother wishes to fix his interest with Miss Millington?'

Phyllida turned to find Ashe right behind her in the hallway. 'I hope so,' she admitted. Jane was holding his hat, cane and gloves, but he made no move to take them. 'I like her very much.'

'I wonder if I could have a word with you before I go, Miss Hurst?'

Phyllida realised she was alone in the house except for the servants. She should ask Jane to sit in the corner of the room, or ring for Anna, but it seemed priggish to insist on the proprieties and no one was there to wag a disapproving finger at her.

She went back into the drawing room and noticed that he left the door open behind him which was, she supposed, a relief. Ashe Herriard seemed to take all the air out of the room. Or perhaps it was just that there was none left in her lungs. She sat down and gestured to a chair, but he remained standing.

'You are going to that warehouse by yourself to buy some of the porcelain, aren't you?' he asked without preamble.

She was, of course. If it was half as good as they were saying, she would buy all she could afford and turn a healthy profit on it. But she had no intention of revealing her plans to anyone, let alone autocratic gentlemen. 'I have not decided, Lord Clere.'

'Oh, yes, you have, I saw it in your face. But you must not go, it is not safe in that area.'

Phyllida got to her feet in a swirl of rose-pink muslin. 'Lord Clere, you have no right to dictate my actions.'

'A gentleman is duty-bound to protect a lady.'

'I have a brother, sir.'

'He seems either unwilling, or unable, to control your activities.' Ashe leaned against a chair, apparently unshaken by either her tone or her frowns.

'As we are alone, my lord, allow me to remind you that I have a business to run. I am twenty-six years old and I do not need *controlling*. But I do need stock of the highest quality and this porcelain promises to be just that.'

'I will buy it on your behalf.'

She sat down again with an undignified thump. 'You? What do you know of porcelain?'

'At least as much as you, I would wager.' Now she was sitting again he dropped into the chair he had been leaning against with considerably more elegance than she had just displayed. 'I was brought up in one of the great trading cities of the East with a grandfather high in the East India Company and I have spent the last three years in the court of an immensely wealthy prince with a taste for collecting.'

'I need to make my own judgement. I know what will sell in my shop, what my limits on price are.'

'Then I will come with you.' He was pleasant, he smiled, he might as well have been made of granite.

'And buy the best pieces from under my nose?'

'Now I know about the collection it will not take me long to discover where it is. I do not need to accompany you, I could cream off the best items tomorrow.'

'Oh…!' Phyllida was not used to being thwarted in her own world. She was limited by her birth, her secrets and the need, endlessly, to make money, but within those constraints, she was in control. This infuriating man who just sat there patiently waiting for her to finish fulminating and give in to him was completely outside her experience.

'You, sir, are no gentleman,' she said with an icy determination to put him in his place.

'Oh, yes, I am.' Ashe Herriard got to his feet, making her clench her teeth because she could not help but note the ease with which he stood. Some wretched feminine instinct was clamouring at her to look at him, to admire him, to exert herself to make him like her.

He came over and held out his hands to her. Puzzled, she put her own in his. Was this some way of admitting defeat in Indian society? Even as she thought it he pulled, bringing her to her feet. 'It is just that I am not an *English* gentleman,' he said and drew her close, as close as a waltz hold, as close as a kiss…

*If he tries, I will slap him*, she resolved. And yet the resolution did not make her twist her fingers free of his hold. Phyllida looked up into the deep-green eyes that always seemed a little amused, at the firm mouth and the chin that hinted at determination, and swallowed.

'I have been brought up to understand the jungle and its dangers. Your East End is a jungle without tigers or cobras, but a jungle none the less. I do not allow women to wander unprotected into such a place. That is not negotiable. But we can negotiate a truce,' Ashe said. 'You will promise me that you will not visit the warehouse without my escort. I promise you that I will not attempt to buy any item until you have made your selection.'

'We cannot go in some smart carriage with a crest on the door.' Phyllida knew she had admitted defeat. 'We must take a hackney.'

'Of course. It would not do to arrive flaunting wealth,' he agreed. 'You know this is sensible and you are a sensible woman, so why are you still unhappy about it?'

Of all the flattering things he might have said to her, *sensible* was not one of them. Phyllida tried to accept it as Ashe doubtless meant it. His fingers were still wrapped warmly around hers, he was so close she would smell sandalwood and linen and man if she was so foolish as to inhale deeply. Her *sensible* brain appeared to have taken a holiday somewhere. 'Because it means going with you,' she blurted out.

Ashe did not appear offended, although his dark brows arched up. 'You dislike me so much?'

'You know I do not. But I do not know what you want from me, why you persist in pursuing our acquaintance. You seek a wife and I am totally ineligible, as we both know. An acquaintance of my brother, a gentleman who dines with us, has no reason to be escorting me in this way. What does that leave?'

'Friendship?' he suggested after just the merest pause. Why did she suspect he had almost said something else?

Phyllida stared at him. 'Men and women are not *friends* in English society. Not unless they are of mature years or closely related.'

'It is the same in European society in India. And as for Indian society—a man risks death for the slightest intimacy with a woman. But why shouldn't we be un-conventional? I enjoy novel experiences.'

There did not seem to be anything she could say. The truth—that she found him far too disturbing to be around—was hardly something she could admit. 'Very well. Can you call for me tomorrow at about ten? And please wear something inconspicuous.'

'Ten it is. And I promise not to look like a rich and over-eager English collector with more money than judgement.'

'Until tomorrow then, my lord.' She gave her hands, that had rested in his for a quite scandalous length of time, a little tug.

'*Ashe*, Phyllida. Friends, remember?' And he bowed his head as he lifted his hands, bringing his lips to her knuckles. The shock, even though she was wearing thin kid evening gloves, shot up her arm as she felt the heat. Her lips parted as though he had kissed them instead of the unyielding ridge of her knuckles. 'Goodnight,' he said, releasing her. 'Thank you for a delightful dinner party. I can see myself out.'

*My friend Ashe.* Phyllida sat as the front door closed behind him and wondered what on earth she had let herself in for. She looked down at her hands, clasped in her lap, then slowly raised the one he had kissed to her lips.

Friends sounded safe. *Do I want to be safe? Or have I just agreed to be friends with a tiger?*

# Chapter Seven

It was 'Mrs Drummond' who was waiting for Ashe when he arrived promptly at ten. She wore a brown wool gown, darker-brown pelisse with braid trim that had rather obviously been re-used from another garment, a plain straw bonnet retrimmed with a bunch of artificial flowers, darned gloves and sturdy shoes. Under the gloves, if one looked hard enough, was the shape of a thin wedding band.

'Good God.' Ashe stopped dead and stared at her. 'That's worse than the outfit you were wearing when we first met.'

'Never mind me,' Phyllida retorted. 'What on earth are you doing looking like that?'

He was wearing a high-necked coat of dull black brocade, tailored in at the waist with skirts to the knee all round. Beneath were tight, dark-red trousers tucked into boots of soft black leather and a sash of the same dark red circled his waist. He had not shaved and his morning beard, darker than his hair, made his skin seem darker, too. And the final touch of exoticism was his hair, freed from its tie and touching his shoulders. As he moved his head she caught the glint of a gold ear stud in his right lobe.

'Don't you like it?' One eyebrow rose. Phyllida could have sworn he had done something to make his lashes even sootier. She wished she dared ask what, it looked a useful trick.

'You look magnificent and you know it,' she snapped. Over her dead body was she going to let him see that he was the personification of every daydream of the exotic Orient. 'Do not fish for compliments, Lord Clere. That is hardly the outfit for where we are going.'

'But I look like a dealer from the East. Someone who knows about Chinese ceramics.'

'We will see who gets the better deals,' Phyllida said. 'Are we acquainted with one another?'

'I do not think so. I will get the driver to drop me off around the corner and I will go in first.'

'Why?' Phyllida picked up her reticule and dropped in the front-door key.

'In case there is any danger, of course.' Ashe followed her out and pulled the door to. Phyllida told the driver where to go and they climbed into the hackney.

'You will deal with that by throttling assailants with your sash?'

'You are more exhausting than my sister,' Ashe complained. 'No, I will stab them with one of the three knives I have about my person.' He settled back against the battered squabs and crossed long legs.

Knives? Gentlemen did not stroll around London armed to the teeth with knives, not these days. He was teasing her, he had to be. Phyllida resisted the temptation to look for betraying bulges in case he thought she was studying his body.

'Who is Miss Millington?' he asked in a rapid change of subject. 'I couldn't find her in either the *Peerage* or the *Landed Gentry*.'

'You can't have her!' Phyllida sat bolt upright and gripped her reticule. 'She is for Gregory.'

'I didn't say I wanted her, I was simply trying to place her.'

'Her father is a prominent banker.'

'Ah, I see. She will come with a substantial dowry and your brother comes with land and title.'

'Exactly. And they like each other, so I have every hope they will make a match of it.'

'Your doing, I suspect.'

'Certainly. It is no secret that our father left Gregory the earldom, a crumbling house, a great deal of entailed land in poor heart and a mountain of debt. We sold off everything that we could and cleared the debts, but that left virtually nothing to live off and certainly no resources to restore the Court and the estate.'

'So you support the pair of you with your dealing and the shop. What happens to you when Fransham marries? You appear to be a notable matchmaker—can you not turn your talents to your own benefit?'

'I will not marry.' Phyllida began to fiddle with a darn on her right glove. 'In my position…'

'Nonsense. Someone will fall in love with you—a professional man, a younger son.'

And then she would have to confess the truth about her past. 'I will not marry,' Phyllida repeated stubbornly. 'I have no wish to.' And even if she could find the right man, and even if he did not care about her birth or her past or the shop, could she bring herself to be a wife to him?

She shivered. Just because she found one man attractive and still dreamt about his kiss and the pressure of his fingers on hers did not mean that if things went beyond kisses that she could bear it. Her body's instinctive reactions, female to male, were one thing, her mind's capacity to overcome horror and memory was quite another. Better never to risk it. It felt as though Ashe was tugging her closer and closer to a cliff edge and she had no strength to resist him.

'We are close.' She pulled the check string. 'If you get out here and walk around the corner to the left, you'll see the warehouse. Tell the driver to take me to the entrance in a few minutes.'

When she entered the warehouse with a nod to the guard on the door and the scurrying clerks, she found men she recognised inside. Taciturn, shabby figures with notebooks, they made secretive jottings as they passed amongst the packing cases and racks. Her fellow dealers spared her curt greetings and assessing looks, their faces as blank as those of card players in the midst of a high-stakes game.

It was not hard to locate Ashe. He was strolling along the crowded aisles, a faint sneer curving his lips, Joe Bertram, the warehouse manager, at his heels. She watched as he stopped and shook his head over a display of just the sort of small items she was interested in.

'Who the blazes is that?' One of the dealers stopped next to Phyllida and jerked his head at Ashe, who was rolling his eyes at a large vase.

'I have no idea,' she said, hardly able to recognise the supercilious Indian gentleman they were looking at. 'But he looks as though he knows what he is talking about.'

'He's putting the wind up old Bertram. Might lower the prices for all of us,' the man said with a chuckle and moved on.

Ashe approached her, paused and produced a slight inclination of the head. His face was expressionless, an aristocrat showing courtesy to a lesser being. Phyllida ignored him and made a pretence of studying some vast urns before going to the small items. Her heart was racing as she picked up the first delicate tea bowl. There was high-quality *famille rose*, some exquisite blue-and-white incense burners, charming unglazed terracotta miniature figures, plates... She would have to consider very carefully and bargain hard.

On the edge of her concentration she could hear Ashe, his voice strongly accented as he condescended to take an interest in a suite of vases. She put the pieces she wanted to one side, added some more as sacrifices once the bargaining began, and looked around for Bertram or one of his assistants. At the doorway there was jostling, laughter, a string of swear words, then Harry Buck and his bullies swaggered in. All around her the dealers faded into the background, like terriers yielding to a bulldog at the bear pit.

Only Ashe, inspecting the base of a bowl, the nervous Mr Bertram and herself were left exposed to the stare of Buck's muddy brown eyes. They flickered over Ashe, visibly dismissed him as a foreigner, over Bertram, who hurried to Buck's side at the jerk of his head, and then fixed on her. Phyllida could feel the stare like the touch of greasy fingers on her skin. Her nightmares began and ended with Buck, his coarse laughter, his thick fingers, the smell of onions on his breath. Why was he here? She was trapped.

She kept her eyes fixed on the bowl she was holding, its sides so thin she could see the ghosts of her fingers through the white porcelain. If it had a mark, it was blurred. Phyllida put it down before it fell from her fingers and pretended to make a note.

'Wot we got 'ere, then?' Buck sauntered over. 'Some dolly mop looking for a nice teapot, eh? Bit pricey for you, darlin', best look down the market. Or I can put you in the way of earning some dosh. Take the weight off your feet.'

Perhaps he wouldn't recognise her. He never had in all the times he had glimpsed her in the East End after that first time and she had taken great care that they were only glimpses. She fought to reassure herself. Why should he recognise in the drably dressed woman in her mid-twenties one terrified seventeen-year-old virgin? How many other desperate girls who needed to earn some *dosh*, bargaining with the only thing of value they possessed, had passed through those dirty hands since then?

But Buck had never been so close, so focused on her alone before. She had always managed to slip away, vanish around corners, merge behind something more interesting when she had inadvertently strayed across his path.

She could smell him now: tobacco, sweat, onions, a cheap cologne. Phyllida gripped the edge of the table and fought the primitive instinct to run.

'I know you, don't I? Where do you deal?' Buck demanded. His shrewd eyes were narrowed on her face.

Phyllida fought for self-possession. If she showed fear, it would only intrigue him more.

He raised one hand as if to take her by the chin and hold her while he studied her face. 'Wot's your name?'

'I do not think the lady wishes to talk. You are distracting her from studying the goods.' The calm accented voice came from her right, then she felt the brush of his coat hem against her skirts as Ashe moved to stand between her and Buck.

'You're not from round 'ere, are you?' Buck said. 'Perhaps you don't know how things go. I was talking to this piece.'

'Things go the same around the world,' Ashe said calmly. 'A gentleman does not trouble a lady.'

'Yeah? Well, I'm no gent and she's no lady.' Buck slammed down a hand on the trestle table beside Phyllida's hip. She flinched away and found one of the bullies had moved round behind her. 'So you take yourself off, pretty boy, before you gets hurt.'

There was a sudden movement, a flash, and a thin knife was quivering in the wood between Buck's thumb and forefinger. The porcelain shivered and clattered together with the force.

'My hand slipped,' Ashe said into the thick silence. 'I find that happens when I am crowded. What a pity if anyone was to fall and break your valuable consignment, sir.'

'Mine?' Buck did not move his hand. His attention had shifted from Phyllida like an actual weight lifting from her chest.

'I think you are the money behind this, are you not? I really do suggest you ask your men to move away. If I were to faint from terror I think I would probably fall against that stand of Song Dynasty wares, which would be a tragedy, considering how valuable they are and the fact that I was prepared to spend a significant sum on that set of vases.'

'You were, were you?' Buck eased his hand away, his eyes fixed on Ashe's face. He was a lout and a bully, Phyllida thought as she fought to get her breathing under control, but he was not stupid enough to lose money to make a point, not if he could save face. No one else could see the knife. And then it vanished as fast as it had appeared, point first into Ashe's left sleeve.

'I was. If we can agree on price. And, if you do not frighten the lady away, I imagine she was about to enquire about the cost of the articles she has set to one side.'

She looked up at Ashe looming large and dangerous next to her. He seemed completely relaxed, but then she was probably tense enough for both of them. He held Buck's stare with his own and the man's wavered.

'Show us your money first.'

'No. We agree a price first. Then I send for the money, then we make an exchange,' Ashe said as pleasantly as if they were chatting over afternoon tea.

'Done,' Buck said with a grunt and moved away, his men pushing past Ashe and Phyllida to follow him.

'Oh, my God.' She unclenched her fingers from the trestle table and painfully massaged life back into them. 'Are we going to get out of here alive?'

'If I spend enough money,' Ashe said with a suppressed laugh. 'Have you chosen?'

'Yes.' Phyllida knew she could not just bolt from the warehouse, which was what every instinct was screaming at her to do. It would draw attention back to her and

Ashe would be curious. She righted a little figure that had been knocked over with the force of the knife blow.

Ashe gestured to Bertram and stood back as she haggled. Her voice shook at first, but the familiar cut and thrust of bargaining soothed her a little and they agreed a price that gave her almost everything that she wanted. 'I'll take them now,' she said, paid, then stood aside while a porter packed the pieces and Ashe negotiated the price of the vases.

'They are Northern Song,' Bertram declared. 'Very rare.'

'No, they are southern celadon ware. Thirteenth century, quite late for Song,' Ashe countered.

*He knows what he is talking about.* It was easy to watch and listen to Ashe, to the rhythm of that lovely, lilting accent, to the fluent movement of his hands as he gestured. He had become less European, more Indian, just by the way he pitched his voice, the way he stood. He did not nod, but swayed his head from side to side in the sinuous Indian gesture of agreement.

Fascinated, she watched, saw Bertram's nervous glances to the back of the warehouse, guessed he was under orders from Buck about the price. Ashe was going to pay in money for coming to her rescue.

'I'll help this lady out with her purchases,' he said when the deal was concluded. 'And I will send for my man with the money. Do not pack them until I get back, we wouldn't want anything to get chipped, would we?'

*Or substituted*, Phyllida thought. But what man with the money?

Ashe summoned the waiting hackney, helped her in and put her purchases on the seat. 'Go around the corner and wait,' he said to the driver. 'I'll be about half an hour. If anyone else approaches, drive off and circle round, I do not want the lady bothered.'

No one approached, but after a few moments Buck strolled out and leaned against the door frame, his eyes fixed on the hackney. He made no effort to approach, but it felt as though his speculative gaze could penetrate the walls and see her, huddled in the furthest corner like a rabbit in a trap.

Twenty minutes later Ashe wedged the box containing his vases on the seat next to Phyllida's porcelain and swung into the hackney. 'All right? I had to make a pretence of going for the cash. If they'd had any idea how much I was carrying...'

'Yes.'

Ashe studied her face and the way she gripped the strap far too tightly, even allowing for the carriage's lurching progress over the uneven cobbles. 'That was Buck again, wasn't it? The man from the quayside.'

'Yes.' After a moment she seemed to force herself to add to the stark monosyllable. 'You might say he's the local lord of crime. He owns the b-brothels, runs the gaming dens, takes protection money from all the shopkeepers.' Her voice was as tight as her fingers on the leather loop.

'You are scared of him.'

'Everyone with any sense is scared of Buck. Except you, apparently.'

'Perhaps I have no sense. Why do you come into this area and risk meeting him?'

'Because this is how I earn my living.' The look she shot him said clearly that he did not understand. 'I have to buy cheap and sell high, so I scour the pawnshops, talk to the sailors, buy from warehouses like this one. But if I had known Buck owned it, I wouldn't have come,' she admitted. 'And thank you. I should have said that immediately. You were... You knew exactly how to treat him. I just freeze, he makes my skin crawl.'

'He's a bully. He won't risk being hurt—in his body or his wallet. A man prepared to stand up to him, someone he doesn't know, armed and unpredictable—he would back down. There is nothing you, or any woman, could have done with him in those circumstances.'

'Yes,' Phyllida agreed, her knuckles almost splitting the thin leather of her gloves. She was still desperately upset by the threat of violence, Ashe realised. All this calm acceptance of what he said was simply a cover.

'Phyllida, it is all right to have been frightened, you can stop being brave about it.'

She shook her head and muttered something he did not catch, beyond one word, *feeble*.

'That is nonsense,' he said sharply and could have kicked himself when her lower lip trembled for a second before she caught it viciously between her teeth. 'Come here.' He turned and, before she could protest, lifted her on to his knees. He untied her dreadful bonnet and threw it on to the seat opposite. There was a tussle over her grip on the strap, then she let it go and turned her face into his shoulder. 'You can cry if you want to, I don't mind.'

Phyllida took a deep breath, but there were no sobs. Ashe put his arms around her to hold her steady from the jolting and waited. 'Thank you,' she muttered.

'Don't mention it. I mean it, you may cry,' he added after a moment. 'I'm a brother, don't forget, I have training for this.'

That provoked a muffled snort of laughter from the region of his shirt front. She was not weeping, he realised, although she seemed to find the embrace comforting.

Sara always used to hurl herself into his arms and sob noisily over the frustrations of life, the little tragedies, the general unfairness of parents. But it was a long time since his sister had cried on his shoulder. As Phyllida relaxed, her body becoming soft and yielding against his, the memory of a sisterly hug faded.

The last time he had held a woman like this it had been Reshmi in his embrace and she had been weeping in bitter, betrayed grief because he had told her he would not take her back with him as his mistress when he came to England. And they had both known that he could not marry a courtesan from his great-uncle's court.

Phyllida stirred, settled against him, taking comfort, he supposed, from his warmth and the strength of the man who had just intervened to protect her. His reflexes, sharpened by the aggression at the warehouse, brought the scent of her, the feel of her, vividly to him. Subtle jasmine, the heat of her body sharpened by fear, the rustle of petticoats beneath the plain woollen fabric of her skirts, soft, feminine curves made to fit his hard angles and flat planes.

His body reacted predictably, hardening, the weight low in his belly, the thrill of anticipation, of the hunt. He would protect her against everything and everybody. Except himself. He wanted her and he would have her.

# *Chapter Eight*

❧❧❧

It would be bliss to stay here, wrapped in Ashe's arms, sinking into the sweet illusion that everything was all right, that she was loved and cared for by this strong man who would sweep her away from all her troubles. *I love you, Phyllida,* he would murmur. *I do not care about your birth or any secrets you keep from me. I will marry you.*

Such a sweet fantasy. Just a minute more. *Or perhaps not.* Phyllida became aware that however gallantly Ashe had protected her at the warehouse, and however brotherly this embrace might have been at the beginning, he was not thinking brotherly thoughts now.

He was aroused. As she snuggled into his lap there was no mistaking the matter, the crude physical reality of male desire. His hands might be still, but his breathing had changed. His body was tense, as though he was holding himself in check. It would not take very much encouragement, she sensed, to shatter that control. She was not the usual unmarried lady, fenced about with rules and assumptions that a gentleman was expected to observe, and she had given him every reason to believe her unconventional and reckless.

The temptation to twist around in Ashe's arms, to seek his mouth, to savour his heat and passion and strength, fled like mist in the sun. He would, she sensed, be a generous, careful lover, but even if she could subdue her fears about making love with him, she could not hide what had happened to her from a man with experience.

And afterwards? Had she really been thinking of risking that hard-won acceptance in society, her good name, simply for the dream of an hour in this man's arms? Besides, Ashe might well reject her encouragement, she told herself. Just because his body reacted to a woman on his lap it did not mean that he wanted *her*.

The shock of the confrontation with Buck, the heart-stopping threat of violence, had disordered her emotions and her judgement.

'Oh, good Heavens, look, we are nearly at Great Ryder Street,' Phyllida said with a brightness that sounded entirely false to her own ears. 'What on earth has happened to my bonnet?' She regained her seat with as much dignity as she could muster and found the hat lying on the dusty floor of the cab. 'Thank you, I am so sorry I allowed my nerves to be so overset.' She swiped at the dust with enough violence to crumple the bunch of artificial violets tucked under the ribbon.

'Where do you want the porcelain taken? Here or the shop?' Ashe asked, as though they had not been entangled in an embrace in a public vehicle, with no window blinds, for the past ten minutes.

'Here, please.' She would not be flustered or allow him to guess how she had so nearly allowed her feelings to overcome her good sense just now. The cab drew up at the kerb, Ashe helped her down and took the key to open the door for her before lifting down her package and carrying it into the hallway.

'You will not go back there.' He seemed to tower over her in the narrow space and she could feel her resolution not to reach for him weakening again.

'The warehouse? No.' She could promise that with heart-felt sincerity.

'Too much to hope that you will not go into that part of London again, I suppose.' Ashe touched her cheek with the back of his hand. 'I have been able to distract Buck twice, I might not be there the third time.'

'I will be careful.' Her own hand was over his, although she had no recollection of lifting it.

'Here, guv'nor! You want to go on, or wot?'

'My coachman awaits,' Ashe said. He stopped at the foot of the steps and looked back. *'Au'voir.'*

*'Au'voir,'* she echoed as she pushed the door closed. The box sat in the middle of the hall, something immediate to do. Something real. Phyllida took a deep breath. 'Gregory! Are you home? I need some help.'

'This is from Lady Arnold.' Anusha Herriard looked up from a letter in her hand. 'She invites us for a few days at the end of the week to their estate near Windsor. I had been speaking to her about Almack's and the importance of vouchers for Sara and she tells me that two of the patronesses will be there, which is thoughtful of her.'

'Ashe and I were going down to Eldonstone,' the marquess said. 'Are these vouchers so important?'

'Essential, Papa.' Sara shook her head at him in mock reproof. 'You have not been paying attention. If you want to marry me off well, then Almack's is the main Marriage Mart.'

'Ghastly expression.' Ashe put down his own afternoon post and shuddered. 'Someone asked me if I was taking part, as though it is a sporting event.' He supposed it might be, if he saw himself as the waterbuck pursued by the hounds.

'There is no hurry for you,' his mother said, passing the letter to her husband. 'Do not look so harassed, Ashe.'

'There is no denying that a daughter-in-law who knows the ropes would be a help for you,' Ashe pointed out. It was one of the reasons for marriage that he kept reminding himself about and his mother's rueful smile only reinforced the point.

'It sounds as though you would have plenty of choice if you come to this house party,' his father remarked as he scanned the sheet in his hand. 'And several of the peers I want to talk to will be there by the look of it. Sooner or later I must sort out my political affiliations and a relaxed country gathering is probably a good a place as any to make a start.'

'So you want to postpone our trip to Eldonstone?' Ashe asked him.

'I would say, yes, but then there is this letter from Perrott.' He handed it across the luncheon table. 'It seems my father had no patience with the ornaments and collections of his forebears and the place is stuffed with crates and boxes filled at random with every kind of stuff. Perrott frankly confesses himself at a loss as to know how to begin to sort it out and what is of value and needs special care and what is not.'

'Poor devil,' Ashe said with a grin. 'He sounds thoroughly exasperated. I'll go by myself, if you like. At least I can sort out Oriental porcelain and ivories for him and have a stab at any gemstones.' His father was expressionless and Ashe tried to assess how many bad old memories the thought of the family home was stirring up. 'Of course, if you want to be the first one to return there…'

'No.' The marquess shook his head. 'I only ever saw the place once. My father and grandfather were at odds, as you know. By the time I came along my father was not received. I went there in the hope the old man would stop my father packing me off to India. I got as far as his study and no further.'

'I'll go, then,' Ashe offered. 'I can manage to postpone my plunge into the Marriage Mart for a few days.' The feeling of reprieve was a surprise. He had not expected to actually enjoy the experience of finding a wife, but neither, he thought, had he been dreading it. Not that Eldonstone, haunted by his ancestors and heavy with the burden of unwanted responsibility, was likely to be much of a holiday.

'We'll have to hire an expert, I suppose,' his father said. 'Get it sorted, cleaned up, catalogued and evaluated.'

There was a murmur of agreement from his mother. No one, it seemed, was eager to tackle the chaos of the big house. The gloom of the town residence was bad enough. 'I have made some progress here,' she said. 'Most of the clutter has been stripped out of the main salon and I had that cream silk I brought with us made up into curtains. Come and see what you think.'

They followed her through into the largest reception

room, full of admiration for the transformation. 'This is just the right setting for a present I have for you, *Mata*.'

Ashe fetched the celadon vases from their packing case and set them on the grey marble of the mantelshelf. The subtle green seemed to glow in the light the cream curtains allowed into the room.

'Now those are perfect. Thank you, darling. Where did you find them?'

'A warehouse in the East End,' Ashe said. 'Miss Hurst mentioned it at dinner the other evening and I escorted her to look around.'

'Miss Hurst?' Sara said. 'Lord Fransham's sister? Why was she interested?'

The plan seemed to present itself fully formed in Ashe's head. 'Because she is an amateur expert in *objets d'art*,' he said. 'Rather more than an amateur, but you won't mention that to anyone, I'm sure. They are somewhat short of funds and she buys items that appeal to her and then sells them discreetly. Auctions and so forth.' He was not going to mention the shop and her other personas. He had promised, and this was quite enough to explain what he was about to suggest. 'You might have noticed that fine suite of cameos she was wearing at the Richmonds' ball. If we were to offer her a fee…'

As he expected, none of his family seemed shocked. 'How clever,' Sara approved. 'I know they are not well off—I was warned not to set my sights on her brother— but that must be a great help. No wonder she always dresses with such style. I was wondering about that shopkeeper in Jermyn Street, where we bought my moonstone, but Miss Hurst would be much better.'

'Certainly,' Ashe agreed, straight-faced. 'We wouldn't want a Frenchwoman.'

His mother was frowning. 'Miss Hurst can hardly go off with you unchaperoned, Ashe.'

'There is Great-Aunt Charlotte in the Dower House. She could stay with her,' Ashe pointed out. 'Or Aunt Charlotte might prefer to come to the house. If I hired a chaise for Miss Hurst and she had her maid with her, I cannot imagine that would be a problem.'

'All I know of my aunt is that she cordially disliked my father,' the marquess said. 'But I can write, see if she's willing to assist us in this, if your Miss Hurst is prepared to oblige us.'

*My Miss Hurst.* Now there was a concept that appealed to him. Ashe kept his face neutral. 'I will sound her out in principle. If Great-Aunt is not willing to have a guest or move to the main house, then we will just have to think again.'

Great-aunt or not, he was going to offer Phyllida a fee that would keep her from the necessity of going into the East End for months. Months while he persuaded her into his bed, months while he enjoyed her as his mistress.

'You want me to come with you, alone, to your family home?' Phyllida sorted through a jumble of emotions. Surprise, a surge of wicked excitement, rapidly suppressed, outrage if this was deliberate plotting, delight that she might earn a fee so easily and in such surroundings.

'I am asking you to accept my escort, with your maid. My great-aunt Charlotte has condescended to move into the main house for the duration  largely out of curiosity, I suspect, but she will make an unexceptionable chaperon should anyone discover your presence.'

'But—'

'I am suggesting a generous fee by the day, as we have no idea of the extent of the problem, and you have the first opportunity to negotiate on items we wish to sell.' Ashe Herriard sat back in the chair, crossed long legs in elegant relaxation and waited. 'Naturally we will not be making it known that we have employed an expert, let alone who it is,' he added.

'I suppose I could develop exhaustion from all the gadding about I have been doing and need to visit a friend in the country for a few days' rest,' Phyllida pondered aloud. A generous fee and time alone in Ashe's company. It was very tempting. But could she trust him? Or, rather more to the point, could she trust herself?

'You would not have to venture anywhere near Buck's territory for months,' Ashe remarked.

Cowardice? Or the perfect excuse to yield to Ashe's persuasions? Whichever it was, that was a powerful argument. 'I will be glad to do it,' she agreed before she could talk herself out of it. 'Gregory is going to the same house party as your family, and so is Miss Millington. Lady Arnold has promised to exert her best endeavours to secure her vouchers for Almack's because she is Gregory's godmother and thinks Harriet will be good for him.'

'And you are not invited?'

'Best not to remind the patronesses about our parents' casual approach to marriage,' she said with a lightness she was finding hard to maintain lately.

'May I ask what happened? I do not mean to pry if it is not something you choose to speak of.'

There was a faint snort from Anna, sitting in the corner with a basket of mending to keep up the appearance of propriety. Phyllida shrugged. 'It is no secret. They were madly in love—or, at least, Mama was—eloped and then Papa just kept vaguely failing to get round to marrying her.

'He made every excuse you might imagine. His father would forgive them in time and then they could have a proper society wedding, he'd run out of funds for Mama's bride clothes, he had to come back to London from Tunbridge Wells where she was in lodgings in order to make money for the rent by gambling. One pretext after another.

'And once Mama was expecting me she was hardly the slender girl who had attracted him in the first place, so she saw even less of him. Finally a frantic letter brought him back to marry her. But, of course, he stopped off for a prize fight on the way, got drunk and surfaced a day later. A day too late, as it turned out, for I had been born the night before.'

'That,' Ashe said austerely, 'is outrageous.'

'Mama put it rather more strongly, apparently. But she loved him, at least enough for Gregory to be conceived. After that we hardly saw him. Money would arrive erratically.'

And then Mama had become ill and so, with no family alive on her mother's side, Phyllida had set out for London to find Papa. But that had cost more than she had imagined. He was not to be located, not immediately, so she had to pay for lodgings and food and gradually she had become more and more desperate until there had been only one stark choice. Sell the last thing of value she had, or starve and fail her mother and brother.

'Miss Hurst?'

She started, looked up and found Ashe watching her, his faint frown at odds with the relaxed pose he still held. 'Sorry. I was just remembering. It was not a happy time. But that is all in the past now. Anna, we must pack and prepare for a trip of— How long, Lord Clere?'

'Five days? We can do the journey in a day, easily, I understand, so that would give you three to assess the situation. I hoped to leave the day after tomorrow at nine.'

'Very well. I will be waiting.'

Phyllida found herself staring rather blankly at Ashe's broad shoulders as he made his way out in Anna's wake. Had she just made a terrible mistake in trusting his discretion? The consequences of this getting out were serious. Not for her reputation, as such, for if Ashe said his great-aunt was to be there as chaperon, she was certain she would be. But she was risking being exposed as a dealer, as not just dabbling in trade, but being deeply immersed in it.

It was, she thought with a sigh, thoroughly unfair. If Gregory pulled off the successful wooing of a mercantile heiress he would be warmly congratulated by everyone and his wife accepted everywhere.

'Penny for them?' Her brother was lounging in the doorway, an amused smile on his face at her abstraction.

'I was just thinking about you. Have you seen Harriet today?'

'Barely ten minutes ago. I took her walking in Hyde Park under the eye of her mama. The approving eye, I flatter myself.' He came and sat down where Ashe had been, another long-legged, attractive aristocrat to grace the little room.

Phyllida's conscience gave a twinge. 'You do like Harriet, don't you, Gregory? Really feel some affection for her, I mean? I like her very much and I would hate to think she was going to end up the loser in a transaction between her parents and you.'

He raised an eyebrow. 'Are you asking if I will be faithful to her?'

'Well, yes, I suppose I am. And kind to her, a proper companion. She is too intelligent and sensitive to be fobbed off while you gallivant about town spending her money.'

'Ouch.' To her surprise he neither laughed it off or became angry. 'You are right, of course. If she was one of those empty-headed little geese who only wants a title it wouldn't matter, but I do like her and I think we could make a go of it.' He grimaced. 'If she'll have me.'

'Are you going to speak to her father?'

'They've asked me to their box at the theatre on Monday. I was going to see how Millington seems towards me then. If he looks amiable, I'll go and talk to him on Tuesday. If he's starchy, I'll expose them all to my many charms and talents for a few more days before I put it to the test.'

'Would you mind if I left town for a while?'

'No, of course not. Where are you going? Amanda Lewis in Essex?'

It was harder to explain than she thought it would be. Phyllida found herself scrabbling round for the right way to word it, almost as though she had a guilty conscience. *This is business*, she told herself. 'Lord Clere has asked me, on behalf of his father, to assess some items at their country seat in Hertfordshire. I would need to leave the day after tomorrow. It should take about five days in all.'

'That's good,' Gregory said. 'I should imagine you'll get on well with the marchioness and Lady Sara. Finding the pace in town a bit hectic and needing a rest, are they?'

'Actually...' *Oh Lord, how to put this?* 'They aren't going. Nor the marquess. Lord Clere is arranging a chaise for me and Anna.'

Gregory, it seemed, was not quite as relaxed as he looked. 'What?' He sat bolt upright. 'Are you telling me you are going off with that rake?'

'He is not a rake! Is he?' she asked, suddenly dubious. 'How do you know?'

'It takes one to know one,' her brother said darkly.

'Oh, really, Gregory! Either come up with some evidence—ruined maidens, drunken orgies or three-day gambling sessions—or stop slandering the poor man. I thought you liked him and, besides, he is not coming in the chaise and his great-aunt will move from the Dower House, so I will be perfectly adequately chaperoned.' *I hope.*

'I ought to go and talk to him about this.' But her brother sat back again, apparently mollified.

'Certainly,' Phyllida said, hoping she did not sound uncharacteristically meek. *Please don't!* 'I really appreciate you doing something so potentially embarrassing for me,' she added with sisterly cunning.

He rolled his eyes. 'I suppose it would be a bit awkward, asking him his intentions like that. Might be open to misunderstanding.'

'Whatever you think best, Gregory,' Phyllida said. 'But the real danger is that anyone discovers why I am away. So, if you're asked, just say that I've gone into the country to stay with friends for five days for a rest. Will you do that?'

He nodded and got to his feet. 'Got to get changed. I'll see you at dinner, Phyll.'

Left alone, she tried to decide whether she was happy that she had persuaded Gregory of the wisdom of this expedition or not. Five days with Ashe Herriard. Was that going to be Heaven—or hell?

# *Chapter Nine*

'**G**ood morning, Miss Hurst.' Lord Clere stood on her top step, looking indecently awake and perfectly groomed, just like the rather handsome bay gelding that was tethered by its reins to the area railings. Also sleek, male and alert was Lucifer, perched on the pommel.

Phyllida, on the other hand, was feeling harassed, wan, decidedly out of sorts and in no mood to be amused by evil-minded crows. It was one thing to agree to hazard one's reputation in the safety of one's own drawing room, but two nights in which to fret over it—in the intervals between fantasising most unwisely about the person of Ashe Herriard—was two nights too long.

'Lord Clere. We are ready, as you see. Come along, Anna, don't keep his lordship waiting.' The street, mercifully, was empty. It had only just occurred to her that to be seen getting into a hired chaise in the company of a man not her brother was more than enough to cause scandal, regardless of her motives for doing so.

'Are you comfortable, Miss Hurst?' he enquired when she was seated and wishing she had thought to add a veil to her bonnet.

'Perfectly, thank you. Anna, pull the blind down on your side. If we can depart as soon as possible, my lord, I would appreciate it. I have no wish to be seen, under the circumstances.'

'Of course.' He closed the carriage door and the vehicle jerked into motion.

*Eleven words. I can hardly convict him of attempting to seduce me with his charm this morning,* she thought as she huddled back against the seat and hoped that no one could see through the glass at the front of the chaise between her and the bobbing backs of the postillions. *But then, all the thoughts about seduction are in your head, your fantasies. Probably.*

Then a rider on a raking bay gelding passed the team and she found herself smiling. Why not have fantasies? The man looked magnificent on a horse and she was not made of stone. Fantasies were safe, much safer than yielding to impulses. In her daydreams passion was safe, romantic, pleasurable. Unreal.

'This will make a nice change,' she said to Anna. 'It is a while since we've driven out to the country. I wonder what Lord Clere's great-aunt is like.'

'An old dragon, I expect,' the maid said with a sniff. 'At least, I hope she is. If she exists at all,' she added.

'Are you suggesting that Lord Clere invented her and that there will be no one to chaperon me?' Phyllida demanded.

'Could be.' Anna pursed her lips. 'Or perhaps that's what you're hoping for, Miss Phyllida. He's the gent you were talking about in the park, isn't he? Handsome as sin, that one.'

'Nonsense. At least, anyone who isn't as blind as a

bat must agree Lord Clere is good-looking. But he is on the hunt for an eligible wife, so—'

'It isn't marriage I'm talking about, Miss Phyllida, and you know it. What's his lordship going to say if you come home ruined?'

*I* am *ruined*. Phyllida bit her tongue more painfully than she had intended as the carriage bounced over a rut. 'I'm not a green girl, Anna. If Lord Clere has any intentions towards me other than the friendship he professes, I am quite well aware that they would be dishonourable ones and I have no intention of ruining all my plans for the sake of a risky dalliance.'

'I'm glad to hear it, Miss Phyllida.' To Phyllida's relief Anna settled back in her corner and turned her attention to the passing landscape, leaving her to her own, not very comfortable, musings.

What if Ashe did make a move, of any kind? Was she strong enough to resist the temptation? He was attractive, attractive enough to break through all her fears and qualms about a physical relationship, at least at first, she thought with a shiver. Kisses and caresses, so long as she remained in control, would be wonderful. But he was a full-bloodied man, passionate, strong. She had no hope of controlling him and then... Phyllida shuddered. She liked him as well, too much for her own peace of mind.

Her sensible self told her firmly that to become involved with Ashe Herriard risked all her plans, all her practical, prudent schemes for her future. But at the back of her mind a small, seductive voice murmured that if she was never going to marry she ought to experience what she was missing. That as an independent

woman she had the right to make her own decisions
about her life.

*And what would the Millingtons say if there was a
scandal?* common sense demanded. *And I'm probably
quite wrong and Ashe has merely been flirting and has
no interest in me at all, that way,* she added firmly. *I
am perfectly safe and the only danger is my overactive
imagination. Probably.*

Lady Charlotte Herriard proved to be a Roman-nosed
spinster of formidable assurance and considerable age
who had no qualms about saying exactly what was passing through her mind at any moment. Ashe and Phyllida
were shown into her drawing room amidst half a dozen
lapdogs that skirmished about their ankles.

'Lord Clere, Miss Hurst, my lady,' the butler announced. 'I will have the tea tray brought up immediately.'

'Plenty of cake, mind, Sparrow.' She set down the
book she had been reading and crooked an imperious
finger at Ashe. 'So, you're Nicholas's son by his Indian
wife, are you? You've got the air of your great-grandfather about you. Come here, Miss Hurst, and let me
have a look at you. Who are you, eh?'

'The sister of Lord Fransham, ma'am.'

'Ah!' She raised a lorgnette and studied Phyllida with
all the arrogance of age and rank. '*Those* Hursts. Your
father always was a fool, even as a child. So you're a
woman of business, are you? Causes a scandal, eh?'

'No, ma'am. I am very discreet.' Phyllida kept a bri-
dle on her temper and thought about the significant fee
she was going to earn.

'You'll need to be, because don't think I'm going to

drag myself over to the house just to act the chaperon all day long! I'll come to play propriety, but you set out to be independent, my girl, and you'd better be able to look after yourself.' She smiled thinly. 'I certainly did.'

Phyllida was digesting that statement and wondering what Lady Charlotte had got up to in her youth as she was waved to a chair, apparently dismissed as a source of interest.

'Clere, bring those side tables over for the tea and then sit here so I can look at you.' Ashe did as he was bid and sat down opposite his great-aunt. 'You going to behave yourself with this young lady or have I got to set a maid to keep an eye on her?'

'I can assure you, Great Aunt, that I would do nothing that Miss Hurst would not wish.' Phyllida knew him well enough by now to tell he was amused by the old dragon, but not well enough to tell whether that was a double-edged reply or not.

Lady Charlotte seemed to have no doubts. She raised one thin grey brow. 'Oh, yes, you do indeed remind me of my father.'

'Not his son, my grandfather?' Ashe asked, apparently at ease under the scrutiny.

The tea tray was brought in before Lady Charlotte could answer him. 'Be so good as to pour, Miss Hurst. And eat some cake and then I can do so and keep you company. My doctor forbids it, old fool.' She fixed her gaze on Ashe again. 'No, you do not have the look of your grandsire, for which you may be thankful. Every family mints a bad penny now and again and he was certainly one. Go and have a look at the Long Gallery and the family portraits and you'll see.'

* * *

Ashe rode on from the Dower House after an agonising hour of interrogation, leaving Phyllida's chaise and his aunt's travelling chariot to follow him. He told himself that the faint feeling of nausea in the pit of his stomach was partly the acerbic questioning of Lady Charlotte and part the consumption of an unwise quantity of excellent lemon cake. It was nothing to do with apprehension over what was waiting for him at the end of the carriage drive as it wound through the shrubberies to the front of Eldonstone House.

He had fought in battles in the heat of the Indian sun, he had dealt with palace plots, he had foiled an assassination attempt on his great-uncle and he could outwit a French diplomat. What was there to set his nerves on edge here other than a house that held no memories for him and a straightforward duty to be undertaken?

Lucifer gave a harsh *caw* and flew down to his shoulder as though seeking reassurance and then the house came into view.

It was an imposing, alien-looking pile of grey stone and red brick, begun, he had learned from his shipboard studies, under Charles II, but owing most of its character from the reign of the first George. Used to small windows, carved grilles and screens and all the details of inward-looking palaces, the expanses of unshielded glass in numerous windows made the house seem almost indecently exposed. Almost as exposed as the English ladies in a ballroom with their revealing gowns, he thought.

The front doors opened as he approached and liveried servants emerged with Perrott in their midst, his red head a familiar sight. 'My lord! Welcome to Eldonstone.'

Grooms ran to take his horse, the staff lined up to be introduced by Stanbridge the butler and Ashe found himself inside his ancestral home.

He turned a full circle in the hallway, swearing softly under his breath in Persian as he took in the smoke-stained hangings on the walls, the lack of ornament or signs of care, the stack of packing cases pushed partly under the arc of the handsome flight of stairs.

Stanbridge cleared his throat. 'His late lordship professed himself uncaring about the state of the house, my lord. He refused to waste money, as he put it, on upkeep or even thorough cleaning and, with a skeleton staff, I regret…'

'I understand. But he lived here?'

'Most of the time, my lord. This is where he mainly, er, entertained.' The butler's face was so expression-less that he might as well have shouted his disapproval.

'Entertained? In this?' Ashe opened a door into what must once have been an elegant salon.

'His lordship's company was more concerned with drinking, hunting and the young female persons who were hired than with the amenities of the house, my lord.'

'So I see. Well, there is no way that my mother and sister are going to come and live in this.' The picture over the mantel was enough to make even Ashe, inured to erotic carving, raise his eyebrows.

'Quite so, my lord,' Perrott agreed. 'However, even the more objectionable items appear to be of some value and I could not undertake to dispose of them on my own initiative. I understand you have brought an expert to assess things?'

'Miss Hurst, who is coming on from the Dower House with Lady Charlotte. We will start work in the morning. Have bedchambers prepared for the ladies, Stanbridge.'

'Certainly, my lord. One of the footmen will attend you in the Garden Suite, the traditional rooms for the heir.' He regarded Lucifer through narrowed lids. 'I will have a large bird cage sent up, my lord. Dinner will be ready in an hour, if that is acceptable?'

Ashe climbed to the first floor, wondering if the best thing would be to set a match to the entire edifice. And yet… He paused on the landing and looked down the sweep of stairs, the proportions of the hallway. This was an elegant, well-made house that had been ravished and neglected. It could be saved, it could become a home if the ghosts that haunted it could be exorcised.

'I am glad I came and not my father,' Ashe said as Phyllida stood beside him in the hall the next morning and stared about her. 'He will have some concept of it as it should be.'

'It needs a platoon of scrubbing women, a good clear-out and a family living in it again and then it will be a lovely house,' she said stoutly, trying not to feel daunted by the gloom, the neglect and the clutter. 'Where shall we start?'

'Here and the drawing room, I thought—then it will at least appear more welcoming. Then the master suite and rooms for my sister. I should warn you, some of the artwork is of an indecent nature.'

'I will avert my gaze,' Phyllida said and Ashe smiled

for the first time that morning. 'You will trust my judgement?' Three days to start to bring some order to this was a significant challenge. 'May I direct the staff to clean and move things?'

'I leave it entirely to you,' he assured her. 'Stanbridge, place everyone at Miss Hurst's disposal and hire additional cleaning women as she directs. She will doubtless need footmen to help her move things. I will go and inspect the stables.'

Three hours after breakfast the next morning Phyllida felt she was beginning to make progress. She had commandeered a long chamber as a sorting room, had directed the footmen to set up trestle tables and was dividing up items from the hall and drawing room into things which just required cleaning and which could then go back, things that seemed beyond repair, items of poor quality and, forming a dauntingly large section, items of some value, but in dubious taste or of an indecent nature.

The tapestries in the hall were fine Flemish work and were being lowered and rolled to go off for cleaning, maids were scouring the marble floors and washing down the walls and she had found some unexceptional pictures to hang.

Phyllida pushed up the sleeves of her cambric morning gown and rummaged in one of the chests brought in from the hallway. It was a good thing, she decided, swiping dust from her nose with the back of one hand, that she had not come here hoping to seduce Ashe Herriard. Not only had she hardly seen him since yesterday, but she must look a complete fright with her hair wrapped up in a linen towel, a copious apron borrowed from Cook and dust everywhere.

A wrapped object proved to be a charming porcelain figure of a lady, caught in the middle of executing a dance step, her hand raised as though to take her partner's hand. 'And where are you, young man?' Phyllida muttered, delving again. 'There you are!' She emerged triumphant and unwrapped the male dancer, tipped him up and studied the base. 'Meissen. Lovely.'

She set them carefully on the table of items to keep and caught her own skirts up with one hand as she raised her other arm in imitation of the lady. 'Exquisite.'

'Indeed.' Fingers interlaced with hers and she found herself turned to face Ashe. 'Shall we dance?'

He was teasing her, of course. There was no need for her heart to pound or her cheeks to colour and no excuse at all for letting her fingers curl into his as he kept their hands raised in the graceful hold. 'A minuet? Sadly dated, I fear, my lord.'

'You forget, I am lamentably behind the times, Miss Hurst. It might be just the dance for me. Shall we try?' He turned her under his arm and she found herself toe to toe with him. A little panicky tug and her hand was free, only to find that allowed him to put both arms around her, drawing her close. 'There are other dances we could enjoy together,' Ashe suggested, his voice husky.

She could not breathe. There was no mistaking his intent. But was he asking her to be his mistress or simply to indulge in a liaison here for a few days? Either of those possibilities should have sent her fleeing from the room and yet, in the fleeting seconds before he bent his dark head and captured her lips, she could not feel outrage or fear or anything she should have experienced. Only desire. Desire mercifully untainted by fear or apprehension.

Phyllida closed her eyes as Ashe drew her close against him. It was not from modesty, but simply for the sheer pleasure of his hard body against hers, the strength of him, the male heat and scent, the deliciously contradictory sensations of safety and danger. Ashe's kiss on the quayside had fuelled arousing dreams, but that had been the merest caress, she realised as her lips parted under his and he took possession of her mouth. Then his attention had been half on the man who had made her so afraid, now he was focusing every iota of his formidable expertise on reducing her to quivering surrender.

Did he expect her to respond? She had no idea how to answer this onslaught, although her hands had curled instinctively around his neck, her lips had parted and her tongue seemed to be doing daringly wicked things without her conscious direction. *He believes me to be a virgin, to be innocent*, she reassured herself as she wondered dizzily if she was about to faint from lack of air, or simple lust.

Ashe seemed to sense her weakness even as her legs began to give way. He broke the kiss and she opened her eyes to find herself still held in his arms. His heavy-lidded gaze studied her face. 'I thought I was not wrong,' he murmured.

*Arrogant man.* The thought flashed into her head as a deep indrawn breath steadied her. What had she been thinking of? This was madness. Delicious, exciting, infinitely tempting, but completely wrong. Besides, it could come to nothing. She liked Ashe, he took the trouble to kiss with finesse and consideration for her pleasure, but she could not pretend to herself that the delight would last were matters to go any further.

'You thought me a lightskirt?' she flashed at him. She would *not* back away. Phyllida stiffened her spine and her quaking knees and did her best to ignore the clamouring instinct to throw herself back into Ashe Herriard's embrace and find out if he could, after all, work magic and banish her memories and her nightmares.

'No. I thought you a passionate woman it would be a pleasure to kiss and I judged you would respond if I did.' He was watching her like a man confronted by an unpredictable danger, calm but poised to evade both a slap on the cheek or a lashing from her tongue.

'And now what?' Phyllida demanded.

'We could do it again?' That wicked mouth was serious, but his eyes were filled with laughter.

'That is not what I meant! Am I to expect kisses whenever you find me alone—or do you have the intention of taking me to your bed, my lord?'

'*My lord,*' he echoed. 'Am I so in disgrace? Would you come to my bed if I asked you? It is what I hope.'

# Chapter Ten

Phyllida hesitated a betraying second too long. 'No! Of course I will not come to your bed!' Her hands were knotted in her apron and she made herself release it, smooth out the creases.

Ashe half-turned and moved to examine the Meissen figures as though to soothe her by putting a little distance between them. 'A pity. I am very attracted to you.'

His long fingers caressed down the bare arm of the dancing lady and Phyllida shivered as though they touched her own naked flesh.

'You told me you wanted to be friends,' she accused.

'I have always been friends with my lovers,' he countered.

'How pleasant for you! I am very conveniently here, am I not?' *And I am a weak-willed woman who has been dreaming of the touch of your lips, the pressure of your hands, the hardness of your body and I am not sophisticated enough in these matters to hide that.* 'And there are no other distractions to entertain you.'

'There are plenty of distractions, Phyllida. Not that any of them are very entertaining,' Ashe said wryly.

'But are you telling me that you feel nothing for me? That I am so far adrift in my reading of you?'

She moved round the packing case, glad of its bulk between them, and reached in for another wrapped object. 'I am a respectable woman, my lord.' *Liar.* 'I cannot afford to allow my feelings to dictate my actions.' The wrappings fell away to reveal a pot pourri bowl. She set it down on the table too hard and the fragile pierced lid rattled like her nerves.

'Then you do have feelings for me?'

'Only the realisation that you kiss very well.' She wiped her hands on her apron and dug into the chest again. If she fled from the room, she would never have the nerve to return and the work steadied her hands. 'I expect you have had a great deal of practice. Or perhaps it is simply that I have had very little and you are actually quite mediocre at it.'

That surprised a chuckle of laughter from him. 'Should I be suffering from any excess of masculine conceit, you, Phyllida, are a most certain cure for it.'

She removed the paper from around a stack of delicate Worcester fruit plates, lips tight on a thoroughly unladylike retort. After an interval when he said nothing, made no move to touch her, she asked, 'You expect feelings in your liaisons, do you?' His face went very still. 'You charm your mistresses with talk of love, perhaps?' She had meant to be sarcastic, to show her scorn for his talk of feelings when all he wanted was to bed her, but the expressionless face was suddenly vulnerable. For a second she thought he flinched.

'Ashe? What did I say?' Phyllida realised she had blundered into something she did not understand.

'I no longer make that mistake,' he said lightly.

'You loved one of your mistresses? What happened to her?' As she asked it she guessed. There was loss, bleak and cold, in those green eyes. 'She is dead.'

'Yes.' Ashe turned away as though to study the porcelain she was setting out. 'All this is European. Is it any good?'

'It is excellent.' If he thought to divert her by changing the subject she would not oblige him. 'And valuable. And that is not important. Tell me about her, the mistress you loved.'

'She was the only mistress I ever had, I suppose,' he said, his attention apparently fixed on the piece of Meissen in his hands. 'Before her there were…encounters. After her, liaisons. I learned my lesson with Reshmi.'

'She was Indian?' Phyllida took the statuette from his unresisting hands. 'Tell me.'

'Her name means *The Silken One*. She was a courtesan at my great-uncle's court. Beautiful, very sweet, gentle. Exquisite.' Phyllida saw with a pang that his eyes were closed, the thick, dark lashes shutting her out. 'I let myself fall in love with her and, far worse, I let her fall in love with me. The mistress of the women's *mahal* spoke to the raja and he showed me that I was simply being unkind to her and that it must stop.'

'But why? If you loved each other—'

Ashe opened his eyes and smiled, the twist of his lips bitter. 'My great-uncle pointed out to me that I was the heir to a marquess's title, that I would be leaving India for England very soon. Did I expect to drag an uneducated Indian girl halfway across the world to be my mistress for as long as I remained besotted with her? I protested that this was love, that I would marry her. He told me not to be a fool and to go away and think about it.'

Phyllida watched him as he wandered across the room to end up with one foot on the hearth stone, his hands braced on the mantelshelf, his back to her. 'So I thought about it. My mother is half-Indian, an educated daughter of a princely house, trained to run a great household, confident and used to European society and yet I knew she dreaded coming here, however well she tried to hide it. How could I uproot the daughter of a peasant from everything she knew—and how could I create such a scandal for my parents with such a marriage?'

'How did she take it?' Phyllida asked, dreading his answer.

'She sobbed and pleaded and then, when I was adamant, cruel because it was hurting me so much, too, she controlled herself, bowed her head, murmured that it should be as her lord commanded. She walked away into the gardens at the foot of the walls and I let her go, thinking she needed to be alone to compose herself.'

'Ashe, she didn't kill herself?'

'No. I tell myself not. She trod on a *krait*, a small, very deadly snake, and died in agony.'

*Oh, God.* Phyllida struggled to find the right thing to say, if the words even existed.

Ashe pushed himself away from the fireplace and came back to stand beside her. 'And when I had stopped wallowing in my self-indulgent grief I understood two things. That I would marry as befitted a future marquess, someone who would be a support to my parents, not a source of embarrassment to make their lives harder, and I would put juvenile fancies of love to one side before I hurt anyone else, let alone myself.'

'Ashe, love is not a juvenile fancy, it is real and strong. It exists.' She took his hand as though she could somehow infect him with that belief. 'Don't your parents love each other?'

'Passionately, without reservation. That sort of love is like a lightning strike, rare beyond belief.' The emotion, the pain, had gone from his eyes as he pulled his hand free. 'Enough of this.'

He would not confide further, not now. She had caught him off balance and he was regretting exposing that emotion and that weakness.

'If you wish to be useful, you could help me unpack these chests,' Phyllida said briskly, as though she had not wanted to weep for him and for that poor girl. *And for yourself. All you can ever be to him is a lover.*

'The tartness of your tongue is a constant delight to me,' Ashe observed, his change of tone startling her so much she almost dropped the set of fire irons she had found packed at the bottom of the chest.

'Then you must give me leave to observe that you are attracted to the strangest things in a woman.' He appeared to have recovered, which she found worrying. All that had happened, she was certain, was that he had buried the pain behind a formidable barrier of charm.

'And whoever packed these things away had the oddest ideas of what could be safely placed with what,' she added, beginning to drag the empty box towards the door.

'Let me.' Ashe strode across the room and lifted it, dumped it outside and took the chisel she was using to pry off the lid of the next one. 'Why are the footmen not assisting you?'

'I have them moving furniture so the drawing room can be cleaned.'

'Then sit down here,' he ordered, placing a chair next to a clear length of table, shrugging out of his coat and rolling up his shirtsleeves. 'And I will lift things out for you to check.'

'Very well,' Phyllida agreed meekly. Her legs were a little tired, to be sure, but it was also a pleasure to watch Ashe working, however unladylike it was to appreciate the play of muscles in his back and shoulders and the way his breeches pulled tight over an admirably trim backside when he bent over. He seemed to find some relief for his feelings in physical work.

The desire to see him naked, to touch him, to run her fingers over those muscles, those tight buttocks, warred with the need to hold him and comfort him. The former he would agree to without hesitation, the latter was impossible.

'To revert to your observation just now,' he continued as he lifted a bronze figure out, grimaced at it and took it straight to the rejects table, 'I have spent a lot of time in a place where I could not converse at all with respectable ladies and then three months on board ship with only my mother and sister for feminine company. It is a pleasure to talk to an intelligent woman who is neither a relative, a servant nor—'

'A concubine?' she murmured and could have bitten her tongue out.

'Exactly.' Ashe dumped the rest of the contents of his box on to the table and pushed a stack of badly chipped delftware towards her.

She pushed it back. 'This is in too bad a state.'

'That's the last of the boxes from the hall. Come and help me explore some of the rest of the house for half an hour.'

If he could act as though nothing had happened, so could she. Phyllida pulled the towel-turban from her head and tried to pat her dishevelled curls back into some kind of order. 'Where is Lady Charlotte?'

'Interrogating Cook. She tells me we need a new closed stove, whatever that is.'

'Expensive.' Phyllida removed her apron and went out into the hall. 'Where shall we go?'

'I thought the Long Gallery so I can inspect my host of ancestors.' Confront them, was a more accurate word, from the set of his shoulders and the tight line of his mouth, unless those were the outward manifestation of her refusal to be his lover or the painful story of Reshmi.

'Do you know much about them?' Phyllida asked as they trod up the staircase side by side. She ought to be feeling apprehensive, going off alone into the depths of a strange house with a man who had just professed his desire to make her his mistress, but instinct told her that Ashe would not force her. The fact that he seemed to have no qualms about offering near-impossible temptation was a truth that she pushed to the back of her mind.

Ashe pushed open the door into the Long Gallery. His body thrummed with unsatisfied desire. He was certain now that he wanted to make Phyllida his mistress and certain too that she could be persuaded. It had been agony to speak of Reshmi, but, strangely, a relief, too. And Phyllida would understand him better now.

He needed her, he realised, for more than the physical release of lovemaking. He liked her and trusted her and he could not let this drop now. But it was a fine balance between leading her into something she truly wanted and forcing her hand. He would take no unwilling woman.

His mood changed from a mixture of arousal and sadness into dark oppression almost as soon as he began to walk along the Gallery. It was uncanny. If he had believed in ghosts, he would think the place haunted by some spectre blowing cold misery over his soul.

Ashe stopped halfway along the long, narrow room and strove for some sort of equilibrium as he studied the life-sized portrait of a man in puffed breeches, ruff and bejewelled doublet. There were so many ancestors, all with his nose, most with the same green eyes that looked back at him from the mirror in the morning. All utterly confident that they belonged here and that he did not. No doubt they were correct.

The Jacobean marquess stared back, daring Ashe to walk on past him towards the most recent portraits at the far end of the gallery

'They are all exceedingly blond,' Phyllida remarked. 'Your portrait will be a pleasant change. Is your father here, do you think?'

'I doubt it.' He could not decide whether she had noticed his withdrawal or was simply ignoring his mood. Ashe walked on slowly, past Cavaliers with ringlets, Carolingian beauties with too much bosom on display and roving, protuberant eyes and into the last century. The house and park began to appear as the background in some pictures.

His pace slowed as he approached the picture almost

at the end. Phyllida peered at the gilded frame. 'I think this is your great-grandfather with your uncle who died and your grandfather.' She pointed at a tight-faced lad leaning sulkily against a tree while his father held a fine bay horse, his elder brother played with a spaniel and a small child held a ball. 'Is that Lady Charlotte?'

'Probably.' He tried to feel some connection with the two men who were so close to him in blood, but he could only feel dislike. The younger had sent his own son off thousands of miles away to almost die on a voyage into the unknown, simply because he resented the boy's likeness to his dead mother and the way he defied him over his treatment of her. The elder had stood by and done nothing to check his wastrel son or protect his grandson.

It would give his father some satisfaction to hang a new family group next to this one, an affirmation that despite everything he had survived, a far better man than either of his forebears had been.

'Do you feel a connection?' Phyllida asked, startling him. He had been so deep in his own brooding thoughts that he had forgotten he was not alone.

'No.' What he felt was oppression, the weight of hundreds of years of expectation on his shoulders. The expectation that he would carry on this line, this name, that he would devote himself to a cause that had not been his and a duty that he would never have chosen.

'Think what it must be like for a royal prince,' Phyllida said, chiming uncannily with his thoughts. 'Not just a name and a great estate, but a whole country to care for and all that on your shoulders because of an accident of birth.'

'How does your brother feel about inheriting a title

and an estate? Or does he simply take it for granted, being the only son?'

She went still, all the energy seeming to ebb out of her. Her memories, he was coming to realise, were not good. Finally she shrugged. 'When Gregory inherited things were in such a bad state that he almost gave up caring, I think. He was too young for the responsibility and he ran away from it to be with his friends. I was angry with him at first, until I understood that it was a form of self-protection, pretending not to care.'

'But *you* cared?'

Phyllida turned her back on the ranks of portraits and crossed to look out of one of the windows that formed the opposite wall. 'I am older than Gregory and I think women are better suited to cope with seemingly hopeless situations. Gregory would have fought if it had been a battle, climbed a mountain if that was what it took, but he could not deal with the daily dragging misery of having no money, a load of debt and no training for what he was facing.'

'It sounds as though your father and my grandfather were well matched.'

'I believe they knew each other.' Phyllida's mouth twisted in a fastidious moue.

'So it fell to you to find a way out of the situation.' Her face was still bleak. He saw how she would look as an old woman, all the colour stripped away, her fine bones and the delicate arch of her eye sockets still holding a elegant beauty. Ashe wondered just how bad things had been, how much strength it had taken to keep fighting until her reputation was established, their finances were under control and her brother finally matured into his responsibilities.

'It fell to me to scheme and nag, yes. You joke about my sharp tongue, my lord—it has been honed on my brother's skin. I just clung to the hope that one day he would grow up, see for himself that if he exerted himself there was a way out.'

'And now he has?'

'I think so. I hope so! And I suspect Harriet will be the making of him. Gregory is not very used to examining his own feelings, but I believe he may be falling in love with her.' She glanced up at him. 'Do not smile so mockingly, I will not accept your assertion that love is so rare, so unlikely.'

'Was I mocking you? But it seems to me that to hold out for romantic love is almost always to doom oneself to disappointment or disillusion.' He went back to the beginning of the gallery to look at the Tudor portraits once again.

'Your parents give the lie to that—one only has to look at them.' Phyllida followed him, refusing to let go of the subject as he had hoped.

'Their story is almost a fairy tale—the hero rescues the princess from a fortress under siege, they escape across a hostile land, fight dacoits, elude pursuing maharajahs. How could they fail to fall in love? The whole thing must have been conjured up by some djinn. My mother jokes that if we ever fall upon hard times she will turn novelist and write tales of dramatic romance and make our fortune again.'

'And you fear you will never find anything as wonderful as they have.' He shrugged. 'And so you will not hope, you will not seek it, because that way you will not be disappointed,' Phyllida observed.

That was too near the knuckle. Ashe glared at a

wooden-faced couple almost obscured by heavy varnish. He would not delude himself that affection, desire or liking were love and he would not risk hurting himself, or another woman, as he had so carelessly with Reshmi.

'I must choose with my head, not with my heart,' he said when he had bitten back the angry retort. 'I cannot afford to drift around, hoping my fancy will fall upon a woman of the right breeding and temperament and connections.'

'Instead you will approach the matter of marriage as you would buying a horse?' Phyllida snapped, suddenly and inexplicably irritable. 'You left out inspecting her teeth and checking for child-bearing hips.'

The hold on his own temper broke. 'And just what have you been doing to marry off your brother that is so different? Making lists of wealth, temperament, looks—and parents who want to buy a title.'

'That is different! Gregory will be ruined if he does not make a good match. Everything that I have done will have been for nothing.' She was sheet-white and there were tears in her eyes.

'And my family have given up everything that was dear and familiar to come here and take up this responsibility. I do not give a damn about this lot.' He swept an arm round to encompass the entire pantheon of ancestors. 'But I will find someone to support my mother socially, help with Sara's come-out, bring my father connections in politics and at court. I cannot play around living some romantic daydream.' *Damn it, I will not feel responsible for upsetting her! She started this.*

'I am going to ride out around the estate,' Ashe said. If he didn't walk away he was going to find himself with a sobbing female in his arms. 'Get one of the footmen to help you and don't lift anything heavy.'

Phyllida watched the tall figure stride out of the Long Gallery. 'I am not going to cry,' she said out loud as the door closed behind him with a thud. 'You don't have to run away.'

It would be pointless to weep just because Ashe had held up a mirror to all the things she had done since their father left them: all the work and the sacrifices and the bitter decisions. What he saw reflected back was a managing, nagging sister pushing her reluctant brother into marriage for convention's sake.

That wasn't true, was it? She found she was curled up on one of the broad window seats overlooking the gardens at the back of the house without any clear memory of how she had got there. If she hadn't been strong, hadn't bullied and cajoled and schemed, Gregory could have ended up like their father.

Movement pulled her out of her introspection. A rider was galloping at full stretch across the parkland beyond the ha-ha. Ashe, of course, riding as though all the devils in hell were after him, Lucifer soaring above him like a dark familiar spirit.

That outburst had not just been the irritation of a man being forced to turn his mind to marriage, she realised as the horse and rider vanished behind a copse of trees. She had touched a raw wound. Love… Ashe did not believe he could ever find it again and his spirit revolted at making a suitable, emotionless, match. Did he realise that was what was wrong? She doubted it. In her experience men would sooner poke out their eyes with red-hot needles than contemplate their own emotional state. His confidences about Reshmi had ended with him putting up the shutters again with a vengeance.

Phyllida put her feet up on the seat, wrapped her arms around her legs and rested her chin on her knees. No wonder Ashe was so straightforward about proposing she should come to his bed. He had decided to put sex and marriage and affection into separate boxes and that way no unpleasant, risky, messy emotions could interfere.

No risk of loving a wife and being hurt by her lack of response. No danger of it with a mistress, someone paid to respond to his body's needs, not his mind.

She ached for his hurt, ached for the walls he had built around his heart. And she feared for herself. It would be too easy, perilously easy, to let liking and desire for Ashe Herriard slip over into something dangerously like love.

# Chapter Eleven

Green, peaceful… Ashe wondered if this was typically English. He reined in and began to look around him at the expanse of parkland that surrounded the house. His anger had evaporated in the clear air, leaving him light-headed, as though he had been ill with a fever and was recovering.

Time enough to worry about that flash and spark of emotion between him and Phyllida just now in the Long Gallery. He knew he had overreacted and he was not certain why, for he could have sworn he had his emotions under control again after his weakness in blurting out the story of Reshmi. Nor could he fathom what he had said to distress Phyllida so deeply. She was not a woman who used tears as a weapon—that anguish had been genuine.

Ashe shook his head to clear it and made himself study the land around him. It was beautiful. The ground rose before him with a mass of curving woodland that clad the upper slopes in soft curves like the bosom of some generous earth goddess. There was a glint of water ahead, and coppices of slender trees of fresh green, unlike the heavy woodlands beyond.

But surely the parkland should be grazed? The grass was almost high enough to conceal large game. And there was dead wood in the coppices, bricks had fallen from the ha-ha and as he approached the lake he saw that it was muddy and overgrown with weeds.

There was money to make this right and surely there were men who would want the work? Had his grandfather really hated the place so much? Ashe rode on, found a hedge and a gate with farmland beyond. That was better. The methods of farming and the crops were strange, but this was well tended, in good heart.

'Can I help you, sir?' A man reined in a stolid cob.

A countryman, Ashe decided, looking at the sturdy, self-possessed figure in corduroy breeches and working boots. 'I am Clere.'

The man doffed his hat, but showed no other sign of deference. 'Then welcome to Eldonstone, my lord. I am William Garfield from the Home Farm. We look forward to having the family back at the house.'

'There's work to be done before then, I fear.' The other man grunted. No doubt he knew what the house was like. 'I know little or nothing about farming in this country, but your acres look in good heart.'

'I've farmed this land for twenty years, my lord, and my father rented it from the marquess before me. I hope my elder son may carry on in his turn. But your small tenants are not in such good shape—the ones who rely on you for repairs to their dwellings and investment in the land.'

Ashe liked the direct look, the honest criticism. 'Have you time today to show me?'

'There's your land agent, Mr Pomfret...' Garfield began.

'Who has connived in the neglect. I would prefer to see for myself before I tackle him.' When the other man gave a brisk nod he reined back to allow him to open the gate.

'We'll begin with the smallholdings then, my lord.'

Ashe followed as he cantered away across the park. This was not what he had come here for, he had never had the slightest interest in agriculture, but something was pulling him to investigate.

'What have you been doing with yourself all day, Clere?' Lady Charlotte demanded from her place at the foot of the dining table. Phyllida, who had been dying to ask the same question, kept her eyes on the cruet in front of her and congratulated herself on having asked for four sections of the dining table to be removed.

'Miss Hurst has been making admirable progress, I have to say,' Lady Charlotte added. 'I am sure she would have welcomed some assistance—or was vanishing into the blue your idea of discreet behaviour?'

Phyllida flinched inwardly. The older woman had no regard for the footmen ranged around the room, no doubt absorbing every word. 'Lord Clere was very helpful,' she said hastily. 'But, really, I get on well by myself.' She risked a glance at Ashe, immaculately attired in evening dress that had, at least, won the approval of his aunt. There was a magnificent emerald in the centre of his neckcloth.

He was smiling, apparently without strain. She reminded herself that he had been a diplomat. 'I have been exploring the estate in the company of Mr Garfield, our tenant at the Home Farm. I found it unexpectedly interesting.'

'I imagine you know very little about agriculture, my lord,' Phyllida ventured.

'Which may be why I find it intriguing. But even I can see that there has been a scandalous neglect of the land and the properties,' he said with a complete absence of his usual faintly amused tone. 'The tenants are living in poor conditions and the land is in bad heart, which reduces their yields and our rents.'

'Pomfret was your grandfather's creature,' Lady Charlotte observed. 'Idle devil. I wouldn't put it past him to have been lining his pockets.'

'I intend to dismiss him tomorrow,' Ashe said. He glanced around the room at the footmen. 'That goes no further, do you understand?' He ignored the chorus of muttered, *Yes, m'lord*, and added, 'I have employed Garfield's second son in his place.'

'High at hand!' his aunt exclaimed. 'Without consulting Eldonstone?'

'I found I did not want to have this continue a day longer. My father will agree.' He glanced at Phyllida and caught her watching him. 'I have discovered, to my surprise, that although I do not care one jot about my ancestors, I do care about the land and the people.'

His great-aunt snorted. 'You give me cause to doubt that you are a Herriard! Every one of them of recent generations has cared more for the name and the standing than for the estate, provided it kept on bringing in money.'

'The land and the people are all that matters,' Ashe said. To Phyllida's ears he sounded even more surprised at himself than his great-aunt had been.

'You can fall in love so easily?' she asked in jest, with some instinct to cut the intensity that seemed to thrum in the air, and then bit her lip. She should not joke about love to Ashe.

'It seems I can,' he said slowly, his eyes shadowed as he met hers across the table. 'With an idea, that is. I felt the connection, the history, the link back for hundreds of years, more closely riding around the estate this afternoon than I ever did reading about my ancestors or seeing their portraits in the Long Gallery.'

'If that means you are going to apply yourself to dragging this estate out of the slough it has fallen into, then it doesn't matter what high-flown sentiments you express about it,' Lady Charlotte said tartly.

'My father always intended to do that, and I to help him. I have no idea what his feelings might be when he comes here. If he dislikes the place, then I suppose he will leave it to me to deal with.'

'You had best find yourself a wife to help you sooner rather than later if that is the case,' Lady Charlotte observed. 'Have you any idea of the duties the lady of the house has towards the estate?'

'No, but I expect you will tell me,' he said with a smile that Phyllida thought a trifle forced.

'I do not need to. Marry the right girl and she'll have been trained to it and she'll need all that experience. This is not just a large house, but one that will need dragging into the nineteenth century. I wonder if there are any of the local misses who would do,' she mused.

'That would save you the tedium of Almack's, my lord,' Phyllida said sweetly to cover a little jolt of discomfort at the image of a flock of local eligibles fluttering around Ashe. Each would bear some valuable piece of adjacent land as her dowry, no doubt.

'I have a strong suspicion that my father is going to desert the field and leave me to squire my mother and sister to that place,' Ashe said darkly. 'I doubt I can escape it. I return to town the day after tomorrow.'

The ladies retired to bed after the tea tray was brought in. Ashe kicked off his shoes and swung his feet up on to the sofa as the sound of Lady Charlotte bemoaning the poor quality of the Bohea tea faded into the distance.

It was some kind of miracle the connection he felt to this place now, as though a key had turned in a lock in his brain, a door had opened and he had recognised the rightness of this estate for him. Home. He was, by some miracle, genuinely a Herriard of Eldonstone and so, he hoped, would his sons be.

Which brought him back neatly to the inescapable fact that he needed a wife. What were the duties of the lady of a great holding like this? His mother was going to have to discover them, fast, and a daughter-in-law raised on just such an estate would be invaluable to her.

If he could only conjure up some image of the woman he wanted. He closed his eyes and tried. He knew what her qualities must be, her breeding, but what would she look like, what would her character be?

The trouble was, the image he found himself painting on the inside of his eyelids was of medium height, had wide brown eyes, a dimple in her chin and was all too inclined to laugh at him, argue with him…kiss him.

*Hell's teeth, I need a mistress. I need Phyllida.* Then he could concentrate on finding a wife. Ashe stood up, found his discarded shoes and took himself off to the library in search of something dull enough to send him to sleep.

By the third evening at Eldonstone Phyllida felt weary with the pleasant tiredness that comes with hard work and a successful outcome. Lady Charlotte had toured the finished rooms, declaring herself delighted with the hall, the drawing room, Lady Sara's chamber and the master suite. Ashe had been nowhere to be found—inspecting leaking roofs and fields in need of drainage, the two women agreed.

'At least now my nephew and his wife and daughter may sleep here without having nightmares,' the old lady pronounced at dinner. 'The sooner Miss Hurst works her magic on the rest of the bedchambers, the better. I declare I have hardly had a good night's sleep while I have been here. There is a stuffed bear in my chamber and my maid has had to turn most of the pictures to the wall!'

'There is a series of prints in mine that I have not inspected too closely, but which I fear may be hideous Chinese tortures and executions,' Phyllida said with a shudder.

'I deal with my bedchamber by the simple expedient of only using one candle and confining most of my activities to the dressing room,' Ashe contributed. He had come in just before dinner looking windblown and energised.

They exchanged horror stories about the house all through the meal. Her companions spoke as though it was an established fact that she would come back and work on more rooms, but Phyllida was doubtful. She would help the family dispose of any items they wished to sell, of course, but she found herself shying away from the idea of continued close contact with Ashe as he pursued a wife with increased motivation.

He had said nothing more about a liaison between them and had not so much as touched her hand. It seemed she was safe now, but she was too attracted to him, she acknowledged as she ate syllabub abstractedly, her gaze fixed on the quite hideous urn on the sideboard. And if she was not careful that attraction could grow and become more. It would be very easy to become exceedingly attached to Ashe Herriard.

'Miss Hurst?' Lady Charlotte said impatiently. 'You are woolgathering! What are you thinking about?'

Phyllida jumped and almost dropped her spoon. 'Lo—' *No, don't even think the word!* 'I am sorry! I was just envisaging lovely expanses of clear walls and polished surfaces, all ready for Lady Eldonstone to decorate as she pleases.'

Ashe, speaking to the footman about the dessert wine, did not seem to notice her stumble. Lady Charlotte gave her a considering look, but made no comment beyond saying, 'If you are ready, Miss Hurst, we will leave Clere to his port.'

Phyllida followed her out of the room, braced for a lecture on either daydreaming at table or, if Lady Charlotte was as perceptive as she feared, committing the heinous crime of falling for the heir when utterly ineligible herself.

But the old lady chatted about local gossip—all of it impenetrable to Phyllida—complained about the new curate's sermons, asked her opinions on roses, then disagreed with everything she said and finally rang for her maid. 'I am for my bed.' She creaked to her feet, waving aside offers of assistance. 'That boy is turning out better than anyone might have hoped,' she remarked just as Phyllida was resuming her own seat and offering up thanks that she could now relax.

'You mean Lord Clere, ma'am? Hardly a boy!'

'No, he is not, is he?' The faded hazel eyes rested on Phyllida's face for an unnervingly long time before Lady Charlotte turned and walked to the door. 'I just hope he knows what he's about, that is all. Goodnight to you.'

'Goodnight, ma'am.' *What on earth does the old dragon mean?* She could make no sense of it and her own thoughts were too uneasy to add speculation to them. If Ashe wanted tea, he would have to consume it alone, she decided, she could not face being alone with him just now. Besides, they had a journey ahead of them in the morning and she should try to get some sleep.

Ashe trod softly up the sweep of stairs. He had no desire to wake anyone up at this hour. As if to emphasise the point the long case clock in the hall struck two.

He was strangely unsettled. He knew he was unwilling to leave Eldonstone and uncomfortable with the prospect of wife hunting, but those sources of discomfort did not seem enough to account for this mood. He would be coming back here as soon as he could and he had accepted that the search for a bride was a priority. There was nothing new there.

His nagging state of physical frustration was not new, either. He could deal with that himself, he supposed, while he brooded on tactics for the seduction of Phyllida Hurst. *No, persuasion*, he corrected himself.

He could live with persuading her to do something she already wanted to, he was not such a rake that he would seduce her against her better judgement.

He padded past the first of the bedchamber doors. His, the vast and gloomy Heir's Suite as Stanbridge insisted on calling it, was inconveniently placed right at the back of the house.

'Let him go!'

Ashe stopped dead in his tracks, the shadows created by his candle swooping wildly across the walls. The silence that had followed that demand was almost more alarming than its suddenness had been. He was outside Phyllida's room, he realised. Just a nightmare? Or could there possibly be something wrong—an intruder, illness?

The knob turned under his hand and the unlocked door swung open silently. The candlelight flickered over the bed and he saw that Phyllida was sitting bolt upright, her face turned towards him, her eyes open

'Phyllida?' She made no reply, so he entered. The door clicked shut behind him, the small noise like a gunshot to his straining ears. Ashe held his breath and listened. They were alone—he could hear her breathing, feel his own heartbeat—but nothing else stirred.

When he reached the bed she did not move and her wide eyes were unfocused. A nightmare after all. Ashe wondered whether to leave her, but as he watched she stirred, put her hand to the top of the covers as though to push them back. No, he would have to wake her, he could not risk her sleepwalking around the house.

Setting the chamberstick down loudly on her bedside table did not rouse her. 'Phyllida! Wake up.'

She gave a little gasp and wriggled back in the bed,

her eyes still staring past him. 'No,' she whispered and raised her hands as though to fend off someone. Some *thing*.

Ashe sat on the edge of the bed and took her firmly by the shoulders. 'Wake up, Phyllida, you are quite safe. I am here.'

Between his palms her shoulders felt thin, fragile, although he had seen her lifting heavy ornaments with ease. It was as though this night-terror had sapped her strength. She blinked and he saw focus and consciousness return like wine being poured into a glass. 'Ashe?'

'You were having a nightmare and I thought it best to wake you.' He kept his voice low and matter of fact. 'Do you sleepwalk?'

'Not for years.' In the warm candle-glow she seemed to lose colour.

'It was a bad dream, I heard you call out. What was it about?' Perhaps if she spoke of it the thing would become less terrifying.

'You,' she whispered.

'*Me?* You were having bad dreams about me?' The shock made him pull back, his hands still cupping her shoulders, jerking her towards him.

'You were trapped under all those portraits of your ancestors, as though they had fallen off the walls and somehow thrown themselves at you. They were talking, gibbering.' She shuddered and he brought her close against his chest for comfort. 'I could see your left hand and you were wearing your father's signet ring. Then you threw them all off and got to your feet, but they were reaching out of the frames for you, all those white hands with the same ring, all reaching, scrabbling.'

Ashe encircled her with his arms and she burrowed

in, her cheek against his shirtfront, her hands sliding under his coat to hold him. At that moment Ashe was as glad of the human contact as she seemed to be. He could well do without that image to come back and haunt his own dreams. As soon as she was settled he was going up to the Long Gallery to face down the spectres himself.

But now the cold finger of superstition was being thawed out by the pleasure of holding an armful of warm, soft woman. 'Thank you for having my nightmare for me,' he murmured in her ear. Strange that she had been so perceptive, so in tune with his mood, despite his reserve and ill temper.

Phyllida gave a small laugh, her sense of humour apparently resurfacing as the dream faded. 'I do not think it works like that, but perhaps I was a lightning rod for it. Thank you for waking me.'

'I was passing.' His hand, of its own volition it seemed, stroked down the supple curve of her back, warm through the thin lawn of her nightgown. His thumb ran down her spine, traced each vertebra, and she arched against his palm like a cat being stroked.

'Ashe.' She wriggled a little and looked up, her head tipped back because she was so close.

He had no idea what she was going to say, nor any conscious intent to kiss her, but he dipped his head and found her mouth with his, and was lost.

# Chapter Twelve

**P**hyllida was all soft, warm, scented femininity against him, every inhibition seemingly lost in the haze of waking from her nightmare. Her arms were around his torso, her breast heavy and rounded in his hand as he palmed it, the nipple hard beneath the thin veil of lawn.

Urgent for her touch on his naked skin, he fought his way out of his coat, ripped off his neckcloth, pulled his shirt over his head, all the time with one hand touching her, caressing her. He caught her up and felt her gasp as her hands pressed against his back, heard the soft whimper of arousal as he bent his head to bite gently along the white slope of her shoulder, into the angle of her neck, up to the alluring soft skin below her ear.

'Ashe.' It was a whisper.

He lifted his head and read the trouble in the darkness of her eyes, the tremble of her lip, smooth and plump, ripe for his kisses. He only had to close his eyes against hers, only had to take her in his arms and use all the expertise he had to overcome her fears and scruples and the thing was done.

*Damn it.* He couldn't do it. *Persuasion, not seduc-*

*tion.* As though it was physically painful he forced his body further away from her. His hands slid down to rest on her forearms, her fingers turned up to clasp his wrists.

All his mistresses before now had been Indian and he had loved the contrast of his pale golden skin on theirs. Now the whiteness of Phyllida's long fingers on his arms was like cream over honey and he bent to run his tongue-tip along one of them.

'Ashe, no. I cannot. I cannot be your mistress.' She pulled her hands back until their fingers meshed as they had in that impromptu minuet days before.

'Why not?' he asked, trying not to make it a demand, calming his breathing as if he was about to take aim with a bow and arrow and must be utterly still. 'When we kiss—'

'I want you. I am not such a hypocrite to pretend otherwise. We spoke of this, Ashe. I have not changed my mind and I thought you had understood that.'

'I had. I do.' Was that a lie? No, he understood her decision, but he was determined to change it. 'When I came into this room I had no intentions other than to make certain you were safe. When I took you in my arms it was to offer comfort and then—' he met her eyes squarely '—then my intentions changed. I have no excuses.'

She should make a fuss, be indignant, make him feel guilt and shame and then he would never tempt her again. 'Yes, there are excuses. Real ones,' Phyllida found herself saying. 'I reacted as though I would welcome your caresses.' She forced herself to as much honesty as she dared. 'I *did* welcome them. I wanted to touch you, to kiss you. Most men would not have stopped, would have argued that I led them on.' *Stop pretending* you *don't want it, you need a real man to show you...* Somehow she repressed the shudder lest he think it was for him.

So close to his naked torso, her hands still on him, she wondered again what would it be like to lie with Ashe. Would his kisses sweep her away so the fear was lost, submerged by a roaring wave of passion, or would he coax her out of her fears, softly, gently, replacing nightmare with pleasure?

Or would she panic when those caresses moved beyond kisses? She closed her eyes, imagining her own screams, her nails ripping down his cheek. And he would know her deepest, darkest secret, that she had given herself, her innocence, to another man, not out of love but for money. Like a whore. *Not* like, the inner voice of her conscience chided her. *You* were *a whore.*

'No, you did not lead me on,' he said as he freed her hands and stood up. 'I take responsibility for what I do and I may want you too much for my own peace of mind, but I am not some rutting beast whose lusts must drive him. Are you all right now? Perhaps you should ring for your maid, send her for some hot milk or chocolate to soothe you.'

'It would take more than chocolate to soothe me after that kiss,' she said wryly. 'And why should the poor woman lose her own sleep because I am restless?' She watched him pull on his shirt and tuck it into his evening breeches, deliberately heaping coals on the smouldering fires he had kindled. The feel of that smoothly muscled back, the memory of the trail of dark hair from his chest down past his navel, the easy breadth of his shoulders—those were going to haunt her dreams for nights to come.

'Goodnight, Phyllida.' He caught up his neckcloth from the back of a chair and draped it around his neck. 'Dream of rare porcelain and precious gems. Sleep well.'

Phyllida slept and, if she dreamed, did not recall it when she woke, wincing, to the clatter of curtain rings.

'Good morning, Miss Phyllida.' Anna sounded indecently bright and cheerful. 'Rise and shine! We're away after breakfast and his lordship has ordered it for eight o'clock.' She came to the bedside and looked down, her smile fading. 'Are you well, Miss Phyllida? You're as white as a sheet.'

'I feel it.' Phyllida struggled up against the pillows and took stock of herself. 'I have a horrible suspicion that I'm going to be sick, Anna.'

The maid whisked the basin off the washstand and dumped it on her knees. 'It's that whiting from last night. We had the leftovers for dinner in the servants' hall and William the footman swore it was off.'

'It tasted all right. Oh!' Phyllida doubled up over the basin with a groan. When the worst was over she lay back, a wet cloth in her hand, and thought back. 'I do hope Lady Charlotte didn't eat any. At her age sickness could be dangerous.'

'Most of it came back down to the kitchen,' Anna said, frowning in recollection. 'That's why there was enough for the staff. But no one fancied it much because the stew was so good. William didn't finish his and Cook got the hump because of him saying it wasn't right, so she took it off the table. I'll go and get you some hot water and I'll let his lordship know you can't be travelling today.'

'No!' She had to get home, safely away from Ashe and all the temptation he offered. 'Lord Clere has to return and I cannot expect Lady Charlotte to spend any more time away from her own home. I'll be fine now. Just bring me my breakfast up here. Some toast, perhaps.'

Phyllida managed to keep down a slice of dry toast and a cup of weak tea, wash and get dressed, although her stomach was cramping and she felt ridiculously weak. Lady Charlotte was in perfect health and unbent as far as to offer her cheek to be kissed before she was helped into her travelling coach for the short ride home.

'In we get.' Phyllida urged Anna towards the chaise the moment the postilions brought it round. She had no intention of standing in the bright sunlight for Ashe to observe her pale, green-tinged complexion. He would probably put it down to a broken night spent fretting over him and simple vanity stopped her admitting to something as prosaic as an upset stomach.

By the time he had waved his great-aunt off and come to the chaise, she was sitting well back in a shadowed corner.

'What an admirably prompt woman you are,' Ashe said. 'The day looks set to stay fair and we'll be back to London in good time.'

'Wonderful!' Her cheerful response must have convinced him all was well for he closed the door, mounted his horse and they set off down the drive.

After ten minutes Phyllida was recalling all too vividly why post chaises were nicknamed Yellow Bounders. This one seemed to have extra-firm springs to make sure that every pothole, rut and stone contributed to the eccentric motion of the vehicle.

She doggedly chewed on the spearmint leaves that Anna had found in the kitchen garden and focused on Ashe's tall figure. But after a while the even cadences of the cantering horse on what must be a smooth verge only emphasised the swaying and jolting of the chaise. 'I've never felt sick in one of these before,' Phyllida lamented.

'Well, you hadn't eaten stale fish before, had you, Miss Phyllida?' Anna pointed out. 'We'll be stopping to change the horses in an hour.'

An hour! Phyllida bit down grimly on another mint leaf and tried to think of anything but her stomach and her swimming head. The only possible benefit of feeling so queasy, she had decided by the time the chaise reached King's Langley, was that it was a most effective antidote to amorous thoughts of Ashe.

'We're stopping, Miss Phyllida.'

'Thank goodness for that, because I do not think my breakfast is going to stay down any longer.' Phyllida clamped a handkerchief over her mouth. As the chaise clattered to a halt in the inn yard she opened the door and stumbled down, clutching the high wheel for support.

'What is wrong?' She had not even seen Ashe, but he was there at her side, his hands supporting her.

'Bad fish,' Anna said. 'She's going to be sick any moment, my lord.'

'Hang on.' Ashe bent and scooped her up in his arms, strode into the inn and snapped, 'A room, hot water, a basin.'

'Please…I can manage…' She glanced around as

best she could over the lace of her handkerchief. This was a large, smart inn, obviously one catering to the carriage trade, not some shabby little place where she could be ill in dingy privacy.

'In here, sir. Oh poor dear. Increasing, is she?' A woman's voice…a stranger. She was settled in a chair, hands—Ashe's—pressed a bowl onto her lap. Somehow her bonnet had gone and so had her pelisse.

Phyllida retched miserably, someone held her shoulders, a damp cloth smelling of lavender was put into her hand as the bowl was removed. She leaned into the supporting arm and smelled sandalwood beneath the lavender.

'Here's a little peppermint cordial. That'll settle you nicely, my lady.'

Hazily Phyllida realised that Ashe must have made his title known to secure prompt service and the woman attending her though she was his wife. And pregnant.

She sipped the cordial and swayed as the room lurched around her. This was ridiculous. She would *not* faint, she was made of sterner stuff than that.

'She is going to faint.' Ashe's voice came from a long way away. 'I had better put her on the bed.'

If she did lose consciousness it could only have been for a moment. Phyllida found herself propped up against pillows and lying on a vast patchwork quilt. 'I am sorry,' she managed.

'Don't you worry, my lady,' the other woman's comforting voice said from the doorway. 'I'll just pop down and get you a hot brick.'

'Where's Anna?' Phyllida asked, scrabbling ineffectually at her bodice. Her stays were like a vice, stopping her breathing.

'She's gone to find an apothecary for what she swears is an infallible potion to stop the nausea. What is the matter? Stays?' Ashe enquired. 'I can't say I've much experience with the things, Indian women have more sense than to wear them, but let's see what I can do.'

With a gasp Phyllida found herself tipped forwards against Ashe's broad shoulder while his fingers dealt efficiently with the buttons at the back of her gown and then the laces of her corset. 'Oh! Ashe, really you cannot—'

'I can,' he said. 'Thought I might have to cut them, but it was a nice easy bow. Now then, how are we going to do this?' He slid her dress off one shoulder, still holding her up from the pillows. 'Then this one…' The corset came away and she took a deep breath. 'There, is that better?'

'Lord Clere and his *wife*, you say? And the poor lady is sick? I must see what aid I can give. In here where the door is open?' A penetrating female voice, a rustle of skirts and Phyllida opened her eyes to see Lady Castlebridge, an earl's wife with the longest tongue in society, standing just inside the door, her expression avid with curiosity. 'Miss Hurst!'

Phyllida laid her forehead on Ashe's shoulder with a faint moan and the impossible hope that she could conceal just how much of her bosom and arms were laid bare. This was utter disaster and she could not think of a thing to do to rescue the situation unless the earth opened and swallowed her up.

'Madam?' Ashe laid her unresisting against the pillows and flipped the counterpane over her. 'I do not believe we have been introduced or you would know I am not married.'

'Well, everyone knows who you are, Lord Clere!' The delight of discovering a scandal right in front of her nose was all too apparent. 'And we had heard nothing of a wife, which is why it is such a surprise to find Miss Hurst with you and *enceinte*, poor dear.' The skirts rustled in to the room and the door clicked shut. 'I am Lady Castlebridge. Naturally, you may rely on my total discretion.'

'Far from being in an interesting condition, Miss Hurst is suffering from food poisoning and was taken ill on the road. We are the merest acquaintances, but naturally I could not leave the lady in distress when she fainted at my feet.' Ashe sounded aloof and faintly puzzled, as though he could not quite believe the intrusion. 'You are a close family friend, it seems. Perhaps you could hold the bowl for Miss Hurst when she vomits again while I go and find out what has happened to her maid?'

Despite everything Phyllida felt a faint flicker of amusement at the sounds of her ladyship's hasty retreat.

'Not that good a friend. I am certain Miss Hurst will want her maid to attend her. Er...perhaps I could find her.'

'Excuse me, madam.' Blessedly, Anna's voice, so polite it verged on insolence. 'Thank you, my lord, I can manage now.'

The door closed. After a moment Anna said, 'They've both gone, Miss Phyllida. He looked fit to strangle the nosy old besom, his lordship did. How are you feeling?'

'Dreadful.' She sat up and opened her eyes. Her stays were draped over the footboard of the bed, presumably where Ashe had tossed them. Her gown was round her waist and only her chemise gave any vestige of decency.

'Who took your stays off?'

'His lordship.'

'Oh, lumme.'

'Exactly.'

'And old sharpnose saw? Here, drink this, Miss Phyllida. I ran down the street to the apothecary.'

'She not only saw me on the bed, in Lord Clere's arms in my shift, she also heard the landlady's opinion that I am suffering from morning sickness.' Phyllida sipped the hot brew and felt it settle soothingly in her abused stomach. 'I rather think I am ruined, Anna.'

'Surely not? You'll be out and about in town tomorrow quite obviously not with child,' the maid protested.

'That is not the point. I am supposed to be staying with friends in Essex. How am I going to account for being in bed in a Hertfordshire inn on such terms with Lord Clere that he removes my underwear in a crisis? I will wager fifty guineas she has already discovered that we arrived together, even if he was not in the chaise.' She threw back the cover and got up. 'The smoke is all it takes, Anna. There doesn't have to be any fire, not when one's position is as ambivalent as mine is.'

*This is a complete disaster*, she thought as Anna did up her gown, bundled the corset under her own cloak and found Phyllida's bonnet and pelisse. Then another thought hit her: Gregory. 'Oh, my Lord.' She sat down on the edge of the bed. 'What is Mr Millington going to say when he hears? He'll never allow Harriet to marry my brother after this. We must get back to London as soon as possible. I must speak to Gregory, find some way of persuading Mr Millington that this will not come to reflect on his daughter.'

'Miss Phyllida!' Anna followed her down the stairs. 'You need to rest.'

'I can rest in the post chaise.' She gathered all her strength and swept into the hallway, praying that her shaky legs would continue to hold her up. 'Good morning, Lord Clere.' She stopped and bobbed a curtsy. 'Thank you for your assistance, but as you see, I am able to resume my journey. Lady Castlebridge! It is quite all right, there is no need to stand back in the shadows, I am not suffering from anything contagious, merely the effects of some bad fish last night. I will see you at the Fosters' musicale, I am sure.'

She made it to the sanctuary of the chaise before either could say a word. Anna called to the postilions to make a start and they rattled out of the yard and turned towards London and disgrace.

# Chapter Thirteen

Ashe found his father and Edwards, his secretary, in the study dealing with a pile of correspondence.

'You have made good time.' The marquess's smile faded as he took in Ashe's expression.

'Sir. Excuse the intrusion, but I need Mr Edwards's advice. What are the laws concerning marriage in England?'

His father went very still, then set down the pen he was holding. The secretary pushed his spectacles firmly on to his nose and cleared his throat, his face entirely blank of expression. 'Banns of marriage must be called in the parishes of both bride and groom over three weeks. This may be avoided, and often is by the Quality, by the provision of a common licence from a bishop. For marriages at very short notice a special licence from the archbishop is required, which in London will involve a personal visit to Doctors' Commons and a not inconsiderable fee.' He glanced at the clock. 'If one is needed, I fear it must now wait until the morrow.'

'Thank you, Mr Edwards, that is very clear. I was not contemplating matrimony within the week.' Ashe moved to the empty fireplace and rested one foot on the fender. 'Would you excuse us for a moment?'

When they were alone he said, without preamble, 'I have compromised Miss Hurst and therefore I regret that I must marry her.'

'Regret?' His father's brows rose.

'She is not an eligible bride. She is illegitimate, she is not received at court or accepted at Almack's and therefore she cannot assist my mother or Sara.' Ashe made himself continue dispassionately down the list. He was not going to fudge what a disaster this was. 'Her brother has no political influence, his lands are a significant distance from ours and will bring no benefit to you or to the estate. She has no dowry. She owns a shop and buys and sells for it herself—in other words, she is a trader and if word of that ever gets out it will mean she is received in even fewer places.'

'Your mother is illegitimate and her father was a trader,' his father said in the quiet tone that Ashe knew disguised tightly reined emotion.

'Yes,' he agreed. 'But she is the daughter of a princess, he was a nabob. You are a marquess. The case is very different in the eyes of society.'

'How is she compromised? Is she with child?'

'No!' Ashe caught up the unravelling ends of his temper. *Guilty conscience*, he told himself. 'No, it was all very innocent and damnably unfortunate. She was taken ill as we returned and fainted in the inn. I was loosening her stays in a bedchamber when Lady Castlebridge, who appears to be a voracious scandalmonger, walked in on us.'

The marquess gave a bark of laughter that sounded as though it was wrenched unwillingly from his throat.

'It is not funny,' Ashe said mildly. He was inclined to kick something. Someone. Probably himself.

'It has all the elements of a farce,' his father countered. 'But there is nothing to be done about it. You are quite right, you must marry the girl and we'll make the best of it.' He narrowed his eyes at Ashe. 'Do you like her?'

'Yes.' Ashe shrugged. 'As far as that goes it would be no hardship to be married to her.' And making love to Phyllida would be a perfect pleasure.

'A special licence would appear to be the best method under the circumstances.'

'No. I have been thinking about this.' All the way back from Hertfordshire. 'I believe less damage will be done if I very publically court Miss Hurst and marry her after a couple of months. There will be no question of her being with child then, which should confound the gossip and retrieve her name somewhat.'

'There is a question of pregnancy?'

'She was casting up her accounts after eating bad fish. The innkeeper's wife assumed she was increasing and said so loudly for all to hear.'

The marquess sat back in his chair and ran both hands through his hair. 'God! And to think I had assumed we could descend on England and sink quietly into society with hardly a ripple.' He gave a huff of laughter that sounded more like genuine amusement. 'We had better go and tell your mother that she is about to acquire a new daughter.'

His father was taking this well. Ashe suspected that his mother, always unconventional, would forgive him, too, and Sara, the romantic chit, would think him in love and happily ignore any snubs that came her way as a result. He would rather they all abused him roundly for allowing this to happen.

And he would be rewarded for not closing a door and impetuously not waiting for a maid by having to marry the woman he desired as his mistress. *No*, his inconvenient conscience reminded him. *If you had not been as intimate with Phyllida as you were, then it would never have occurred to you to stay in the room, let alone loosen her gown and remove her stays, and you know it.*

He had always assumed duty and honour went hand in hand. It seemed that in this case his honour demanded that he default on his duty. *You reap what you sow*, he thought bitterly as he went to find his mother. He would do the honourable thing by Phyllida Hurst—now he had to find a way to do his duty by his family.

As for Miss Hurst, she would be delighted at a marriage beyond her wildest dreams and it should not be too much trouble to put an end to all those hidden elements of her life that proved such a risk. The shop must go, the stock be sold—she could have no objection.

'Gregory! Oh, you are home, thank goodness!'

He appeared in the doorway of the back parlour in his shirtsleeves, a pen in his hand, his hair on end as though he had been raking his fingers through it. 'Welcome home, Phyll. I have good news for you.' She stepped into the light from the open drawing-room door and he saw her face clearly. 'You are ill! Anna, what is wrong with Miss Phyllida?' He strode forwards, dropped the pen and took her arm.

'Anna, please go and ask for tea to be sent up. It is just bad fish, Gregory. I have been sick in the stomach, that is all. Come into the drawing room, we must talk.'

She let him guide her in, seat her on the *chaise* with her feet up, wrap a shawl over her legs. 'Give me that bonnet. Can you manage the pelisse? You should be in bed.'

*Don't fuss*, she wanted to shout. *Don't make me feel any worse than I already do*. 'Thank you. Gregory, what is your good news?'

'Harriet has accepted me!' Despite everything she felt a glow of pleasure at the genuine warmth and happiness on his face. He *did* care for Harriet.

'Thank goodness! How wonderful, Gregory.'

'And Millington has been all that is generous and welcoming. Very straightforward about settlements and what he expects and none of it unreasonable. I was just working through the papers when you got home. He wants certain guarantees for Harriet's future and trusts for the children and so forth.'

'He sees your true character, Gregory,' Phyllida said warmly, feeling the guilt like a knife in the stomach. 'But I am sorry, I have done something so imprudent that I fear Mr Millington may withdraw his consent to the match.'

*'What?'* He stared at her. 'What on earth could you have done? Is it Clere? I knew I should never have allowed you to go off with him!'

'Gregory, sit down, please. It was the most awful combination of circumstances and not Lord Clere's fault at all.' She explained what had happened at the inn while he paced up and down the room, swearing under his breath. 'I must go and speak to Mr and Mrs Millington before they hear of this in any other way.'

'Lord, yes.' Her brother sank into a chair and rubbed his hands over his face. 'I'll come with you, of course, they must see I support you completely. But where is Clere? He should be here with a special licence in his hand, telling me how he intends to safeguard your honour.'

'I have no idea where Lord Clere might be.' Phyllida closed her eyes, overcome with weariness. 'I escaped from the inn before we could speak of it. I do not wish to marry him.'

But she did need his help to calm the scandal and safeguard Gregory's betrothal. She had expected him to overtake them, stop the chaise, demand that they discuss it there and then. Now she wondered with a shiver whether Ashe simply intended to ignore the whole thing and brazen it out. She was on the knife-edge of respectability as it was, a completely unsuitable wife for him, but surely there was something he could do to help?

'Be damned to that!' her brother exploded. 'You must marry him. I am going round there right now and if he is not prepared to do the right thing he can name his seconds.'

'Gregory—' The knock on the door cut her short. *Ashe.*

'A letter for you, Miss Phyllida.' Jane had remembered to put it on the silver slaver and presented it with a flourish, all crisp expensive paper and heavy red seal.

Phyllida knew that seal. She broke it, spread open the single sheet with hands that shook and read out loud,

> *'Miss Hurst,*
> *I trust you will have recovered sufficiently from your indisposition to attend Mrs Lawrence's party this evening. I am reliably informed that Lady Castlebridge will attend, as will the Millington*

*family. I intend to silence the lady and reassure
those whom you hope will be your future in-
laws in a manner that I trust will meet with your
approval.*
*I remain your obedient servant,*
*Clere.'*

'He is going to propose and announce it there and
then,' Gregory said, mopping his brow with his handkerchief. 'Thank heavens for that.'

'I do not wish to marry him and there is absolutely
no reason why I should,' Phyllida protested. 'If I just
explain to the Millingtons, and then carry on as though
nothing has happened, it will quickly become apparent that the cause of my sickness is exactly what I say.'

'You cannot refuse an offer of marriage to the heir
to a marquisate,' Gregory protested. 'Besides, the mud
will stick.'

'I most certainly can refuse him. It would seem as
though I had schemed to entrap him! My only concern
is your marriage to Harriet and if we can convince the
Millingtons that there is no truth in this, then all should
be well.'

Gregory looked ready to argue the matter all day and
night if necessary. 'I am going to rest until this evening,'
she said wearily and cast the shawl aside. 'I cannot talk
about this any more now.'

'Miss Hurst, I am very pleased to see you again.'
Mrs Millington shook hands with a beaming smile. The
gossip had not reached her yet then. 'Lord Fransham
will have told you the happy news, I have no doubt,' she

added in lowered tones as Phyllida joined her and her husband in a quiet corner of the reception.

'Indeed, yes. I understand there is to be no announcement until Miss Millington's twentieth birthday next month, but I am very happy for both of them. She will make Gregory a wonderful wife and I know him to be deeply attached to her.' She plied her fan and tried to see if there was any sign of either Lady Castlebridge or Ashe in the chattering crowd that filled Mrs Lawrence's large salon.

'Are you quite well, Miss Hurst?'

She snatched the opportunity. 'To be frank, Mrs Millington, I am feeling somewhat fragile. An internal upset caused by bad fish,' she added in a whisper. 'Do you mind if we sit down?'

'Of course not. Mr Millington, do find a waiter with a glass of wine for Miss Hurst, she is not feeling quite the thing.'

She waited until he came back with a glass and when he would have moved out of earshot put one hand on his arm to detain him. 'Please stay, sir. I must confess I had a most unpleasant encounter this morning and it has quite shaken me. I was taken ill at an inn where we had stopped to change horses. I fainted and was observed by Lady Castlebridge being assisted by Lord Clere, who also happened to be there.' She did not have to act to produce the quaver in her voice. 'She leapt to the most appalling conclusions when she found him supporting me in a bedchamber and I fear so much that any scandal will reflect most unfairly upon my brother.'

'That woman,' Mrs Millington uttered in tones of loathing. 'She lives for gossip and has the most unpleasant, snubbing manner. Why, I would not believe a word she says, my dear Miss Hurst, if she swore the sky was blue.'

Her husband, Phyllida saw, was less certain. 'There is bound to be talk.'

Mrs Millington frowned, the import of the story obviously beginning to sink in. 'That is true. There was nothing more that might have made things worse, I trust?'

Phyllida could feel the blush mounting in her cheeks. 'Lord Clere was loosening my clothing and the landlady assumed I was *enceinte*.'

'What? Oh my heavens, the scandal! What is Clere doing about it?'

'I have no idea,' Phyllida said. 'He is an acquaintance of Gregory's, but—'

'Here he comes,' Mrs Millington said, sounding not a little flustered. 'And there is Lady Castlebridge.'

As a lady should, Phyllida showed no sign of having seen the approaching viscount, but continued to exchange meaningless pleasantries with the Millingtons. To her relief, they were continuing to talk to her. *So far.*

'Miss Hurst.' Did she remember his voice as being as deep, as carrying? Heads turned. The little group around Lady Castlebridge watched, agog. 'I am so relieved to see you here. Are you quite well now, ma'am?'

'Well?' What was he doing? Why on earth was he speaking in such carrying tones? The entire reception would hear.

'After your collapse this morning at the inn.' An expression of dismay that she knew perfectly well was feigned crossed his face. 'My apologies, ma'am, I should have realised that no lady would wish it bruited abroad that she had been taken ill.' His voice was hardly any less carrying. 'But it appears you were correct and the effects of the bad fish have worn off.'

'Lord Clere.'

He turned to Mrs Millington and bowed. Phyllida introduced them hastily.

'Ma'am?'

'You were able to assist Miss Hurst this morning?'

'Ineptly,' he said with a laugh. Phyllida realised that all eyes were on them and that Lady Castlebridge was frowning in apparent confusion. 'I should have done better to have laid Miss Hurst down on a settle until her maid came back from the apothecary. But what must I do, but catch her up in my arms—a fine sight for Lady Castlebridge to come across, indeed.'

So that was how he was going to try to play this! All she could do was to join him in brazening it out. 'Mrs Millington, I cannot tell you how embarrassing it was,' Phyllida said brightly. 'There was the landlady, giving her opinion as to why I was ill, for anyone to hear, the gallant Lord Clere with an armful of fainting lady *en déshabillé* and dear Lady Castlebridge not knowing what to do for the best.'

She turned and appealed, smiling, to the bridling countess, 'Confess, ma'am—was it not the most complete farce? If I had not been in the middle of it all and feeling so unwell, I would have been in ripples of laughter.'

'It had all the appearance of a most irregular situation,' her ladyship snapped. All around people were joining in with Phyllida's laughter and her lovely scandal was turning on its head.

'Exactly.' Phyllida forced a chuckle. 'Oh dear, I should not laugh, I know, for there is poor Lord Clere, who has hardly set foot in London, suspected of elopement or worse.'

'Miss Hurst,' Ashe said with considerable warmth. 'Any gentleman of sense would surely wish to carry you off.'

Phyllida found herself in the midst of a crowd. Ladies enquired sympathetically about her health, shooting dagger-glances at Lady Castlebridge who, it seemed, had made one bitchy remark too many to win friends. The men slapped Ashe on the back and told him what a slow-top he was not to have carried off Miss Hurst while he had the chance.

'That,' Mrs Millington remarked close to Phyllida's ear, 'was a masterly piece of strategy on Lord Clere's part. I can only hope it was enough.'

'Indeed,' her husband muttered. 'If this does not die down, I must reconsider Harriet's position.'

'Of course,' Phyllida whispered back, her stomach cramping with nerves. 'I do understand, but I am certain… If you will excuse me,' she added, more loudly, 'I think I should sit down. Perhaps I was a little ambitious in coming out this evening after all.'

'I hope I may take you driving in Hyde Park tomorrow,' Ashe said. Several young ladies pouted in chagrin at not being asked. 'Eleven o'clock?'

'Thank you, the fresh air would be delightful.' He bowed and strolled off, leaving Phyllida to wave her fan to and fro and try to congratulate herself on a lucky escape. Because, of course, she could not marry Ashe Herriard, she did not *want* to marry him and to feel at all disappointed that she was not now compelled to was positively perverse.

She cast a glance up at Mr Millington's stony countenance and tried to convince herself this was going to be all right. It must be, for Gregory's sake.

## Chapter Fourteen

'I should wait and have a word with Clere.'

Phyllida adjusted her bonnet before the drawing-room mirror and wondered if her brother had reformed rather too far. 'There is absolutely no need. We discussed it last night and you heard yourself how cleverly he turned the gossip on Lady Castlebridge.' Gregory was still hovering. 'Go and take Harriet out for a walk as you promised. It is a lovely day.'

'Clere should marry you,' he said stubbornly. 'For your sake and...'

'Why? You making a good marriage is one thing, but it simply isn't an option for me. And I do not need to— the Millingtons are being understanding, are they not?'

Gregory shifted uncomfortably and then unfolded the letter he was holding in his hand. 'This came from Harriet first thing. She says her father was difficult at breakfast time. Apparently he mentioned our own parents' scandal and then made some remark about Clere's family, the fact that his mother was not born in wedlock and is half-Indian. He seems to think that makes Clere likely to be a bit lax about propriety.'

'He will withdraw his consent?' Phyllida dropped her gloves in agitation.

'He hasn't gone that far. I think if you stay in London and scotch the rumours of pregnancy and Clere continues to pay court to you in a respectable manner, that might set his mind at rest.' Gregory's normally cheerful countenance was set in an unfamiliar expression of resolve. 'If he does forbid it, then Harriet and I will elope.'

'*What?* Gregory, no! Her father will cut her off, you'd be penniless.'

'I'd manage and Harriet is willing, she says so in this note. We love each other.'

'Gregory, no, you must not do anything so rash. I will lay this scandal to rest, I swear. Now promise me you will do nothing irregular.'

He shrugged. 'Not unless I have to.'

To Phyllida's relief Ashe was prompt, although she was too agitated to admire the handsome curricle he was driving.

'We must talk,' he said as he drove up the hill of St James's Street towards Piccadilly.

'We *are* talking.' Her stomach dipped in apprehension.

'I do not mean social chit-chat. Where can we avoid the crowds?'

'Cross the Serpentine. I will point out the less-frequented routes where we will still be visible. And I agree, we need to talk. Urgently.'

He did not reply and she glanced sideways at his profile, very aware of the groom perched up behind them.

'Harris, you may get down here and wait.' Ashe drew up just inside the gate, waited for the man to descend from his perch and then urged the pair into a smart trot. 'Now then, how are you feeling?'

'Confused,' Phyllida said with a snap. 'Anxious.'

'I mean in the aftermath of the fish.'

'Perfectly fine, thank you. And my nerves have just about recovered from that outrageous play-acting at Mrs Lawrence's party. I have persuaded my brother not to call you out, but I am worried—his future in-laws are taking this very seriously. Mr Millington has dredged up the scandal with our parents and, forgive me, has even referred to your own family's unconventional background.'

'Hell.' She glanced sideways and saw his mouth was a thin line. Then he smiled at her. 'I am delighted that Lord Fransham is prepared to stay his hand. One hardly wishes to meet one's future brother-in-law in a cold field at the crack of dawn.'

'What?' Phyllida almost dropped her furled parasol. 'We need to behave like indifferent acquaintances until people believe there is nothing between us and I must stay very visible until it is obvious that there is no question of my being with child, but there is absolutely no need for you to marry me.'

'Smile,' Ashe said, reining the pair back to a walk. 'Someone you know is approaching, I think.'

'Lady Hoskins.' Phyllida produced an amiable expression and kept it steady under the stares of Lady Hoskins, her son and daughter. 'What a lovely day, is it not?' Once they were out of earshot she said, 'This is so embarrassing.'

'They will all get used to me courting you,' Ashe said calmly, looping his reins as they turned to cross the bridge.

'My lord... Ashe, stop this.' He reined in and turned to her, one eyebrow raised.

'I do not mean the carriage! I mean this nonsense about marriage. You know perfectly well that I am a completely unsuitable wife for you.'

'I compromised you. You know it, I know it and Lady Castlebridge knows it.'

'And the fact that I do not wish to marry you, you do not wish to marry me and your father must be tearing his hair out at the thought of me as a daughter-in-law means nothing to you?'

'It is a matter of honour. My family is in absolute agreement with me. And nothing would calm the Millingtons' nerves more than the assurance their daughter will be related by marriage to a marquess.' He sounded quite calm about the whole thing.

Phyllida wondered distractedly if this was actually a nightmare, one of those frustration dreams where the dreamer is thwarted at every turn and with the added torment of wanting to do exactly what he said and knowing she should not.

'Arguing with you is like trying to reason with a cat,' she said in exasperation. 'You just sit there, calm as you please, licking your whiskers and purring to yourself and not attending to a word I say.'

'Licking my whiskers?' At least he sounded taken aback.

'You know what I mean. And if you are so determined to marry me, why did you not appear on the doorstep with a special licence in hand?'

'And confirm the scandal? Have everyone watching your figure for months in expectation of a seven-month baby? With a leisurely courtship honour is satisfied, your reputation is unharmed and society will simply conclude that the incident at the inn brought us together and roused my interest in you.'

'Your honour may be satisfied, Ashe Herriard, but what about mine? Do you think a woman enjoys knowing she has entrapped a man, however unwittingly?'

'Nonsense. You were so far from entrapping me that you refused all my persuasions to become my lover.'

'Really?' Perhaps insult would convince him how insane this scheme was. She could hardly tell him why she could never marry any man. 'I hardly felt over-persuaded—you had not even begun on the inducements. Where were the offers of jewels and gowns and a luxurious apartment that I gather are a standard part of the negotiations? Or did you think that we could meet in the rooms over the shop and save money?'

Ashe flicked a rein and the pair began to walk on. 'If I had thought you were a woman who could be swayed by mercenary considerations, I would have raised the subject immediately.'

'So you thought your kisses were enough, did you?'

'I had hopes that you did not find me entirely repellent,' he admitted. 'I cannot imagine what gave me that impression,' he said mournfully.

*Wretch.* 'I do not, and you know it, so you may stop play-acting,' she said, smiling despite everything. 'Why I like you I cannot imagine. You order me about, organise my life, attempt to seduce me—'

'No,' Ashe interrupted. 'Never that. I tried to persuade you. Seduction involves bedazzling someone until they do something against their better judgement.'

'So, you would not seduce me into becoming your

mistress, but you will compel me to become your wife? It is a fine distinction I do not understand.'

He reined in again and this time shifted on the seat so he was three-quarters turned to her. His eyes were hooded and intense as he studied her face. 'What will compel you is your understanding of what society requires and your need to protect your brother's engagement to Miss Millington from scandal.'

'And what of the many reasons against you marrying me?' Phyllida half-expected him to deny that her birth, her unconventional way of earning her living, her lack of influence or wealth mattered. She would not believe him, of course, but it would be soothing to her pride and that was very much in need of something to heal it.

'I put them in the balance against what honour demands and the scale tips most definitely to marriage,' Ashe said with flattering honesty. That was one thing she could never hold against him, he had always been truthful with her.

Honesty or deceit. There was one way out of this, a way that would safeguard Gregory until his marriage was concluded *and* save her reputation. She could lie to Ashe, pretend that she agreed, allow the courtship to progress and then jilt him. Society would doubtless agree that it would be a lucky escape for him.

'I see,' Phyllida said slowly as she turned the idea over in her mind, trying to see beyond her instinctive feeling that this was a dishonourable thing to do. But if it saved Ashe from an unsuitable marriage, freed him to make a match that was everything his duty to his family demanded, then where was the dishonour in that? And she was hardly living a life of open, honest virtue now—she deceived the *ton* every day of the week.

'Very well,' she said with a show of reluctant capitulation. 'How do you propose we carry out this courtship?'

'As publically as possible.' He did not sound rapturous over her surrender, but then, what did she expect?

'In that case, in the interests of openness, I suggest you drive back towards the more populated parts of the park. How long do you suggest we should wait before you are overcome with a passionate, if unwise, desire to marry me?'

'Four weeks?'

'Four weeks it is.' The Millingtons, she knew, had been happy to have Harriet marry Gregory fairly shortly after their betrothal was announced. She had four weeks of simulating a growing love. Then there would be a few weeks after she 'accepted' Ashe, during which time Gregory would be married and then she could develop cold feet, or a nervous collapse or some other excuse for quietly breaking it all off.

Four weeks in the company of a man she was perilously close to wanting to make her own, a few weeks of pretending to be a happily engaged bride-to-be. She could not bring herself to look beyond that.

Phyllida was not happy and he did not trust her capitulation. Ashe turned the curricle and tooled it back over the bridge and along the now-crowded Rotten Row.

He was getting the same prickling between the shoulder blades that he had come to recognise as a diplomat when someone was lying to him with skill and conviction and yet he knew, deep inside, that it was a front.

She had accepted him and she was planning something. Probably to jilt him as soon as she felt safe to do so, Ashe thought with a grim twist of his lips. That would solve the problem of her unsuitability, but his pride rebelled at such a reprieve. Or was it simply pride and would it be so much of a reprieve? He glanced across at Phyllida's profile. She was smiling slightly, her eyes darting from side to side, her hand lifting every now and again to greet acquaintances, acknowledge other waves.

Why had he not noticed before that her nose was very slightly upturned at the end or that her lashes were really ridiculously long? Probably because he had been focusing on her mouth with the intent of kissing it, he acknowledged.

'What are you staring at?' she asked. 'Have I a dirty spot on my face or is my hair escaping?'

'I was admiring your eyelashes,' Ashe admitted. She turned and laughed and something inside twisted with a kind of pleasurable discomfort. Ridiculous, to be so captivated by a laugh, especially when he strongly suspected Phyllida was laughing *at* him. Yes, it would hurt more than his pride if he allowed her to escape his net, he realised. 'They are very long.'

'So are yours.' She studied him openly for a moment before turning back to watching the crowd. 'But yours are darker than mine, which is unfair. Ashe, when you were dressed as an Indian at the warehouse, had you put something on them?'

'Kohl,' he admitted. 'You can have it if you like, I doubt I'll need it again in this country. When I was at my great-uncle's court I found it handy on the occasions I wanted to pass unnoticed as an Indian on diplomatic missions.'

'Was it dangerous, that work?'

'Sometimes.' He had the thin knife scar over his ribs and the nick out of his collarbone to prove it.

'Will you be going back to Eldonstone Hall soon?' Phyllida asked after a moment, as though that was a logical continuation to his answer. He supposed it was, if she was wondering how he intended to fill his time now without the stimulus of intrigue and danger.

'Perhaps, for the odd day or so. But I will need to be here, courting you, don't forget.'

'What about the unsorted objects? I do not think I had better go there again, not until our betrothal is announced.' Then she answered herself before he could reply. 'Have Perrott pack up all the items we weeded out and any more of the indecent objects and paintings that he discovers and send them to London. I can assign them to the right dealers and auction houses for you in my guise as Madame Deaucourt. That will at least save your mother and sister the worst of it when they visit.'

Thinking about her work had meant she had relaxed in his company again, Ashe realised. 'Thank you, I will do that.'

He watched as she greeted some more acquaintances. Ambivalent as her position might be, Phyllida knew everyone who was anyone in society and knew, too, how to navigate its shoals and rapids. It made him think of the less pleasant social obligations. 'I have been taking dancing lessons,' he admitted. 'It was rather worse than learning Persian, but I think I have the waltz under control now, as well as the others, so will you dance with me?'

'That was very fast,' she exclaimed. 'Or did you dance in India? Of course you will have done, English society in Calcutta must have had regular dances.'

'I usually managed to avoid them, although I could stumble through a cotillion and the country dances if I had to,' Ashe admitted. 'But I learned to dance at court in Kalatwah.'

'Will you show me?' Her eyes were wide, her lower lip caught between her teeth as she turned to him, full of interest.

'In India men dance with men and not for a female audience.'

'Oh.' She sent him a sliding, sideways look full of speculation. 'You must not demonstrate for me, then? It would be improper?'

'Very improper. So, not until we are married.' She had not answered his question. 'Will you waltz with me?'

'I have not been approved by the patronesses,' Phyllida said and the laughter vanished from her eyes.

'You aren't approved by them for *anything*,' Ashe countered. 'Why should you care about this? If they won't let you into their stuffy club, one more infraction will not make any difference.'

'True.' Her lips curved into a reluctant smile. 'But everyone knows I do not dance.'

'Dance with me and they will see you have changed your mind. You know you want to—you enjoy it, don't you?'

'You could tell? Oh, yes, so much. But then gentlemen started getting warned off by their mothers in case they forgot my situation. So I stopped.'

He imagined the subtle snubs, the gradual realisation that this was happening. Or perhaps it had been sharp, like a slap in the face. Now if anyone tried to wound Phyllida in his presence, he would call them to account for it. His conscience jabbed at him. So he was the only one to be allowed to hurt her then, forcing her to do what she did not want?

'There is Lady Castlebridge,' Phyllida said, her voice tight.

'Excellent.' Ashe began to rein in, ignoring Phyllida's hand closing hard on his left forearm.

'I don't want to talk to her,' she hissed.

'Oh, but I do.' The curricle came to a halt beside the open carriage Lady Castlebridge was occupying with three other ladies of a similar age. 'Lady Castlebridge, good day to you. Ladies.' He gave them the look that Sara described, amidst giggles, as his *seducer's smoulder* and they fluttered their plumage a little and smiled back.

'Miss Hurst, fancy seeing you with his lordship. Are you quite well now?' Lady Castlebridge asked, her eyes narrowed on Phyllida's face.

'I believe Miss Hurst feels better for the fresh air,' Ashe said before Phyllida could reply. 'I was just congratulating myself on the very mischance that led us to meet,' he added. 'It is probably most ungentlemanly of me to be grateful that a lady was indisposed, but I suspect that she would not have agreed to accompany me to try out my new curricle if had not been for that chance encounter at the inn.'

Four sets of feminine eyebrows arched upwards. Phyllida's unobtrusive grip on his arm developed claws. 'I certainly realised you were a safe pair of hands, my lord,' she said demurely.

Ashe bit the inside of his cheek hard to stop himself laughing. 'Good day, ladies.' He raised his whip in salute and drove on. 'For goodness' sake, Phyllida, you almost had me losing my countenance then. I think we had better be seen with my mother as chaperon as soon as possible.'

'Hmm.'

It was one syllable that held a wealth of meaning. 'You do not want to meet her? You must, soon.'

'Yes, of course. I am sure she is delightful, but she will not welcome me as a prospective daughter-in-law, will she?'

'If she likes you, she will accept you whether you are a duke's daughter or a flower seller,' Ashe said with perfect truth. As soon as he said it he spotted the danger. The corollary was, of course, that if Anusha Herriard decided that Phyllida was wrong for her son then she would move heaven and earth to stop the match and the woman beside him was quite sharp enough to realise that. 'And it is no use you play-acting in order to give her a disgust of you. She has seen you and heard enough about you to see through that.'

'I have told you, my lord, I am resigned to my fate,' she said as sweetly and meekly as she had addressed the carriage full of ladies.

*And I trust you no more than I do Lucifer,* Ashe thought. He would just have to give Miss Hurst something to think about besides plotting to get rid of him.

They conversed with excruciating politeness all the way back across the park to pick up Ashe's groom, then on even blander topics on the drive back to Great Ryder Street.

At a word from Ashe the groom jumped down and went to the horses' heads and he dismounted himself to hand Phyllida out of the curricle. She was relaxed, he saw, confident now that she had arrived home unscathed, probably pleased with the little barbs she had slid under his skin.

He escorted her up the steps, then took her hand and raised it to his lips. That was unconventional enough behaviour these days, he knew, but she accepted it readily enough after a quick glance to ensure that his body hid what he was doing from the almost-deserted street.

Phyllida was wearing short kid gloves. It was the work of a moment to roll the one he was holding down her hand until her palm was exposed to the sweep of his tongue, slow, insinuating, deliberately lascivious.

'*Ashe.*' She froze, her hand rigid in his, the scent of the jasmine water she had dabbed on the pulse point of her wrist filling his senses as he sucked the swell at the base of her thumb right into his mouth.

'You are mine now, Phyllida.' He rolled the glove back, freed her hand. 'And I hold what is mine and I do not let it go. Remember that.'

# Chapter Fifteen

*On my own front step...* Phyllida stood, her right hand cradled in the left at her breast, staring up at Ashe. Her pulse was thundering in her ears, her whole body felt sleek and tight and as wet as the flesh he had just sucked into his mouth in a blatant erotic statement that she had no answer for. No words at all.

It took an effort of will to unclasp her hands, to reach for the knocker, her eyes still locked with his, to bang it down and then stand there, waiting, waiting until the door opened.

'Clere!' Gregory opened the door wide. 'Do come in.' Despite his tone his eyes were hard.

'Thank you.' Ashe stood aside courteously to let her past. Phyllida made her unreliable legs move, crossed the threshold and went straight into the drawing room and the nearest couch, throwing aside gloves, bonnet, parasol before she collapsed on it, hands over her face.

Behind her she heard the door close and Ashe's voice, pleasant and normal, just as though he had not been wreaking indecent havoc on her nerves a moment before. 'I hope you will be the first to congratulate me, Fransham.'

'Cong… You are marrying Phyllida?' She could almost hear his jaw drop.

'You feel I should have asked your permission first? But Miss Hurst is of age and very independent.' Ashe sounded friendly and not in the least bit apologetic.

'No, no not at all. Delighted.' The relief in Gregory's voice was clear. 'But last night…'

'If a match had been announced last night, then it would have been quite obvious that something untoward had occurred.'

'But it hadn't.' Gregory sounded suspicious again.

'Of course not, but your sister had been at Eldonstone engaged on an activity she does not want to be public knowledge. She *was* found in my arms, her gown *was* disarrayed. People have such nasty minds. Now they will see a perfectly conventional, respectable courtship taking place. I have compromised Miss Hurst, I will marry her—but not with any unseemly rush.'

'Then you have my blessing.' By the sound of it Gregory was pumping Ashe's hand enthusiastically. And no wonder. He would be round at the Millington house immediately, telling them the good news that Harriet would be sister-in-law to a viscount, the heir to a marquess. Phyllida kept her eyes closed and tried to get her unruly body under control.

How could Ashe speak so piously about an *unseemly* rush? Unseemly! What he had just done verged on the indecent and now she wanted more, wanted him, and he knew it perfectly well.

'I must go now. Shall I call tomorrow so we can have a preliminary discussion about the settlements?'

'Yes, certainly. About three suit you?' Their voices became fainter as they went to the front door.

Phyllida lay back against the sofa cushions and tried to work up the energy to be indignant. Gregory did not control her money, she did. If Ashe wanted to discuss settlements, he could do it with her and her lawyer.

But just now she did not feel as if she could add up a simple column of figures, let alone work her way through the complex maze of a marriage settlement—and one she intended to wriggle out of the moment she could.

'Phyll? Are you all right?' Gregory bounded in, full of enthusiasm, and perched on the end of the couch.

'Just tired, that is all. It has been an eventful few days.' Should she tell him what she intended? No, too risky, she thought, studying his open, cheerful face. He would never be able to stop the knowledge colouring his reactions to Ashe.

Her hands lay in her lap, curved palm up, the swell at the base of her right thumb pinker, plumper than the left. The Mount of Venus, they called it on fortune-telling charts. She had thought it just a pretty name, but Ashe had known its sensual potential and had used it ruthlessly. What else did he know that he was prepared to use in her undoing?

There were whispers amongst some of the more daring ladies of erotic pictures and books from the East. Lady Catherine Taylor had confided that she had found just such a volume high up on a dusty shelf in her grandfather's library, but had been too flustered to do more than take a few shocked peeks inside. The next day it had vanished. Others spoke of stone carvings in private collections.

Her imagination presented her with images of Ashe surrounded by beautiful Indian women all highly skilled in the erotic arts, of him studying ancient love texts, viewing carvings, refining his technique...

What would it be like to lie with a man who made love instead of using her bodily brutally for his own gratification?

'Phyll? You are very flushed. Shall I ring for tea or should you go and lie down, do you think?'

'Luncheon,' she said with decision. 'And then I shall do the accounts.' There was nothing remotely erotic about debit and credit columns. 'Tomorrow, please do not commit to anything with the settlements. I would prefer to go through any proposals with my lawyer first.' Old Mr Dodgson could prevaricate for weeks given the slightest encouragement.

'Yes, of course,' Gregory agreed amiably. 'I've enough to do working through all the stuff for my own wedding. I don't imagine for a moment there will be any problem once they realise you are to marry Clere. They want St George's, which is fine with me.'

'And in only a few weeks' time? Until this blew up Mrs Millington appeared very calm about a wedding at such short notice. There must be so much to organise.'

Gregory grimaced. 'It seems Millington simply throws money at it. His secretary could organise the invasion of a small country, from what I've seen of him, and he has hired two lady assistants for Mrs M. who spend all their time planning flowers and drafting lists. I can scarcely get a word with Harriet because she's being fitted for her bride clothes, which is why they are quite relaxed about us exchanging notes.'

'So where will you live?' Phyllida sat down again, all thoughts of luncheon and the accounts forgotten.

'After the visits we are being organised into, you mean? Apparently we will be away for about three weeks and by the time we get back the town house will be transformed.'

'*Our* town house?' No wonder Gregory looked faintly stunned. 'But we rented it to Sir Nathaniel Finch for three years.'

'He has been persuaded that the alternative offered by Mr Millington, at a lower rent and a longer lease, will suit him admirably.'

'What a wonderful father-in-law to have.' It seemed she had succeeded beyond her wildest dreams in finding the right match for her brother.

'He will do anything for Harriet, I think. And it is also very clear that if I am not a good husband my body will be found in several pieces, widely scattered.' Gregory coloured up and regarded his boots with rapt attention. 'Not that I would ever do anything... I mean...I'm in love with her, Phyll.'

'And that is wonderful.' She jumped up and went to kiss him. 'You see—all our troubles are over.' *Until Ashe Herriard realises I have no intention of marrying him.*

The next day's post brought a letter from Lady Eldonstone. She was most grateful to Miss Hurst for offering to handle the unwanted and undesirable items from the country house, she wrote. She wondered if Miss Hurst would care to come and stay for a few days to expedite that and to get to know the family.

It was a charming note, friendly and informal, and

quite definitely an order. That was where Ashe had got his assumption of command, perhaps. Phyllida wrote that she would be delighted to come the next day as Lady Eldonstone suggested and was most appreciative of the offer of the family carriage to collect her and her maid.

Phyllida had thought her poise equal to the most trying social occasion, but she found her hands were trembling as she walked up the steps to the big Mayfair mansion. It would be bad enough if she really had any intention of marrying Ashe, but while she had some scruples about deceiving him, she felt thoroughly guilty over accepting his parents' hospitality.

The Herriards were waiting for her in an airy reception room decorated in cream and greenish-greys. The celadon vases that Ashe had bought at the warehouse gleamed on the mantelshelf, flanking the family group before the hearth.

Lord and Lady Eldonstone were seated, their son and daughter standing beside them. It seemed they had been looking at a book the marquess was holding open on his lap. Lady Sara bent slightly forwards, her hand on her father's shoulder. Ashe was smiling. They looked beautiful, poised, exotic and so at ease with each other that tears came to Phyllida's eyes.

To have grown up in a family like that, with so much obvious love and affection, would have been wonderful. The money and the insecurity would have seemed trivial, if only they had been together like this. She swallowed and blinked hard. What on earth would the marchioness think if she stood there with tears pouring down her face?

'Miss Hurst, here you are.' Lady Eldonstone came forwards, holding out her hands, and caught Phyllida's as she was about to sink into a curtsy. 'None of that, please! This is just a family gathering.' She did not release her, but looked deep into her eyes. 'Is everything all right?'

The blinking had obviously not been hard enough. 'Some dust just now in the street. The wind caught it and it went on my eye, ma'am.'

'Then come and sit with us and I will ring for tea. Oh, you are here already, Herring. Take Miss Hurst's things, if you please, and send in the tea. Now,' she said, hardly waiting until Phyllida was relieved of bonnet, pelisse, gloves and parasol. 'You know my son, of course.'

*Of course.* 'Lord Clere.'

He bowed as his mother continued, 'And this is my daughter, Sara, and my husband.'

'Lady Sara, Lord Eldonstone.' She attempted another curtsy and this time it was the marquess who took her hand and guided her to a chair.

Ashe's sister sank down on to the footstool beside the chair, as exquisite as a piece of amber with her blond hair, golden skin and creamy yellow gown. 'Sara, please. We are going to be sis… Friends, are we not?'

'I hope so. I am Phyllida.'

'Ashe has told us all about you.' She seemed not to notice Phyllida's blush. 'And he says you worked so hard making a nice room for me at Eldonstone. But he is being very stuffy about showing me what is in the boxes that have been sent down. Are they very naughty?' she asked, low-voiced, as her parents were distracted by the arrival of the tea tray.

'Distasteful, is how I would describe them,' Phyllida said.

'Then Ashe should just have had a bonfire and not made you look at them!'

'Unfortunately some of them are valuable and there were all sorts of things mixed up together, so I had to sort them out. This is a lovely room, Lady Eldonstone. The silks are exquisite.'

'Thank you. I seem to spend all my time throwing things away but gradually a rather fine house is emerging. The silks are one of the things I managed to pack and bring with us in quantity. Which reminds me, Nicholas, we have been invited to a fancy-dress ball the day after tomorrow. We must all go in Indian dress. I am sure we can find something that will suit Miss Hurst.'

'But I have no invitation—it is Lady Auderley's masquerade ball, I assume?'

'And you are not invited? I shall tell her we have a house guest and that you will accompany us.'

'But she... Lady Auderley is one of the hostesses who has never received me,' Phyllida said, wishing the exquisite silk carpet would envelop her.

'Because of your birth,' Lady Eldonstone stated bluntly. 'Well, if she does not receive you, she must have the same objection to me. When I consider some of the rakes and loose screws I have been introduced to in the noblest of houses here, that is completely hypocritical.' Her chin was up, her eyes were sparking like flint struck against iron and she looked ready to pick up a rapier and run Lady Auderley through on the spot.

'I really do not wish to cause you any embarrassment—'

'I will not have anyone in this family—' the marquess cleared his throat and his wife changed tack neatly '—or who is a guest of the family treated like that.'

'You outrank her, *Mata*,' Sara said with a giggle. 'And she is in love with Papa, so you could arrive on an elephant, let alone with a charming guest such as Phyllida, and she will not object.' She turned to Phyllida, who was torn between the desire to sink gently into oblivion and fascination with the marchioness. 'All the ladies are in love with Papa,' Sara explained.

'Not with Lord Clere?' Phyllida ventured.

'Papa is safely married. They can flutter their eyelashes all they like, whereas with Ashe their husbands would become agitated and lock them up.'

'I do not think you have quite grasped how things work in English marriages,' Ashe drawled. 'The wives do as they like and the men have duels about it afterwards. Is that not so, Miss Hurst?'

'As an unmarried lady I could not possibly comment,' she said demurely.

'Of course. You will have been living a life of blameless, chaperoned respectability,' he murmured as he passed her a plate of biscuits.

'Naturally, Lord Clere.'

'We must see what we can do about that,' he replied, making her choke on a biscuit crumb. 'We are decided, then?' he said to the family. 'Miss Hurst will join us at the masquerade to give us a tally of three Indian beauties.'

'Shall we find clothes for Phyllida now, *Mata*?' Sara said. 'She would look lovely in jade green.'

'I think I should start to prepare those items for the sale room,' Phyllida interjected. 'The specialist sale I told you about, Lord Clere, is in two weeks' time and, if we delay much longer, we will miss the catalogue.'

'Very true. If you have finished your tea, I will come and assist you, Miss Hurst.'

She could hardly protest that the last thing she wanted was to be in one room alone with Ashe Herriard and a quantity of erotic art, not in front of his mother and sister. 'Thank you,' she said politely and smiled despite the urge to wipe the satisfied expression from his face.

He showed her into an empty room at the back of the house where the crates had been stacked on arrival from Eldonstone. 'The ones of, shall we say, esoteric content are in the boxes marked with an X, according to Perrott, who added a note to say that he did not know what we were paying you, but that it was not enough.'

'When one does this sort of thing for a living one cannot afford to be too nice about it,' Phyllida said prosaically. 'We must list each item and it had better be in my hand as the auctioneer is expecting them to come from Madame Deaucourt and he knows my writing.'

'I will unpack them, call out a description and you can list it.' Ashe set paper and ink in front of her at a desk and went to the first crate. 'Small bronze of a group of satyrs, signed *Hilaire*.'

They began to work steadily, although Phyllida did wonder what on earth any society lady with her ear to the keyhole would make of it.

'...six naturalistic carvings in ivory of phalli, possibly French. Size, improbable.' Startled, she glanced up to find Ashe eyeing one of the objects with scepticism. 'Well, I ask you! Have you ever seen...? No, of course not.' He slammed the lid down on another completed crate. 'This stuff is about as erotic as a plate of boiled cabbage.'

'If you say so.' Phyllida drew a neat line and wrote a new heading for the next box.

Finally Ashe hammered a crate closed. 'That, thankfully, is the lot. I just hope it was worth the work.'

'It will make a thousand, possibly,' Phyllida said, running her pen down the list.

'Pounds?'

'Guineas. Gentlemen will pay high figures for erotica.'

'They'd do better to spend it on flesh-and-blood women.' He sat on the edge of the desk next to her, one booted foot swinging, took the pen and put it firmly back in the standish.

'You do not enjoy looking at it?' she asked boldly, thinking of the tales of Indian love texts.

'Nothing is as arousing as being close to a lovely woman, touching her skin.' His fingers ran slowly over the back of her hand. 'Watching her pupils dilate.' He held her eyes with his. 'Seeing the colour come up under her skin as though an artist has brushed it with the palest wash of rose.' His other hand lifted to caress her cheek. 'That stuff in the boxes is for men who don't have a woman or who are incapable of making love to one if they have.'

'I thought India was famous for its erotic texts.'

'Those are for a man and a woman to use together. In the Far East they call them pillow books. You will enjoy them.'

It was a promise that had the fine hairs standing up all over her body. Phyllida shivered. 'When we are married.'

'Why wait that long?' His fingers slid up into her hair, capturing her, holding her for his kiss.

'Not here,' Phyllida said against his lips. 'We cannot—'

'No,' Ashe agreed. 'Not here.' His tongue, firm and insistent, caressed along the seam of her lips, wanting entrance.

'I mean, not at all. Not until we are married.' It had to be said, but it was a mistake to open her mouth at that moment. The words were swallowed by his kiss and she let herself go with them, unable to resist the urgings of her own feelings, needing to touch him, hold him.

He broke the kiss, not she. And it should have been her, she knew it and could not find it in herself to feel guilty. *He's mesmerised me*, she thought, her hands still fastened on his lapels, her back arched against the chair rail. But, no, she could not blame him. *Persuade, not seduce*, Ashe had said. He was showing her what she wanted, needed as much as he did. It was up to her to resist.

# Chapter Sixteen

'Are you frightened of consequences, of becoming pregnant?' Ashe asked with the directness she was coming to expect from him. 'It is such a short time until we will be married that it need not worry you.'

*I cannot because I am not a virgin and there is no way I can explain to you why that is so.* How would he react when he realised? With revulsion? Would he blame her, think her wanton? It would be hypocritical of him, of course, but men held women to different standards than they applied to themselves.

Might she deceive him into thinking her a virgin? She had no idea how to go about that. Besides, she shrank from the deceit. *I cannot because if I do lie with you now and you believe me a virgin, then nothing is going to persuade you that we must not wed.*

Phyllida rested her forehead against Ashe's shirt-front and tried to find some composure, some strength of will. It occurred to her that, of all the reasons she had for not making love with him, the fact that society would say it was immoral mattered not at all.

'No,' she said after a while. How long had she been

sitting there? Ashe was warm and strong and she could hear his heartbeat and his hands around her felt so good she could stay like this for ever. 'No. I want to. You know that, of course. But, no.'

'Very well,' he said, his voice a deep rumble against her ear. 'I see I must be patient. But you will let me know if you change your mind? There are many things that would give us both pleasure that would still allow you to go up the aisle a virgin.'

'Stop it!' Phyllida pushed back against his chest and he let her go. She swung round and got to her feet, retreating to the far side of the room while he remained sitting on the edge of the desk.

'I am merely trying to persuade you of the joys of marriage,' Ashe said mildly.

'*Marriage* being the operative word! And I do not believe this has anything to do with me and my feelings. You are trying to reconcile *yourself* to the marriage by telling yourself if the physical side is good, then that is all we need to worry about. Your confounded sense of honour is telling you that you must marry me, but you do not want to. Not with your head— *that* knows how unsuitable I am—and certainly not with your heart, because I do not believe for a moment that you are in love with me.'

'Love?' Ashe stood up abruptly. 'Why did you have to drag that into it? Why is it that women must imagine all relationships are about love?'

'I did not drag it in,' she said and felt sick. *Because I am so close to loving you. I didn't know it before, but I do now.* 'It is one factor in a relationship, that is all. Women talk about love because we understand that emotions are important, too. It is not some sinister plot to entrap the entire male population—why should we want to do that when you men are mostly as insensible to your emotions as an illiterate man is to literature!'

She wrenched the door open, stalked out, shut it behind her, remembering just in time that this was not her house and slamming was out of the question, then realised she had no idea where to go. Her room, if she could find it? Back to the salon to face Ashe's family?

'Are you lost, my dear?'

The lightly accented voice made her jump. 'Lady Eldonstone. I was just wondering where I should go now I have finished with those crates.'

'Let me walk with you up to your room. I am sure you would like to get rid of the dust and the ink stains. Then we can go to Sara's room and see what she has found for you to wear to the masquerade.'

'Thank you, I should like that.'

'And it has the added benefit of removing you from my son before you are moved to tell him he is so impossible you will not marry him,' the marchioness said calmly halfway up the stairs. 'Careful, my dear, you will trip.'

'Ashe is… Lord Clere… That is, we had a slight disagreement, but I am sure it is normal.'

His mother sighed. 'Men are sometimes inclined to think with their heads and certain parts of their anatomy first and their feelings a long time later. At the moment Ashe is doing what he believes to be right. I hope you will not take it amiss if I say that it may take him a while to accept that he is doing what he cannot bear *not* to do.'

'I do not take it amiss, Lady Eldonstone, I simply find it impossible to accept,' Phyllida said as they reached the door of her room. Which was a mercy. If he was truly attached to her, then to leave him would hurt him. It was better this way, she had to believe it.

'Ah well, we will see. I had to run away from Ashe's father before he realised he was in love with me. It was quite dramatic—I was dressed as a youth and he dragged me off my horse and kissed me in the middle of a group of very confused Bengali traders.' She sank down on to the *chaise* at the foot of the bed and curled her legs up under her with enviable ease.

'I should imagine that would cause a stir in the middle of London,' Phyllida suggested as she poured water into the basin to wash her hands. But she was going to jilt Ashe, she was determined on that. If he was truly his father's son, he might make that very difficult indeed—but it would be pride, not love, that was going to make him refuse to give up.

'It caused a stir on the banks of the Ganges,' Lady Eldonstone said with a reminiscent smile. 'Shall we go along to Sara's room? I have had a very civil note back from Lady Auderley who will be delighted if you accompany us to her masquerade.'

Phyllida told herself that the more she was accepted, the better it was for Gregory and that she should swallow her pride with good grace. 'Thank you for asking her, I am sure I will enjoy it,' she said politely as her hostess opened Sara's door, then stopped dead on the threshold. 'My goodness, how beautiful you look.'

Sara was twirling in front of the long glass, her skirts flaring out in a bell of shimmering, heavily embroidered golden silk that revealed her legs, clad in tight dark-brown silk trousers, almost to the knee. Her bodice, which left a hand's span of bare flesh between its hem and the waistband, matched the skirts and her hair, covered by a transparent scarf of dark brown, hung in a long plait down her back.

'Do you like it?' She came to a halt and a jangle of golden bracelets fell down her arms to collect at her wrists. Her ankles had bands of little bells tied around them and her earrings gleamed with more gold.

'I think it is stunning. But all that bare skin at your midriff is very daring.'

'I wondered about that,' Lady Eldonstone said. 'I think a jacket over the bodice, Sara, we do not want the ladies fainting away with shock.'

'I was thinking more of the gentlemen having heart attacks,' Phyllida said as Sara put on a jacket that was cut open to expose the front of the bodice and then buttoned tightly from below her breasts to flare over her hips.

'*Mata* will be wearing blue, so I thought this be best for you.' Sara gestured to a pile of green silk on the bed, its colours ranging from darkest fir to palest grass, the embroidery glittering gold in the light from the window. By candlelight it would be spectacular. 'I think we are about the same size.' She held up the bodice for Phyllida to see.

'Try it on.' Lady Eldonstone kicked off her slippers and assumed what appeared to be her favourite cross-legged position on a sofa.

'I'll help you undress.' Sara propelled Phyllida behind a screen and began to unbutton the back of her gown. Unused to having a sister, Phyllida felt almost shy shedding her clothing, especially when Sara said, 'You need to take off everything. Stockings, chemise, the lot.'

'No stays?'

'Goodness, no. The bodice is tight enough to keep everything in place,' Sara said, ruthlessly tying and tweaking.

'Trousers feel very strange.'

'The absence of them feels stranger, believe me,' Lady Eldonstone said. 'I felt positively indecent when I had to start wearing European clothes. And don't forget, skirts were still wide then. I was in constant alarm that the wind would flip everything up.'

'It certainly makes the most of my bosom.' Phyllida peered down at a cleavage she had not known she possessed.

Finally Sara finished. 'No, do not come out. I do not want you to see yourself until the night of the masquerade. *Mata*, do come and look. Doesn't Phyllida look lovely?'

'Exquisite.' The marchioness came round the screen and studied her. 'Ashe will be enchanted. I will find jewellery for you. Now, Sara, help Phyllida change again. The day after tomorrow, in the afternoon, we will turn my bedchamber into the women's *mahal*—the women's quarters in the palace,' she explained.

'All afternoon?' Phyllida turned her back so Sara could lace her stays.

'It will take us hours to get ready. Baths, our hair, the henna for our hands and feet, dressing, choosing jewellery. We will have dinner up here and the men can wait in suspense to see us.'

*And we, them*, Phyllida thought. She had some idea of how Ashe would look from the subdued Indian costume he had worn at the warehouse. What he might wear for a masquerade, she could not imagine.

* * *

The next day was occupied with finalising the list of items for the specialist sale. Phyllida visited the auctioneer disguised with severe clothing and French accent. Ashe and his father spent most of the day closeted in the study, working on estate papers, and only reappeared for dinner.

Phyllida found herself coming to like the Herriards more and more. They were unconventional, affectionate to each other, intelligent and their outsiders' view of the world she was so used to was constantly entertaining. Sara and her mother treated her as though she was already one of the family and it was all too easy to slip into the comfort of having a sister and a mother after years of fighting to stay afloat with no close female support.

The morning of the masquerade Lady Eldonstone had announced that after luncheon her rooms were to be considered out of bounds to all males.

Phyllida had no idea what to expect, but after half an hour she was convinced that she had strayed into the world of the Arabian Nights. The dressing room was filled with fragrant steam as three baths were prepared, separated by filmy curtains. They wallowed and soaped and scrubbed, then emerged wrapped in towels to have their hair brushed and braided. Once their skin was completely dry, Sara and her mother set to work painting elaborate patterns on palms and feet.

'Will it wash off?' Phyllida surrendered her palm, trying not to flinch as the pen tickled.

'Eventually. It just fades away. This isn't very strong henna.'

Then there was the lengthy process of going through jewellery boxes to select three sets of ornaments. Phyllida tried her best not to gawp at the gold and silver and gems, but she could not resist exclaiming over the set of Burmese sapphires that Lady Eldonstone selected for herself.

'They are very fine, are they not? A bride gift from my uncle, the rajah. Sara, the yellow diamonds for you and for Phyllida, the emeralds, of course.'

'But…Lady Eldonstone, they are far too valuable to lend to me. If I may borrow some bangles and earrings, that would be perfectly adequate, I am sure.'

'You are one of the family, Phyllida, and you will wear the Herriard gems.' Lady Eldonstone quelled her protest with a raised hand. 'It may not be known yet, but you will marry Ashe. Not to dress you accordingly would be to insult you both. Please, humour me in this.'

There was nothing to do but surrender. They ate a light dinner, then, finally, dressed. Phyllida was given sandals to wear, heavy earrings with emerald drops were fixed in her ears, bangles slid up her arms and clasped around her ankles and a gold chain with a single emerald hung around her neck to dip between her breasts. Then the veil was pinned in place over her hair.

'Now you may look,' Sara said, turning her so all three women were reflected in the long pier glass.

'That is not me.' It could not be her, that exotic, bejewelled silken creature with the wide eyes and the curving form.

'Yes, it is,' Sara assured her. 'We would make any maharaja proud, would we not, *Mata*?'

'We would indeed. Now, if this was the women's quarters of the palace we would go and spy on the men

through pierced marble screens, move our skirts so our
perfume would waft down to tease them, but we must
do our best with the staircase.' She handed masks to
both young women and slipped on her own. 'Everyone
will know who Sara and I are, but you, Phyllida, will
be a mystery. Ashe will be so jealous of the admiration
you will provoke.'

Phyllida had no doubt Ashe would prove to be exceedingly possessive, but she doubted that his feelings
were engaged enough for jealousy, which was a good
thing. If he channelled as much energy into anger as he
did into passion, he would not be a good man to cross.

'Will they be in the hall?' she asked, wondering how
the staircase could give them a secret view of the men.

'Of course,' Lady Eldonstone said with a certain
smugness. 'Naturally, we are late.'

They walked to the landing, their sandals making
only the softest sound on the carpeted floor. Phyllida
found the wide skirts and tight trousers strange and yet
liberating to move in. When they reached the banisters
Lady Eldonstone put her finger to her lips and leaned
over, Sara and Phyllida on either side.

Beneath them, pacing slowly on the marble floor,
were the two men. Ashe, his hair loose on his collar,
was wearing a golden-brown coat, with tight trousers
beneath of bitter orange and a sash of the same colour.
As he moved the long line of buttons down the front
of the coat glittered gold. Beside him his father wore
dark green with black trousers and sash, the spark of
green fire from his coat buttons surely that of emeralds.

The marchioness plucked a flower from the vase
that stood in an alcove at the stair head and dropped it
over the rail. It spun down and landed on the floor be-

tween the two men. As one they looked up and smiled and then, in unison, put their hands together as if in prayer and bowed.

'Like this.' Sara showed Phyllida as the ladies turned to go down the stairs. 'We do not curtsy or shake hands. The depth of the bow signifies respect for rank or age.'

It seemed a long way down to the hall and the waiting men. Phyllida hung back to let her companions go first and the marquess came to the foot of the stairs, his hands held out to them.

'How do you manage to look more beautiful every day?' he asked his wife as he bent to kiss her cheek. The emotion just beneath the surface caught at Phyllida. This truly was a love match. 'It is no wonder we have such a lovely daughter.' He smiled at Sara and Phyllida saw he had an emerald stud in his earlobe. 'Miss Hurst. You look—'

'Enchanting,' Ashe finished for him. 'Magical.' Phyllida put her hands carefully together and bowed her head and he did the same, the skin around his eyes creasing as he smiled at her. He had a diamond in his ear and looked, she decided on a wave of longing, indecently glamorous.

'Will we have an armed guard?' she asked, needing to cut the tension that flowed between them. 'We are all wearing the most beautiful gems and jewellery. I imagine we are a footpad's dream come true.'

'We are all armed,' Ashe said.

Of course, he seemed to be able to conceal knives anywhere about his person and his father no doubt did the same. But 'All of you?'

'Naturally. Sara and I have these.' Lady Eldonstone flipped the thick braid of hair over her shoulder and withdrew an ornamental pin that proved to be a long, and probably lethal, skewer. 'Would you like one? I think there is a small one that would be hidden by your hair.'

'Oh, no,' Ashe said. 'You have both been trained to use the things. Phyllida would probably impale a dowager or run an ambassador through, just by turning her head too fast.' He put on his mask and became even more mysteriously exotic. 'I promise to rescue you if you are set upon by footpads.'

Phyllida shivered, partly aroused by the promise in his heavy-lidded gaze, partly in reaction to the potential for violent action in his lean, muscled body.

The carriage was at the door. The marquess began to usher his wife and daughter out, but turned as Ashe said, 'With five of us the ladies' silks will get crushed. I have ordered the chaise and we will follow you.'

'Unchaperoned?' But the marchioness did not appear to find it shocking, or to hear her, and the footman was already closing the door of the larger carriage.

'Do I need a chaperon?' Ashe asked as the chaise drew up.

'Not for you, you wretched man! What if someone sees us arrive?' Phyllida demanded as he handed her in.

'We will be right behind the others, don't fuss so.' He reached forwards and tweaked her veil evenly about her shoulders. 'You are nervous, that is all. Calm down, Phyllida. You look utterly ravishing. No one will know who you are, you can relax and enjoy yourself.'

'Calm down? I am alone in a carriage at night with a man who keeps trying to seduce—I am sorry—*persuade* me to sleep with him. I am laden with a fortune in someone else's gemstones and gold. I am wearing a gorgeous outfit that feels positively indecent for some reason I cannot quite put my finger on and you, you patronising man, you tell me to *calm down*?'

Ashe moved to sit beside her. Phyllida stiffened, but the seat was too narrow to shift away. Through the thin silks the heat of his thigh was like a brand against her skin.

'When I make love to you, Phyllida, neither of us is going to get any sleep,' he promised, his voice like a tiger's purr in the semi-darkness. 'That is a promise. Those clothes feel indecent because wearing them you are more aware of your body and of what your body wants. As for the jewellery, I will protect both you and it.'

'And who is going to protect me against you?' she demanded, trying to keep the quaver out of her voice.

'Why, no one,' Ashe said and lifted her so she was sitting on his thighs. His arms closed around her. 'I want your hands on me, Phyllida. I want to strip those silks from your body and cover it with mine.' She gasped as his mouth found the angle of neck and shoulder and his tongue slid insinuatingly up to the soft skin beneath her ear. 'I want to make love to you until you beg me for mercy.'

They were in a carriage, driving through the streets of Mayfair, minutes away from a crowded ballroom. There was nothing Ashe could do to carry out his threats, his promises, surely? But she wanted him to. With a groan Phyllida ran her hands into the thick silk of his hair and captured his head, holding him as though to prevent the delicious torment his tongue was wreaking ever stopping.

He said something in a language she did not understand, his breath hot, and then his mouth was over hers and she was straining against him, her breasts in the tight bodice aching for his touch, her nipples, without chemise or corset, fretting against the silk lining.

'Ashe. Oh, Ashe, *yes*.'

What she was agreeing to, begging for, she was not sure. If this was madness then she did not care, for to-night they were both mad.

## Chapter Seventeen

The jolt of the carriage stopping jerked Phyllida back to reality and sanity. 'I mean, *no!*' she said as she scrambled off Ashe's lap with more haste than dignity.

'Certainly this is neither the time nor the place,' he agreed smoothly as the carriage door opened.

'It will—' The sight of the rest of their party waiting at the foot of the steps choked the words off unuttered. Phyllida fussed with her mask until Ashe was out of the carriage and waiting to hand her down, then descended with a smile fixed on her lips.

Already they were attracting attention. She heard the name *Eldonstone* murmured, saw that the glances from the other guests filing in through the front door were intrigued or approving, and relaxed as much as a woman could do whose heart was pounding, whose knees were knocking and who was mentally castigating herself for an idiot.

If that had happened anywhere but on a short carriage journey, she would have surrendered to Ashe's demands. *Oh, be honest with yourself,* she scolded. *It is not* surrender *and you cannot put all the blame on him.*

*You want him, you are simply not strong-willed enough to resist him.* Was it inevitable that sooner or later her attraction to Ashe would begin to overcome her fears, her doubts? With the feelings that were growing inside her for him, how could she ever find the strength to deny him?

The great ballroom was already crowded as the Herriard party made its way in. The noise and the conflicting scents and odours and the colour hit Phyllida as a physical blow. She had never been to a masquerade on this scale.

'I almost feel we are back in India,' Lady Eldonstone said with a laugh as a Crusader knight in silver knitted-string chainmail bore down and asked for a dance. 'All this colour and noise! Why, yes, sir, I have this dance free.' And without a backwards glance she stepped on to the floor.

'Curiously liberating, the effects of these masks,' the marquess remarked. 'No introductions, no names. How am I going to keep an eye on our two young ladies?'

'We will use our common sense, Papa,' Sara promised.

'No stepping out on to balconies or the terrace, no little alcoves,' Ashe warned.

'Brother dear, is that what rakes do, lure young ladies into those places?' she asked, all wide-eyed innocence behind her mask.

'It is, as you very well know.'

A tall Pierrott in a skintight costume presented himself in front of Sara. 'Fair damsel, may I have the honour?'

'Lay one wrong finger on her and I'll tear your arm off,' Ashe said pleasantly as his sister took the man's proffered hand. Her partner shot him a startled glance and hastened on to the floor to join a set on the far side.

'May I?' The marquess offered his hand to Phyllida.

'Thank you.'

'Deserted, abandoned,' Ashe said with a heavy sigh.

'You will manage to console yourself, I have no doubt,' Phyllida said sweetly as his father bore her off. She made herself catch his eye and almost gasped. Despite the mock-dramatic tone of his words his expression was not amused, but intense, almost hot. Phyllida followed her partner, feeling as if she had been rescued from a blaze.

Lord Eldonstone was an excellent and amusing partner. Gradually she found herself caught up in the dancing and the atmosphere, swept from one partner to another, relaxing with the anonymity, even though she recognised several familiar faces behind the disguises and was certain she was recognised in turn.

She tried to keep an eye on Sara, but every time she caught a glimpse of her she was behaving just as she ought, dancing in an elegant manner and not romping like some of the young ladies regrettably felt free enough to do. It was hard to miss the Herriards—even in the midst of such vivid and extraordinary costumes and all the jewellery of the *haut ton* they stood out with an exotic glitter. And so did she, she realised as yet another gentleman sought her hand for the dance and she overheard envious whispers from women admiring her costume and gemstones.

And it was bliss to be dancing after so long denying herself the experience. Her feet were beginning to ache, but she did not care. And now it was the waltz, the forbidden dance, the one she had never done in public.

The broad-shouldered Cavalier with the chestnut curls of his wig falling over the velvet of his coat bowed before her. 'Madam, I am honoured that—'

'There you are.' Ashe appeared by her side with a charming smile and more than a whiff of brimstone about him, she could have sworn. His sudden appearance certainly made the other man stiffen. 'Thank you for entertaining my partner, sir, but I must claim her now.'

'But—' The other man eyed Ashe's smile and apparently decided on a strategic retreat. 'My pleasure, sir. Ma'am.'

'That was rude,' Phyllida chided as Ashe took her in his arms.

'It was necessary. Did you see the size of his feet?'

So he was in the mood to jest, was he? It was certainly a relief not to be dealing with his sensual intensity. 'And yours are smaller? And can you waltz? The last time we spoke you had only been having lessons.'

'Simple.' She glanced up at him and realised she was not safe after all. His eyes glinted behind the mask and the smile on his lips was pure sensuality. 'I hold you in my arms and we move together. Rhythmically.'

He was not talking about dancing. Phyllida set her smile into one of bland innocence and pretended not to understand him. 'Excellent. The orchestra is very good, don't you think?'

'When you speak I hear only your voice,' Ashe murmured and swung her into the dance. 'When I breathe I smell only your scent. When I look at a woman I see only you. Do you still believe I am reluctant to marry you?'

'*Ashe.*' He did not mean it, could not, but the dark

honey of his voice, the heat of him so close, the circling strength of his arms, made the passion in the words a physical thing, invading her body, lifting her spirit, bringing tears to her eyes.

They danced as if alone. In silence, in harmony. Phyllida's eyes were closed as though she could trap this moment, hold it, keep it for when she left him and the pretence that they were a couple would be ended for ever.

'Phyllida.'

She blinked and opened her eyes. The music had ceased, couples were chatting as they waited for the orchestra to organise themselves for the next tune of the set. She should chat too, make light social conversation, even flirt a little. But she could not. *I love him*, she thought and swallowed back the tears. *I love him and I could have him. Would it be so wrong of me?*

'Phyllida?' he said again, his voice questioning. 'Am I such a bad dancer?'

'No.' She could have him, but only if she told him the truth, that she might not be able to make love, not fully. Might not be able to give him children.

She found her courage and her voice and laughed. 'You are excellent. But I have longed to waltz and that was magical. Such a beautiful melody, was it not?'

'Beautiful,' he agreed, but his eyes told her it was not the music he was speaking of.

Suddenly shy, Phyllida blinked and looked around. 'What a crush!' On the far side of the room a flash of gold and amber caught her eye. Sara, leaving the ballroom. But the ladies' retiring room was at the other end. 'Ashe, I may be being foolish, but I think Sara just left the room and I can think of no good reason why she should go through that door.'

He turned, frowning, but the glimpse of gilded silk had vanished. 'Are you sure?' But he was already striding off the floor.

Phyllida followed and caught his arm. 'Slowly, do not draw attention.' They reached the door, solidly closed. 'Stand in front and face the room, let me go first, then follow in a minute. The last thing we need is any kind of fuss.'

She opened the door, shielded by Ashe's broad back, and slipped through, to find herself in a narrow passageway. There was light ahead and the sound of voices so she ran along it to where it opened out on to an inner service lobby. She paused, just before the opening. The voices, it became immediately clear, belonged to Sara and the chestnut-haired Cavalier.

'Kindly escort me back to the ballroom, sir. This is not the way to the refreshments and well you know it!'

'Don't pretend you believed that. A little minx like you doesn't parade about, covered in paste jewellery and with her tits hanging out and not expect a man to take an interest.'

'They are yellow diamonds of the finest water, you ignorant oaf. And as for my costume, I would have you know, this is the court dress of Kalatwah!' Sara sounded furious, but not at all alarmed.

'Then let me have a feel—ow!'

Phyllida whipped around the corner to find the Cavalier doubled up, clutching his groin, and Sara pulling the stiletto out of her plait. She tossed the man's elaborate wig aside and tugged off his mask. 'No, put the pin back,' she cautioned Sara. 'I know who he is. It is Lord Prewitt and he is a toad, but we don't want to kill him...'

'Don't we?' Ashe, mask discarded, stalked past Phyllida and seized the gasping Cavalier by his cravat. 'Name your friends, Prewitt.'

'Ashe.' Phyllida tugged at his arm. 'If you call him out, there will be a scandal you won't be able to control.'

He dropped the gasping baron, who fell with a thud and stayed sprawled at his feet. 'You suggest I simply kill him here and now?'

'I suggest you make him very sorry, here and now. Perhaps he would like to apologise first and promise not to say a word of this?'

'Got carried away,' Prewitt gasped. 'Wouldn't dream of mentioning it. Sorry.'

'You will be.' Ashe hoisted him to his feet, waited until the man was standing upright by himself, then hit him square in the mouth. He raised an eyebrow at Sara. 'Enough?'

'Enough,' she agreed. They turned and walked away, back to the ballroom.

In the good light Phyllida saw the girl's face, the unshed tears and the way she bit her lip to stop it trembling. 'Ashe, find your mother, ask her to come to the ladies' retiring room. I think Lady Sara should go home.'

'Of course.'

He vanished into the throng and Phyllida guided Sara down the room, chatting brightly. 'Such a noise, I am not at all surprised you have a migraine. Let us go and sit down quietly.'

'I didn't realise,' Sara whispered miserably. 'I honestly believed he was taking me to the refreshment room.'

'You dealt with him very effectively,' Phyllida consoled her. 'Look, there is your mama.' And Lord Eldonstone, looking like the wrath of God at Ashe's side.

'No harm was done, except to shock her,' she explained as Lady Eldonstone put her arm around Sara's shoulders. 'I do not think anyone has noticed anything amiss and Ashe dealt with the man—he will not dare speak of it.'

'Miss Hurst feels that tearing him limb from limb would be counter-productive,' Ashe said, his voice hard.

'And she is probably correct,' his father agreed. 'Unfortunately. Ashe, will you see Miss Hurst home? I will take your mother and sister now. If some of the party remain, it may quash any speculation.'

Ashe watched them walk away, then took Phyllida's arm and steered her into exactly the kind of alcove that his sister had been warned about finding herself in with a man. 'Are you all right? You were marvellous back there. You dealt with Prewitt, you made Sara feel better, but it must have been a shock.'

'No.' *No, discovering that I am in love with you, that was a shock.* This had all happened so fast that she'd had no time to reflect on just what that realisation would mean, other than that it was certain to be painful. Love him or not, she was not going to marry Ashe Herriard. In fact, loving him made her even more determined. She produced a smile because he was still watching her, his unmasked face serious. 'I am fine, truly, just worried that this might shake Sara's lovely trusting nature.'

'I would have said she was perfectly awake to all the tricks rakes play,' he said ruefully. 'But she is obviously not up to snuff for London society.'

'The unmasking dance!' someone called and the orchestra struck up a waltz.

'Well, Phyllida, shall we be unmasked waltzing in front of everyone? One more step in our public courtship?'

If not here and now, then soon he would move the progress of their wooing further along, push her closer to the moment where she must break her word for his own sake. Break her heart for both of them. And this would give her another perfect waltz in his arms.

'Why not?' she said with a lightness she did not feel. 'It is probably my duty to help you perfect your steps.'

'It was not me treading on my partner's toes,' Ashe said as he resumed his mask and led her onto the floor.

'I never did! What a fib,' Phyllida protested as they passed a small group of matrons, masked and with dominos over their gowns, but otherwise in ordinary evening dress. She saw the quick glances, the exchange of looks, the arched brows and knew she had been recognised, the ineligible Miss Hurst dancing an unsanctioned waltz with the highly eligible Lord Clere. The word had spread that he was courting her, she could tell from the way they were being watched.

It was probably even more entertaining for the gossips than the aborted scandal of their encounter at the inn, for that was an ordinary, squalid piece of tittle-tattle whereas this, if Ashe persisted in his gallant sacrifice, would certainly give the old tabbies something to exclaim over.

'I see we are being watched.' He had noticed them, too.

'I am not surprised. You look quite magnificent in

that attire.' A fact he knew perfectly well, judging by the satirical curve of his mouth.

'Of course. I come from the land of the peacock.' The music began, he took her in hold and launched into the dance.

This time Phyllida kept her eyes open and her wits about her. They might not have been noticed last time, but this time they were definitely under scrutiny. 'There are at least two of the patronesses here,' she said after studying the faces around the edge of the dance floor.

'What can they do?' Ashe asked, executing a particularly ambitious turn. 'Is it like an exorcism and they will stalk onto the floor, sprinkle us with bad claret and pronounce us unfit for Almack's? Or perhaps it will be more military and they will strip off our epaulettes and demote us to the ranks.'

'Idiot!' Phyllida fought the urge to giggle helplessly. 'I think I will just receive the cut direct from them. You, of course, being male and beautiful, will probably be all right.'

'Are you attempting to tease me, Miss Hurst?'

'Me?' She opened her eyes wide at him and he swept her close, far too close for decency, so close that her breasts brushed his chest. Then they were dancing with perfect decorum while she fought to control her breathing and he made unexceptional small talk without the slightest indication of being affected by the woman in his arms.

'Beast,' she muttered. Ashe grinned at her and her heart contracted. She liked this man as much as she loved and desired him. She would adore to be married to him, to have his children, to share the heat and the humour he generated. She had been contented with her life, accepting of its restrictions, happy with the unconventional freedoms she had created for herself. Now she felt like a prisoner who had been taken outside the gates for a while and who must turn and walk back of her own free will.

The music stopped. All around them partners stayed close, waiting for midnight. With the first stroke of the clock Ashe lifted his hand to her mask and she to his. He bent close and she did not retreat, feeling the heat of his breath on her lips, watching his eyes, green and mysterious, still shadowed by the black velvet.

Then the last stroke and he pulled her closer as they took away their masks. He would kiss her now, in front of everyone. Claim her. Phyllida held her breath as they stood like statues in the middle of laughter, cries of recognition and a pattering of applause as their fellow guests were unmasked.

'Breathe,' Ashe murmured and stepped back, lifted her hand in his and kissed her fingertips. 'I am not going to create *that* much of a stir tonight.'

The party was obviously set to continue into the small hours. Ashe took Phyllida to find their hostess and thank her. 'A delightful ball, Lady Auderley. I regret that my parents were unable to take their leave of you, but my sister developed a severe migraine and had to return home.'

Her ladyship was gracious, offered sympathy for Sara's malaise and smiled, only slightly maliciously, at Phyllida. 'You look delightful, my dear. So many people have commented on how striking you and Lord Clere look together.'

'Thank you, ma'am.' Phyllida smiled back modestly. 'But I must thank Lady Eldonstone for kindly lending me this beautiful costume and her jewellery.' *Remind her she is dealing with the patronage of a marchioness.*

'So gracious of her,' the older woman replied. 'I hope we will have the pleasure of entertaining you here again.'

Phyllida waited until they were back in the carriage before she finally made up her mind. 'Ashe, I must speak with you, tonight.'

As the carriage moved off the flickering torchlight played across his face and she saw he understood her to mean more than speech. 'We will go to the apartment over the shop,' she said and pulled the warm velvet cloak more firmly around her shoulders. 'We will be private there.'

# Chapter Eighteen

$At\ last.$ Ashe said nothing, only pulled the check-string and leaned out of the carriage window. 'Drop us off at the top of Haymarket, we will walk. Tell the staff to lock up and leave the front door locked, but unbolted. They can all go to bed.'

He pulled up the window as they moved off again. Phyllida looked pale, but it was probably only the effect of the heavy shadows. So, she had decided to stop resisting and come to him, to accept that the marriage was inevitable. His body was already primed, heavy with desire, his blood hot with the aftermath of the encounter with Prewitt, the exhilaration of the dances with Phyllida. But there was something more than the prospect of satisfying his desires, of securing her acceptance. Somewhere along the line he had developed feelings that ran deep for this provoking, secretive, unusual woman.

'You have made a decision?' he asked, wondering at the nerves that made him suddenly short of breath.

She raised her head from her contemplation of her clasped hands and said, 'Yes.'

For such a firm syllable it sounded anxious. Nerves, too, no doubt, Ashe thought, deliberately making no move to touch her. He wrestled, briefly, with his conscience. He ought to take her home, send her up to bed with a chaste kiss on the cheek. But instinct was telling him to make certain of her. If she gave herself to him, then she would be committed to this marriage.

It was only a short drive. The carriage pulled up and he helped her down, sheltering her with his body from the bustle that still crowded the pavement. The crowd that was out here, at this time, was no company for a lady. Several women caught his eye and threw out unsubtle lures. They were not called Haymarket Ware for nothing and this was their prime hunting ground as he had learned, very early in his night-time explorations of this new city.

'I should have told them to turn into Jermyn Street,' he said. 'I had forgotten about the quantity of whores that infest this area.' Against his protective arm he felt her flinch. Presumably her forays into the East End had all been in daylight and she had not seen the worst of it, or perhaps the poor drabs who serviced the slums were less brazen and gaudy.

'It doesn't matter,' Phyllida said. 'It was more discreet. Besides, we are almost there.' They turned into Jermyn Street, passing the shutters of the numerous luxury shops, the pavement dimly lit by the light from the apartments above. 'These are mostly lodgings and chambers for gentlemen,' she explained. 'I had thought of doing up the rooms above my shop and renting them out, but I find them valuable for sorting stock.'

He bit back the comment that she could let them out

along with the shop once they were married or sell the lot. Something told him that giving up her business was not going to be easy for Phyllida.

'And last year, when Gregory and I seemed to be arguing about his gambling and parties the whole time, they made a peaceful refuge,' she admitted.

'He has settled down now, with a vengeance.'

'I know. I hardly believed it at first. He said he looked in the mirror, realised he wasn't getting any younger and began to think about what he was doing with his life. He met Harriet at just the right moment and what is so wonderful is that they truly seem to be in love.'

'You had no hopes of that when you were looking for a rich wife for him, though. Why are you so pleased about it now?' A group of young bucks, more than a trifle top-heavy after an evening at their club, were weaving along the pavement towards them. Ashe moved Phyllida into a doorway and stood in front of her.

One of them stopped. 'Hey, look, it's Clere! Come and join us, we're off to find some company, if you know what I mean!' He roared with laughter at his feeble sally, then peered past Ashe into the shadowed alcove. 'Ah, see you've got your own. Good man!'

'Another night, perhaps, Grover,' Ashe said, forcing joviality into his voice.

They reeled off down the road, waving and shouting advice as they went.

'I am sorry about that.' He handed Phyllida down the step again.

'Perhaps every lady should be taken out to the Haymarket at night at least once to see what gentlemen are truly like.' There was an edge to her voice that puzzled him.

'I am not given to rampaging drunkenly through the streets seeking out cheap whores, if that is what you mean.'

'I am sure you are far subtler and have much more expensive tastes,' she responded politely.

'That was not what I meant. I do not court a lady I am not faithful to, nor would I marry one and keep a mistress.'

'Oh.' Then, more softly, *'Oh.'*

Ashe looked sharply at Phyllida, but her face was unreadable in the shadows. Surely that little exclamation had not been one of dismay? Surely no woman *wanted* her husband to take a mistress?

'Down here,' she said, turning into an alleyway before he could put the question into words. She led him into a yard and up to what must be the back door of the shop. 'Wait while I get the key.' She bent, there was a scrape of brick on stone, then she straightened with the key in her hand. 'Ugh. I hide the spare behind a loose brick and I encourage a nice slimy puddle just in front of it to help keep it safe.'

She let him in, shaking her fingers fastidiously as she did so, but turned before the inner doorway and led the way up a narrow flight of stairs and into a room that covered, Ashe estimated, the whole area of the shop below.

'There is a tinderbox on that table. Can you light the candle? I always fumble for ages with it and end up breaking a nail.' Phyllida went to close the curtains and then fidgeted about the room, her jewellery and the golden embroidery on her clothing making her look like an exotic moth in the gloom.

*Lord, but she is nervous*, Ashe thought as he struck a

spark and nursed the wick into flame. He must be very, very careful, gentle, this first time for her.

The wick flared up and he touched it to the other candles around the room. It was not the bleak storeroom he had feared it might be, but a strangely practical, very feminine den. The walls were hung with tapestries, tattered and worn, but rich with shades of old rose and blue and gold. The curtains at the window were deep-red velvet, obviously salvaged from some grand suite of bed hangings. His feet sank into carpets, spread to overlap and cover the wear and holes.

There was a desk and chair, a deep armchair, a daybed and a bookcase overflowing with books. 'This is a beautiful room,' he said. 'It reminds me of chambers in my great-uncle's palace, snug, private little caves of luxury.'

'The luxury is threadbare and not all it seems. Few things are what they seem.' There was that bitter note in her voice again, as though she was mocking herself.

'Phyllida, what is wrong? You know I would never force you. It would make me very happy to make love to you here, but if you want to leave, I understand.' Ashe pulled out the desk chair and sat down. Not a gentlemanly thing to do when a lady was still standing, but he did not want to loom over her.

'I need to tell you something.' She sat down on the end of the daybed with an inelegant thump as though her legs would not hold her up any longer. 'You will not wish to marry me once you hear what it is.'

'That I very much doubt,' Ashe said robustly, even as he tried to ignore the stab of apprehension in his gut. *Debts, that was all, nothing to worry about there.*

Phyllida stood up again and this time he rose too,

something in her face warning him that she was serious. Whatever this was, she was not exaggerating its importance to her.

'I am not a virgin,' she said, as though pleading guilty in a court of law.

Ashe blinked. That was not so bad. 'Neither am I, oddly enough.'

Her lips thinned. 'Men appear to set much value on virginity.'

'Are you still involved with him? Am I likely to meet him?' She shook her head vehemently. 'Then, if you can refrain from comparisons which would wound my pride, I do not see it as a problem.' As soon as he said it, he saw the attempt to introduce some humour into the exchange was a mistake.

'Hardly! You do not understand, and I am not explaining it properly.'

'Was there a child?' Ashe struggled to understand, to read the messages her voice, her rigid body, were sending him. He tried to take her hands, but she batted his away.

'No, thank God.'

And then he realised. 'Phyllida. Were you unwilling? *Mere jaan.' My darling.* He caught her in his arms, held on to her despite her attempts to twist free, cradled her against his chest until she stilled and let her head rest against his breast. *'Sahji, jaani.'* He murmured the love-words as he stroked her hair. 'Tell me who it is and I will bring you his heart and his manhood on a platter.'

'It was a long time ago. When I was seventeen,' she said, her voice so low he could hardly make out the words.

Worse and worse, if anything could make it so. So young, so innocent.

Phyllida straightened. 'Let me go, please. I...' He opened his arms and she sat down again, her hands tightly clasped. 'You sit down too, Ashe. I told you because you had a right to know and because I do not think I can make love, not without it all coming back, not without panicking. I am sorry I let you believe that was what I asked you here for tonight.'

He sought for the words to say this right. 'When I kiss you, you respond, Phyllida. In the carriage, when I caressed your breast, that was not feigned, the fire I felt in you. When that man attacked you, hurt you, it would have been nothing like making love with someone who cares for you.'

'I don't... I cannot marry you, not knowing if I can bear that part of it. I should have told you at once, when you proposed this marriage.'

'You did not know me very well. Now, I think, you trust me rather more.' It was not a question, but she nodded. 'You know I would never force you, Phyllida.' That time he did want a response and steeled himself for her hesitation. He had been a rogue, to put it at its lowest. He had done his best to persuade her into his bed, despite her reluctance. Then it had almost been a game, now he was not certain he could forgive himself.

'Of course I know.' She seemed startled that he had to ask and, as she looked at him, her unhappy face softened into a smile of such tenderness that his heart melted. 'But it might come to that, or not have children.'

Ashe got up and walked to the window, needing to move while he absorbed that realisation. An heir. The son to whom he would hand the estate that would be saved from decline, the title he would one day hold. The daughters, the other sons. He had never given them any thought, except in the abstract. Suddenly they were tangible, ghost children who might never become real.

'Then I will abandon persuasion for seduction,' he said. 'We know I can kiss you, hold you, even caress you a little and you are not afraid. It was a terrible wound, but it was not fatal—you will heal with the right medicine. We will take all the time it needs and you will be in control.' He knew he sounded confident. Inside he was unsure, but determined. He had committed himself to this woman and he was not going to abandon her now. Ashe walked back and hunkered down in front of her, took her hands. 'Will you think about it?'

'I will not marry you unless…' She took a deep breath and looked at him. 'I have never been with any other man, you understand, so I do not know if I would be able to make love. I might be creating a problem that does not exist.'

'No one would be unaffected by such cruelty,' Ashe said. 'But if you learn that making love has nothing to do with what happened, then I believe you will be able to separate the two.'

She nodded. 'I did not expect you to be so understanding. I did not know how to tell you, although I knew I had to.'

This was what had been behind the ambiguity he had sensed in her agreement to marry him. She had not decided if she could tell him of this and, being a woman of honour, would not marry him unless she did.

Phyllida leaned forwards and linked her hands behind his neck. 'Shall we try? Make love to me, Ashe.'

He did not answer, simply letting her pull him closer

until he could caress her mouth with his, gently, deeply, increasing the demands of his tongue as she began to melt against him. He pushed just a little ahead of her tentative responses until he felt her relax entirely, begin to tease him a little with nips and sucks and the wandering caresses of her fingers at his nape.

Ashe eased back and unbuttoned his coat, let it fall to the ground, then took her in his arms again and kissed her while his fingers dealt with the fastenings at the front of her tight jacket. She did not resist when he slid it from her shoulders to reveal the swell of her bosom above the constriction of the *choli*, so he kissed across the creamy skin while his fingers caressed her bare midriff.

If she would relax a little he could ease her back on to the daybed, but there was still a tension in her that warned him that might be a step too far. How could he reassure her?

He lay down himself, on his back, and smiled up at her. After a moment she gave a little nod, as though she understood, and bent to kiss him. She was endearingly clumsy, he thought, then realised with a shock when she changed the angle of her mouth and her position on the bed that his reaction was, to put it mildly, patronising. She was thinking too hard, but she was working out what pleased her and, he realised as he fisted his hands in the covers to stop himself grabbing her, she was working out what pleased him at the same time.

Her hand brushed his right nipple, almost certainly by accident, but he was so tense that the sensation shook a groan out of him.

'Ashe?' Phyllida's eyes were wide and dark in the candlelight. 'Did I hurt you?'

'No,' he lied. This was exquisite torture.

'Don't you want to get on top of me?' she worried.

*Yes.* 'No,' he lied again. He could hear the fear threading through her voice. That bastard would have thrown her down, crushed her with his weight, trapped her. Somehow he had to let her feel in control, as if she could escape at any moment.

'Do you like it when I do this?' He cupped her breasts boldly, let his thumbs find the nipples tight under the silk.

'Oh, yes.' Her lids drooped, her lips parted in a sensual sigh that had his already-hard body almost arching off the bed. He found the ties at the waist of her skirt and loosened them until he could slip his fingers down over the curve of her belly. The delicate skin shivered and twitched to his touch, but she did not fight him. 'Ashe, I…*ache.*'

'Good.' He tugged gently to bring her down to lie beside him and buried his face in the angle of her neck, filled his senses with jasmine and the betraying scent of her arousal. *Slowly*, he told himself. *So slowly.* 'Will you let me pleasure you?'

'How?' She stiffened, curled away from him. 'You won't—'

'No. I won't move from lying here beside you. Just let me touch you.'

He could feel the effort it took her to trust him, to let him brush the nest of curls, to ease one finger between the soft, damp folds. He found what he sought and stroked, just *there*, as her hips came off the bed with the shock of it.

'Ashe!' Phyllida had expected discomfort. Whatever a man did there, however gentle, would hurt, surely? But the shaft of sudden, shocking pleasure lanced through her as if a lightning flash had run from his fingertip to her womb, to her breasts, to every quivering nerve in her body.

'*Priya,*' he said, his voice husky. 'Sweetheart. Just let go, allow yourself pleasure.'

*Allow?* She twisted, frantic with not knowing how to deal with the onslaught of delight when she had expected pain, out of control in a way she had never imagined, overcome by her own body's reactions, not his strength. She was aching and needing only the heat of Ashe's body next to her, his arm holding her safe, his wicked, wicked fingers driving her insane.

'I don't know how,' she gasped.

'Let go,' he repeated. 'Your body knows.' And he kissed her and suddenly the pleasure peaked into an almost-pain that made her cry out against his mouth, arch her body hard into his hand to make it last for ever and then she lost herself, utterly, as she clung to him, knowing she was dying, not caring.

'Phyllida?' Ashe's voice, soft and dark as the caress of black velvet, as sensual as sin, as gentle as... *the man I love.*

'What happened?' She was still lying beside him on the daybed. In his embrace, still dressed, although her clothing was disordered. Her body thrummed with a deep, sensual relaxation and quivered with tiny aftershocks of pleasure.

'That was an orgasm.'

She blushed. She knew the word, had even looked it up in a dictionary. 'But that is something men experience.'

'Both partners in lovemaking can experience it.'

He pulled her close, shifting her position so her cheek rested comfortably on his chest.

'But you did not.'

'No. I can wait.'

Phyllida looked down his body. He was clearly aroused. It hurt men to be in that condition and frustrated, she had heard that somewhere. 'Can you?' She put her hand on the hard ridge, the thought of which had so frightened her, and he gasped. She had the power to make Ashe groan, to arch into her hand as though begging her. If he could give her pleasure with a touch, could she do the same for him?

'Let me.' Before Ashe could protest she tugged at the ties of his trousers, slid her hand inside. She had expected the hardness, the heat. She had not realised the skin would be soft, that it would be so sensitive that it seemed to grow as she closed her fingers around it.

She was clumsy, she knew that. Clumsy and shy, but not afraid of him, or of what she was doing. After a moment of resistance Ashe fell back on the bed and let her have her way with him. He moved into her hand, showing her the rhythm he needed, giving her the confidence that she was not hurting him and she could be firmer, bolder. He gasped, his body arched, he thrust hard into her circling fingers and then fell back on the bed as the heat flooded over her fingers.

Phyllida curled into his body, loving the total relaxation, the musky scent, the way the feel of him changed in her hand as his body calmed. After a minute his arm tightened around her and he pulled her close so he could kiss her. 'I'm sorry, sweetheart, that must have shocked you,' he murmured.

'I liked it,' she mumbled into his shirt front, too shy

to meet his eyes. 'Ashe, I think it might be all right after all. When we do it properly, I mean.'

'That *was* properly,' he said and sat up. 'There are all kinds of ways to make love —think of a banquet, lots of dishes. Some great solid roasts, some sweet fluffy concoctions, some rather sinfully sweet, others dangerously spicy.'

He was on his feet, investigating behind a screen. 'Is there water in this ewer? Yes, rather dusty, very cold, but it will do. And a towel.' There was the sound of splashing behind the screen. Phyllida sat up and pulled the coverlet over her bare toes.

'Ashe, do you want to do it again?' That had been wonderful beyond words and the relief of knowing that she could lie in a man's arms, be intimate with him and enjoy the experience, was huge. But whatever Ashe said, sooner or later sex would involve the same act that had taken place in the tawdry room in the Wapping brothel, the act that had taken her virginity. The act she had been paid for by Harry Buck.

# Chapter Nineteen

What she had done would brand Phyllida a whore. Any man would say so, she knew that. She had allowed Ashe to think she had been forced, when in fact she had taken money, removed her clothes, lain on that bed and had done nothing to resist. The fact that if she had not then she would have starved, that she needed the money to find her father, to make him come back, or give her enough money to get food and medicine for her mother, food and shelter for all of them, did not alter the fact of the transaction that had removed her claim to be a woman of honour.

It made her angry, that double standard, but that was the way things were. And if she had to do it again, if someone's life depended on it, if Gregory was in trouble and it was the only way to save him, then she would sell herself again without hesitation. Her screams, she had learned in the course of that one bitter night, would only fuel the excitement of the man taking her.

'I only used half the water.' Ashe emerged from behind the screen. 'Do it again? I would like to very much, but not tonight. And the next time, then we will talk about what other dishes on the menu you would like to sample. You choose what we do, when we do it. The control is yours. There is no need to rush anything.'

She shot him a look of gratitude as she passed him, then went to tidy herself. No wonder she loved him. His past had not, she guessed, been blameless—she recalled the amusement with which he had told her he was not a virgin—but he was a decent, honourable man and she was thinking about deceiving him about something he would believe touched on that honour.

Phyllida wrestled with her conscience. She had not meant to make love when she had asked him here, only to confess that she was not a virgin. Ashe's closeness, his response, had overset all her scruples, swept away everything but the desire to be in his arms.

Now she knew how wrong, how weak, that had been. Ashe wanted to marry her out of honour. There were many reasons why she was the wrong bride for him and Ashe believed he knew them all and could make it work despite them. He admitted he was attracted to her. He even knew now that she was not a virgin. His parents and sister seemed to like her and were prepared to welcome her into their family. The benefits to her and to Gregory were too numerous to name.

*I love him and I had let myself dream I could marry him. Ashe and love and children. Ashe for as long as we lived.*

*So,* temptation murmured, *do not tell him the truth. How would he be harmed by the secret?*

But shouldn't a marriage be based on honesty and truth? Phyllida argued back as she fiddled with the ties on her skirt and trousers, reluctant to emerge until she had come to some conclusion. If she did not love him, she suspected it would be much easier—never mention her past. But she did love him and so she felt compelled to tell him. If he reacted badly—and what man wouldn't?—she would have lost him for ever.

*But I should not be marrying him in any case*, she reminded herself with bitter realism. *Marriage is a dream, happiness with Ashe is a dream. Those children will never be born.* Phyllida leaned back against the wall, her hand pressed to her mouth to stifle the sobs that seemed to come from nowhere.

*Oh, Ashe, my love.* She should never have spoken of children, never have let him be so certain she would marry him. Now, even though he did not love her, she would hurt *him*, not just his pride, when she broke this off.

'Are you all right?' Ashe did not sound impatient.

'Yes.' She found her voice and managed to strike a light note. 'I must admit to feeling a trifle bemused,' Phyllida admitted. Ashe chuckled. He had made her dizzy with his lovemaking. Perhaps that was why it was so difficult to think clearly and logically, to resolve to end this here and now. They were going to make love again, she knew that. It was as inevitable as sunrise.

'Ashe, what is the time?' She made herself come out from behind the screen. It was hard to meet his eyes, although she felt warm and safe with him. Her guilty conscience, she supposed.

'Three. Time to go home. Here is your jacket.' He held it out to her, then stopped and touched one finger to the top of her left breast. 'What is that? A birthmark? I meant to ask when you took off your jacket, but I became…distracted.'

'Yes.' Phyllida squinted down to where his finger

traced the coffee-brown mark the size of a strawberry.
'Luckily it is towards the side so, if I am careful, the
bodice of a gown covers it.'

'But why would you want to hide it?' Ashe helped
her into the jacket. 'It is a perfect heart. Charming.'

'It is a blemish.'

'Nonsense. It looks fascinating on your white skin,
tantalising. Promise me you will not cover it up any
more.' He bent and kissed it, then pulled her sides of
the jacket together and began to do up the tiny buttons.

'Very well.' It would not be a problem, not with her
evening and half-dress gowns and if Ashe liked it she
was too flattered to resist. She would only need to remove some of the trim or turn under the edge of the
bodice. There were a few days left before she had to
end this. In day gowns, with their higher necklines, it
would never show in any case.

'Ashe, stop that or we will never get back!' He
laughed and ceased tickling between the button holes.

'Come along then. Before you tempt me unbearably.'

Phyllida was sitting sewing with Sara the next afternoon when Gregory called. Lady Eldonstone had
insisted that she sit down and rest after a morning supervising the despatch of crates to the auction house
and it had seemed a good time to alter the neckline of
some of her evening gowns so that the heart-shaped
birthmark could be seen.

The lack of logic in doing something that could only
inflame Ashe's enthusiasm for lovemaking, and entan-
gle her even more in the deception she was caught in,
did not escape her. It was as though she was two people: one sensible, honest Phyllida who should be cold-

bloodedly planning the break with Ashe for his own
good, the other a dizzy girl in love who could not think
beyond the next moment in his arms.

Sara rang for refreshments and Gregory sat down,
all long legs, tight pantaloons and gleaming Hessians.
'You are the picture of a perfect London gentleman,'
Phyllida teased him. 'So neat and tidy and respectable-
looking. And such a smart new crop!'

He grinned at her good-naturedly. 'Harriet likes it.
Which brings me to why I am here. You and I have
been invited to a family dinner party tomorrow evening, I'm afraid.'

'Afraid? But I thought you got on very well with
Harriet's family.'

'I do, but a long-lost uncle has appeared back in
town. He's Mrs Millington's brother and a bit of a black
sheep, apparently. He's been safely off in Jamaica working as a land agent or some such thing and I suspect they
all hoped he'd stay there. Anyway, we've been invited
to dilute the family tensions a bit, I suspect. There's
a couple of cousins and a great-aunt coming as well.'

'It will be very awkward if he decides to stay, won't
it? Or perhaps he has reformed,' Sara remarked. 'Would
you care to pour yourself a glass of sherry or Madeira,
Lord Fransham?'

'Thanks, I will. Millington was all for showing him
the door, apparently, but Mrs M. wants to give him another chance, hence the dinner party.' Gregory went to
the decanters while Sara poured tea.

'I will have to ask Lady Eldonstone if it would be
convenient. She may have plans for the evening,' Phyllida said. It sounded an awkward situation, but if she
could help the Millingtons, she would. Everything was

back on course for the wedding and she felt nothing but gratitude to them for their tolerance.

'We aren't doing anything tomorrow night,' Sara said. 'I know because Papa is going to a lecture at the Royal Society and Mama said this morning that it would be good to have an evening at home recovering from all our gadding about.'

Phyllida asked her hostess's leave and, when her brother had gone, went back to removing the lace from the neckline of her dark-green dinner gown. That would do nicely for the Millingtons' dinner. It was a little formal, perhaps, but formality was sometimes a help in sticky social situations.

Ashe was rather less obliging about her plans than the marchioness. 'I had hoped to spend the evening with you in Jermyn Street,' he murmured in her ear later.

'I wish we were,' Phyllida whispered back under cover of a singularly dreary piano sonata. Lady Eldonstone had insisted on attending a musicale that evening. 'I will miss you.'

At seven o'clock the next evening Phyllida emerged from the Eldonstones' carriage outside the Millingtons' house.

She mentally squared her shoulders for a fraught dinner party and wished Ashe was with her. Gregory was concerned for Harriet and she suspected that she would have to spend the time making vacuous small talk to the other relatives, all bristling with disapproval over the return of Mr Phillip Wilmott.

'Oh, do wait a moment, ma'am, that cloak isn't quite fastened.' The maid Lady Eldonstone had lent her was poised in the carriage doorway just as a dark figure strode out of the shadows into the pool of light cast by the door lantern. 'Here, take care, you!'

The man barged into Phyllida, pushing her back against the carriage. *A footpad, so brazen, to attack right on a Mayfair doorstep?* Too shocked to feel fear, she grasped her reticule, ready to strike out at him. The cloak slithered off her shoulders to the ground.

For a moment she thought him a stranger, then, as the light caught his face, she knew him. *Harry Buck.*

''Ello, darling,' he said on a coarse chuckle. 'Thought there was something familiar about you.' She flinched as his eyes went from her face to her bosom exposed by the plain, low neckline of her newly altered gown. 'I remember that. Thought I couldn't be wrong.' Her hand flew to the birthmark, but it was too late, he had seen it.

The maid was screaming for help, the front door flew open as the driver swung down from the box seat, whip in hand. Buck vanished, as abruptly as he had come.

If the carriage door had not been under her hand, she would have fallen, for all the strength seemed to have vanished from her legs. It was her worst nightmare made real. Harry Buck, the man who had bought her virginity, had recognised her, tracked her down.

And then, just as she thought she would faint, the butler was hurrying down the steps. 'Miss Hurst! Are you all right?

Phyllida forced herself to stand straight and think. 'Yes. He must have been drunk. Most unpleasant, but no harm done. Please do not alarm Mrs Millington by saying anything.'

Somehow she reached the house, was announced, greeted. Somehow she managed to get to a sofa and sit before her legs gave way. Apparently her horror and fear were not imprinted on her face, for no one paid her any heed, other than to introduce her to the dubious relative, Mr Wilmott. She kept her face rigidly expressionless and inclined her head, hoping Mrs Millington would simply think her shy in the presence of an acknowledged black sheep.

Mrs Millington had abandoned all correct form for her table setting, apparently anxious to separate the young ladies from her brother. Phyllida found herself making conversation on one side to an elderly cousin who turned out to be a stockbroker and on the other to Mr Millington. She must have made some sense in what she was saying, and apparently she ate and drank in a normal manner, for no one asked her if she was all right.

On sheer will-power she got through the endless meal and back to the drawing room. Gregory, in a brave attempt to support his future in-laws, engaged Wilmott in conversation. Phyllida felt fainter and fainter until eventually she could not stand it any longer. She got up and went to Gregory's side. 'Gregory, I am sorry, but I think I must go back now.'

'Yes, of course. I'll just say goodnight to Harriet.'

She turned on her heel and almost fled to Mrs Millington. 'I am so sorry, ma'am, but I have such a headache. Would you think me very rude if Gregory took me home? I am sorry to drag him away, but—'

'My dear, I will send for your carriage at once.' Fussed over, wrapped up, Phyllida drove back through the darkened streets, shaking with horror.

Ashe was crossing the hallway as she came in, a book in his hand. He grinned at her. 'Good evening. Was it as sticky an evening as your brother feared?'

'Worse.' She looked at him standing there. The man she loved, her lover. The man who still intended to marry her because she had been too weak to end this when she should have done. 'Ashe, I must speak with you.'

'Of course.' He opened the door of the library for her. 'There is no one else at home. What is wrong?'

'I cannot marry you.' As soon as she said it she knew she was right and she should have refused from the first. Now Buck had recognised her she knew she dare not marry and try to keep this a secret from Ashe.

She could not tell him what she had done, could not bear to see his expression change, the liking and the desire ebb away to be replaced by revulsion when he discovered she had not been the victim of some predatory man but had deliberately sold herself. Made herself a whore. She had heard him speak of those Haymarket whores, knew what he, what any man, would think of a woman who did what she had done.

She would have to do what she had always planned once Gregory was settled: leave London altogether and retire to the Dower House.

Ashe became very still as he stood in front of the cold grate. Then he put down the book he had been holding. 'Why not? Is it because of what you told me the other night? Or what happened between us?'

'No,' she lied. 'I was wrong to accept your plan to rescue me from the scandal. I only agreed thinking I would refuse in the end, but I allowed myself to become...more involved than I intended. I can see there is no need for you to protect me any more. The gossip has died down, no one will be the slightest bit surprised if your interest in me wanes. We are completely unsuited to each other and it is foolish to condemn ourselves to a lifetime of an indifferent marriage.'

'Unsuited and indifferent. I see. I had not realised I could be so wrong in my perceptions of either my own feelings or of yours.' He looked as though he was listening to a dry political speech, his face a mask of concentration with no emotion to be seen. 'So making love with me was a way of overcoming your fears?'

'The bad memories. Yes,' she agreed. If he believed she was simply using him, then he would be less inclined to fight, more convinced that he must not marry her.

'I am happy to have been of use.' He raised his eyes to her face and she saw with a shock just how angry he was. Angry, rigidly controlled and dangerous because of it. If she had been a man and had made him this furious he would have struck her, she realised, but she felt no fear, just total misery. Ashe would not hurt her even though he thought she had used him, used his body, in a calculated attempt to deal with her nightmares.

'I will go home first thing in the morning,' she said, striving for a control to match his. 'I will explain to Lady Eldonstone that I realised we would not suit. She can only be relieved.'

'She will be disappointed to have been mistaken in you,' he said. 'As I am.'

'I did warn you, right from the start, that I am unsuitable for you.' Best to make certain, to sever the fragile bond that had grown between them out of desire and liking and what she knew, on her part, to be love. But Ashe did not love her, thank God. He would not fight for her beyond all reason.

'But you had to be noble about it, had to do the honourable thing, even if that overrode your duty to your family,' she added with the intention of throwing oil on the flames.

It worked. Ashe stalked forwards as she retreated before him, until she was backed up against the door with nowhere to go. 'Attempting to do the honourable thing is part and parcel of my duty to my family, to my name,' he ground out. 'And I had thought that I had found a woman worthy of that name, one who would stand by me and my family and fight to bring it, and the lands, back to where they should be. I was wrong.'

He stood back and Phyllida turned before he would see the tears or read in her eyes that her heart was breaking. She left the room without a word and climbed the stairs to her bedchamber. Some foolish part of her was straining to hear the door open behind her, Ashe's voice calling her back. But, of course, it did not happen.

It was quite extraordinary, how much a breaking heart hurt, Phyllida thought as she stood passive while the maid unpinned her hair and removed her gown. Mama, loving foolishly and too well, had died of a broken heart. Her daughter was not going to have even that release, she was going to have to live with the wounds for the rest of her life.

# Chapter Twenty

Lady Eldonstone was kind and regretful and exceedingly courteous when Phyllida made her difficult confession that she did not think she and Ashe were suited and that it would be best if they did not meet again. Phyllida was certain that beneath the tranquil poise the older woman was concealing considerable anger that her son was being spurned by someone who had every reason to be grateful to him.

She took herself off before breakfast, back to Great Ryder Street and the news that Gregory was staying with the Millingtons for a few days, presumably to bolster the family while they decided what to do about the return of their prodigal relative.

'You all right, Miss Phyllida?' Anna asked, peering closely at her as she took her valise. 'You look as if you've been awake half the night crying.'

'Nonsense, of course not.' *Just all night, alternating between tears and frozen indecision. What to do? Where to run?* 'I have got a cold coming or something, that is all.'

'I'll make you up my remedy,' the maid said. 'Oh,

and there's a letter for you. I was just about to get Per-
kin's boy to take it over to you.'

Phyllida picked it up. Not a hand she recognised,
ordinary paper, thick, clumsy writing. She trailed into
the drawing room and sat down, opened it with no curiosity. A bill, she supposed.

A large engraved card fluttered out and she picked
it up from the floor.

*Mr Harry Buck's House of Pleasures for the Dis-
cerning Gentleman.*

Below that was printed in the heavy black handwriting. *Three o'clock this afternoon. Come back to work.
Don't be late. I'll need a little sweetener to keep this
secret all to myself.*

Phyllida dropped the card as though it had moved
in her hand. It lay at her feet, as dangerous as an adder.
Overcome by nausea, she staggered to a bowl on a side
table and was violently sick.

'Lord love us! What's the matter now?' It was Anna,
fussing and anxious.

Phyllida closed her eyes and dragged her hand across
her mouth. 'Don't know, something I ate perhaps. I'm
sorry, I'll wash the bowl, you shouldn't have to.' In a
minute, when she could think, when she had stopped
shaking.

'Nonsense. You come up to bed now, my lamb, and
I'll send for the doctor and his lordship.'

'No! Not Lord Clere!'

'Your brother, I meant. Now come along, you lean
on me.'

'All right. Thank you, Anna. Don't send for the doctor, I will be all right presently. And don't worry Greg-

ory, Miss Millington needs him. But I will lie down for a while, then I have to go out this afternoon.'

'In this state? You'll do no such thing, Miss Phyllida. It's bed for you.'

Ashe ate his breakfast wearing his best diplomatic face while his family pretended valiantly that nothing was wrong, that they'd never had a houseguest and that they were not desperate to know just how affected he was by Phyllida's defection.

He then strode off to Brooks's club, mentally kicking himself when he realised he was averting his eyes from the turning off St James's Street into Jermyn Street.

He already knew enough members to make negotiating the entrance hall and finding a quiet corner to bury himself behind a newspaper a trial, but the club was used to gentlemen seeking peace and quiet after a hard night and no one seemed offended by his curt nods of greeting.

The newsprint swam in front of his eyes, the words meant nothing. *Damn the woman.* He had lost a night's sleep alternating between anger and aching arousal.

Phyllida didn't want him, she thought marriage to him would be a life sentence to unhappiness and she didn't even desire him. Their love-making had simply been an exercise in getting over a traumatic incident in her past.

It was only hurt pride, of course, this sick ache inside. That and unsatisfied lust. He had been used. Used to get her out of a scandal, used to conquer her fears, and now she no longer needed him so she simply walked away. It seemed that her disinclination to marry him overcame his title, his wealth and his prospects.

Ashe folded the newspaper with savage precision and slapped it down on the table beside him. He needed to hit someone. He didn't care if they hit him back, he just needed the outlet of violence.

A waiter came at the crook of his finger. 'Are there any boxing salons near here?'

'Yes, my lord. Quite a few. Gentleman Jackson's is the prime one, of course. I'll give you the direction, shall I, my lord? Or any cabby will take you there.'

'I'll walk.' Ashe took the slip of paper and gave the man a coin. 'Thank you.'

He spent an hour pounding hell out of a punch bag, then sparred with one of Jackson's assistants, the great man being booked for the day. It was some help, the ache of the bruises where punches had landed were a distraction from the internal ache. He ate a hot pie and drank porter in the Red Lion down an alleyway off Pall Mall, making himself focus on the taste and texture of the food as he had on the mechanics of the bout he had fought.

When he had finished he walked north with no fixed idea of where to go, just needing to move.

'My lord!'

He stopped dead and turned. A woman in a plain gown and cloak was hailing him. A maid by the look of her. Then he saw it was Anna, Phyllida's woman.

'Oh, my lord, I was coming to find you.' She panted to a halt beside him. 'Then I saw you cross St James's Square…'

Ashe looked around him and found he was almost in Haymarket. 'What do you want?' he asked curtly.

'It's Miss Phyllida. She came home this morning

looking as if she'd been crying her eyes out, but she said it was just a cold coming on. Then she'd no sooner opened her post than she was casting up her accounts and shaking like a leaf.

'I got her to bed, but she said she had to go out later and off she went, wearing those awful clothes she puts on to go down east. And she'd said she wasn't doing that any more.' Anna took a deep breath and looked him in the face with something very like accusation in her eyes. 'Something's wrong, my lord, and I'm betting it's to do with you because she told me you wouldn't be round any more and bit my head off when I asked why. So what have you done to her?'

'Nothing. Your mistress has decided she wants nothing more to do with me.' He turned on his heel and walked away. He'd be damned if he was going to be interrogated by some maidservant in the public street.

Two yards. *Phyllida crying her eyes out. Well, she rejected me, not the other way round.* Five yards. *Sick, shaking. She deserves it. I feel sick.* Ten yards. *Going east. Into the slums, into the dangerous world of Harry Buck and his ilk.*

Ashe looked back. Anna was standing where he had left her, but when she saw him stop she ran to him. 'My lord?'

'What post?'

'Just one letter. She didn't say who from.'

'Where is it?'

Anna screwed up her face in concentrated thought. 'Don't know. She didn't have it when I took her upstairs. I'll be guessing she dropped it in the drawing room when she took ill.' She put her hand on his arm.

'Please, my lord, do you think there was something in the letter?'

'I don't know, but it is the only clue we have. Come on.'

Anna found the card under the sofa. Ashe read it, once in stunned disbelief, the second time in cold anger. *Come back to work.* She hadn't been raped, she'd been a whore. Phyllida had lied to him, she had hidden this disgraceful secret and only the danger of exposure had forced her to break off their relationship. He could have ended up married to her—and then what would have happened when one of her former clients turned up?

*To hell with her, she deserves everything she gets.* Ashe ripped the card in half, then made himself look at it again, made himself start thinking with his head and his heart about the real woman, the woman he knew and not the one who had wounded his pride.

Phyllida had been genuinely inexperienced and nervous when he had made love to her. This creature Buck had most likely used her only once. And now he was blackmailing her to get her back to his brothel, into his power.

It would not just be money he'd be after. Phyllida might not realise it, but Ashe could read between the lines and the danger she was in made him cold with fear for her. How she had ended up in this mire could wait for later.

'Have you heard of Harry Buck?' he demanded.

'Yes.' The maid went pale. 'He's a dangerous thatch-gallows, is that one.'

'Where's his brothel?'

She gawped at him, then seemed to realise he was

serious. 'He's got half a dozen of them, so I've heard, but I don't know where they are.'

How long would it take him to scour the slums of the East End of London without help, without local knowledge? Even if he found her brother and explained all this, there was no guarantee Gregory would know where to go. He seemed to have visited the gaming houses, but there was no hint he habituated brothels in such a rough area.

Then he recalled Phyllida asking about his name and whether Ashe was the same as Ashok. She knew an Indian trader in the docks by that name and he, she'd said, was a rogue, but a good-hearted one.

'I'll find her, Anna,' he promised. 'You stay here in case she makes it back without me.' Then he ran.

There was no-one at the Town house as he pushed through the front door, up the stairs to find his pistols and his knives. He went down again three at a time and out into the square to find a cab. 'The docks,' he snapped at the toughest, biggest driver he could see. 'Double your fare if you get me there fast.' He wedged himself in a corner and began to load the firearms. If Phyllida was harmed, someone was going to suffer.

She knew roughly where to go, somewhere in the maze of alleys and courts wedged between Butchers Row, Pillory Lane and New Street where the noise and smells of Smithfield Market did battle with the stench of human waste, over-stuffed graveyards and tanneries. She had stumbled though this area once before, shaking and sore, horrified at what had happened, her fingers cramped around the coins Harry Buck had given her.

It was only later that Phyllida realised that she had been lucky, that Buck had kept his word and used her for that one occasion only and had not simply turned the key in the door and kept her captive to use again and again.

A plump girl with a red shawl, her breasts uncovered almost to the point of indecency, looked a likely person to ask. 'Can you tell me the way to Harry Buck's house?'

'What, looking for a job, are you?' The girl ran a scornful eye over Phyllida's drab gown and brown cloak. 'Prime bit of crack you are, I don't think.'

'Heard 'e needs a cook.' She flattened her vowels, dropped her aitches. 'I'm a good cook.'

'Yeah? Well, his cunny warren's just up there.' The whore jerked her head in the direction of Smithfield. 'The best house, that is.'

'Thank you.' Phyllida made her reluctant feet move. She had no idea how she was going to get out of this, but she had to do something before Buck told the world that the Earl of Fransham's sister was a common whore.

The nausea came back when she saw the house, three storeys of respectable-looking brick turned black by years of soot and grime. The front door was clean, though. Red, glossy and flanked by torchère holders that would blazon its presence to all those seeking it.

Phyllida climbed the steps and banged on the knocker. A panel slid back, a broken-nosed face scrutinised her. She stared back, recognising one of Buck's regular bodyguards. 'Mr Buck asked me to meet him here,' she said.

''E did, did 'e? You must 'ave some interesting tricks if he wants you.' The panel slammed shut and then, with the sound of bolts being drawn, the door opened. 'Come on in then, the boss is along 'ere.'

He peered at her as he opened a door on the first floor. 'You're that dealing woman, ain't yer?'

'Yes,' she agreed as she hesitated on the threshold, summoning enough courage to step into Harry Buck's lair. 'I'm a dealer.' *Not a whore.*

'What's that?' Buck demanded sharply as she walked in. 'What you say, Jem?'

'It's that dealer woman from the warehouse, guv'nor. You know, bought the Chinese stuff when that Indian geezer got lippy with you.'

'Nah, this is a bit of laced mutton, this is.'

Phyllida looked up from the swirling patterns of the Turkey carpet and saw Buck lounging in a chair beside a wide desk.

'What you doing all got up like a dowd, darlin'? You wasn't looking quite so drab last night, off to dinner with your smart friends.'

The bruiser closed the door behind her. Phyllida straightened her spine and looked Buck in the eye. She was not going to give him the satisfaction of seeing just how he made her feel. But the memories kept swirling back like thick, putrid fog to cloud her brain.

*You're a pretty one. Think I'll break you in meself. Don't see why I can't have a treat now and again. Thick fingers, unwashed body. Pain and shame.*

'I am here. What do you want to close your mouth?'

'Money, darlin', like I said.'

'How much?'

'Hundred.'

She could find that easily enough. But it wouldn't

end there, she knew. 'And that will be that? You will keep your mouth shut?'

'Don't be a silly girl. I'll want that every month. If you ain't got it, you can come 'ere and work for it on yer back. You pay or you work and I stay quiet.' He leered at her. 'You was a scrawny little thing back then, but I remember those eyes, all big and round, just like when you looked at me in the warehouse. That mark like a heart on your tit. I've a good memory, I 'ave. So I had you followed and thought about it 'til I remembered who you was.'

'Blackmail is a serious crime.' And blackmailers were never satisfied—she knew that. Buck would never go away.

'Send me to the nubbing cleat, it would,' Buck agreed, baring his teeth in a grin. 'But who're you going to tell?'

*No one*, was the answer to that. She needed time to think now she knew what he was demanding, time to find some kind of lever that would counteract his threats. Could she find out something to threaten him with, blackmail him in return? But Harry Buck had probably committed every crime and sin in the book and he was still out on the streets. No one seemed able to touch him.

'I can't find that kind of money all at once. You'll have to give me time to get it together.'

Buck studied her, her gaze sliding like a greasy finger over her face and down over her body. 'Nah. I know that's a lie. So we'll start tonight, shall we? I'll get me hundred out of your body. There's one of me little parties here this evening. They'll like you, my gentlemen will.'

'Oh, no.' Phyllida reached for the door handle, jerked at it and found herself facing Jem's broad chest.

'Oh, yes,' Buck said. 'The lady's staying, Jem. Put her in one of the rooms upstairs and lock the door— don't want 'er straying and 'aving an accident, do we?'

She tried to push past him, knowing even as she shoved at the sweat-stained frieze coat that it was hopeless. Jem picked her up and slung her over his shoulder as easily as he might a child.

The room he dumped her in was quite obviously one used to entertain clients. She wondered, as she stared around at the tawdry red velvet, the huge bed and the mirrors, if this was the one she had been taken to before. It was all a blur, the only real thing in her memory Buck's face above her, his weight, the pain and the sheer helpless terror.

Well, she was not a helpless girl now and she was desperate enough for just about anything. Phyllida pushed up the window and leaned out, hands braced on the filthy sill. She was three storeys up, overlooking a back alleyway. There were no ledges, no drainpipes within reach. This window and the locked door were the only ways out of the room.

She took off her cloak and one half-boot, held the thick fabric in front of the mirror and hit it hard with the heel. The glass shattered into a radiating pattern of long, knife-like shards. Phyllida picked one out at the cost of a cut finger, dragged back the cover from the bed and began to cut the sheet into strips.

# Chapter Twenty-One

'You'll do it?' Ashe asked in Hindi.

The tall Indian smiled. 'Of course, my brother. You are the enemy of Buck, he is my enemy. We are allies, are we not? And I do not like that man's dealings with women.' He used a foul word and spat. 'Come, let us hear what my men have discovered.'

Ashe suspected that Ashok—he admitted to no other name—was as much a criminal as Buck. He might not deal in women, but Ashe could smell raw opium, and the heavy locks and the glint of weapons everywhere he looked argued precious contraband hidden in the warehouse that was Ashok's headquarters.

He had been remarkably easy for a man who spoke Hindi to find. The first group of Indian seamen that Ashe saw had been startled to be addressed in their own language by a man dressed in the height of fashion, but Ashe's colloquial speech seemed to win them over and they led the way to Ashok without any further persuasion.

Ashe had explained what he wanted, had swallowed liquid opium from the other man's own cupped palm, exchanged a number of highly coloured items of gossip about Calcutta and was now sitting cross-legged on a heap of silk rugs, drinking sherbet while using all his diplomatic training not to take Ashok by the throat and shake him into urgent action. But this was the Indian's world, his men and, Ashe was acutely aware, his own best and only chance of getting into Buck's headquarters and removing Phyllida.

'Oh yes, my brother, she is still in there. I have the place watched, always, as is prudent with an enemy. Your lady went in—pale, in a dull brown cloak—and has not come out. Now we wait until evening.'

'No. She is in danger. Even as we sit here talking they could be—'

'Wait until evening, then customers come. That's who they want her for. You are just another English gentleman and so the door will be opened to you. My men attack at the back door and others follow you in through the front.' The Indian reached for a sweetmeat. 'When you find Buck, you will have a duel with him?'

'That is for gentlemen.' Ashe slid the knife from his sleeve and delicately trimmed a rough edge on his nail. 'He is not a gentleman.'

'Ah.' Ashok smiled. 'No, he is not. And we do not want the magistrates getting their hands on him, he knows too much about me. Perhaps he will have an accident. While we wait, your lady admired some pearls I have, the last time we did business, but she said they were too expensive for her. Perhaps you would like to look at them?'

*My lady. Is she?* Ashe pushed aside the thought. The future consisted of whatever time it took to get Phyllida out of there. After that he would try to work out just what she meant to him and discover what he meant to her.

* * *

Waiting was the hardest thing, Phyllida thought as she stood behind the door. The window opposite was wide open, curtains flapping. The posts at the corners of the bed were not part of the structure, she had discovered, merely supports for manacles. With a shudder at the thought of how they had been used, she had tugged one free of the brackets that held it, then jammed it across the window opening before tying the long tail of plaited sheets to it.

The makeshift rope would not hold her weight, she knew, but it served its purpose if it drew her captors to the window and gave her the chance to slip out the door.

It seemed hours before the household began to stir. Footsteps outside had her tensing every muscle, but they passed by. Women's voices, low male replies, a shriek of laughter, the bang of the knocker.

Then, with shocking suddenness, loud shouting, a crash from far below, screams and the report of a pistol. *A raid by the magistrates?* She hardly dared hope.

The door opened without her hearing any footsteps. Phyllida braced herself to run. The man strode towards the middle of the room and as he did so a big black bird landed on the sill with a harsh croak.

'Lucifer!'

The man spun on his heel. 'Phyllida!'

'Ashe. *Ashe.*' She fell into his arms laughing and sobbing.

'Are you all right? Have they—?'

'No. No, just very frightened,' she admitted.

'But not so frightened you could not think,' he said with a glance at the open window, the shattered mirror and stripped bed. 'Clever. That could have worked.'

'You!' Buck burst into the room behind them, blood on his face, a wicked knife in his hands. He waved it at Phyllida. 'You bitch, I'll gut you.'

'You'll go through me to do it.' Ashe drew a long blade from his sleeve. Feet pounded along the corridor, voices shouting in a foreign tongue coming closer.

Buck looked like a cornered rat. He bared yellow teeth at Ashe. 'Some other time. You'll pay.'

He was at the open window in one long stride, threw a leg over the sill and ducked out, his big hands grasping the sheet rope. Lucifer gave a sharp *caw* and flapped away into the alley.

'No! It won't hold,' Phyllida shouted as Buck vanished from sight.

There was a sharp cry from the bird, a scream of 'Get away from my eyes, you—' from below the open window, then a sickening thud.

The room filled with silent, turbaned men. One man leaned out of the window and spoke to Phyllida in a language she did not understand, then, as suddenly as they had appeared, they melted back, leaving her alone with Ashe.

'Oh, God. I've killed him?' She had never meant it as a trap, had never meant to do more than create a diversion.

'You are responsible for nothing. He lived the life he chose and he died of its consequences,' Ashe said harshly. 'If anyone killed him, it was Lucifer. Come on.'

'Where are his men?' She followed him into the corridor and down the stairs.

'Engaged in a battle royal with your friend Ashok and his followers in the basement, by the sound of it.'

She saw the way his eyes went to the head of the

lower stairs, the tension in his body. 'Go. I will be all right here now.'

'No.' He turned away and led her to the front door. 'That is Ashok's fight now. We agreed he would deal with Buck and his men, and he'll take the spoils of that. My part was to find you.'

'What would you have done if Buck had not fallen?'

Ashe took her arm and strode up the street towards Smithfield. A hackney carriage stopped at the top of the road and he hailed it, then turned to look down at her, but he answered only obliquely. 'He touched you, threatened you, put fear in your eyes. Now we get clear of here before someone calls the law.'

He would have killed Buck, she saw it in the cold, hard glitter of his eyes, the set of his jaw, and offered up a silent prayer of thanks that in the end it had been an accident and there was no blood on Ashe's hands.

'Now what happens?' she asked as they sat back on the battered squabs of the carriage and it rattled into motion.

'I take you home and we say nothing to anyone of this. I will speak to Ashok in the morning, make certain everything is tidied up.'

*Make certain Buck is dead, you mean*, she thought, but did not say it. 'I had not realised that Ashok was more than a trader,' she ventured. It seemed that Ashe was not yet ready of speak of what now lay between them.

'In his way he is as hard and as ruthless as Buck,' Ashe said. 'You will not go into the East End again, too many people have taken notice of you now.'

Part of her wanted to defy him, simply because he was giving her orders, but she knew he was right and she would have come to the same conclusion herself. 'I was going to get a manager for the shop, once Gregory was settled. I will do that now; there is a man at one of the auction houses who I have in mind.'

'And what will you do to occupy yourself?' Ashe asked.

The tiny flame of hope that had flickered into life when he had taken her in his arms in that sordid room wavered and died. Ashe was not going to say they could put it all behind them, carry on as they were before she had met Buck again. But then, how could he? He had learned that she had sold her body, had been prepared to keep that from him at the risk of a scandal that would tarnish his whole family if it came out. And she had always known, deep in her heart, that a marriage was impossible.

'I will do what I always planned, go and live in the Dower House.' There was silence between them, a heavy stillness that felt physically hard to break. After a minute she said, 'I will tell you what happened, when—'

'No. I do not want to hear. It is not my business.' Ashe was looking out of the window as though Leadenhall Street was of abiding fascination.

'You saved me just now. You know what he was going to do.'

'I would have done the same for any woman I knew to be in that danger,' Ashe said politely, as though she had thanked him for rescuing her parasol from a gust of wind.

*I love you.*

They sat without speaking until the hackney turned into King Street and passed Almack's. They would be in Great Ryder Street at any moment.

'I would not have married you. I never intended to,' Phyllida said hurriedly. 'I knew I could not because of what had happened, how it happened. I was wrong not to have been stronger right from the start, never to have allowed you to kiss me, never to have let this farce of a courtship go on as it has while I let myself dream.

'You will not hear my story and I understand why not. You are very angry and I have put you to a great deal of trouble, let alone embarrassment and danger. But I want you to realise that I would never have compromised your honour by becoming your wife. I could never have married you and kept this a secret from you, even if your honour had not mattered to me.'

Her house key was in her hand now as the carriage drew to a halt. Phyllida pushed the door open and jumped down before Ashe could move. She stood on the pavement and took a last, long look at his face. 'I love you, you see. Goodbye, Ashe.' Then she turned and hurried up the steps, thrust the key in the lock and was inside before she heard his booted feet hit the pavement.

*I love you, you see.* The door slammed shut. *Goodbye.* That had been final.

'You getting back in, guv'nor, or is this it?' the cabby demanded.

Ashe gave him the address and climbed inside again. *Is this it?* the man had asked. Was it? He should be glad. Phyllida was safe, he was saved from a highly unsuitable marriage, the slums were free of Harry Buck, an unsavoury predator upon women who had met his just desserts.

*I love you.* She did not mean it, did she? He had not tried to attach her emotionally, she had made no attempt to cling to him, to plead with him. Her eyes as she said it had been dry.

Why had he not let her tell him her story? If she could bear to tell it, then he should have the patience to hear it. Then he realised that it would have taken courage for him to sit and listen, that it mattered to him, more than an abstract story of an everyday outrage. It mattered because Phyllida mattered.

Sara was alone in the drawing room when he walked in. 'Whatever have you been doing? You look as though you have been in a fight!'

'That is because I have been in a fight.' He sank down on the sofa beside her and leaned his aching head on the cushioned back. 'And don't worry Mata by telling her.'

'Of course not. Did you win?'

'I think so.'

'Excellent.' She picked up her embroidery and let him rest.

'Sara, may I ask you something shocking? Something I should not even dream of speaking of to you?'

'Is this something else I should not be telling Mata about? Of course you may.'

Ashe sat up, rested his elbows on his knees and studied his clasped hands. 'What would drive you to sell yourself? To give your body to a stranger, a man who revolted you. Hunger?'

'No!' He felt the movement as she shook her head vehemently. 'I would rather starve.'

'Money?'

'Well, the money would be a reason, otherwise why do it? But...' She fell silent for a while, thinking. 'I

would do it if it would save Mata from some awful
danger. Or for you or Papa. If one of you were sick and
there was no money for a doctor and medicines, then
nothing else would matter.'

She said it earnestly, obviously meaning it. After a
moment she moved close to him and put her hand on
his arm. 'Is that why you were in a fight?'

'Yes. She was very young.'

'Oh, poor thing,' Sara said compassionately. 'Is there
anything I can do to help her?'

'No, she's safe now.' *I have broken her heart, but
she's safe.* Ashe got to his feet. 'I'm going out, probably won't be home for dinner.'

Fransham, when he finally ran him to earth, was
at White's, dozing over a newspaper in a quiet corner
of the library. 'Clere! Have a drink.' He waved to the
waiter and tossed the paper aside. 'You're looking uncommonly serious.'

Ashe had washed, changed, combed his hair, before
he had left home, but it seemed he had not been able to
scrub away the darkness in his mind. 'I wanted to ask
you something personal, something you probably don't
want to talk about. Only it affects Phyllida and I need
to understand.' Understand not only Phyllida, not only
what had driven her to that desperate act, but himself.
How he felt for her, why he ached inside, why he felt
worse than he had when Reshmi had died.

'All right.' Gregory sat up and poured a couple of
glasses of brandy. 'Ask away, I can always punch you
on the nose if you get too personal.'

'Phyllida told me about your parents, why they didn't
marry until after she was born. But what happened

when your mother died? She didn't seem able to talk about it.'

Fransham's face clouded. 'God, that was an awful time. She told you how unreliable our father was? Well, the time he spent with us got less and less—and so did the money. And then Mama got sick. Consumption, the doctor said. We did the best we could. I was fifteen and I got a job with the local pharmacist, just a dogsbody, really, but he paid me in medicine. Phyllida was seventeen and she ran the house and nursed Mama and kept writing to Papa.

'He never answered, so in the end she scraped together enough money for the stage and set off to London to find him. She came back a month later, looking ghastly, and said he'd died in a tavern brawl. Knock on the head and too much drink. She'd seen the lawyers and they said there was some assets and more debts. I was the earl, and that kept the creditors at bay for a bit, but it was too late for Mama. She died a week after Phyll got home.'

'If she took only enough money for the stage, how had she lived in London?' Ashe asked, knowing the answer only too well. She could have turned around and gone home when she didn't find her wastrel father at once, but she had hung on, kept searching even though she was starving.

'Got some odd jobs, I suppose. I never asked, what with Mama and the news about Father.' Gregory scrubbed his hand over his face. 'I should have thought. She was as thin as a rake, took her ages to put the weight back on.'

So she had sold herself for the money to stay alive while she found her father, because if she did not then her mother and brother would starve. And the world would think—*he* had thought, damn it—that what she had done dishonoured her. And she believed that if she married him it would compromise his honour.

'I have fallen out with Phyllida,' Ashe said bluntly. 'I've hurt her and I doubt she'll open the door to me now.'

'Do I need to name my seconds?' Gregory asked and set his glass down with a snap.

'No. You need to give me your door key and eat dinner out. In fact, I suggest you go and beg the Millingtons for a bed for the night.'

'The devil you say!' But Gregory was pulling the key out of the pocket in the tail of his coat.

'Don't ask and I won't have to lie to you. Thanks.'

'You had better be intending to marry her,' Gregory warned. 'I've been a damned slack brother, but I mean to do the right thing by her now.'

'I can ask. Only Phyllida can accept,' Ashe said and pocketed the key.

# Chapter Twenty-Two

A she let himself into the house in Great Ryder Street
with the care of a burglar. The ground floor was
silent, but he could hear the murmur of voices from
the basement, the clang of copper pans. Soft-footed,
he moved to the top of the stairs and listened. Three
feminine voices, none of them Phyllida's.

They were devoted to her, he knew that from observing Anna. Whether that devotion would move them to
fillet him with a boning knife or help him, he had no
idea, but he could hardly be alone and uninterrupted
with Phyllida unless they knew he was there from the
start.

'Good afternoon.'

The cook dropped the ladle she was holding and the
little maid gave a squeak of alarm. Anna jumped up
from the chair by the range where she had been mending and marched up to confront him. 'What did you do
to her? You got her away from Buck, I'll say that for
you, but she's shut herself away in her bedchamber and
she won't talk to me, or come out. If you've hurt Miss
Phyllida, you rakehell, his lordship will beat your brains
out and we'll cheer him on!'

'I didn't *do* anything to her,' Ashe said and sat down in a chair by the kitchen table, neatly unsettling Anna who did not seem to know how to deal with gentlemen lounging at the table, stealing Cook's still-warm jam tarts. 'I managed to say the wrong things, not say the right ones, and comprehensively put my foot in it with her. So, yes, I've hurt her, but not the way I suspect you mean, Anna.'

He laid the key on the table. 'That's Lord Fransham's, by the way. He knows I am here and he won't be in now until tomorrow.'

'So that's the way it is,' Anna said and sat down too.

'If you're all going to eat those tarts, I'd best put the kettle on,' Cook said, suiting her actions to her words. 'Get the tea caddy, Jane.'

'Are you in love with Miss Phyllida?' Anna demanded. Ashe raised his eyebrows at her tone, but she was not to be intimidated and sat there glaring at him while she waited for an answer.

*Am I?* 'Do you think I'd tell you before I tell her?' he asked. 'I do not mean her harm, that I promise you.'

Cook passed him a cup of tea and pushed the plate of tarts closer. 'Well, get your strength up. You'll need it,' she added darkly.

She could not stay in her room for the rest of her life. Nor the rest of the day, come to that. Phyllida swung her legs over the edge of the bed and ran out of energy to stand up.

This would not do. Life had to go on and Gregory would be worried and the staff would fret if she hid herself away like a lovelorn adolescent. There was much to be done, that would help. A manager to find for the shop, the Dower House to whip into habitable shape, Gregory's wedding to plan for.

Goodness, she would be so busy she would forget Ashe Herriard in a few days. Oh, who was she deceiving? Not herself, obviously. Phyllida lay down again, curled up into a miserable ball and stubbornly refused to cry. A girl was entitled to mourn for a day when her heart was broken, she told herself with a rather hysterical attempt at humour.

The door opened. 'Go away, Anna. I do not want to be disturbed.' It closed again, but there were soft footfalls, the sound of breathing. 'Anna, *please* go away. Tell Cook I will not be down to dinner and say to Lord Fransham that I have a headache.'

'Lord Fransham will not be in to dinner. He is staying the night with the Millingtons.'

*Ashe?* Phyllida uncurled and sat bolt upright. 'What the devil are you doing here? I said goodbye and I meant it.' How could he come and mock her like this?

Ashe sat down on the side of the bed. 'I was shocked. I was shaken and I was horrified and above all I was hurting and I had no idea why,' he said abruptly. 'Then I made myself think. No woman sells herself unless she is desperate, or foolishly thinks prostitution is an easy way of life. And you are neither stupid nor wanton. I ought to have had that clear in my head. I recalled what you had said about your father, how your family had been abandoned and so I asked Gregory about the time just before your mother died.'

'You told him what I did?' It would kill Gregory to know she had been driven to that.

'No, of course not.' Ashe scrubbed one hand across his face. 'I might have made a thoroughgoing mess of this, but he has no idea why I asked him. What he told me made sense and I knew why you had no choice. Damn it, Phyllida, if a man fought and killed for honour and to protect his family, then everyone understands, thinks he's a fine fellow. If a woman puts herself through hell for her family, sacrifices everything short of her life, then she is called a whore and is ruined.'

He twisted round to face her fully. 'I should have had that straight in my mind and I should have told you that was what I thought, there and then. What you did for your family was courageous and honourable. When you wanted to tell me about it, I should have listened and reassured you and comforted you.'

He thought her courageous and honourable? He was apologising to her when she had taken advantage of him, hidden the truth from him?

When, lost for words, she simply stared at him, at his beloved face, taut with pain and self-recrimination and regret, he stood up. 'I don't imagine you can forgive me for that. Like an arrogant fool I told Gregory to stay away tonight, that I had been clumsy, but that I would make it right with you and that I would marry you. I was wrong to presume. Insensitive. I am sorry, Phyllida.'

He had his hand on the door before she could find her voice to stop him. 'Ashe, I love you.' His back to her, he stayed where he was, as though he could not turn. 'I would forgive you anything, understand anything. You do not have to marry me and make that sacrifice. Just knowing you understand and do not condemn me for it, that you forgive me for letting this masquerade of a courtship go on as long as it has, that makes so much difference.'

'Why would it be a sacrifice?' he asked and his voice, always so confident, always so strong, was unsteady.

'For all the reasons we have rehearsed before. Sooner or later the strain of that, of my birth, of my secrets, they would crack such a marriage. I would rather not have you than ruin your life.' He had praised her courage just now. This, if he did but know it, was the hardest, most courageous thing she had ever done, sending away the man she loved.

'None of it would matter if I loved you,' he said and turned, his voice quite firm again, his eyes green and calm and certain. 'My family like you, soon they will love you as a daughter and a sister. And, with love, we can face down any whispers about your birth.'

'But you—' Ashe did not lie to her, she felt that deep in her bones. Her heart, so heavy, suddenly became light, the beat so fast she felt dizzy with it.

'But I do love you. It took a lot of pain to make me realise just why I felt the way I did. What I had thought was love before was only a faint shadow of the real thing. You loving me, despite everything, is a miracle I do not deserve. But perhaps our children do.' His beautiful, expressive mouth curved into the first smile she had seen, it seemed, for days. 'Marry me, Phyllida. Let me love you. Shut all your secrets away so they will wither and die in the darkness and come and live in the light with me.'

'Yes. Oh, yes, Ashe.' She found she had scrambled off the bed, all anyhow, her arms held open to him, and he was in them and they held each other so tight she could not breathe, but it did not matter, because Ashe loved her.

Ashe set her back a little and grinned. 'That feels as though a huge weight has just lifted off my heart. Do you want to go and tell Gregory and my family, start to make plans for the wedding?'

'No.' She laughed at the surprise on his face. 'You sent Gregory off for the night. You meant to stay here with me, did you not?'

'Yes, but I already said it was arrogant and insensitive of me to assume that is what you would want.' He was running his fingers over her cheek, tracing her lips, stroking her hair as though he had just found her after a long absence.

'It is exactly what I want,' she murmured and stood on tiptoe to kiss him. 'I want to show you how much I love you. I want to feel how much you love me.'

'You are not afraid?' Ashe murmured into her hair.

Phyllida swallowed. 'A little. Parts of it will not be… will hurt, I know that.'

'No, they won't,' Ashe said with complete confidence. 'For a start, no one has ever made love to you before and, even if they had, they were not me.'

'Of all the arrogant creatures!' she protested, laughing uncertainly as he attacked the fastenings of her crumpled gown.

'Not at all. I know what I am doing—don't frown at me like that. There have been other women, but you are the last one. The last and only.' Her gown fell to her feet, her corset dropped away. 'As I was saying, I have been learning to *make* love so I could pleasure the woman I *do* love.'

Ashe shrugged out of coat and waistcoat together,

yanked off his neckcloth and pulled his shirt over his head. 'There is a time and place for leisurely undressing, but this is not it. You, my darling, need sweeping off your feet and that is precisely what I am going to do.'

His boots went flying, his breeches were kicked off, Phyllida clutched rather desperately at the front of her shift as she found herself confronted by a naked, fully aroused, man. 'Oh, my.' Her eyes felt wide as saucers.

'All yours, indeed.' Ashe said as he stripped the shift from her, deposited her on the bed and straddled her hips. 'This is the frightening bit, I imagine. I promise I won't squash you.' He slid down her body and she felt her legs opening instinctively to cradle him. He took his weight on his elbows and looked down at her. 'All right?'

'Yes. Yes, perfectly all right.' And it was. There was no point of resemblance at all to how it had been with Buck. This was Ashe and he loved her and he was going to pleasure her. She reached up and freed his hair from the tie, ran her fingers through the silky weight of it, gasped as he bent his head and let the ends tease across her breasts.

He kissed her mouth, a fleeting caress, then slid down her body until he could kiss her breasts, nibbling the tips until she gasped and then sucking and swirling with his tongue until her hips lifted off the bed and she writhed against him, her fingers laced into his hair as though she did not know whether to hold him captive there for ever or push him away to end this exquisite torture.

'Ashe. Oh, please...'

He moved to the other breast, shifted his weight so he could slide one hand down between her thighs where she ached and throbbed and needed him, needed him desperately to do those wonderful things that he had the other night.

When Ashe left her breasts she gasped in protest, but he only murmured, 'Sweet, so sweet,' and possessed her mouth again while his fingers slid and teased and pressed and she panted into his mouth, so close to the bliss, so close.

Then his weight and heat had gone, leaving her reaching for him. She opened her eyes and saw his dark head where his hand had been, his hair fanned out over her thighs, startling against the white skin. He pushed firmly but gently to open her and then kissed her there, even as he slid two fingers into her. Shocked, she tensed. It would hurt, she had known it would...

'Oh.' It was a murmur, a gasp. Instinctively she tightened around the intrusion, arched up against his mouth, sobbed wordless pleas that he would never stop, never, because it was almost there, that wonderful sensation that transcended reality.

He moved, too fast for her to protest at the absence of his lips, his hand. He was over her, holding her, whispering what she knew were love words although she did not know the language. His hips moved in the cradle of her thighs and he filled her in one long stroke and she shattered, broke, heard her own voice crying out.

Phyllida came to herself to find the pleasure was not waning, only changing. Ashe moved within her, his body part of hers, his gasps of pleasure hers as well as his. She curled her legs around his hips, tilting up until he was as deep as she could take him, and clung to the broad shoulders, slick with sweat, kissed him wherever